Praise for Alex' Choice:

Life's revelations continue for Alex Jorgenson in this engaging sequel to *The Treasure of Stella Bay*. Set in middle-class Ontario in the sixties and early seventies, readers have a front row seat into Alex's life challenges, his triumphs and tribulations, as he grapples with maturity, independence, and love. Alex' Choice is an emotional, funny, and delightful novel that peers into the tough decisions of a young adult life.

Barry McArthur, Toronto

Alex' Choice is a well-crafted novel with some lovely characterisation and a clever narrative, suitable for a wide range of readers and it is, like *The Treasure of Stella Bay*, a good read. His portrayal of a young man growing up, struggling with maturity, coping with the opposite sex, leaving home, adjusting to new schools and university, and then keeping the older generation, including parents, 'onside', is second to none. His writing reminds me of Mark Twain and some aspects of Dickens but without the heaviness.

Jordan brings into play the emerging sexuality of a young man and his girlfriends, but does it in a way that is readable, acceptable, and brings the storyline forward and at speed.

Doug has drawn some wonderful characters: sensitive yet courageous Alex; the voluptuous Eleanor; the wholesome Sandra; his parents – wry Professor Jorgenson, and his mother, the pragmatic Victoria.

Doug draws in the smaller characters at suitable points: brother Oliver, especially in The Cave In – a brilliant way of developing a sense of drama earlier on and at the same time bringing the new reader into the story line of *The Treasure of Stella Bay*: the recovery of the treasure and the near drowning with the treasure; the reintroduction of 'Old Man O'Reilly'; the cast of other supporting characters: Reverend Farquharson, and his wife Clara, and his best friend, Hugh, – what a great invention. I liked the chapter devoted to Tony the Beagle, the failures with the football team, and track, the crisis of the fire, and of course, finally, the choice.

David Bradley, Whitby, U.K.
Author, *William Bradley's Handcart*

Alex' Choice

By Doug Jordan

— Alex' Choice —

Copyright © 2024 by Doug Jordan

All rights reserved. This book or any portion thereof may not be reproduced or used in any manner whatsoever without the express written permission of the publisher except for the use of brief quotations in a book review or reference.

First Printing in this form: 2024

ISBN 9 781304 326393

AFS Publishing
A division of AFS Consulting
Ottawa Ontario
Visit afspublishing.ca

Cover illustration by Katy Dockrill, design by Jeffrey Primeau

Katy Dockrill
Illustrator
katydockrill.com

This is a work of fiction. All the characters in this book are the creatures of the mind of the author. The locales are real places but may have different names than actual in many cases; some 'facts' have been adapted to suit the story. The events are made up, probably. Any presumed association of the events and personages in this story to real people are themselves in the mind of the reader.

Dedication:

To Marlene,
Whose ghost walks many of these pages

TABLE OF CONTENTS

Kingston, 1973 .... **9**
   1.   Kingston, 1973 June 11

Stella, 1964 .... **13**
   2.   Stella, 1964 October 15
   3.   "That Went Well" 22
   4.   The Cave-In 25
   5.   The Story 29
   6.   Old Man O'Reilly 34
   7.   Return to The Fort 39
   8.   Alex' Reasons 42

Amherst Island, 1963 .... **45**
   9.   Amherst Island Public School, September 1963 47
  10.   Hugh McPherson 51
  11.   Sandra Farquharson 61
  12.   Boy Scouts 65
  13.   Hugh's News 71

Amherst Island, 1964 Fall **81**
  14.   Napanee High School 83
  15.   On the Buses 87
  16.   Head of the Household 91
  17.   Snapping Turtle 95
  18.   Tony Meets his Maker 98
  19.   Goodbye Stella Bay 105

Peterborough, 1965 - 1969 .... **111**
  20.   Edmison Heights 113
  21.   Adam Scott CVI 118
  22.   Pen Pals and Preoccupation 124
  23.   Landscaping 129
  24.   Body Building 132
  25.   Athletics 136
  26.   Scouts 140
  27.   The Cottage 148
  28.   Girls 162
  29.   Scholastics and Conflicts 167
  30.   Eleanor 171
  31.   Driver's Test 184
  32.   Grade XIII Finals 190

Kingston, 1969 – 1973 ....**203**
    33.   The Road to Queen's 205
    34.   Orientation..211
    35.   Graduation Weekend..217
    36.   First Year Queen's..224
    37.   Canada Bread..242
    38.   Second Year Queen's 250
    39.   Sean O'Reilly..256
    40.   Cashway Lumber..259
    41.   Civic Holiday 270
    42.   Portsmouth Tavern...277
    43.   jThe Incident at the Bank 283
    44.   The Heart Attack 287
    45.   Distance...292
    46.   The Summer of '72 306
    47.   Roommates..312
    48.   Montreal House 318
    49.   The Rooming House...321
    50.   The Emergency Room..324
    51.   The Choice...330
    52.   Graduation Day 342
    53.   Yes or No?..353

List of Maps

Figure 1: Map of Kingston and Surrounding.................... 20
Figure 2: Map of Amherst Island....................................... 21

Forward/Dedication

Despite what many readers personally familiar with my life might think, this is not a memoir, it's a work of fiction, though, as Mark Twain remarked, rather obviously, much of fiction is at least in part autobiographical. Most of the adventures set out in this narrative never happened, or certainly never happened in quite the way described. So too the characters in this book – they never existed, they are fragments and amalgams of people from my own life, including myself.

The story takes place in small town Ontario in the period of 1963-1973, more particularly, Kingston, Peterborough, and the tiny village of Stella.

This is a sequel to *The Treasure of Stella Bay*, being the further adventures of Alex Jorgenson. It was never my intention to write a sequel – I thought the adventures of the 12-year-old Alex (my 1960s Tom Sawyer) was enough. But many of my readers began to ask, not clamouring exactly but wondering, what happens to Alex next? So, almost against my will, ideas began to percolate in my mind while I was doing other things. Fragments began to form into clumps while other fragments seemed to have no home, some never made the final draft. But I still didn't have a story arc, something that builds to a climax and a resolution. Until one day in May, it came to me, a series of events that connect this story to key elements of *The Treasure of Stella Bay*.

This may not in fact be the sequel my readers had in mind. If they were looking for the further adventures of a 12-year-old boy on bucolic Amherst Island they may be disappointed. I couldn't see writing a continuous series of Hardy Boys mysteries, in which the protagonists never age. Instead, I felt I needed to take the story through the next five or ten years of young Alex' life, the rest of the 1960s, through high school and maybe university and the early 1970s.

It's not necessary to have read *The Treasure of Stella Bay* before embarking on this one. I wanted *The Treasure of Stella Bay* to stand on its own and *Alex' Choice* to stand on its. Naturally, I had to bring some of the elements from the TSB story into the present novel in order for the new reader to make sense of the relevant references and see links in the plot and the characters. I tried to do that as seamlessly as possible so as not to annoy the impatient reader irritated with 'Readers' Digest' prose. I haven't been able to bring all the characters from the TSB forward into this one but surely you will be curious to find out, or maybe not, what happens to Peter Jorgenson, and Victoria, and little brother Oliver; Hugh and Sandra; and Old Man O'Reilly.

    I hope my book appeals to readers of all ages. *The Treasure of Stella Bay* was about a 12-year-old boy but was actually intended for mature readers who were themselves 12 once. Similarly, *Alex' Choice* is not a YA (Young Adult) genre fiction: it's for anyone wanting to relive their late teen years, to acquaint, or reacquaint, themselves to the late 1960s, or recall their struggles with emerging sexuality and making choices that would affect the rest of their lives.

    If my dear wife of fifty years, Marlene, were still with us I hope she would have liked this book. I hope she would have smiled when she recognized the people in the story.

    Doug Jordan, Ottawa
    2023 December

KINGSTON, 1973

— Doug Jordan —

1. Kingston, 1973 June

ALEX JORGENSON STOOD ON THE NORTHEAST CORNER of Union Street and University Avenue looking south at the row of towering elms of the boulevard. He was in a pensive mood. Today was graduation day. And then some.

This wasn't the first time he had stood at that corner and wondered what would happen in his life. Ten years earlier when he was eleven or twelve while visiting his dad, Dr. Peter Jorgenson, Professor of Psychology at Queen's University, he had studied this intersection and wondered what his future would bring. He ha d plans then, just as he had plans now, only some of those plans hadn't quite worked out. Older now, and tempered by his disappointments, he took his education to heart and tried to practice his new-found stoical philosophy. He found Marcus Aurelius much more to his bent than Mark Twain, his father's preferred philosopher. Peter Jorgenson was a humourist, and even specialized in the psychology of humour. Alex got more of his father's quips these days than he did when he was twelve but he figured he took more after his mother in temperament – serious and practical, rather than ironic.

Regardless, here he stood on the corner of Union and University, studying the clean outlines of Dunning Hall and reflecting on the many hours he had attended classes there studying Political Science and Economics. But he thought he was done with Dunning and looked west on Union Street to Sir John A. Macdonald Hall where he had thought to spend the next three years studying law, and on his way to becoming a lawyer.

It had been a ten-year twisted journey to get here. He never imagined the obstacles and surprises he had encountered. He had gone to Queen's, as he expected, as Peter and his mother, Victoria, expected, but many other hopes and dreams had not turned out quite as hoped. His father had said life is full of disappointments, but they should not be the end of your dreams. Failure was character-building, he'd say.

Peter was full of homilies like that, sort of a living Benjamin Franklin. Alex didn't always appreciate his dad's advice – was it character-building when his parents announced they would be moving to Amherst Island where he had no friends, nor roots, nor prospects? He had to admit, though, it had turned out alright.

But today he was graduating with a Bachelor of Arts degree.

With one last look, he turned and, walking east on Union Street, joined the gathering throngs of new graduands in caps and gowns working their way to the new Jock Harty Arena where his parents would be waiting to watch him graduate. He could hardly believe that Sandra would be there too. His heart fluttered a bit at the thought of her. He had been very sure of her when they were the closest of friends in Grade Seven at Amherst Island Public School. But now, after a ten-year twisted and torturous journey, he was less certain. As he had discovered, even though he had made his choice, dreaming and hoping didn't mean things would turn out the way he wanted.

Instinctively he reached into his pocket, feeling for the ring he knew was there.

Today would be even more than his graduation day.

Stella, 1964

2. Stella, 1964 October

"I DON'T KNOW, PETER," VICTORIA SAID, "Alex is going be pretty upset. You know how hard it was on him when we moved to Amherst Island three years ago."

"Yes, dear, I know. But he will survive and, it's character.."

"Don't give me that 'character building' spiel, it isn't going to wash this time."

"That sounds like it isn't going down well with you either, Victoria."

"Listen, Peter, I understand that you are ambitious and this opportunity at Trent is in line with your academic interests, but this is very disruptive to the whole family.

"Alex is too young to understand career ambition.

"And don't use any of your wry humour on him to soften the blow. Sometimes I wonder if you actually understand psychology even though you teach it."

"Ouch, okay. Silence may be more persuasive than argument. Perhaps you should tell him. I'll just stand by and look concerned." But he said this with smile. Victoria scowled.

It was October of 1964, Thanksgiving weekend. Dr. Peter Jorgenson had just accepted a new position at Trent University as Full Professor, Psychology, with the opportunity to pursue his research into the psychology of humour. Victoria couldn't quite understand why Peter was willing to leave the ancient and prestigious Queen's University, Kingston, to go to that newly created university in Peterborough, so new it didn't even yet have its own campus, operating instead out of rented institutional buildings in downtown Peterborough. But she ultimately accepted Peter's need to advance himself in his field. She smiled wryly to herself with that old cliché – if Peter wanted to be outstanding in his field, why didn't he take up farming? – Amherst Island was the perfect place for that. She loved him, and she supported him, and she was grateful that his career allowed her to stay at home and raise their two boys, Alex and Oliver. She had been a paediatrics nurse at Kingston General Hospital but she much preferred being a stay-at home-mom; she believed caring for her boys was her true calling, at least for now. But she had her doubts and worries. In the back of her mind she wondered what she would do when the boys no longer needed her. Alex had just started first year of high school, Oliver two years behind. She needed to make some plans of her own. But that could wait a couple of years. Now she had to inform the boys their lives were about to change, and she worried they might not take the news well, especially Alex who tended to brood and take change hard.

"We might as well get to it," she said.

"Boys," Peter called, "please come down to the dining room. Your mom and I have something to tell you."

That got Alex' attention. The only time the family met in the dining room was for Sunday dinner or for a family conference. This was Saturday, Thanksgiving Dinner wasn't until Monday. Something was up. He wondered if Oliver had got himself mixed up in something again.

He glanced at the back of his bedroom door as he was about to leave, taking courage from the picture of Sandra Dee mounted there.

As he stepped into the hallway he called down to Oliver's room.

"Come on, Oliver, Dad's calling us."

"Yeah, I heard him and now I'm a bit worried. Maybe Tony's in trouble." Tony was their three-year-old beige and white beagle.

"Where is he by the way?" Alex questioned, "Has he run off again?"

"No, he's right here with me on my bed."

"Better bring him downstairs with us. He may as well face the music too."

The boys stepped lightly into the dining room, not at all sure what was up. Tony was quieter than usual; he must have sensed a mood change too.

"Sit down boys, we need to have a conference," Peter said.

The boys took their usual places at the dining table; Tony dove under the table.

"Oh," remarked Alex, "is Tony in trouble? It's not always our fault he gets off the clothesline. He's very clever at tricking that clip and getting away."

"No, it's not about Tony, is it Victoria?"

That was Victoria's cue to step into the conversation. She glanced at Peter with a minor look of annoyance and began.

"You remember, boys, when we moved to Stella three years ago, we thought Amherst Island was an ideal place for our little family to call home."

Victoria paused for a moment, looking at Alex. Alex figured he was supposed to say something.

"Yeah, I wasn't too happy about it, leaving our place in Kingston and coming to this god-forsaken island," he said, with a gentle smile. "At least, that's what I thought at the time. But it turned out pretty well."

"Yes, it did," said Victoria. "You've had three wonderful years at Amherst Island Public School, you've made a lot of friends, you even discovered that treasure in Stella Bay and created a lot of excitement."

"Yes but, now" replied Alex, "my best friend has moved away, and I never realized I'd be on a bus four hours a day going to High School in Napanee."

"Yes, well, that was a surprise to your father and me too. We were blinded by the idyll of Amherst Island and didn't think about all the impracticalities of living on an island."

Peter looked at Victoria with one eye-brow raised – 'island idyll'? that was interesting language coming from his usually practical wife – but didn't say anything.

"We thought we would spend the rest of our days here," Victoria continued. "It's so peaceful here, and we all love swimming off the dock in Stella Bay, and the boat, and, um. And well, we've even adapted to living with the ferry schedule."

"Well," retorted Alex, increasingly agitated with this conversation, "I'm not sure I'm going to adapt too well to a daily trip to Napanee and back and that damned ferry."

"Now Alex," Peter retorted, "your Mother and I hadn't figured on that but there's no need for you to be getting upset."

Silence filled the room for a minute. Oliver hadn't said anything. He was still worried the conference was about something Tony had done, or maybe himself, and he wasn't about to implicate himself prematurely. Peter wondered how Victoria's praise of life on Amherst Island was helping announce the news.

Victoria continued, her face unsmiling.

"You know that your father is a professor at Queen's and, well, what you probably don't know, there's a new university that just opened in Peterborough, and well, they've been talking to your father."

Victoria stalled for a minute. Alex still didn't know where this conversation was headed.

"Where's Peterborough?"

"You know where it is Alex. We've driven through it a few times on our way to visit your Grandpa and Grandma Jorgenson in Orillia and my parents in Bailieboro."

"Yeah, but usually we just go along Highway 401 to Toronto to Hwy 400 to Barrie, except when Dad wants to take the 'scenic routes' through the back country."

"Well, anyway," Victoria continued, "Trent University has offered your father a wonderful position and promotion in the Arts Faculty as Head of the Psychology Department."

"Oh," said Alex. His mind was racing to consider all the implications of this bombshell statement.

Oliver just looked at Alex, blankly, but with mounting trepidation, waiting for some clue from his brother as to what was going on.

The old clock on the dining room mantle clacked slowly, loud in the silence of the room, competing with Alex' beating heart.

"Your father has decided to accept their offer.

"It's wonderful career move.

"Peterborough is a lovely town. There's a new housing development in the north end of town, near where the new campus is going to be built.

"We'll buy a brand-new house with all the modern amenities."

Silence rained a few moments more.

"So, we're moving to Peterborough," Alex bluntly summarized.

Alex' Choice

"When will all this happen?"

"Well, your dad is traveling to Peterborough on Monday, leaving right after Thanksgiving Dinner.

"Your dad starts work on Tuesday at Trent."

Alex looked at his father. "You mean you've already resigned from Queen's?"

"Yes, son," Peter replied.

Alex was a bit surprised that all this planning must have been going on for weeks now.

"When will we be moving to Peterborough?"

"Well, Son," said Peter, now obliged to take the floor, "I'll start looking for a house, probably in that new development your mom mentioned, and if it's built in time we will move in just before Christmas.

"You'll be able to finish your school term here in Amherst Island..." Alex interrupted.

"You mean Napanee. Only Oliver goes to school here now."

"Yes, I realize that. And you will start your next term at your new schools in Peterborough."

"Oh," said Alex, his mind racing with all these implications.

"Will you be gone for three months?"

"No Son, I'll be home every weekend. Peterborough is only a two-hour drive from here.

"You can be the man of the house while I'm gone Mondays to Fridays."

At that point the penny must have dropped for Oliver.

"What? What are you saying? We're moving away from here?!

"What about my school? What about all my friends?

"I don't want to leave here. That's no fair."

With that, Oliver jumped up from the table, knocking over his chair. He turned and stormed out of the room, letting the swing door to the dining room swinging violently, Tony hard on his heels. He stomped across the kitchen and disappeared around the corner.

Peter and Victoria exchanged glances, then looked at Alex.

Alex shrugged.

"May I leave now?"

Peter nodded.

19

Figure 1: Map of Kingston and Surrounding

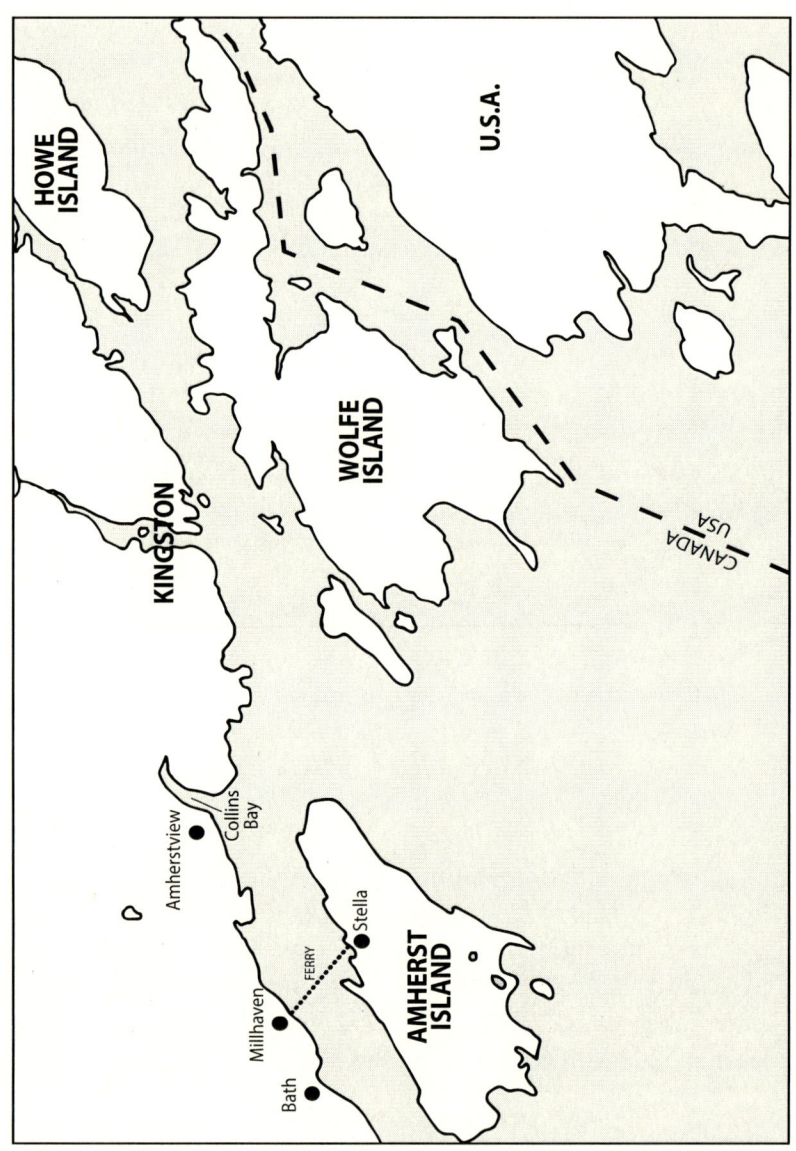

Figure 2: Map of Amherst Island

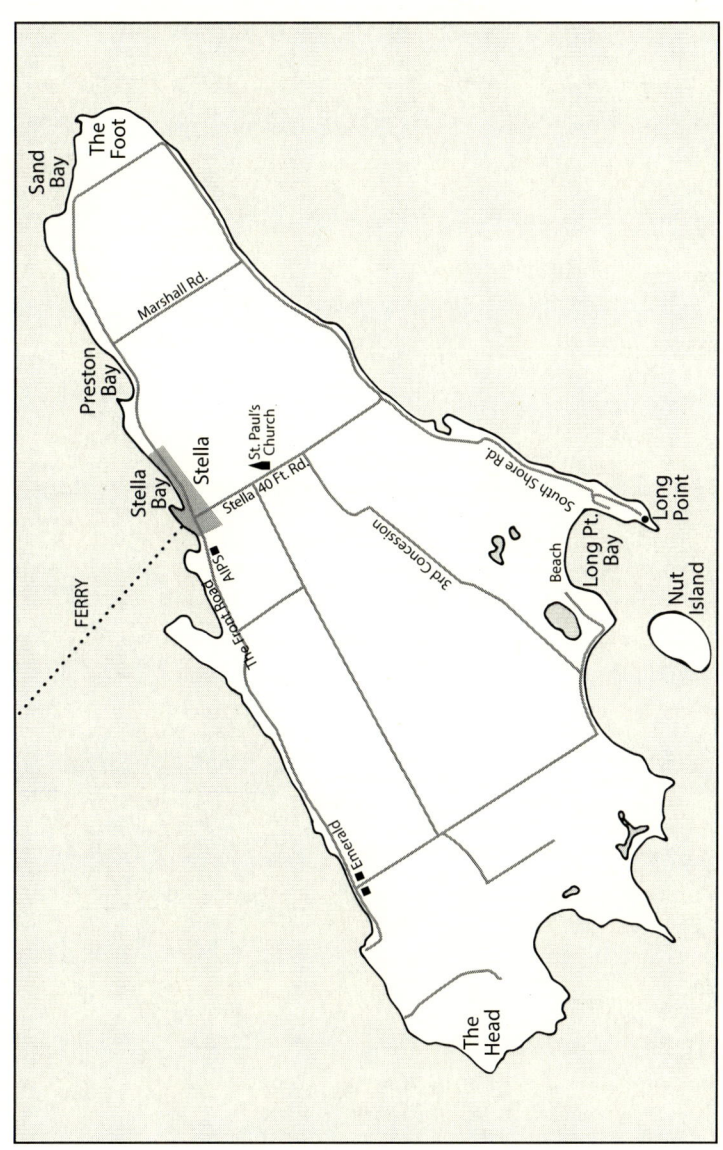

3. "That Went Well"

"THAT WENT WELL," Peter observed with his usual irony. "At least you didn't promise them another dog."

Victoria glared at Peter. "I didn't expect Alex' reaction," she said, "I never thought he'd be sanguine about this news."

"More phlegmatic, I think, Victoria, but at least not melancholic.

"Still, I was a bit surprised at Oliver's choleric response."

"This is no time for your silly word games Peter," Victoria replied, only slightly miffed. "But I was totally surprised at Oliver. These sorts of things usually just roll off his back, but he was very quiet and then exploded."

"Maybe it's best we leave him to process the news in his room," said Peter, sagely.

The parents talked amongst themselves for another thirty minutes until Victoria decided it was time to check on the boys.

She climbed the stairs to the bedrooms, first stopping at Alex' room. Alex was lying on his bed leafing through a copy of *Mad Magazine*. He didn't seem very troubled by the news. Victoria figured there was more going on in his head than he was letting on and she intended to have a chat with him later, but for now she needed to see to Oliver.

"Is Oliver in his room, Alex?"

"I don't know Mom."

Victoria walked down the hall and knocked on Oliver's door. She called his name. There was no response. Gingerly, she turned the knob and opened the door.

"Alex, he's not here. Where do you suppose he is?"

She began to feel alarmed.

"He's not in his room," Victoria exclaimed, her voice rising with anxiety.

She called his name but got no answer.

"Oliver, where are you?"

Peter called up from the foot of the staircase.

"What's the matter, Victoria?"

"I can't find Oliver, and he won't answer when I call."

"Maybe he's hiding somewhere in protest," remarked Peter.

Victoria was not amused, firing a dagger at him with her eye.

"Check his closet. And the attic," Peter said, "I'll take a look in the garage and tool shed."

"I'll check the dock, Dad. Sometimes he likes to go there and brood."

That was news to Peter; he never thought of Oliver as a brooder.

The two of them left the house by the side door, and then in different directions to look for Oliver. Where could he be? And for that matter, where was that beige and white beagle?

As Alex crossed the lawn, he noticed that only his three-speed Raleigh bicycle was lying on the lawn; Oliver's 20-inch green Supercycle, with whitewall tires, was missing.

"Dad," he called to Peter, "I think Oliver might have gone down the lane to be with his friend Janey Clarence and her sister."

But Alex also thought of another place Oliver might have gone. He jumped on his bike, but before he headed down McDonald's Lane he stopped at the top of the embankment of Stella Bay in front of their house and checked the dock. Oliver wasn't there but Alex studied the far shore and in particular, the spire of St. Albans Church.

He could hear barking way off in the distance. Sounded like a hound, but was that Tony? Beagles have a compulsion to run and chase their noses but the distant barking continued in one place. Maybe Tony had a squirrel up a tree.

Alex whipped his bike around and raced down McDonalds Lane. When he reached the corner of the Lane at The Front Road he squeezed the hand brakes hard, pulling the bike to a sliding stop and a cloud of dust. He glanced up the road to The Stella Forty Foot Road to see if by chance Oliver might be at Johnson's General Store, but he saw no sign of Oliver's green bike.

Alex turned his bike east on The Front Road and raced to St. Alban's Church, passing the old brick houses and overgrown fences, avoiding the broken-down sidewalk but riding on the left shoulder of Stella Road, racing past Neilson's Warehouse, then around the side parking lot at the ancient little red brick church. He made no effort this time to hide his course.

He braked hard, leapt off, and, guiding his bike, picked his way through the brush at the back of the church.

There was the green Supercycle, just as he suspected, leaning against a tree, and there was Tony on a tumbled down pile of railway ties and 4x4 cedar posts.

Alex was alarmed at the sight. Instead of the carefully stacked timber that disguised the secret hideout beneath, there was a pile of rubble and timber all askew. And there was Tony barking frantically at was once the entrance to 'the fort' Alex had burrowed out of the timber pile three years ago.

This had been Alex' hideout when the Jorgenson's had first moved to Stella. It had served as the headquarters of 'The St. Albans Secret Society', of which Oliver was a junior member.

Alex wasn't surprised that Oliver had come to the fort in his anger and upset but why was the roof all caved in?

Tony had stopped his barking when Alex arrived but he continued to stand on the top of the broken pile, whining.

Alex called Oliver's name, but he already realized where he was. Under that pile of rubble.

He scrambled over the pile and called Oliver's name again. There was no answer, but as Alex cleared some of the boards and beams away he could see one arm of Oliver's blue jacket, the rest of him apparently under some of the timbers. He couldn't move any of the big pieces and realized he needed help to get Oliver out.

'Oh my god, I hope he's alright,' Alex thought to himself in alarm and emotion.

He picked his way down the little path the boys had made over the years to the hidden rock jetty where they moored their motorboat out of sight of other boaters.

Alex stood on the jetty and hollered across the bay to his father standing on McDonalds Lane at their house.

Peter heard his name and then could see Alex waving from the opposite shore. He clambered down to the dock and called back across the water.

"Alex, what are you doing over there?"

"I've found Oliver!"

"Dad, call the Emergency Response Team and send them to St. Albans Church, right away!"

4. The Cave-In

PETER RAN BACK TO THE HOUSE AND HOLLERED to Victoria,

"Call Frank Gohm and have him wrangle the volunteers and meet me at St. Albans Church."

"Why?" yelled Victoria in reply, "what's wrong?"

"Alex has found Oliver."

"Is he alright?"

"I don't know. I'm taking the boat over there now."

Peter jumped into the family fishing boat, untied it from the dock and frantically gave the pull cord of the little six-horsepower motor a pull. Blessedly it started on the third try. He turned the bow towards the opposite shore and gave that little motor all the gas he could.

Alex continued waving to his dad as the little boat drew closer and then pointed to the tiny hidden cove. He guided his dad into the space and helped him climb out of the boat and quickly tie up.

"The fort is just up here," Alex said pointing the way along the grassy path.

"Fort?" Peter quizzed. But Alex didn't answer him.

As soon as he saw it Peter was instantly alarmed.

"What the devil happened here?" he asked, almost rhetorically.

"I don't know Dad, but you can see Oliver buried at the bottom of these timbers. I can't move them."

"Yes, I see, Alex, and it's probably better we not try until the volunteers arrive."

It took only minutes before Frank Gohm and the Rescue Vehicle arrived at the church, but it seemed like ages.

"Peter, where are you?" Frank called.

"We're around at the back down near the water. There's been a cave-in and Oliver is trapped under some rubble."

Frank and his crew arrived a minute later crashing through the brush. Tony set up a new hew and cry.

"What's all this" he said, eyeing the pile of timber and rubble.

"Alex says it was their old hideout."

"Who knew?" Frank remarked, rhetorically, glancing around at the pile, wondering. But he could see at a glance this was just the thing for a gang of 13-year-old boys. It was only about three feet high, though the sandy floor had been dug out some. Only kids could have crawled into the small opening that must have served as a door, a piece of canvas hanging from the ends of some of the beams.

"Let's take a look. Is Oliver talking?"

"No, he's not. I can see his arm but he's not moving."

At that moment Victoria arrived in the family Oldsmobile and ran through the brush towards the noise of the crew and the barking dog.

"What's happening?" she exclaimed. "Where's Oliver?"

Immediately she knew Oliver was under that pile. She screamed and rushed at the pile of timber and began clawing at the large pieces of wood and scraps.

Peter intercepted her, gently pulling her away from the rubble.

"Victoria, leave it to the crew. You can't do anything and you might disturb the pile.

Victoria stared at Peter with uncomprehending eyes, anguish and despair on her now tear-streaked face. Slowly, as Peter held her tight and away from the pile, she began to collect herself. She was a Red Cross Lifesaver and knew panic was never helpful in a crisis.

Frank took charge. He sent the crew members back to the Rescue Vehicle to retrieve tools that could lift and cut some of those timbers. This cave-in wasn't much different from a collapsed burning building and they had trained tirelessly in this sort of rescue.

Crew members cautiously jostled various of the fallen beams and timbers to see what was unstable and what needed to be moved to get Oliver out. They carefully removed as many of the loose boards as they could but were wary of the heavy railway ties. A couple of those ties had fallen in to the hollowed-out cavern below; one was over Oliver's head and one on his torso.

Once they had reinforced the sidewall beams and removed all the overhead boards and beams they were able to lift the tie that was across Oliver's head, then the one over his chest. Frank scrambled into the space and felt for Oliver's breath and pulse.

"He's alive but unconscious. That tie must have given him a crack on the skull, judging from all the blood. And I'm not sure about his ribs."

"Careful boys. Two of you fetch the stretcher and then we'll carefully lift him out of that hole. We'll have to be very careful with his back and neck.

"I'll call the ferry and tell them to hold it on this side so we can get him to hospital in Kington."

"Already done, Captain," said one of the crew. "I did that as soon as I heard the alarm call."

"Okay, good."

Victoria was sobbing gently now. Peter was teary-eyed too.

"It's all my fault," said Victoria. "I didn't handle that family conference very well. I was worried about Alex and I wasn't paying attention to Oliver."

"It's not your fault Mom," Alex said. "We built this fort very sturdy, and I don't see how it could have caved in by itself. Something else must have caused this.'

Frank perked up his ears at that.

"That's interesting, Alex. Once we've taken care of Oliver, we will undertake a thorough investigation and figure out what happened here."

The crew members then proceeded to remove all the timbers from what was one wall of the fort. They cleared a space for the stretcher and set it down beside the unconscious Oliver. Frank carefully put his hands around Oliver's head and neck. Another crew member held his right shoulder.

"This doesn't feel right Captain, may be a broken collarbone or dislocated."

Another crew member cradled Oliver's other shoulder, another secured his hips, and another grasped him by the ankles. Oliver was a boy of only 90 pounds; they could easily lift him but wanted to minimize any jarring.

"On my count of 3 and Lift," said Frank. The crew nodded.

"Slowly now, one, two, three, and lift."

Victoria could hardly look but as they lifted Oliver onto the portable gurney, settling his head and neck in the collar brace that was positioned there, he was jostled slightly and he cried out.

Victoria rushed to his side.

Oliver began to open his eyes.

"Oh honey, you're awake, oh my God Oliver, you are awake."

"Sorry Mom," he whispered.

She went to kiss him on his cheek but Frank interceded.

"Better not to touch him Victoria and jostle his neck. I think he's alright but better we not take chances."

"Yes Frank, I know you're right.

"Thank you."

Frank proceeded to strap Oliver to the gurney, making his head and neck secure in the collar. Then he secured his arms across his body, and Oliver cried out again.

"Yes boys, I think that shoulder is injured."

Frank continued to strap Oliver's hips and legs to the gurney.

With that the crew repeated their procedure to lift the gurney and carry it to the rescue vehicle, but this time with only two crew.

"One, two three, and lift."

The crew picked their way back through the brush and settled Oliver in the back of the Rescue Vehicle.

One of the crew members said, "hey, we'll take the bikes back to the house in our pick-up truck."

Alex said he'd take Tony home in the motorboat. Tony, barking at the Rescue truck, showed every sign he wanted to get in with Oliver. Alex turned and called Tony, excitedly, "Want to go for a boat-ride, Tony?" Tony reluctantly followed Alex back to the fallen-in fort and down to the motorboat, all the while looking back.

Peter and Victoria followed the Rescue Vehicle to the ferry launch and crossed with it to the mainland. There were dozens of other cars waiting to cross as well but they were denied. The emergency took precedence. The islanders understood perfectly, they knew the drill. The non-comprehending visitors were less generous.

5. The Story

THE EMERGENCY TEAM AT KGH rushed Oliver into an examining room, leaving Peter and Victoria fretting and pacing in reception. After what seemed a long time, the white-coated doctor on duty emerged and reported his findings to the worried parents.

"He's had a nasty cut on his forehead that took a dozen double sutures; I don't think he will have any serious scarring. He's had a concussion; we will keep him in the hospital for observation, but I think he will be alright.

"We've taken a series of x-rays to see if anything is broken. His neck and back are fine. He doesn't have a broken shoulder as The Rescue Officer thought, but he does have two cracked ribs and he will have some nasty bruising on his shoulder and chest in the next few days. He'll be pretty sore, but he's going to be fine in a few weeks."

Victoria slumped in her chair in relief.

"Oh, thank you doctor."

"I'm not sure what exactly was the situation he got himself into to cause all those injuries but it needs to be investigated. He's talking now and he keeps saying 'Old Man O'Reilly'".

Peter and Victoria looked at each other. Not him again. They thought they were done with that sorry excuse of a human being.

The next day the Ontario Provincial Police showed up at the hospital to interview Oliver.

"We've been over to the ruined 'fort' and we've interviewed Alex, Mrs. Jorgenson. Now we need to hear from Oliver as to what happened. Is he able to talk to us now?"

"Yes, officer, he's fully awake and his usual talkative self. We have a good idea what happened, but I suppose you'll want to hear it directly from Oliver."

"Yes, Ma'am, we will."

"Apparently, he keeps mentioning 'Old Man O'Reilly'; that's the old coot who was mixed up with the treasure of Stella Bay episode, summer before last."

"That's right Sergeant Foster," Peter said, "I remember you led that investigation at the time. We haven't seen him since."

"That old coot had a real hate on for young Alex at that inquest last year. Mean bugger," Sergeant Foster observed.

"I hear John O'Reilly has turned over a new leaf since he was released from prison, getting the family farm back in shape."

"Yes," said Peter, "and he's a member of the Volunteer Rescue Team now. Apparently, he's read the riot act to his uncle, old Nelson O'Reilly."

"Let's go in and see what Oliver has to say. You two can sit in if you want."

The three of them entered the Paeds 3 private room where Oliver was resting. The OPP Officer pulled up a chair on one side of the bed, Victoria protectively on the other side; Peter sat at the end of the bed.

"Hello Oliver," said the OPP Officer, "I'm Sergeant Foster from the Amherstview Detachment of the OPP."

"I remember you from the inquest over Alex's treasure," responded Oliver.

Peter was relieved. Oliver seemed to be his old extroverted self.

"That's right, young man, that was me."

"Now, can you tell us what happened at your fort at St. Albans Church?"

"Yeah, well, I was very upset with my Mom and Dad because they said we have to move to Peterborough and so I ran out of the house and grabbed my bike and rode over to St. Albans to hide in our fort and think.

"I was mad and racing and I didn't pay attention like Alex always warned us, and just drove my bike into the St. Albans parking lot without first checking if anyone was around."

"Wait a minute, what do you mean by 'us'?" Sergeant Foster asked.

"The other boys in The St. Albans Secret Society: me and Alex of course, and Hugh and Fuzzy and Thursty."

"You mean a club of boys would meet at the fort behind the church?"

"Yes, that's right. We're always supposed to make sure there's nobody seeing us going on past the church to the back.

"Anyway, I jumped off my bike and pushed it through the brush and propped it up against the tree like always and came over to the entrance to our fort, moved the plywood cover to the entrance and crawled inside. I sat in my usual spot and kinda brooded for a while. There was enough light coming through our portholes that I didn't bother to light any candles, and besides I kinda liked being in the dark."

Victoria sighed. She was both anguished and angered that this was the first she had heard of a fort.

"Did you know about the kids having a fort over there, Peter?" she exclaimed.

"No, I didn't, Victoria, but I'm not surprised, many twelve-year-olds have some sort of retreat to hide out in; and we've given the boys a certain amount of freedom to roam in safe Amherst Island."

Sergeant Foster cut off this conversation. "Let the boy continue his story, please."

"What happened next, Oliver?" asked Sergeant Foster.

"Well, I thought I heard a noise, like maybe footsteps rustling the leaves, but maybe it was Tony. He had followed me out of the house and raced with me down McDonald's Lane. He's not supposed to but I didn't care. Sorry Mom. I crawled over to the porthole that faces the church and looked out.

"I could see a grizzled old man looking at my bike. He touched the seat and handlebars, picked it up and examined it.

"Then he looked over to the fort. I hoped he would think it was only a pile of junk, but Tony was standing on the roof and he must have been curious. He walked over to it. I held my breath. Tony was barking and baying his head off."

At that point Victoria sucked in her breath. Sergeant Foster looked at her and Victoria recovered herself.

"Then what happened, Oliver?"

"Well, by then I thought the old guy was Old Man O'Reilly and that made me really nervous."

"What made you think it was Nelson O'Reilly?" Sergeant Foster asked.

"He had grey hair under some kind of cap, and a gray scruffy beard, and ragged old overall jeans and red plaid shirt. He wore the same clothes at the inquest."

"You mean the inquest I held when Alex discovered the chest in Stella Bay?"

"Yes, that's right."

"And what happened next?"

"I was getting scared.

"But I got even more scared when he came over to the entrance to our fort. He pulled aside the canvas cloth we use as a door and peered inside but I don't think he saw me. I had crawled back to the far corner of the fort where it was really dark, and his eyes wouldn't have been used to the dark. He stuck his head in further but he couldn't fit his body in. He shoved some but that loosened some of the timbers and some pieces and dirt fell in.

"I held my breath harder and then the old man pulled his head out of the door.

"Next thing he climbed on to the roof of the fort. He took a kick at Tony and Tony ran off. The roof shifted again and more dirt fell in through the cracks.

"Then he jumped up and down on the roof, twice.

"And that's when the whole roof started to cave in. I put my hands up over my head but one of the ties hit me on the head and I blacked out."

"What happened to the old man?"

"I don't know; like I said I must have blacked out."

"Right.

"Are you sure the old man who jumped on the roof of your fort was Old Man O'Reilly?"

"I think so sir, but I can't be sure. I haven't seen him for more than a year and was only looking at him through our porthole and then I tried to make myself as small as I could when he started to look in at the door."

"Why do you think he did that, Oliver?"

"Maybe he saw me and my bike and thought I was Alex."

"What happened next?"

"What happened next was that I started to come to when they lifted me on the stretcher. And then I saw my mom.

"And then the Volunteers drove me here to KGH."

"Okay son, I guess that's about it.

"If you think of anything else, tell your dad to call me; we'll talk again."

"What's going to happen to Old Man O'Reilly?"

"If we can be sure it was Nelson O'Reilly, he'll be arrested and charged with reckless endangerment."

"Oh."

Sergeant Foster and Peter left the room while Victoria gingerly hugged her little man.

"What's next, Sergeant Foster?" Peter inquired.

"Well, we'll go and pay O'Reilly a visit and see if he can account for his whereabouts on Saturday afternoon. If he's got a good alibi, there's probably not much we can do. Even if he doesn't, I'm not sure there's much of a case against him. He could claim he didn't know there was anybody inside the pile of timber and he didn't try to wreck the pile, he just stood on it and it caved in."

Peter shrugged, "it sounds like just another O'Reilly episode of 'he said-he said', and O'Reilly gets off again."

"Maybe," said Sergeant Foster with a reciprocal shrug. "But we'll put some questions to him and put on the pressure."

6. Old Man O'Reilly

OLIVER WAS DISCHARGED FROM HOSPITAL Monday morning. The Jorgensons had an early Thanksgiving Dinner; not surprising – Sunday Dinner was always at 12:00 Noon, sharp, so naturally, special dinners were at noon too, even though on a Monday. Late that afternoon Peter had to leave for Peterborough.

"What are we going to do about that O'Reilly situation?" Victoria asked, a bit petulantly.

"Nothing for now, Victoria. We have to leave it in the hands of the police. When I get back on Friday I'm sure we'll have some news from Sergeant Foster."

Tuesday, the boys were back in school and Oliver was the talk of the Amherst Island Public School playgrounds, with his bandaged forehead and the story of the caved-in fort. Even Alex had to field a shower of questions from kids on the school bus to Napanee High School. Half the questions were about Old Man O'Reilly – did he really cause the cave-in? – but Alex was more in mourning over the loss of the fort. He knew they could never go back to the fort again – everybody knew about it now, and it was wrecked. But he also knew that since he and most of the members of the Secret Society, except Oliver, were in Grade 9 now, they rarely went to the fort anymore. Now never.

Sergeant Foster paid Nelson a visit at the O'Reilly farm on Tuesday and on Saturday morning, with Dr. Jorgenson returned home from Trent, he called on the Jorgensons to report on what he had discovered.

"Well folks," he began, "I'll cut to the chase. I don't think we've got enough to proceed with charges on Nelson. He's got an alibi for his movements on Saturday afternoon; I don't believe him, or his alibi, but I'm pretty sure the Crown Attorney will decide there's not enough to take him to trial."

Victoria exclaimed, "That's ridiculous!"

Peter studied Foster's face and offered a philosophical shrug.

"Oh Peter," she said, "you always concede the point too easily."

— Alex' Choice —

"Now, Mrs. Jorgenson, don't be too hard on Professor Jorgenson. He's quite right. Sometimes the law doesn't seem like it meets out justice but due process is there to protect the innocent, not to shield the guilty. It's the same brush."

Victoria went silent. Sergeant Foster continued his story.

"I went to the O'Reilly farm and met with John and his wife, Vera. They weren't happy to think Nelson was on the wrong side of the law again. They said that as far as they knew, Nelson wasn't home last Saturday and they didn't know where he was.

"They turned to their two boys, Shamus and Sean, who were lurking in the background. 'Do you know where your uncle was last Saturday afternoon?' and Seam replied, 'I think he was up at Keith McEwen's camp.'

"That made my ears perk up – McEwen's camp is only a couple of lots over from St. Albans Church."

"I asked if Nelson was at home now and Vera sent Shamus down to Nelson's shed by the shore to fetch him.

"When Nelson arrived at the house, his face scowling as usual and carrying that big chip on his shoulder, I asked him if he could account for his whereabouts last Saturday afternoon. Of course he resisted, 'What's it to ya?' I said, 'just answer the question, Nelson.'

"He growled again, 'I was at Keith McEwen's camp all afternoon, fishing in the channel."

"And Keith McEwen will vouch for that?

"'Yep,' he said, insolently.

"You better be telling the truth here, Nelson. I'm going to be checking with Keith.

"'Fat chance of that today, he's gone back ta Kemptville,' he sneered.

"Insolent so-and-so.

"John asked what this was all about, and I explained that there had been a cave-in of an old construction site behind St. Albans Church and Oliver had been trapped and injured in the rubble. I told him we think Nelson had something to do with that. Oliver was seriously injured.

"John O'Reilly turned red with anger. 'Well this is the last straw,' he muttered, glaring with anger. Vera nodded grimly in agreement. It was plain they believed it possible Nelson was somehow involved in this latest calamity.

"I checked at Keith McEwen's camp but there was nobody there, no truck, no sign of anybody.

"I got his number in Kemptville and gave him a call. Keith wasn't there but I left a message with the woman who lives with him. She said he would be coming back to Amherst Island on Friday.

"This morning I paid Keith a call at his camp. He corroborated Nelson's story that the two of them had been fishing in the channel all day.

"I tested him, 'All day Keith? He was never out of your sight?'

"'All day,' Keith replied, but he wouldn't make eye contact with me.

"'Anyone else here last Saturday who can corroborate that?'

"'Nope', said Keith, eyes still cast down.

"I'm pretty sure he's lying about at least some of this story but without anyone else to corroborate it, I have to accept this alibi.

"So, there you have it.

"We're not going to be able to take this any further unless somebody else comes forward with new information.

"I'm sorry."

After a few minutes, Sergeant Foster took his leave.

"Well isn't that just a wonderful how-do-you-do?" exclaimed Victoria, frustrated once again with police impotence.

"Now Victoria, sometimes we just have to accept things as they are."

"But this is the third time we've had trouble with those O'Reilly's and nothing is done about it. First it was our boys being bullied by Sean and Shamus, then there was Nelson causing Alex and Sandra to be dragged down in the Bay with that booty chest, and now this. Sandra and Alex almost drowned and now Oliver has a cracked skull. It's just not right."

"I know, Victoria, but The O'Reilly family have made a fresh start – Sean and Shamus are back in school, and in Scouts; and John is active on the Rescue Squad.

— Alex' Choice —

"I'll tell you what, I'll give Frank Gohm a call and see if he will come with me to visit John and see if there's anything that can be done."

"Can I come too?" chimed in Oliver.

Alex scowled at his feisty little brother. He wanted to blame Oliver for exposing their fort, but part of him also wanted to get back at Old Man O'Reilly.

Peter called Frank Gohm and the two of them drove to the O'Reilly farm.

Vera met them at the side door of the old farmhouse.

"I expect you want to talk to Nelson. Well, he's not here."

"Well, actually," Frank said, "we'd like to speak with John."

Vera's nervous anxiety flicked on, "You don't think John had anything to do with this?"

"No, no, Mrs. O'Reilly, nothing like that," said Frank, "we just want to see what we can do to help John and you with your problem."

"You're right about that. Nelson is a big problem.

"John's down at the barn, do you want me to call him or you just go down to the barn?"

"We'll go down to the barn," said Frank.

Peter and Frank picked their way along the path to the barn. Peter made mental notes: this place looked so much better than the last time he had paid Vera O'Reilly a visit when Sean and Shamus had been bullying Alex and Oliver. The weeds and wild hollyhocks and raspberry canes had been cut back, the lawns had been mowed, the yard to the barns had been cleared of cow paddies; the barns had been mucked out and the fences rebuilt.

"Some real progress is being made here, Frank," Peter commented.

"Yes; John's been working hard."

They found John sitting on a stool under a cow, milking.

"Hi John," Frank said.

"Hi yourselves," John replied, "I've sorta been 'specting you."

"Say John," Frank asked, "how many head do you have now?"

37

"Twenty cows milking, a dozen yearlings, half of them steered. I'll keep the heifers, take the boys to the abattoir in a couple of months, for veal. The girls I'll sell for milkers. Even with Vera and the boys helping I can't handle more than 20 cows milking by hand. I've been talking to the De Laval fella about getting milking machines set up in here."

"Wow, that's great," Peter exclaimed.

"Say, John," Frank continued, we wanted to talk to you for a bit about what can we do about Nelson. We all know …"

John cut Frank off at that point.

"Say no more Frank. This latest episode with your boy, Professor, is the last straw. Vera and I read the riot act to Nelson and we drove him off the farm. We told him he was no longer welcome here. And what's more we told him to get himself off the Island too.

"He left on Tuesday. He's got some friends in Kingston and some distant relatives on Wolf Island. I'm sure he'll end up as a vagrant on the streets of Kingston, selling pot to Queen's students, and spending most of his time at the Montreal House. But I can't worry about him anymore. He's incorrigible and he's caused this family more than enough grief. Enough."

Frank and Peter looked at each other. Peter was about to give a little lecture on hopefulness and rehabilitation but then thought better of it.

"Well, John, I suppose that's for the best," said Frank. "I'll tell the Rescue Team and the OPP Detachment what's happened, and they can be on the lookout for Nelson if he tries to come across to Amherst Island on the ferry. We can't technically prevent him from traveling over here but we can certainly discourage him.

"I'm sorry for troubling you John," said Peter.

"If there's anything the boys and I can do for you," Frank said, "just let us know.

"See you next Wednesday for training session."

With that they all shook hands and silently hoped that was the last they'd see of Old Man O'Reilly.

7. Return to The Fort

THE TUESDAY FOLLOWING THANKSGIVING, Alex returned to his caved-in fort. He wanted to examine the damages for himself, without a crowd of people around. It was very likely that was the end of it – no longer a secret hideout and would be seen by the town and the church as a hazard.

He rode his bicycle over to St. Albans after school, stopping first, out of habit, looking to make sure nobody was around to see him. He pushed his bike through the brush and leaned it up against the parking tree. Alex wended his way to the remnants of the fort – it was a disaster. He studied it reflectively, imaging how it used to look. He studied. The roof material of plywood and sand had been pushed over the far side of the woodpile, some had fallen into the cavern; two of the heavy black railway ties – the ones that had pinned Oliver down – had been pitched over the far side too and out of the way. The walls of timber and ties on the near side had been removed in order to lift Oliver onto the stretcher. The hidden inner cavity was nothing but an open pit now.

He jumped into the pit to take a closer look. Ha! The hidden cubby hole in the remaining wall was still intact and the tin 'strong-box' in place. Alex pulled it out of the wall and examined its contents – everything undisturbed: the candles and matches, the knives and forks, the *Mad* magazines and the copies of *Playboy*.

He put the box on the floor beside the block of wood that usually served as his seat in his fortress chamber, now exposed to the sunlight; he sat down and let his mind mine his memories.

He remembered when he first discovered the abandoned pile of building materials three years ago when the family first arrived in Stella and he was allowed to tour Stella Bay in the family outboard on his own. He remembered the thrill of stowing the boat in the little cove out of sight of prying eyes. He saw right away the potential of the pile of timber being excavated and converted into a secret hideaway. He had 'borrowed' tools from the family tool shed and began digging out the interior.

He couldn't keep his secret hideaway a secret very long: his brother Oliver had been watching Alex traveling back and forth across the bay from the family dock and eventually pestered Alex to reveal his secret and take him to it.

Soon after that Alex managed to tell his best friend, Hugh, about the fort, and was persuaded to take him in the outboard to the hidden bolthole. Rambunctious Hugh bumped the roof with is head, bringing down sand and dust from the low ceiling. Alex and Hugh reinforced the roof with pieces of 2x4 and resolved never to walk on the roof.

They returned the next day by bike, Alex warning him not to go straight into the parking lot but always stop to make sure there was no one else around.

"Who else knows about this place?" Hugh asked.

"No one," said Alex, "except my brother."

"How're you going to make Oliver keep a secret? He's younger and he talks a lot to all his girlfriends in the school yard."

"Yeah, but I told him this fort at St. Albans Church was our meeting place for our secret society."

"Secret Society? Who else is in your secret society?"

"Nobody. I just told Oliver that to reinforce this should be a secret place."

"Can I be a member of your club, Alex? Do you have a name for it?"

"I call it the St. Albans Secret Society."

"Hey, we could invite some other guys to become members."

So Hugh and Alex invited Walter Taylor (but everyone called him Fuzzy) and Billy Thurston (but everyone called him Thursty) to join on pain of death from mysterious causes if they should ever tell anyone else about the fort and the Secret Society. They drew up a charter with roles and rules – No Girls Allowed – and signed it in blood with their thumb prints.

Alex laughed to himself at this memory. He himself had ended up secretly bringing Sandra Farquharson to the fort. He excused himself with this indiscretion because Sandra had become a very special person in his life.

— Alex' Choice —

Alex had one more look around the wreck of his fort and realized the finality of his loss. He would never be coming back to this fort again. He also realized this wasn't the only thing he had lost recently. And that's why he thought the family move to Peterborough might not be such a bad thing.

He picked up his 'strong box' of magazines and supplies and walked back to his bike; he rode out of the St. Albans parking lot, and he didn't look back.

In fact, once the police had released the scene, a group of congregants from St. Albans Church got together and cleared that old pile of timber and junk and hauled it to the dump.

8. Alex' Reasons

ONCE THE CAVE-IN EXCITEMENT had settled down, Victoria's thoughts returned to the pending move to Peterborough. She began to puzzle herself why Alex was not evidently very upset about the announcement. She expected him to be the one troubled, not Oliver.

Oliver was the hero of Amherst Island Public School now, with his wounds and his encounter with Old Man O'Reilly. With all this attention he seemed to have forgotten his upset with moving, his buoyant optimism returning.

Alex on the other hand remained a mystery. He was up at 6:00 and on the school bus by 7:00 in time to catch the ferry for the mainland at 7:30. He did his chores without complaint, and except for his weekly Scouts meeting, he hung around the house.

She decided she needed to have a wee chat with him.

"Alex, Son, I don't see you hanging out with your friends much anymore. Everything okay?

Alex mumbled some sort of answer, but Victoria wasn't going to let that go. She continued.

"You haven't said too much about our pending move to Peterborough. Do you want to talk about it?"

"Not really," Alex replied.

Victoria decided to wait. After a quiet couple of minutes Alex said,

"Well, I think it might be better than living here."

"Why is that, Alex?"

"Well, things aren't going too good for me now."

"Oh?"

"You know. Everything has changed: Hugh has moved to Cobourg, and Sandra is boarding in Odessa; I hardly know anybody who is going to Napanee High School; even Sean O'Reilly is going to Regiopolis in Kingston."

"And?..."

"And there's a lot of Indian kids who go to NHS from the Deseronto Reservation. They all hang out together in one part of the school, and all the Napanee white kids hang out elsewhere."

"Oh?"

— Alex' Choice —

"And I just don't fit in."

"Yes dear, but I'm sure you'll make new friends, kids from Bath, and Adolphustown."

Alex raised an eyebrow and stared at his mom.

"Ma-om!"

"I know, I'm trying too hard to soften it."

"And besides, I won't make new friends there because we're moving to Peterborough."

"Right," said Victoria, smiling at her mistake.

"Anything else?"

"Well, I'm sure not going to miss those four hours on the bus every day."

"Yeah, that's a problem. I'm sure your dad and I would have tried to figure out another solution if we were staying here.

"Yeah, and you know what else?"

"What, dear?"

"Because I have to take the bus at 3:30 I can't play for the Napanee Golden Hawks football team."

"Oh," said Victoria. "I didn't realize that was so important to you. I know you like football, and your father takes you to Queen's games all the time."

"Yeah, Mom. My dream is to play for the Golden Gaels one day."

"Hmmm, I see.

"Maybe you will be able to play football at the new high school in Peterborough next year."

"Yeah, that's what I've been thinking."

"Is that why you seem okay with moving to Peterborough?"

"Yeah."

"Well son, I hope that turns out for you.

"But, just remember, you've had some wonderful years here on Amherst island."

"That's true."

"Let's think of the top ten memories you're going to bring with you to Peterborough."

"Well, of course there was the discovery of the treasure, and then there was saving Sandra from drowning, and the fort, and the school newspaper. And,"

"Yes, you've had a lot of adventures, especially in Grade Seven"

"Yeah, last year in Grade Eight it was quieter."

"I suppose, but surely there were good things in Grade Eight too..."

"Yes, Mom."

"You like to write. Why don't you get a journal and record your time on Amherst Island? You can show me your journal if you like, and we can put it in your memory box."

So, Alex 'borrowed' one of his father's hard-covered note books, and began to write: Alex' Journal. He thought he ought to start with his Grade Eight year, still fresh in his memory.

Amherst Island, 196

Amherst Island, 1963

— Doug Jordan —

9. Amherst Island Public School, September 1963

ONCE ALL THE EXCITEMENT OF THE TREASURE and the inquest had settled down, Grade 8 was anticlimactic. The boys of the St. Albans Secret Society were grateful their fort remained undetected, but they had to be vigilant, and with Winter soon coming, they would have to stay away until spring.

Alex was already thinking ahead to high school:

He knew he was pretty smart and also a good runner, but being the fastest in his four-room school in Stella was not much of a test. And he had always been the smartest kid in his class, at least he was until Sandra Farquharson came to Amherst Island in Grade 7. Would he be good enough to go to Queen's? And would he be good enough to play football for the Golden Gaels? He tried to calculate the years ahead: It was 1963 and just beginning his final year of Public School. Next year he would be going to Collins Bay High School, or maybe the new Ernestown Secondary School, and he would finish Grade 13 in 1969; he would be ready for Queen's, maybe. It seemed a long way off to Alex.

Alex' dad stopped by his room as he often did and found Alex at his desk deep in thought.

"What are you thinking about, Alex?" he asked, gently.

Alex always had mixed feelings about these dad questions. He loved his father and admired him, and usually he enjoyed their conversations – he made it pretty easy, even about sex, but sometimes Alex found the conversations confusing. Sometimes the Professor's questions were not about what Alex thought they were about, so he always felt he had to be on his toes. This might be one of those times, but he was in a mood to say what was on his mind.

"I was just thinking about my life, Dad. What's going to happen this year and then next year I'll be going to high school. And how will I do in school against all those other kids, and track.

"And will I be able to play football and then will I be good enough to play for the Queen's Golden Gaels, and,.."

"Woah, woah, slow down a bit Son. That's a lot to be thinking about.

"Don't wish your life away, or worry about tomorrow. You need to enjoy today."

Alex had heard this speech before. Instead of worrying about the future, his dad always reminded him, focus on today.

"When you were my age, Dad, did you think about the future a lot?"

"Yes son, I did. I used to worry a lot too. But my dad always warned me to take things one day at a time. He said it's okay to make plans, but you also need to live in the present. You never know what cards life is going to deal you.

"Your Grandpa Jorgenson had a great sense of humour. He always saw the irony in what happens in a life, and cautioned not to take life too seriously."

"You have a good sense of humour too, Dad."

"I guess I do. I know I'm pretty quick with my tongue. Sometimes it gets me in trouble. People don't always get what I'm saying; sometimes I'm not sure myself what I'm saying. That's the thing about language and the brain – things come into our heads and we don't realize how that happened and we just blurt things out."

'Oh boy,' thought Alex, 'here it comes, a lecture on the psychology of language or something'.

Peter caught the look on Alex' face and quickly changed course.

"We were talking about your future."

"Yes, but Dad, do you worry about the future now?"

Peter could see that Alex had something on his mind and was curious as to where Alex thoughts were going.

"Yes Son, I still think about the future, and I think about you and Oliver, and your Mother, and about my teaching at Queen's and my research, and career, but I don't worry as much anymore. I guess I'm just grateful things are going pretty well for me, and my life. My father was right – worry is a waste of energy."

"Do you think I have a good sense of humour, Dad?"

"I don't know, Son. You're pretty smart and you make quick connections, but your thinking seems more cerebral than intuitive. You take things a bit too seriously."

"Am I more like you, or like Mom?"

"That's a good question, Son. I think you are a mixture of the two of us. Your mom tends to live very much in the present, she doesn't think too much about the future, just takes it one day at a time. She's pragmatic and present whereas I tend to think about possibilities, the future. Both of us try to stay positive.

"See, you're like me that way, but serious like your mom."

"Oh, so what should I do about that."

"Well Son, there's not much you can do about it, it's likely part of your core personality. But you can try to pay attention to what's happening as it's happening and enjoy it. Even find the irony in the situation, especially if things aren't going the way you want them to."

Alex was beginning to lose the train of Peter's argument.

"Okay Dad, I'll try."

"That's good Son; if you can sort of talk to yourself while you're in the moment instead of thinking about the future it will be better for you. You'll feel lighter and you will be happier. Just don't do it out loud, people will wonder."

Alex picked up Peter's little joke and smiled but didn't reply. They sat on the bed, just being together, savouring the moment.

Peter sensed they weren't quite finished their conversation, and he wanted to reinforce the thought for his serious son.

"So what are you looking forward to this year, Alex? Never mind Grade 13, just focus on Grade 8. You know, Grade 8 is in many ways the best year of your schooling."

Alex was surprised at this.

"How so?"

"Well, you're thirteen years old and starting to feel self-assured. Grade 8 kids are the oldest in the school and so all the other kids look up to you."

"Except Oliver!"

Peter smiled: "See, who said you don't have a sense of humour?" and winked.

"You and your classmates are the kings and queens of the school. You'll find the schoolwork is a bit easier than Grade 7 – it will be mostly review and reinforcement of concepts you already know. The teacher's main job is to prepare you for going to high school next year. So that's why you should just relax and enjoy it.

"So, what are you looking forward to this year?"

"Well, I was thinking I'd like to finish first in my class this year. I was annoyed that Sandra and Hugh beat me at the end of the year last year."

"Yes, we know; but your mother and I were not disappointed in you Alex. Sometimes we think you are a bit too competitive. It's okay to be ambitious and to try to do your best, but you don't have to *be* the best all the time. As you get older you will find there is always somebody who is smarter, or faster, or handsomer than you, but that shouldn't stop you from being the best version of yourself you can be."

Alex could feel another lecture coming on and Peter checked himself.

"I think you were a bit distracted with Sandra; maybe you learned a few lessons from that."

"Yeah, no girls."

"Hmmm, well that's going to be pretty difficult Alex. Girls take up more and more space in a guy's mind as he gets older, and now that you are a teenager...

"and besides, it's not Sandra's fault. She's a nice girl and you two make a fine pair."

Alex thought about that for a while.

"I'm also looking forward to Christmas, and I don't have to do a school play this year."

Peter smiled at the memory of the play Alex had written and directed: 'All I want for Christmas'.

"And I want do well at the track meet next spring.

"And maybe I'll earn my Queen's Scout Badge."

"I don't know about the Queen's Scout Badge, Alex – you just turned 13 and you might have to wait another year.

"Anyway, that's a lot to look forward to. So enjoy it as it comes to you. And if dark clouds come your way, well, that's life. You will have to look for the silver lining in that too."

"Okay Dad, I will," said Alex, wondering what a silver lining was, but wanting this conversation to be over.

Peter took his cue and rose from the bed.

He glanced at the poster of Sandra Dee on the back of Alex' door.

"Pretty girl." And walked out.

10. Hugh McPherson

ALEX' BEST FRIEND came into his life at a critical moment, two years previously. Alex had just moved to Amherst Island from Kingston – his family felt the need to live a more bucolic rural life, though Alex never quite understood why bucolic was such a good thing since he had no friends and had to face the ordeal of starting into Grade Six in a new school, Amherst Island Public School. But what Alex didn't realize at the time, another new kid had just moved to Amherst Island and was going into Mrs. MacAskill's Grade Six class too.

Hugh McPherson's father was the new Manager at the Bank of Montreal on Amherst Island. Alex had been feeling sorry for himself when his own family moved to Amherst Island, but he was astounded when he discovered this was Hugh's fifth school and third town. Hugh said it was bank policy to move managers around. Alex had a sense of this because his grandfather had been a banker and that's why Alex' dad had moved a lot as a kid. He said it was character building.

Alex wasn't sure what that really meant but he did think Hugh was quite a character. Hugh was a bit taller than Alex, muscular, with a big head and thick blonde hair. Hugh was smart like Alex, and a fast runner, though Alex was faster; but more than that, Hugh was self-confident and outgoing. Unlike Alex, he easily struck up conversations with almost anyone. Did he get that way from moving so often, Alex wondered?

It was only a few weeks into the Fall of Grade Six that Hugh had persuaded Alex to show him his fort, and a month after that he persuaded Alex to invite Fuzzy and Thursty to join the St. Albans Secret Society.

Despite his inherent social reluctance, by Grade 8, Alex was nevertheless the undisputed leader of St. Albans Secret Society and for that matter in AIPS.

Hugh and Alex became the closest of friends. They did everything together – swimming off the Jorgenson's dock, boating around the bay and even up the channel toward 'The Foot', and bicycling all over the island, from 'The Head', where you could almost see Prince Edward County, to 'The Foot'.

The only thing Alex was annoyed with was the way Hugh teased him about Sandra Farquharson. Sandra was a nice girl, and also a good friend, though Alex realized he felt differently about Sandra than he felt about Hugh. In fact, he didn't think he felt anything for Hugh; Hugh was just his best friend.

It also annoyed him that at the end of Grade Seven, both Hugh and Sandra finished with higher marks than Alex. Well, it was going to be different this year.

When Alex and Sandra found the treasure, and they almost drowned in the effort, Hugh was very proud of his friend. Hugh was sorry he hadn't been there for all the excitement, but he was happy to bask in Alex' reflected glory. Alex, on the other hand, was a bit embarrassed at all the attention.

The two of them pedalled all over the Island, Alex in his three-speed red Raleigh bike, Hugh on his three-speed CCM. Hugh lived west of Stella on The Front Road near Kerr Bay. He would often meet Alex at Johnson's General Store and decide on their route that day. They brought their lunch pails and on good weather days their bathing suits. When they rode down The Forty Foot Road to the South Shore Road they had to ride past St. Paul's Presbyterian Church, that beautiful stone edifice to God tucked in behind tall stately maple trees. Reverend Farquharson, Sandra's father, was the minister there, the manse next to the church. Hugh never failed to call out, "Hey Alex, I see your girlfriend!" but Alex didn't take the bait anymore, though he always kept his own eye peeled.

They often raced down the narrow roads of the open countryside, imagining they were doing the Tour de France.

"Hey, Alex, race you to Concession Three," and off they'd go at breakneck speed. Hugh, with his longer levers, usually won these contests.

On warm Summer days they'd pedal to Long Point Beach and enjoy the warm shallow waters of the bay. It was completely different than the deep cool water of Stella Bay diving off the dock. Alex was a good swimmer, and an accomplished diver; Hugh was neither.

Labour Day Saturday, the last weekend of summer before they had to face the start of the new school year on Tuesday, they arrived at the beach and were amazed to see Sandra there with her best friend, Rebecca, frolicking in the shallow water. Sandra was wearing her one-piece white suit with the ruffles along the bust but Rebecca was wearing a two piece yellow polka dot affair, not exactly a bikini but nevertheless showing more skin than the boys were used to. Hugh dropped his bike and then his shorts – he had his bathing suit on under his shorts – and raced to the water, splashing his way into the shallows and throwing up water with his flashing feet and scooping hands.

"Hey Hugh, watch it, we don't want to get our hair wet," Rebecca shouted.

"Too late for that!" he shouted back, splashing more water at them.

Alex was surprised the girls were laughing at these antics, as if they didn't really mind getting their hair wet even though they protested loudly.

'I don't get girls', he thought to himself.

"Come on, Alex, get your trunks and get in the water," Hugh demanded, excitedly.

"Okay, hold your horses, I gotta put them on first."

Alex didn't like wearing his trunks under his shorts, he found they were too tight and chafed his skin. He went behind some bushes, the usual changing area, and pulled off his shorts and underpants and struggled to pull up his tight trunks.

"Hey Alex," Hugh yelled, "I can see your willy!"

The girls squealed in fake alarm and laughter.

Embarrassed, Alex finished pulling on his trunks and tying the string, and raced over to the beach. And kept on racing, diving into the shallow water and then coming up for air, taking strong strokes out to the deeper water of the bay. He turned around and called back to the three friends frolicking in the shallows.

"Come on out, the water's fine here, and I can still touch bottom.'

With that Sandra started to work her way to deeper water, first walking, then half walking and swimming. When she got to Alex she jumped on him and wrapped her slim legs around his waist.

She whispered in his ear, "my hero."

Alex was thrilled and confused but not for long as in another minute Rebecca and Hugh had arrived. The four of them leaped and clamoured around, bodies bumping into bodies.

Alex wanted more separate time with Sandra and so turned to swim to deeper water, calling her. "Come on, Sandra."

But she didn't like to swim to deeper water and instead headed back to shore. Hugh and Rebecca followed her in. The three frolicked and splashed in the shallows as Alex watched from the deeper water; he was pretty sure Hugh was paying more attention to Sandra than to Rebecca.

Alex joined them in the shallows, but for Alex the fun had gone out of the games.

The four of them dried off in the sun, the girls stretched out on their towels; the boys hadn't brought towels, instead sat in divots they had scooped out for themselves in the sand. They opened their lunch boxes. They each had their favourite bottles of pop: Sandra had cream soda, Rebecca 7-Up; Alex and Hugh had Pepsis. The girls had lovely egg salad sandwiches and peaches for dessert. The boys had peanut butter sandwiches and potato chips, which they were glad to share with the girls.

The girls laughed at the boys' lunches: "I bet your mothers didn't make those lunches for you!"

They lounged on the sandy beach for a while, soaking up the last of the summer sun, the girls on their towels, the boys in hollowed out beds in the sand.

After a while Sandra declared she thought she was getting sunburned; red-headed Rebecca thought so too; they put their blouse and shorts on over their suits, mesmerizing the two boys.

"I think it's time we headed home," Sandra said and so the four of them collected their bikes and headed back on Third Concession to The Forty Foot Road. They bid Sandra goodbye at the manse and the three others continued on to Stella. At The Front Road, Hugh headed west to Kerr Bay and Alex and Rebecca rode in silence to McDonalds Lane, thinking their own private thoughts, though Alex couldn't imagine what thoughts Rebecca might be thinking.

***

— Alex' Choice —

The winter passed somewhat uneventfully, except for the serious freeze-up in January when the ferry was locked into the Amherst Island dock for three days, isolating the mainland.

By Spring, Hugh and Alex were itching to get their bikes out of the garage again and launch another season of the Tour de Amherst.

On one of their rides in the west of the Island, pedaling past the hamlet of Emerald, wide open fields with hundreds of sheep, and on toward 'The Head" where the Front Road shrinks down to a single dirt track, they decided to ride to the very end. A grassy lane turned off to the left going south. They picked their way along the narrow lane, fencing on two sides, some of which were ancient dry walls, with much of the limestone slabs fallen into the ditch. They had to ride their bikes very slowly using the lowest gear. Alex was about to get off and walk, or turn back, but Hugh pressed on.

They turned a bend in the lane and there saw a flock of several dozen sheep all milling around and pressing into the steel wire swing gate. When the boys approached the gate, the sheep set up a mewing and baaing din.

"Hey Alex," Hugh shouted, "I think they want to get out.

"Maybe they need water and they're trying to get to the next field.

"Let's let them out!"

"Wow! Hugh. We can't do that!"

"Sure we can, and we should. Their owners aren't around and the sheep seem to want to move on."

With that Hugh dropped his bike on the ground and ran over to the gate. He flipped up the stopper on the top of the gate and pulled the gate towards the lane. The sheep immediately started out the gate and headed on up the lane.

Hugh closed and re-latched the gate and the two of them remounted their bikes and followed the sheep. When one of the sheep on the edges of the lane tried to leave the flock, Hugh would pedal harder along the edge and turn the wanderer back into the flock. They shouted and whistled at the stragglers. The ewe at the head of the flock kept moving on.

"Hey Alex, we're just a couple of sheepdogs now," Hugh laughed.

Alex wasn't laughing but he did feel the excitement of the situation. The flock carried on down the lane but eventually came to a stand-still. Alex looked to the old ewe at head of the flock and realized they had come to another gate.

"I think they want into that field, Hugh. You go ahead on and open the gate; I'll stay and make sure nobody tries to go back."

Hugh laid his bike down on the trail and picked his way through the flock to the gate. It was a wooden slat gate but the stopper was the same as the previous gate. He lifted the big latch and swung the gate into the field. The lead ewe pushed ahead into the field and the rest of the flock followed her. They headed straight to a water hole.

"See, I was right," chirped Hugh.

"Okay, let's get out of here," Alex called.

Hugh pulled the gate shut and refastened the latch, picked up his bike and started on up the lane.

"Wait a minute Hugh. I don't think that lane goes much further."

"It's supposed to go all the way over to Second Concession."

"Yes, but I don't think it ever got finished. We better go back."

They turned their bikes around and retraced their course.

As they passed the previous gate Hugh said, "Gee, the owners are going to wonder how their sheep got into the next pasture."

By June the boys were getting pretty antsy. School work had ground to a halt and the only thing they had to look forward to was the School District track meet and graduation day. They had pedalled every road and trail on the island and found every bay and point, every inlet and mysterious cave; they had thrown rocks and skipped stones into Lake Ontario until they began to think they'd shovelled half the island into the lake.

One day as they met at Johnson's General Store after school they bought a ten cent ice cream and wondered what they'd do next. The ferry had just landed at the pier and the boys pedaled the short distance to the ferry to see the passengers drive their pick-up trucks off, or walk themselves off. A couple of them pushed their bikes down the ramp.

Hugh looked at Alex with that wild look he got at times with some sort of adventure in mind.

"Let's go to Amherstview," he blurted.

"Geez no, Hugh, I'm not allowed to go off the Island by myself."

"What's the difference Alex? We're just going for a bike ride, only on the other side."

And with that Hugh pushed his bike down the ramp and on to the ferry. Alex figured he had no choice but to stay with his friend and keep him out of trouble. The ferry operators paid them no mind.

The two leaned their bikes against the rail where bikes were to be stowed and climbed the circular metal staircase to the upper deck. They watched Stella receding and Millhaven landing getting ever closer. The wind blew in their hair and they felt the coolness of the air over the water.

They disembarked on the mainland, jumped on their bikes and pedaled east along the Bath Road towards Amherstview. They then realized the Bath Road, or officially the Queen's Highway 33, was a lot busier than The Forty Foot Road on Amherst Island. They had a tiny, paved shoulder to ride on but the cars were very close to them as they whizzed by, 50 miles an hour. The big transport trucks hauling cement powder to Kingston were huge up close and when they passed by the boys they produced a tremendous wind current.

The boys were unnerved but neither wanted to admit it and turn back. They had a mission and they pedalled on.

Amherstview was further down the road than they remembered – it seemed a short trip when they were traveling by car with their parents.

They turned into Nicholson's Point Road, relieved to be out of the traffic. They drove along the shore road looking across the channel to Amherst Island on the other side. They reached the east side of the point and stopped at a little look-out to see how much further they had to go. Making a telescope out of their two hands they were able to train their eyes on Collins Bay and the empty runways of Kingston Airport. They waited for what seemed like ages to see an airplane take off or land, but none came or went. They came upon a gut wagon at the corner of Edgewood Road and the Bath Road and sated themselves on Hostess Potato Chips and Pepsis.

"Hey, Hugh, I think we better forget about making Amherstview."

Hugh didn't object. They crossed the busy highway and mounted their bikes for the trip back to the Millhaven Ferry pier, gaining the landing just as the Amherst Islander was about to depart for its 6:00 pm run. They pushed their bikes aboard, stopped to catch their breath.

Just then, Professor Jorgenson, on his way home from the University, strolled over.

"Fancy seeing you boys on the ferry."

He glanced at Hugh and turned a hard eye on Alex. Alex studied his feet. He figured he was in for it now.

Glancing up, he noticed the smile in his dad's eye. And he relaxed. Peter winked and said, "I won't tell your mother if you want to keep this to ourselves."

"Yes, Dad."

They disembarked and Hugh pedaled hard for home. Alex raced behind the family car for the short ride to McDonalds Lane and home. They pulled into the yard at the same time.

"Alex, where have you been?! It's six-thirty and you know supper is at five."

"It's alright Victoria, the boys were waiting for me at the ferry,"

"Well, alright then, but don't you be making a habit of it."

Alex and Peter exchanged conspiratorial glances.

"Every day, Victoria, you be sounding more and more like an Islander."

Victoria caught Peter's jibe and snapped her tea towel at him.

"Sit down you two for supper. It's already way overcooked."

"Alex, first wash those filthy hands."

***

— Alex' Choice —

Hugh was a pretty fast runner, though not quite as fast as Alex. The first day at School in Grade Six when both Alex and Hugh were new to Amherst Island Public School, Hugh had challenged Alex to a race to the end of the school yard at the back. Alex didn't really know what racing was but as he ran he realized Hugh was pulling ahead of him so Alex just pushed himself harder. He found that if he raised himself on his toes and the balls of his feet instead of his heels he could go faster. And as he picked up speed and moved ahead of Hugh, Hugh pushed himself harder. The cedar rail fence at the back of the yard was coming up fast. Alex touched the rails first; Hugh crashed into the cedar rail fence and tumbled right over it. Alarmed, Alex looked over the fence, concerned for his rival. Hugh glanced up at Alex and winked.

"Hey, Alex, you're sure a fast runner."

"You're pretty fast yourself."

Ever after that, each recess, except in winter and whenever the weather was not good, Alex and Hugh would race to the back of the schoolyard.

Hugh and Alex were teammates on the AIPS 4x100 Relay Team in the District track meets in Grades Six and Seven. They surprised their coach, Principal Clarke, and maybe themselves when they won the race in 1962 and helped little AIPS to win the overall District Meet.

In their Grade Seven year they had high hopes to repeat their Grade Six miracle but this year they didn't have the Gohm twins to anchor their team. Hugh ran lead-off and Alex was the final leg, with Bobby Simpson and Conrad von der Laden running the middle legs. But disaster struck when Alex left his mark too soon and Conrad couldn't catch him before Alex ran out of his passing box and was disqualified.

It was a huge disappointment for Alex.

The ever-supportive Hugh did his best to cheer up his disconsolate friend. Alex shrugged off Hugh's hand on his shoulder. He didn't want any sympathy, and he certainly didn't want anyone to see he had tears in his eyes.

Coach Clarke took Alex aside to offer consolation. He understood competitive athletes but he also knew this was a teaching moment – you can't let a failure poison your other triumphs.

"Hugh's right Alex. You are a great sprinter. Sure, you're disappointed you were disqualified in this relay but it could have happened to anyone. Imagine how Conrad feels that he couldn't reach you in time. How would you feel if Bobby Simpson had dropped the baton from Hugh? You would have been disappointed of course but I bet you would have been the first to tell Bobby it's alright.

"You need to forgive yourself too. There'll be another race."

With that Hugh hollered, "We'll get 'em next year!"

11. Sandra Farquharson

BY THANKSGIVING OF 1963 Alex final year at AIPS was well underway. The inquest over the treasure Alex had found in Stella Bay had been dealt with; the Island folk had no sympathy for Old Man O'Reilly's claim and the excitement had died down. Victoria welcomed the return to the quiet of the sleepy little village but she also noticed that Alex had grown increasingly quiet too. One Friday afternoon Alex arrived home promptly from school and went straight to his room, barely saying hi to his mom. She decided she needed to have a chat with her pensive young man. Oliver wasn't about – probably still straggling home from school and visiting with the girls on McDonalds Lane and Peter would be another two hours before he would be home from Queen's.

She waited a minute, dried her hands on her apron, and climbed the stairs to initiate a little visit. She tapped on Alex bedroom door.

"Got a few minutes?" she queried, gently.

"Sure Mom," Alex replied, unenthusiastically. He was lying face down on his bed, a book propped up on his pillow.

"Mind if I sit down?" Victoria asked.

"Sure, go ahead."

He repositioned himself to make room for her as she settled at the foot of his single bed.

"You're getting a bit big for this bed. Maybe we should be getting you a larger one. Perhaps next year when you go on to high school."

Alex figured his mother didn't come into his room to talk about beds so he just waited for her to continue.

"You've been pretty quiet since the inquest has been over."

She waited for some sort of response from Alex but nothing was coming.

"Is everything all right with you? Are you feeling well?"

"I'm fine Mom."

"Well, you don't seem to have your usual energy. Maybe we should see the doctor."

"I don't need to see the doctor. I'm fine."

Victoria waited.

Alex knew he was supposed to fill in the empty space. "Just been doing a lot of thinking."

"You and the Professor had a little chat the other day…" She let her sentence tail away.

Alex looked at her more closely then, wondering what his father might have said to his mom.

"Yeah, we talked a bit, mostly about me just enjoying my year and not worrying so much about the future."

"And.."

"and well, that's a lot easier said than done.

"and besides, it's the present I'm mostly bothered about."

"Oh?"

Victoria waited.

"Well, things are not the same as last year."

"How so? You're still best friends with Hugh aren't you?"

"Yeah, but school's not the same this year.

"You've still got Mrs. MacAskill as your teacher. And you like her. And you don't have to be bothered with being the classroom monitor."

"Yeah, but I kinda miss that. Now a Grade Seven kid does it and I just go and take my seat."

"Did she give you a seat by the windows?"

"Yeah, I'm in the third seat."

"Where is Hugh sitting?"

"He's in the second row of the Grade Eights, at the back. He sits right in front of Gary Gohm in the last seat; Glenn Gohm sits at the back in the first row by the windows."

"How many kids are there in that class?"

"Well, there's 37 kids altogether, 19 Grade Sevens and 18 Grade Eights. There's three rows of six nearest the windows for the Grade Eights, and three rows from the cloak room for the Grade Sevens."

"I can see why Mrs. MacAskill kept you separate from Hugh. You two were separated in Grade Six because of the talking."

"I know. I wanted to be by the window this year, but I kinda miss where I was sitting last year in Grade Seven, in the first row by the cloakroom near the front."

"Where is Sandra sitting this year?"

Alex could feel her studying his face for his answer.

"She's in the first seat in the row next the window. I have to look through Mary Beth's head to see her."

"I guess you're not exchanging notes with Sandra this year…"

"No."

"And more than that, she hardly talks to me anymore. She doesn't come over to talk to me at recess. She just hangs out with the girls. And even at Johnson's Store she spends all her time with her girlfriends.

"And we don't go on bike rides anymore."

Victoria was starting to get the picture.

"You're missing your girlfriend, aren't you?"

Alex was surprised at that.

"She's not my girlfriend. She's just my friend. We just hang around together. And last year at school we were involved in so many projects – the Christmas Play, the Hallowe'en Party, the school newspaper, and the track team…

"Now, nothing."

"I know son, and you miss all that activity. When you're thirteen it's hard to think about the girls as friends, never mind as more than friends. But I think we both know there was a strong affinity between the two of you."

Victoria paused and retrieved an image of Sandra. She had a lovely face, high cheekbones, straight, slightly perky nose, thin lips, white skin, fair, not quite blonde, hair. She was tall and slim, taller than Alex and yet she didn't slouch, always nicely dressed in skirt and blouse, with a cardigan over the blouse. She was engaging and polite in a genuine way, the perfect picture of a Minister's daughter, which of course, she was. The Reverend Blair Farquharson of St. Paul's Presbyterian Church.

"Maybe her parents have spoken to her and have advised that she put more distance between the two of you."

"Or maybe they blame me for almost getting Sandra drowned last summer."

"Oh, Alex, I don't think that's it. Is that what you think?"

"Yes Mom. If I hadn't been so excited about that damn treasure… I shouldn't have tried to pull it up on my own. I should have told Dad and Mr. Danaher about my discovery so they could have raised it properly."

"Yes son, I can see how you might have got carried away.

"But it wasn't your fault that Sandra got her arm all tangled up with that rope. And it wasn't your fault that Old Man O'Reilly came along when he did and startled you.

"You mustn't blame yourself, Alex."

"Yes but, I think that treasure business has come between the two of us.

"I miss the old times, Mom."

Victoria could see her son was upset. She wanted to hug him but figured that might be awkward for this thirteen-year-old. She thought she would let the thought lie for a few minutes.

"You know, Son, nothing ever stays the same. You have to just keep those good memories in your head and let the future come what may.

"If you and Sandra are meant to stay friends it will just happen. You're both only thirteen, and you both are likely to make lots of other friends over the next ten years – high school and university. Don't rush it, Son. You've got a lot of growing up to do before you need to worry about how you and Sandra are to be together."

Alex began to think his mom wasn't so different from the Professor after all. And besides, she just didn't understand what it was like to be thirteen.

It was almost like she was reading his mind.

"You know, Alex, I was thirteen once."

She waited a few minutes.

"There was this boy in my class in our little school in the tiny town of Bailieboro. I thought he was everything. And now, I don't even know where he lives. Somebody said in California."

With that her mind drifted away with her thoughts.

As the year went by, Alex' restless heart grew a bit quieter. Rather than pining in his room he paid more attention to his other friends, the Secret Society, and of course his best friend Hugh.

And he had Scouts to occupy his mind. Except that the Scout Troop met every Friday at St Paul's Church, and Sandra lived at the manse.

12. Boy Scouts

SEPTEMBER IS LIKE NEW YEAR – everything starts up again, new school year, Sunday School, Boy Scouts meetings, new goals. Every Friday evening, at least in good weather, Alex would pedal over to St. Paul's Presbyterian Church. And every Friday evening Alex would catch himself studying the windows of the manse, hoping for a glimpse of Sandra.

She had told him last year that sometimes she would peek out her bedroom window looking to see him, but never let on, so this year, despite her increasing distance, he hoped she was still behind that curtain.

But somehow, he doubted it. He was sure there was a gulf between them now and his heart ached to think of it.

Still, he was devoted to his Scouting and worked hard every Friday on the rituals and his badges. His plan was to become Patrol Leader of Eagle Patrol by the end of the year. He knew Glenn, and Glenn's twin, Gary, was going to be sixteen at the end of the year and would be going up to Rovers, maybe, the following September. Alex was already Seconder and he figured if he got his First Class Badge, Mr. Burke, the Scout Master, might look favourably on him. Did he have the right stuff – the leadership skills – to be Patrol Leader. He wondered.

Having leadership wasn't something a 13-year-old kid thought about – you just went out and played with other kids. He never thought about the fact that he seemed to have a lot of ideas about what to do; it didn't really occur to him that a lot of the time other kids would wait to see what he was going to do next, or ask his opinion first.

But when your dad is a university professor in psychology, sometimes you find yourself thinking about things most other kids didn't think about. Like goals. And leadership.

So being a Patrol Seconder at 13 and hoping to be a Patrol Leader at 14, and maybe even Troop Leader one day, replacing Fred Jones, seemed perfectly natural to him.

He was a bit alarmed however on the first meeting in September when he saw his nemeses Sean and Shamus O'Reilly in the Church Hall. 'What are those two doing here? Are they signing up to become members of the Amherst Island Scout Troop?'

Instantly, Alex' history with Sean, and his younger brother Shamus, raced through is mind: Sean and Shamus intercepting Alex and Oliver on their way home from Sunday School and Sean giving Alex a bloody nose, and then Oliver too; and Sean and Shamus and their Uncle Nelson – 'Old Man O'Reilly' – stopping their old beat up pickup truck, and picking a fight with Alex on his way home from Scouts one Friday evening – it was a good thing Frank Gohm and the Gohm twins came along when they did; and then, so surprising, Sean diving into Stella Bay and helping Alex bring Sandra to the surface.

And now here they were at the Scout meeting.

Sean was about the same age as Alex, or perhaps a bit older, and somewhat bigger. Shamus the same age as Oliver. Even so, Sean would have to start as a Tenderfoot in the Amherst Island Scout troop.

Alex recalled his first meeting two years previously when he was a Tenderfoot himself joining the Scout Troop.

Mr. Burke repeated the ritual. Sean and Shamus stood at the front of the Troop at the open end of the horseshoe formation. After the Troop Leader administered the breaking of the flag ceremony, Mr. Burke called upon Gary Gohm, Raven Patrol Leader, to come forward.

Gary turned to his Seconder and passed the patrol staff with triangular black flag to him, then marched up to the top of the horseshoe, 'broke the formation' between Beaver Patrol and Wolf Patrol, and marched down the centre of the assembly to face Mr. Burke.

Mr. Burke said, "I'd like to present Tenderfoot Sean O'Reilly. Do you accept him as a member of Raven Patrol?"

"Yes sir," said Gary. He offered Sean the Scout handshake; this confused Sean, not expecting Gary proffering his left hand, but recovered awkwardly and thrust his own left hand out to accept his Patrol Leader's hand. Gary told him to follow him, and with that did an about-face and marched back up the centre of the formation; Sean had the presence of mind to follow him and take his place in Raven Patrol beside Gary.

— Alex' Choice —

Mr. Burke then repeated the procedure with Shamus, assigning him to Beaver Patrol.

Alex was relieved neither of the O'Reilly boys were assigned to Glenn Gohm's Eagle Patrol. It hadn't quite dawned on him that Mr. Burke was fully mindful of the dynamics of the O'Reilly brothers joining the Scout troop, well aware of the history of Sean and Alex.

It was curious thing however when his little brother Oliver graduated from Cub Scouts to the Scout Troop that year. He often thought of Oliver as his little brother, as, just that, little. They were only 21 months apart and in reality, Oliver wasn't much smaller than Alex. And mostly, they got along well, even though Alex was often irritated with Oliver's constant chatter. He was grateful for Oliver's companionship all those times he didn't have anybody else to be with, especially those first few months when they moved to Amherst Island. Despite being annoyed with Oliver, he'd always look out for him. Well, almost always – if Oliver wanted to lollygag at Sunday School instead of getting home quick so as not to be late for Sunday Dinner, well, that wasn't Alex' fault. And of course he agreed – insisted even, over the objections of Fuzzy and Thursty – to have Oliver belong to the St. Albans Secret Society.

But somehow Oliver jumping up to Scouts was different. Alex liked that he had three hours on Friday nights when he didn't have to bother about Oliver.

Still, he was very moved at the joint Cub Pack/Scout Troop meeting the third Friday in September when three Cubs went up to the Scout troop. It was amazing to see his mother, Victoria, as Akela of the Cub Pack and the way she interacted with Paul Burke, the Scout Master. He was chuffed to see the respect Mr. Burke accorded his mom.

He was proud of his little brother too – Oliver was an accomplished Cub Scout with many badges. But he also felt a bit protective of him – it was curious to Alex, and pleasing in an odd way, to see Oliver was a bit nervous about the whole ceremony. Oliver was not his usual flamboyant and outspoken self.

The Scout Troop was paraded in its horseshoe formation. The Wolf Cub Pack was arranged next to it in its pack circle.

Akela called Oliver's name.

"Wolf Cub Oliver, please join me here in the circle."

"Now come with me."

Together the two walked to the edge of the Cub Pack circle, crossed to the Scout Troop formation, then broke the horseshoe formation and walked to the head of the Troop where the Troop Leader and Scout Master were standing.

"Mr. Burke," she said in a strong voice, "I'd like to present Cub Scout Oliver Jorgenson who wishes to join the Amherst Island Scout Troop."

"Do you recommend Cub Scout Oliver as an honourable and diligent member of your pack, worthy of serving the Amherst Island Scout Troup?"

"I do," replied Akela firmly.

With that, Mr. Burke extended his left hand to Oliver, who, at first confused, accepted it in his smaller left hand.

"Please stand next to Mr. Jones."

Akela turned about face and returned to the Cub Pack circle.

She repeated this ritual with two other Cubs.

Finally, she dismissed the Cubs and they all left the room, leaving the Scout troop to continue its meeting.

Mr. Burke then called Oliver to stand in front of him.

He then called on Gary Gohm, Patrol Leader of Raven Patrol to come to the head of the formation.

"Mr. Gohm, will you accept Tenderfoot Oliver Jorgenson to be a member of Raven Patrol?"

"Yes sir," said Gary who then shook Oliver's hand. He turned and marched to the top of the horseshoe, broke it and marched around to his place at the head of Raven Patrol.

Alex was very pleased for Oliver. Raven Patrol was almost as good as his own Eagle Patrol. He was a little concerned though that Oliver would be in with Sean O'Reilly.

After the meeting Sean O'Reilly came over to Alex. Echoes of Alex apprehension of Sean O'Reilly, the bully of Amherst Island, shivered through him.

"Man, that was so cool," Sean declared with enthusiasm.

Alex knew what he meant, the parading rituals, the salutes, the flags, the majesty of the ceremony, was all very moving.

"I'm glad you let me join the Scout Troop, Alex."

— Alex' Choice —

"I had nothing to do with that, Sean."

"Yeah but, after what Shamus and I did to you last year, well, you could have told Mr. Burke you didn't want me, and I'm sure Gary and Glenn would have agreed."

"Yeah, well, their older brother Frank was Troop Leader here once and he must have figured Scouting would be good for you and Shamus."

"Yeah, I know, Mr. Gohm has been over talking with my dad a lot, and about joining the Volunteer Fire Brigade.

"Well, thanks all the same."

With that, Sean offered Alex his left hand in a Scout handshake, and of course, Alex took it.

Later that year Paul Burke was married at St. Paul's Presbyterian Church, Reverend Farquharson presiding.

Though the boys of the Scout Troop weren't invited to the service they wanted to celebrate their Scout Master.

Alex talked with his mom and Dad about the pending nuptials – he wanted to do something for Mr. Burke but he couldn't think what that could be. Victoria suggested the boys organize a colour guard for the bride and groom.

"Great idea," said Peter.

"What's a colour guard?' asked Alex.

"It's a ceremonial thing that military organizations and police forces often do to honour one of their own. Enlisted men, decked in full dress uniform – maybe a dozen or so – each carry a flag on a staff, like the Red Ensign on the flagpole you use at Scout meetings."

Alex was beginning to perk up to this idea.

"The flag-bearers form an aisle, with members on two sides. When the celebration exits the hall, the members raise their flags and form an arch and the celebrants march through the canopy."

"Way, cool'" said Alex with mounting enthusiasm.

"But where would we get enough flags and poles?"

"Well," replied Victoria, "I'll contact District and see what they have in their storeroom. And I think there's an old Amherst Island Scout Troop flag somewhere in the basement of the Church."

"And I can get some poles and flags from the Queen's Marching Band," piped in Peter.

"and I think the Volunteers have a community flag."

"I'm sure we can put this together," said Victoria.

Alex was excited now.

"And we've got to keep this a secret.

"I'll get Gary and Glenn aside at school and we can work out the detail for the boys from the troop. I'm sure we can get a dozen boys who will want to help."

As the date of the wedding drew near, Alex and the other Scouts showed up on Tuesday night after the Cub Scouts meeting so that Akela Victoria could rehearse the boys with the lineup and the raising of the flag poles.

The Saturday of the wedding arrived. The boys assembled in the parking lot in their full Scout uniforms – shorts and knee-high socks, shirts with lapel pockets and epaulets, and badges and regalia of course, and four cornered peak hats with the wide brim, just like the Mounties. Even though it was February, luckily it was mild that day and St. Paul's is sheltered in a gentle vale from the wind that blows off Lake Ontario.

The wedding ended and bells pealed from the belfry; the boys had lined up at the side door of the church that faced onto the parking lot. As Mr. and Mrs. Paul Burke exited the building the boys snapped to 'Alert' and raised their flags to form a canopy. The bride laughed in surprise and glee, and smiled from ear to ear at the troop of Boy Scouts. Mr. Burke was delighted.

A camera man onside snapped a picture. It appeared later that week in the Amherst Island Flyer and in the Amherst Island Public School Times.

As the bride and groom were whisked away for the reception at Victoria Hall, the boys packed up their flags and poles and stowed them in the church hall.

"Man," said Sean to Alex, "that was amazing. I'm so glad I joined up with this Scout troop."

Alex was puffed too, but he had to say, "Yeah, that was great, but don't think that's something that happens every week."

Sean winked back at him.

Alex looked at Sean and thought to himself, this was a different boy than the one he knew less than a year ago.

13. Hugh's News

THE SCHOOL YEAR FINALLY CAME TO AN END and for the Grade Eights it marked the end of their AIPS careers.

Considering all the questions Alex had for himself in September, it turned out Grade Eight had been a pretty good year. He had decided not to think about things so much and just allow himself to experience the year as it came. And that's about how it turned out. Maybe, he thought to himself, the Professor had given him good advice, though it wasn't always easy follow it. But he still had a few questions as the year drew to a close. Like, who would be the Valedictorian? And, what would happen to Gary and Glenn Gohm? And what about Sean O'Reilly?

THE DISTRICT TRACK AND FIELD MEET came mid-June as it did every year. Mr. Clarke, the Principal, and Mr. Monaghan, the janitor, were there to coach, as was Miss Blake to guide the girls. Mr. Clarke had been very pleased with his Grades 7 & 8 team the last two years, winning the District Championship. He figured AIPS had a good chance to do well again: they still had many of the same athletes as the previous year. Alex and Hugh would form the nucleus of the team and Conrad von der Laden, Shanks, was back running middle distances. They didn't know if they had a good field man but maybe Jaime Bowen could do shot put and hammer throw. They weren't allowed to do discus and javelin.

The girls' team was a mystery. Sandra had surprised herself at the 1963 meet when she won the high jump and third in long jump; and the girls relay team surprised themselves winning the 4x110 yard relay race. Rebecca and Jennifer were back to run the relay but the Grade Six firecracker, Tanya, had found a spot in Grade 7 in Amherstview Public School, leaving a big hole.

Mr. Clarke, studying his young charges, said to Miss Blake, "I don't know Miss Blake, the girls seem different this year somehow; and they don't seem as enthusiastic and fiery as last year."

"Well, I don't know about fiery, but I do know there's a bit of tension amongst the girls this year, some kind of girl's rivalry is going on.

"And, take a look at them, Mr. Clarke; they're mostly Grade 8 girls, their young bodies are changing – they've got hips now."

Mr. Clarke took a closer look, "ah, I see what you mean."

Mr. Monaghan smiled sagely.

As for the boys' relay team, Bobby Simpson had graduated last year; Conrad had failed Grade 8 – too many missed school days – but he was still eligible this year; he had acquitted himself well in the relay and said he'd give it a go again this year. But that still left a hole in the team; Alex and Hugh had to recruit another runner for the 1964 team. Jaime Bowen in Grade Seven seemed an obvious choice but he was a heavy weight, not a sprinter.

"What about Oliver?" queried Hugh. "He's a pretty fast runner. He's only in Grade 6 but he's allowed to run relay."

His brother Oliver on the team hadn't occurred to Alex; he always seemed a lackadaisical kid, not very competitive.

"Okay, I guess. But you have to ask him."

Hugh took Oliver aside one afternoon in the schoolyard and put it to him.

"Alex and I were wondering if you would like to be on the boys' relay team. Shanks is going to run third like last year but we don't have anybody fast enough or available to run second leg. Jaime could do it but he has to be home to do chores on the farm every day after school so he can't practice the relay with us. And getting those baton passes down fast is the key to the race. You remember what happened last year when Alex ran out of the passing lane because Shanks couldn't catch up to him in time."

"Yeah, I remember. Alex was sure upset. But I'm not sure about this. I'm only in Grade 6 and Alex is very fast and very competitive and I'm afraid I won't be good enough."

"Oh, I think you're fast enough. And besides, if you run second, I'll be passing the baton to you and you'll pass it to Conrad, and you won't have to worry about Alex. And we'll train hard and I know Alex will be okay if we all try our best."

So it was decided.

The boys practiced their passes religiously and got to be more and more confident and quicker. Alex was especially mindful of his disastrous result in last year's meet. He was determined not to repeat it and hoped for a red ribbon this year.

— Alex' Choice —

The girls only won a few of their events: Sandra finished third in High Jump, and third in Long Jump. Rebecca came third in the 440. But Tonya won all the sprints for Amherstview.

Alex won his three events and Hugh won the 440, and the Hop, Skip & Jump. Now it was time for the relay, the final event of the day. Alex was almost sick with anxiety.

Peter, watching from the bleachers, noticed the look on his son's face. He spoke to Victoria.

"Alex is way too tense. He's probably not going to do well unless he relaxes. Maybe you should go and have a little chat with him."

"You're the psychologist, Professor, why don't you go and settle him down."

"Yeah, maybe you're right. You're almost as tense as he is."

Peter winked at Victoria and she realized Peter was right. Maybe Alex got his competitiveness from her.

Peter made his way down from the stands and across track to the infield.

"Hey, Alex, got a minute?"

Alex looked at his father, a little annoyed and embarrassed that he had come into the infield with the team.

"Alex, I imagine you are pretty excited about the next event."

Alex wondered where this was going.

"It's natural to be all keyed up before a big race, but what you should know is that all the great athletes make a big effort to stay as relaxed as possible. They don't bounce up and down, they don't hold their bodies tight and clench their fists."

Alex looked down at his fists.

"They just 'relax'. They concentrate on their breathing, breathing as normally as possible, not short, fast breaths; they clear their minds of everything else going on around them; they focus on the race ahead. So, Alex, just visualize what is going to happen – you're going to leave your start line at just the right time, you're going to accelerate slowly in your lane so Conrad can catch up to you; he's going to pass the baton smoothly to you and then you're going to turn on your burners and see nothing but the finish line coming up fast to you; you're going to see your chest breaking through the tape first."

Alex was quiet for a moment. "Yeah, but, what about Oliver. I don't know if he's fast enough, and this is his first time and what if he drops the baton?"

"Oliver is not your concern, Alex. Hugh will make a good pass and Oliver will take care of himself. But it is not for you to worry about that.

"Only positive thoughts. Okay?"

"Yes, Dad."

"Now, concentrate on your breathing."

Peter left Alex to do as he had said; he knew standing over Alex wasn't going to help. He rejoined Victoria in the stands as the field judge brought the teams together for final instructions and then sent them to their stations.

At the last minute, Conrad told Coach Clarke that he thought he had pulled a muscle in his last race. Mr. Clarke hollered over to Jaime Bowen.

"Jaime, get over here. You're going to have to substitute for Conrad.

I know you haven't had a chance to practice with the relay team but you're going to have to do the best you can."

The gun sounded and Hugh was out of his blocks as if shot from a gun. He rounded the bend, boring down rapidly on young Oliver but he was ready; Oliver took the baton smoothly and held his own down the back stretch. Oliver passed the baton to Jaime who kept up with the pack coming to the top of the last turn. Alex held himself back at his start line as long as he could and started off slowly to make sure he took the baton from Jaimie in the passing box. But Jaimie was bearing down on Alex much faster than Alex had anticipated and was almost on Alex heels as Alex picked up his pace. Alex took the pass awkwardly but once he secured it in his hand he turned his attention to the race itself. He could see he was in third place but he had already beaten the two boys ahead of him in the 100-yard-dash earlier and he was sure he could do it again. He lifted himself up on the balls of his feet and found another gear; he stormed past the runner on his right side and was almost up to the boy in the inside lane at the top of the stretch. There the two of them battled all the way down the stretch but as they neared the tape at the finish line Alex leaned

– Alex' Choice –

in and thrust his chest ahead of the other boy. The red ribbon was his.

Hugh was already at the finish line cheering and urging his friend on. Alex looked around for Sandra but she was nowhere to be seen.

Everyone felt the triumph of the moment.

Amherst Island Public School didn't win the overall meet, but Alex felt vindicated.

YEAR-END BROUGHT YET ANOTHER annually anticipated event – report cards. Alex was always keen to see how he had done. He wasn't apprehensive, as many of the other kids were, partly because, no doubt, he always expected to do well, and he always drew the appropriate approvals from his doting parents. Oliver was somewhat less achievement-oriented it seemed, but equally, rather blasé about his results. Or maybe he sensed his parents, especially psychologist dad, were more concerned with his self-esteem than achievement. In any event, Oliver's self-esteem seemed pretty secure.

But this year was especially significant for Alex: not only was he keen on coming first, after surprisingly finishing third in Grade 7 behind Hugh and Sandra, but this year, being Graduation from Public School, the first-place finisher would also be Valedictorian at the Graduation ceremony. Alex wasn't ashamed to admit he liked the attention that would come with that lofty title, Valedictorian, but he was a bit apprehensive to have to stand in front of all the other students, and their parents, and the teachers, and give a speech. An 'Address', Professor Jorgenson called it.

He thought he had a good chance at getting the award. The school year activities were much less than in Grade 7, and, as his dad had predicted, the Grade 8 curriculum was not as demanding as Grade 7, mostly review. He found he was not nearly as distracted by the allure of Sandra Farquharson and had gradually become comfortable with their new relationship – occasional, rather than constant. This allowed Alex the frame of mind to spend more time on his books in his room after school, and less time fretting.

Sandra herself seemed quieter this year, and more distant. She always did well in the quizzes but she didn't seem as eager to put up her hand and answer Mrs. MacAskill's questions. She was a polite young lady, the daughter of the Minister after all, but this year some of the fire and enthusiasm seemed to have gone out of her. What would this mean for her studies, and results?

Hugh was his usual self, it seemed to Alex – active and confident. If anything, he had thrived sitting at the back of the class with the Gohm twins, and the other actors in the class. He was a beacon. And a threat, academically.

Graduation was going to be on the Tuesday afternoon of the final week of school in June. Report cards would be issued on the last day. The week before Graduation Day Mrs. MacAskill asked Alex to stay after class for a few minutes.

Alex' heart raced. Whenever he had to face authority figures he became involuntarily nervous. Not actually scared, but a bit apprehensive. He was pretty sure he hadn't done anything wrong, but he knew this meeting was likely significant. Maybe she was going to ask him to be Valedictorian.

After class, Alex lingered at his desk, waiting for all the other kids to leave, and then made his way to the front to stand beside Mrs. MacAskill's desk.

"Now Alex," she began, "as you know, next week is Graduation Day and it is long the tradition in all British schools that the student with the highest average marks in the graduating class be named Valedictorian and is to give a keynote address at the ceremonies."

Alex nodded.

"Alex, you will have the highest average marks in the class this year, and I am very proud of you and your achievement.

"However, I am not naming you Valedictorian."

She gave Alex a minute to let that comment sink in. She noted the surprised look on his face but he said nothing.

"I'm sure you are disappointed and probably wondering why I am not making you Valedictorian. Well, I'm going to tell you, and in strictest confidence. When you get your report cards next week I don't want you comparing marks with anybody else.

"I'm going to be asking Sandra Farquharson to be Valedictorian and I hope she accepts. Her marks are very close

— Alex' Choice —

to yours, but she will be second. However, I don't want her to think that she is undeserving of being Valedictorian.

"Now, you deserve to know why I have chosen Sandra.

"I wonder if you have noticed that Sandra is much quieter and less enthusiastic in class this year."

"Yes Ma'am, I've noticed. And also, she doesn't spend anything like the time she used to spend with me, only with her few girlfriends. I thought maybe she didn't like me anymore."

"I don't think that's it, Alex, but I do think that incident you and she had last summer – that treasure chest and her almost drowning – affected her in some way."

"Yeah, I think she blames me for that, though my mom says that's not true."

"I agree with your mom, I doubt very much Sandra blames you for what happened – in fact, you saved her life – but she has been traumatized by it.

"So, I think, if she is Valedictorian, she might feel accomplished and not feel she is second to you again."

"Oh, I see," said Alex. "I agree with that. I don't want Sandra to feel bad about herself."

"So, you are okay with my plan?"

"Yes, Ma'am.

"But does Mr. Clarke know about this?"

"Of course he does, and so does Mrs. Fleming in the Office, but nobody else will know."

"Okay, good."

"And even better," Alex added, "I won't have to give that speech."

Mrs. MacAskill smiled at him.

"I like your sense of humour Alex, just like your father."

The following Tuesday afternoon the graduates and their families, and the teachers and staff, crowded into the small, overheated gymnasium/theatre. The seventeen graduates, including the Gohm twins, finally, and Sean O'Reilly, paraded up to the front of the stage in their ill-fitting sports jackets, crooked neckties, and running shoes, and the girls in their crinoline-lined skirts and white blouses with patent leather shoes, to receive their Grade 8 Diplomas.

Then came the moment people, well, some people anyway, had been waiting for. The Valedictorian. The name of the recipient had not been printed in the program to add to the drama.

Principal Clarke then called for the audience's attention.

"And now I would like to present to you the Valedictorian of the 1964 graduating class of Amherst Island Public School, Miss Sandra Farquharson."

Hugh looked at Alex in surprise, but Alex just smiled gently back and turned his eyes to Sandra.

Sandra gathered her skirts around her and made her way up onto the stage.

She began to speak. "The topic of my address is "On Gratitude' and she looked directly at Alex. Then she turned her eyes to the rest of the audience and gave her address.

ALEX WAS IN FOR MORE SHOCKS that Graduation Spring. The Grade 8s were told that they wouldn't be going to the new high school in Odessa as they had thought. Instead, kids from Amherst Island would still be bussed as before to Napanee High School. This was very distressing to Alex because it meant he would be on the buses for four hours every day. It also meant he wouldn't be able to participate in any of the extracurricular events after school, and that meant he wouldn't be able to play football.

Some families dealt with this commute problem by finding boarding spaces with families in Napanee, Monday to Thursday, and come home for the weekend, Friday to Sunday. Peter and Victoria were unhappy with this idea and persuaded themselves that Alex would just have to bear with the bussing until they found another solution.

Then Alex found out from the kids at Johnson's store that Sandra was going to be billeting with another family – the United Church Minister's family – in Odessa and would be attending the new Ernestown High School in September.

At least Alex still had a few other friends from AIPS going to Napanee High School: Walter Taylor and Billy Thurston, and especially his best friend, Hugh McPherson.

School was out and the St. Albans Secret Society was meeting at the hideout with a pack of cigarettes to celebrate Dominion Day before going back to the Municipal Park by the

— Alex' Choice —

school to watch the fireworks. Half the Island had gone to St, Paul's for a special church service, even though July 1 fell on a Wednesday that year, but that didn't include any of the members of the St. Albans Secret Society as none of their families were Presbyterians. After the Church service there was a huge family and community picnic which lasted all afternoon and into the evening. All the families brought picnic hampers with sandwiches and fried chicken and large bowls of potato salad and Jello salad that melted in the heat of the day if they weren't kept in a cooler. There was a big fire pit and the church was selling hotdogs. Johnson's General Store brought a portable freezer stuffed with tubs of ice cream and were scooping ice cream cones all day. And then many strawberry deserts after.

And there were all sorts of amusing events staged throughout the day: Potato sack races, three legged races, eggs in a spoon races; a scavenger hunt. By evening the picnic began to break up and form into a sort of a parade. Seemingly out of nowhere appeared a bagpiper, and a guy with a fife and *another with a drum. Together they began to walk up The Forty Foot Road to the Corners, flags flying, Union Jacks, Red Ensigns, and even the new red Maple Leaf banner, and then turn left onto The Front Road to arrive at the Municipal Park.

Alex and the boys talked enviously amongst themselves, wishing their families belonged to the St. Paul's Congregation. St. Albans Church was too small to organize a Dominion Day event so the Church was pretty quiet. Maybe that was a good thing since at least it allowed the boys to congregate undetected at their fort. Still, their cigarettes and potato chips and root beers didn't taste so good against the thoughts of hot dogs and strawberry shortcake.

In Canada it didn't get dark until almost 10:00 on July 1, only ten days after the summer solstice, so it was a long wait at the hideout before they could pull themselves together and join the parade to the school for the fireworks display. Fuzzy Taylor had a pocketful of firecrackers and was itching to let them off but Alex warned him the noise would draw attention to their location.

As they sat there glumly waiting, but yet happy they had the exclusivity of their hideout, Hugh said, his voice quiet, "I'm sure going to miss all this."

The boys all nodded in agreement, though not quite sure why. Then Alex looked at Hugh, a bit puzzled.

"What do you mean Hugh? We'll be able to do all this again next year."

"Yeah, maybe so, but I'm not going to be living here next year."

Silence filled the room as the boys digested this information.

"What do you mean Hugh, 'you're not going to be living here next year'?"

"My dad is being transferred again. It's a career move."

"We're moving to Cobourg next month just as soon as Dad finds us a new house. They want me settled before starting high school in September."

"Shit," said Alex, and that surprised everybody.

"I mean, Hugh, you're my best friend,

"and the Secret Society won't be the same."

"I think this is the end of everything."

The boys nodded in agreement.

"And it's going to be so hard for you, Hugh."

"Yeah, maybe, but I'm used to it. I've moved a few times already. It's been three years here in Amherst Island, almost a record.

"But, you know," Hugh remarked with a glance at Alex, "it's character building."

He didn't say he was going to miss Alex and the boys, but maybe that didn't need to be said.

AMHERST ISLAND, 1964 FALL

— Doug Jordan —

14. Napanee High School

"So you see, Mom, I'm not too sorry to leave this place."

Victoria was amazed at all these thoughts her pensive son had about his last year, and especially the last few months. And she was a bit chagrined that she hadn't really paid more attention to what was troubling him. She wondered if he had put all this in his journal – he hadn't shared it with her. She had noticed occasional episodes of mopiness – and she knew his relationship with Sandra was probably behind some of them – but it had never occurred to her that Alex felt so strongly about playing football.

"I'm very sorry Alex all this has come down on you. It's not at all what we expected. Maybe you will get a fresh start when we move to Peterborough.

"It's too late for you to play football for the Napanee Golden Hawks – and as a Grade Niner, it's pretty unlikely you would have got much of a chance to play anyway – but maybe you'll be ready for the Adam Scott Lions next year."

"Yeah, Mom, that's what I was thinking too."

"In the meantime, Alex, you need to make the most of your time at Napanee High School and add that to your memory bank. You've had some wonderful times here on Amherst Island. Don't let the last few months spoil it for you.

"Besides, with your father away at Peterborough during the week, I'm glad to have your help managing this household."

"Okay, Mom, I'll try, but that School is really different from what I'm used to."

"How so Alex?"

"Well, for one thing, it's really big."

"Well, yes, compared to little Amherst Island Public School."

"and we don't get recess."

"Hmmm, I know."

"And, we have to move from class to class, not stay in one class. We have a locker for our stuff, not a cloak room in our own classroom. Miss van Alstyne is our home room teacher but we only have her for fifteen minutes at the start of the day for opening exercises. She's nice enough but then we have six other teachers, one for each course, and I'm nervous about Mr.

Thomson, our math teacher. I miss Mrs. MacAskill. It feels like I don't have any place of my own, except for that locker."

"And..."

"And, there's the big cafeteria where we have our lunch. Most kids bring a lunch pail and buy milk, but I'm glad you send me with money so I can buy a hot lunch every day, even though the other kids think we must be rich."

"Oh?"

"Yeah, it makes me feel different. Fuzzy and Thursty bring their lunch, mostly soggy peanut butter and jam sandwiches. I'm glad I don't have to do that."

Victoria paused for a while, smiling to herself thinking about her son with his cafeteria tray and plate of spaghetti, milk carton and pie.' She was glad Alex got a good hot meal at lunch after having been on the buses for two hours in the morning. But she wished he didn't 'feel different'.

"So, what else is different about your high school?"

"Well, the kids all group together in different parts of the cafeteria or in the halls. I kinda expect that the older grades keep separate from us Grade Niners, but that's not what I mean. There's basically three groups of kids at the school – the townies, who live in Napanee; the bus kids, who come from all over the place, seem to stick with the other kids on their buses.

"Just like all the kids from Amherst Island stick together?"

"Yeah, I guess, but there's all the kids from Bath, and Adolphustown, and Hay Bay, and Deseronto;

"and then there are the Indian kids."

"You mean the natives? What about the natives?"

"They're alright I guess, but they stick to themselves and they look different from us and it makes you feel strange."

"Well, Alex, that's not unusual to feel a bit strange when you're with people or situations you're not used to.

"I see that you're having to deal with a lot of change, and you're not someone who adapts quickly" – she gave him a knowing smile – "not like your brother, Oliver. You remember how you felt when we first moved to Amherst Island."

"Yeah, new place, new school, no friends," he said, with a bit of a smile. She smiled back at him. They both knew things had turned out pretty well after that.

— Alex' Choice —

"You know Alex, everybody who ever graduated from Grade 8 in a small public school to Grade 9 in a big high school felt pretty lost at the beginning. You move from the head of the school one year to a nobody the next."

"Is that how you felt when you went to high school?"

"Absolutely. The public school in Bailieboro was small – about the same size as Amherst Island Public School but it was an old school, a two-story brick building. My father used to drive me there in the pick-up truck from the farm on Rice Lake when I was little but by Grade 4 I had to walk; it was a pretty long walk and I missed a lot of school on bad weather days. But for Grade 7 and 8 I had to go to school in Millbrook and that was way too far to walk. My older brother used to drive me there in the farm pickup truck and pick me up at the end of the school day. But then I went to high school in Port Hope – Central High. At first I was quite intimidated – it was so much bigger than even Millbrook Public School – but I got used to it. My brother drove me every day but sometimes he couldn't because of farm chores. My father wanted me to quit school after Grade 10 – that was pretty common in those days. There was a wealthy woman living in a big house in Bailieboro who needed a maid. My father wanted me to take that job. In fact, I did that for a few summers – I lived with the old lady in her house and sent my wages home to my father to help with the farm expenses. But my mom insisted I finish high school and then go to Nursing School."

Alex was fascinated with this lengthening story. He knew something of his mother's history but didn't realize how precarious it must have been for her.

"Why didn't you take a school bus to Port Hope High School?" he asked, innocently.

"There weren't any in those days. If you couldn't find your own way to school, you didn't go to school. That's why most kids dropped out after Grade 8 or Grade 10 and went to work."

Alex was pensive for a minute, then he asked,

"You took nursing at Peterborough Hospital, but how did you meet Dad if he was going to Queen's?"

"When I graduated from Nursing School I needed to get a job. I could have stayed on at Peterborough Hospital but I wanted to get further away from home – Peterborough seemed too close to Bailieboro to me. So I applied to Kingston General Hospital and got hired. I thought this was the big time. Not as big as Toronto of course but more interesting than Peterborough."

"And of course you know the story of how I met your dad, at the Oscar Peterson concert."

"How old were you then Mom?"

"I was twenty when I moved to Kingston in 1947, met and married your dad by 1949, and you came along in 1950."

Alex knew these dates but now they seemed to take on different meaning. He was 14 now in Grade 9. His mom was only seven years older than he was now when she finished her education and was working. This must have been what she meant in their last conversation when she said a lot can happen in the next ten years of your life.

He began to think he had it a lot better than what his mother had to deal with when she was 14.

And besides, soon everything was going to change.

15. On the Buses

'I WONDER WHY THE BOYS LIKE TO SIT AT THE BACK OF THE BUS," Alex wondered. He didn't much see the point of it. He figured the only purpose for the bus was to get you to school and that being the case, any seat on the bus will serve the purpose. And since they were on the bus for two hours, the best seat is where it was quiet and you could do something useful. Like your homework. Or read.

But, as Alex discovered, you couldn't really do your homework on the bus. The seats were too narrow and you could hardly fit your notebook on your lap. And the bus was bouncy so you couldn't really write in the notebook, or sketch, and certainly not draw straight lines. So you had to do your homework at home. The only work you could do on the bus was to review the textbooks and catch up on reading assignments, especially that stupid Shakespeare play, A Midsummer Night's Dream.

The boys at the back thought anyone doing homework on the buses was pretty nerdy, and as much as Alex liked being a good student, he didn't think of himself as an egghead and didn't want anybody else to think so either, especially the boys at the back.

Most of those kids were in the senior grades. Some of girls vied for their attention. Monica, for one, and her best friend Candace; Alex knew them when they were in their last year at Amherst Island Public school and he was in Grade 7. Monica and Candace were not on the Track Team, but they made good cheerleaders. They were in Grade 10 now and they sure seemed to seek the attention of the Grade 12 boys in the back row. And they got it too. Alex noticed that the two of them always pulled their skirts up higher once they got on the buses, and undid the top two buttons of their blouses. The other girls just rolled their eyes and sat in the middle rows.

Fuzzy and Thursty tried to sit near the back rows too but the older kids just ignored them, they weren't about to pay much attention to Grade Niners.

Alex sat in the front rows and tried to ignore others around him. Alone with his thoughts he sometimes wondered what Hugh was up to in his new school in Cobourg, He figured Hugh didn't have to take a school bus but he didn't know for sure. Maybe he would ask him the next time he wrote him a letter.

He also wondered how Sandra was doing. He knew she could walk to school because the people she boarded with lived only a few blocks from Ernestown Secondary School. Alex didn't write her letters – he didn't know her address in Odessa – and besides he expected to see her on the weekends when she was back home on Amherst Island. But it rarely happened, only the few chance encounters at the manse on Friday Scout nights.

Since he couldn't do much homework on the bus, he always had a book with him, and when he wasn't feeling nauseous, he read. He went through a lot of them. Even though he was getting too old for them he'd finished all the Hardy Boys books (Nancy Drew too but he didn't want anybody seeing him reading those). He read Tom Sawyer, and Treasure Island, and Kidnapped, The Jungle Books and Coral Island, and anything else he could get his hands on, but he liked those boys' adventure stories best.

The problem with reading on the buses was, it made his stomach a bit queasy. He'd found it difficult to keep his eyes on the right lines of the text, and after a while he'd feel a bit headachy, and his eyes would narrow, and his stomach didn't feel right. So he'd put his book away. It was better in the morning than in the afternoon on the return trip. Being tired at the end of the day seemed to make it worse.

His mom told him one remedy for motion sickness was to sit in a front seat where he could see the road ahead allowing his brain and his inner ear to reconcile. And if that didn't work, Peter bought him a package of Gravol.

So Alex sat at the front of the bus. The driver asked him if he wanted to be the monitor but Alex declined. Still, he watched how the driver used the pedals and his mirrors.

He also found he liked to pay attention to where the driver's route took him. He took note of the various landmarks – the churches and the graveyards, and intersections; he liked the turns in the roads, and the fields, and apple orchards and especially the shoreline of Lake Ontario. It was like he had a map in his mind. He liked the idea of exploring the countryside. Whenever they passed a sideroad he wondered what was down that way.

— Alex' Choice —

The school bus took the grand tour of Amherst Island. The morning run started at Johnson's Store at the corner of Forty Foot Road and Front Road and headed east; it turned down McDonald's Lane and Alex had the option of getting the bus in front of his house or waiting until it had done the circuit of Amherst Island and catching it on its way back at Johnson's store. Usually he waited, except in bad weather, thus saving himself 30 minutes riding round the island; he already knew every inch of the island from his many road trips with Hugh on bicycles. The bus continued east along the Front Road to 'The Foot' then south to South Shore Road, then west to the Forty Foot Road, North to Third Concession Road and then west towards 'The Head'; north again on Emerald Road to the tiny hamlet of Emerald, then east along The Front Road to Stella and the ferry.

The bus had to be at the ferry pier by 7:30 or miss the ferry and be late an hour getting the kids to school. The bus had priority boarding and the ferry waited a few minutes longer if the bus was late. On the mainland the bus turned southwest along the Bath Road to pick up kids in Bath. The Bath kids generally segregated themselves from the Amherst Island kids. They sat on the right-hand side of the bus and the Islanders on the left. Since Alex often sat in the first row on the right he'd collect dirty looks from the Bath boys, or tolerant looks from the girls. The older Bath boys never sat on the back row because the Amherst Island boys had already claimed those seats. Fuzzy and Thursty and the other junior Island boys claimed the next few rows near the back and that created a needed buffer between the senior Islander boys and the senior Bath boys. Monica and Candace, sitting in rows between the two factions, didn't seem to mind the extra attention they got, except for the glares from the Bath girls.

The bus then turned north on Regional Road 7 picking up kids long the way, with a few side trips on country roads to pick up the farm kids not on the main route. RR #7 took them to Hwy 2 and they'd pick up more kids in Morven and along the Highway until they reached Napanee. All in all, the bus was punctual and almost always arrived at Napanee High School by 9:00, in time for the kids to get to their lockers and get to their classes to start their day.

Alex rather liked the morning bus ride, but the afternoon ride had much less appeal. His school day was out at 3:30 but he still faced a two-hour return trip home. If he stayed on the bus he would be the last passenger to be delivered, instead he would get off at Johnson's Corners and walk home, beating the bus by 20 minutes. By the end of October Alex was beginning to lose the novelty of the daily drive. He couldn't imagine five years of this.

His dad had said when they moved to Peterborough, they would be living quite close to his new high school, within easy walking distance. Alex thought to himself, 'what am I going to do with all that extra time?'

16. Head of the Household

DR. JORGENSON HAD TAKEN UP HIS DUTIES as Department Head, Psychology, at Trent University in Peterborough Tuesday after Thanksgiving. The family was to stay behind in Stella until Peter could get settled into his new role and find a house for the family. This meant Victoria, until they could all be reunited in a few months' time, would be managing the household in Stella. But then, she mostly managed the household anyway.

In Alex' mind, this meant he had to step up and take care of his mom while his dad was away, Monday to Friday. With the excitement of the fort cave-in and Oliver being in hospital with concussion, Alex felt a lot of responsibility for the household fell on him. Nobody asked him to do that – oh, maybe Peter casually said, 'you take care of your mom while I'm gone' – but nobody but Alex took that remark seriously, least of all Oliver.

Peterborough was about a 2-hour drive from Kingston, even less to Amherst Island, except for the uncertainty of the ferry. Peter would try to get away early on Fridays from Trent and be home in time for dinner. Victoria even relaxed her regimen for Peter and held dinner until he got home, not her usual 5:00 o'clock sharp rule. If Peter made the 5:00 pm ferry they would have dinner at a respectable 5:40, though Peter would have preferred another half an hour to enjoy a martini after his drive. If he missed the 5:00 ferry it would then be the 6:00 o'clock ferry and dinner would now be 6:30. And this put a lot of pressure on Alex who had Scouts at 7:00 at St. Paul's. In October he could still ride his bike to St Paul's, even though he would be riding home in the dark at 8:30; but by November with the return to Standard Time Victoria wouldn't allow it.

Saturday mornings Peter and Victoria would be lined up early at the ferry to be off to Kingston – Collins Bay actually – to do the grocery shopping at the Dominion Store. Between the shopping and the ferry there was little left of the Saturday.

"Now, Alex," said Victoria, "you keep an eye out for Oliver while we're gone. And don't let that dog get off the clothesline."

So the boys didn't see much of their father on Saturdays either, except maybe a little fishing off the dock in the afternoon.

Victoria wasn't happy about this and began to figure ways to preserve some of their time on Saturdays.

One Friday evening she said, "Peter, since you usually don't get home until late on Fridays anyway because of that damned ferry, why don't you go grocery shopping on your way home and I'll have a nice dinner waiting for you when you get here."

"And a martini?"

"Sure. I can feed the boys at 5:00 and you and I can have an adult dinner at 7:30 or so."

She looked at Peter with what appeared to be a twinkle in her eye, and Peter was quick to interpret the language unspoken, unusual though it might be.

"What about my Scout meetings on Friday nights?" queried Alex in minor alarm.

"I'll see if the Gohms can drive you. I know it's out of their way but they offered before and I'm sure it won't be any bother."

Alex seemed content with that solution but then Peter picked up the obstacles and postulated, "I wonder if Oliver would prefer to visit with Janie and Rebecca; I'm sure he won't want to hang around here while his parents are talking over dinner."

Victoria began to think her shopping efficiency idea was beginning to get complicated, but Oliver came to the rescue by agreeing enthusiastically with spending the evening with the girls down the lane.

So it was decided. Peter would do the shopping on Friday evenings in Collins Bay on his way home, leaving Saturday mornings free for whatever the boys wanted to do with their migrant dad.

The only problem with this plan was that Peter didn't always shop as thoroughly as he might, considering there were two growing boys at home. The result of this was that Alex had to make frequent trips to Johnson's General Store by bike to pick up milk and bread and dish detergent and many another thing that they had run out of by Wednesday.

It also seemed to drain Peter of whatever energy he had left on Fridays; the unspoken contract of an adult evening rarely was consummated.

After a few weeks of this experiment Victoria proposed they go back to their previous routine of Saturday shopping.

— Alex' Choice —

Alex was okay with this plan, especially as it meant a return to the old Saturday night pattern of hamburgers or steak with chocolate mallow cookies for dessert instead of whatever novel menu his dad had dreamed up on his shopping adventures. Only Oliver objected because he liked his Friday evenings with Janey and Rebecca playing Crazy Eights.

While his dad was away in Peterborough Alex paid close attention to his mom. He always took his responsibilities seriously and did his chores without complaint, but now he was more vigilant than usual. He put Tony on the clothesline first thing in the morning and then gave him fresh water and kibble. He supervised Oliver getting dressed in the morning, even though he himself had to be out of the house at 7:00 and down by the ferry by 7:30 and Oliver didn't leave for school until 8:15. He'd take in the laundry from the clothesline when he got home from school, and this got harder and harder on his fingers as October chills gradually became December cold. He set the table for dinner, always noting the missing place where his father usually sat; he chided Oliver to help with the dishes each evening. He sat with his mom watching tv in the evening rather than stay in his room as he usually might reading his books, after he had done his homework.

He often found it hard to get to sleep at night, even though he was dead tired from his long day, up at 6:30 and in bed by 9:30. He'd hear his mom wandering around downstairs doing her own evening chores before she started for bed around 10:00, and he heard every strange sound of the night, wondering if he should lock the doors, something they never did on McDonalds Lane normally.

With the first snowfall of December he shoveled the porch and walkway without being asked, telling Oliver to get outside and help. But he looked at the long gravel laneway and shuddered at the daunting task ahead. In truth the laneway wasn't that long, but was double wide; it still looked like a lot of work without his dad. Victoria noticed him leaning on his shovel in worry; she called Mr. Danaher and asked him if he wouldn't mind plowing out their laneway with his pick-up truck fitted with a blade. Of course that was no problem. All the neighbours were willing to give Victoria a hand since Peter was away.

Victoria herself may not have been as reliant on Alex' help as Alex imagined, but that didn't change Alex' sense that he had to be the man of the house now his dad wasn't around. Curiously, when his father came home on the weekends Alex was surprised at the mixed feelings he experienced. He was glad to see his dad of course, but the weekends didn't have the same feeling as before when Peter was there every day. There was now the anticipation on Friday of his dad coming home, and then a rush of family activity on Saturdays, and then a vague anxiety on Sundays anticipating Peter departing again after Sunday dinner. Victoria didn't like him driving in the dark so Peter would leave at 3:00 to catch the 3:30 Ferry and be on the road to Peterborough at 4:00, though in reality, after the switch to Standard Time in October, the sun had set by 5:00 or so and Peter would be driving in the dark anyway. Still, the weekends carried a little bit of dread and Alex felt a strange resentment that his dad had come home causing this perturbation in the Monday to Thursday routine.

Victoria felt it too and she and Peter sometimes had words about how he was failing to discipline the boys adequately. They hadn't always agreed before about discipline – Victoria was somewhat regimented and stricter than Peter, while Peter, the psychologist, would often treat conflict situations as teaching moments – but now that Peter was away five days out of seven the contrast in styles seemed stark. Alex often found himself taking his mother's side, vaguely thinking it might be better if his dad didn't come home at all.

She took the opportunity one Sunday evening after Peter had left for Peterborough to have a little chat with Alex.

"You know, Alex, I get the feeling you've been a bit upset with your father these past few weekends."

"Yeah, I've noticed I'm snarky with him,

"and I think you're right when you discipline Oliver."

"Yes, I thought so.

"It's stressful for all of us, your father included, because our family routines have been upset. But Alex, it's not permanent. We'll be moving to Peterborough at Christmas and we'll all be together again in our new house as a family."

17. Snapping Turtle

RUMOURS OF AN ANCIENT SEA MONSTER lurking in Stella Bay had persisted for decades. And this wasn't an unreasonable prospect as the bay was a haven for water animals. It's deep water at the channel shrank to shallows at the bottom end and provided homes for reeds and waterlilies, frogs and ducks. Bass abounded and in the deeper water, walleye, and even muskalonge. And turtles, though the only turtles they ever saw were the gentle painted ones sunbathing on rotting logs. But the rumours persisted that there was a giant snapping turtle that patrolled the shores of Stella Bay.

This didn't deter the boys from diving off the dock at their end of the bay and swimming out to the raft. They just willed themselves not to think of monsters that might lie in the deeps.

The last weekend of October Peter had finally dragged the family fishing boat ashore and stored it away in the garage, cleaned the motor and gas tank and hoses and stowed them away in the garage too. The boys could no longer tool around the Bay to examine the flora and fauna they might find there. And now that the fort was demolished they didn't stop by St. Albans anymore either.

The water was too cold to swim of course but not too cold to fish. Except Peter had stowed away their fishing gear too.

Undeterred, Oliver found himself a four-foot stick and fastened some extra fishing line from the tackle box to the end of it. He got a bobber and a hook from the tackle box and threaded a dew worm onto the hook leaving the tail to dangle and wiggle to attract the fish.

He dropped his line in the water off the end of the dock and patiently waited, dangling his feet in the water too, even though it was pretty cold. It was a nice sunny Saturday; the parents were in town grocery shopping so sitting on the dock of the bay was the perfect way to while away the hours, waiting for the parents to come home with the weekly bounty.

"Fishin' for panfish, Oliver?" Alex asked, as he settled down beside Oliver at the end of the dock.

"I'm going to catch me a big old muskie," replied Oliver.

"Not with a worm and that bitty fishing pole, you're not."

"More likely you're going to get the attention of the Monster of Stella Bay."

"Do you think, Alex?"

"Sure, Oliver. Everybody says he's in there somewhere and he's probably hungry, fattening himself up before the winter hibernation."

"I don't really believe that old story, Alex. We've lived here for three years and swam off this dock and the raft a thousand times; and drove the boat around the bay and in the reeds at the end of the bay, and we've never seen anything but ducks and painted turtles."

"Yeah, maybe, but you remember this summer the momma duck had five babies but at the end of the summer she only had three. What happened to the other two?"

"Do snapping turtles eat ducklings?"

"Sure they do.

"Toes too."

With that Oliver quickly pulled his feet up on to the dock.

A few minutes later he saw his bobber wiggling on the surface.

"Hey Oliver, you've got a bite."

The next second the bobber dove underwater, and the pole jerked in Oliver's hands. And the next second Oliver was pulled off the dock and into the water. He let go of his pole and popped back up to the surface sputtering and gasping for breath.

Tony took to barking and baying at Oliver thrashing about.

Oliver was a good swimmer, though not as strong as Alex, but his Fall clothes were heavy and now very heavy with the weight of the water.

"Geeze Oliver, are you okay?"

Oliver's only answer was to thrash the water even more frantically, but he wasn't making much progress towards the dock. Alex threw off his jacket and shoes and dove in to rescue his brother. He grabbed him by the back of his collar and began to stroke his way to the dock.

"Just relax Oliver and float on your back, and kick."

They made it to the ladder at the side of the dock. Alex positioned Oliver by the first step and Oliver was able to pull himself out of the water. Alex followed him.

— Alex' Choice —

Once they realized they were safe, Alex began to laugh.

"What's so funny Alex, I almost drowned."

"More than that, Oliver," Alex replied, "you almost got devoured by the Monster of Stella Bay!"

"Geeze Alex, that's not funny. I'm never going to swim in this bay again."

"Well, we better get up to the house and put on some dry clothes before we freeze to death."

As they climbed the steps up the bank and crossed McDonalds Lane to the house the parents arrived home.

"Why are you boys soaking wet?" Victoria called, slightly alarmed.

"Oliver was fishing off the dock and got pulled in by the Monster of Stella Bay," answered Alex, still chuckling.

"Alex," Victoria blurted, "I thought you were minding Oliver."

Alex felt a bit guilty at that,

"Yeah Mom, but I didn't know the Monster of Stella Bay was going to grab Oliver's line."

"I suppose not."

"So there really is such a thing," commented Peter in his usual wry way. "Was it a giant esocid or a 'stupendimus'?"

"Geeze Dad, I think it was a big snapping turtle.

"Anyway, Oliver says he's not swimming in the bay anymore."

"That's probably right, Alex," deadpanned Peter. "We'll be living in Peterborough next year; but I'm pretty sure the Kawarthas have their share of sea monsters."

"Come on Peter,' interjected Vitoria, "let's get these kids out of those wet clothes and dried off."

18. Tony Meets his Maker

PETER WASN'T HAPPY TO HAVE BEEN PROVEN RIGHT but he knew when Victoria brought Tony home that this might be a short-lived love affair. Beagles are one dimensional dogs – they follow their noses, oblivious to everything else.

Tony was to be tied to the clothesline in the side yard. Beagles are high energy dogs, bred to run and chase all day long. So he needed exercise. Being tied to a tree like Max the German Shepherd down the lane wasn't fair to the Beagle and the boys would never be able to give him enough exercise with a walk about McDonalds Lane a few times a day. The dog needed to run and that wasn't really possible, even in a quiet village like Stella.

Peter dreamed up the idea of tying Tony to the clothesline and letting the dog chase himself up and down a hundred feet of overhead dog run. It wasn't an original idea of course but it was novel to the boys and Victoria nodded in agreement.

She did her laundry Mondays and Fridays and Tony would just have to wait until the laundry was taken off the line on those days.

The clothesline was a double steel wire line connected with a pully screwed into the willow tree by the channel between Amherst Island and the mainland; the other end of the line was fastened to a post by the back stoop near the kitchen side door. Peter got a short length of rope and tied a bowline loop around the steel clothesline. Truth be told he needed Alex' help tying the bowline. He tied a bowline at the other end of the rope with the loop passing through the leather grip of the dog leash. The leash was then clipped to Tony's collar.

The first time they hooked up the contraption and clipped the leash to Tony's collar he just sat there, worrying the leash with his mouth. Oliver tried to persuade him to race down the length of the clothesline.

"Come on Tony," he called enthusiastically and started to run down the length of the clothesline. Tony leaped and started to chase Oliver but as soon as he felt the tug on his neck from the leash he stopped.

Eventually Tony learned to chase Oliver down the length of the clothesline but soon showed little enthusiasm for this game.

"Nevermind boys," Victoria declared. "he'll get the knack of it eventually. Let's just leave him now."

The family walked to the side door of the house and in. Tony followed them, fighting the leash as he went but then stalled when he had reached the end of his rope. He sat down and cried for a minute but his family didn't come back. After another minute or two of loneliness he began to whinge and then to howl. The mournful cries got louder and louder until Victoria had had enough, and, mindful that the neighbours probably had had enough of this baying too, unfastened the leash from the collar and brought him into the house, painfully aware that Tony had learned another lesson, and not a desirable one.

Tony did get the knack of life on the clothesline. He explored the limits of his freedom and got to know the realm of his backyard defined by the extent of his leash on the 100 feet clothesline, until he got bored and began the crying for attention from the household.

He learned something new however when one day an intrepid or ignorant rabbit ventured into the yard and within range of Tony on the clothesline. He set to baying and the rabbit took off down the yard. Tony took off after him and raced to the end of the clothesline where he suddenly found himself caught up short and flat on his back. Oliver howled with laughter at this Vaudeville act. Hardly injured except possibly to his pride, Tony tried again, more cautiously perhaps, standing on his hind legs and straining against the rope.

Maybe he was a slow learner, or perhaps his impulses were faster than his brain, but it took three or four repeats of this racing after rabbits only to end up on his back before he accepted his limit. He still chased the rabbits to the end of the line but knew that he should apply his own brakes before the rope applied them for him.

He'd been out on the line for quite a while one day when it occurred to Victoria that she hadn't heard much complaint coming from the yard. She looked out the kitchen window to see what was going on and what was going on was that Tony was digging a burrow for himself. Peter explained that while dogs liked a cool den to curl up in, Beagles, like the cousins, Bassetts and Dashhunds, were varmint trackers and they would dig down rabbit holes, or groundhog holes to drag vermin back out into the open air and present their prizes to the masters.

Peter built him a doghouse under a tree in the yard, within reach of the clothesline, with a cloth cushion inside, a lounge for his midday nap. Curiously, Tony hardly ever used it. He preferred to sleep in the dirt at the door of the doghouse. He might have slept on the roof like that other famous Beagle, if he could only figure how to do that.

After a few months of life on the clothesline Peter decided he should inspect the rope to see about wear. And a good thing he did because the rope was frayed to threads from being pulled along the steel wire clothesline. The solution was the installation of a guide set that attached to the top and bottom lines of the clothesline pulling the two lines together and running along the lines on little pully wheels. He attached the rope to the middle of the guide and Tony could run the line with the pullies rolling along the clothesline. At first the new setup constrained Tony with its extra resistance but after a while he found he could actually run faster along that hundred-foot runway.

It was around this time Tony learned his Houdini trick.

After another afternoon of too much quiet Victoria decided it was time to see what Tony was up to. She looked out the kitchen window and cast her eyes up and down the line to catch a glimpse of her dog; but there was no dog, only an empty collar hanging from the rope to the clothesline. At first, she was puzzled and then alarmed. Where was that damned dog? Soon enough she got a phone call.

"You missing a dog?"

"Yes I am, my tawny and white Beagle."

"Thought so. I've got him here."

"Oh thank you. I'll send Oliver over right away to get him."

She detached Tony's collar from the line rope and sent Oliver down the lane with the walking leash to retrieve the dog.

Victoria was curious to know how he had escaped. She refastened the dog collar to the line rope and fastened the collar over Tony's head. She went into the house and watched him secretly from the kitchen window. She ignored Tony's whigning

Alex' Choice

and crying for a few minutes and then she watched as he backed himself to the end of the line and then, straining mightily, backed himself out of the collar. She ran to the door to catch him but he was already at the door waiting for her. He'd had enough adventure for one day.

The next day Peter visited Canadian Tire in Kingston and bought a harness affair that fit over Tony's head and around his shoulders, fastened with a strap around his girth. There was a clip at the top of the harness that allowed a leash to be attached. Tony couldn't get off the clothesline anymore.

But he still got away, often twice a week. If the clip on the harness wasn't fastened right when one of the boys, or even Peter put the dog out, he'd manage to get off the line and away. More often he'd just squeeze out the door when someone opened it and away he would go following his nose and whatever scent he had picked up.

He was a good dog and liked to play with the boys. He was well trained. He knew how to sit, roll over, and beg. 'Come' was a bit more challenging and 'Stay' needed a lot of reinforcement. But mostly when he was in the yard with the boys he stayed around; he'd come into the house or go back on the line when the boys had other things to do. The problem came when, after the play, the boys forgot to tie him up again or put him in the house. He'd also learned he could push open the wooden screen door if no-one had fastened the hook, slip out and off over the dales. It might be an hour before anybody noticed he was gone. The giveaway was his baying across distant fields, or a phone call from one of the neighbours. And besides that, the many sheep farms on the island didn't appreciate a Beagle squeezing himself through the fences to investigate the sheep. At least he didn't try to herd them. For that matter, the border collies and Shelties often chased him off, and occasionally the ram and the donkeys sent him packing.

All the neighbours in McDonalds Lane and on The Front Road got to know Tony, and most of them liked him, except the ones who kept a few chickens in their yards. Some put out a bowl of water for him, and at times they would report that Tony had helped himself to Max' or somebody's food dish.

"Don't you feed that dog?" they asked good naturedly.

Cars often sped up and down The Front Road, especially on weekends, and they might not have time to brake if a little white and tan dog should go racing across the road in front of them. So every time Tony was on a tear, Victoria felt the anxiety of what might happen.

It was Wednesday, November 11th, 1964, Remembrance Day; she got a call from the owner of Johnson's General Store.

"Mrs. Jorgenson?"

"Yes?"

"It's Pearl Johnson over at the store."

"Yes?"

"I've got Tony here."

Before she could even say 'thank goodness' something told Victoria this wasn't the whole story.

"He's been hit by a motorcycle. The guy came tearing 'round the corner from the ferry and accelerated east on The Front Road. Tony came from out of nowhere racing at top speed across the road. He just plowed right into the wheels of the motorcycle. That cyclist didn't even see him. He braked hard after the dog hit the motorcycle, saw the dog lying on the road, and then just took off again. Coward."

"What about Tony?" Victoria cried in anxiety.

"I'm sorry, Mrs. Jorgenson, he's dead. Broken neck I think."

"Oh my God," cried Victoria.

"I'll send the boys over right away. The Professor's not home and we don't have a second car."

"Alex, Oliver, come down right away, please."

There was something in their mother's tone that alerted them; something serious must have happened.

"Boys, Mrs. Johnson says Tony's been hit by a motorcycle. Scoot over there right away on your bikes and bring him home."

The boys jumped on their bikes and raced to the General Store. It only took three minutes. Mrs. Johnson was sitting on the bench at the front of the store with a cardboard box on her lap. A few customers were standing around whispering.

Alex asked, intuitively, "Is Tony in the box?"

"Yes, Alex?"

"Is he dead?"

Alex' Choice

"Yes son."

"Can I see him?"

"Yes son, of course."

Alex leaned his bike against one of the front pillars of the store. Oliver stood frozen in place. Alex looked into the box. Tony was still, his eyes still open. He didn't seem to have a mark on him.

Alex eyes started to well up with tears. How could he be dead? He looked perfect. Surely Tony was just unconscious and would soon wake up and jump out of that box.

"I guess I'll take him home now.

"Can I have the box?"

"Of course son."

So Alex climbed back on his bike and Mrs. Johnson passed him the box with Tony and settled it across the handlebars. Alex and Oliver rode home slowly, hardly able to see the road for their tears.

They arrived at the house and Victoria was waiting for them on the lawn. She ran down the few yards of the lane to meet the boys.

She took the box from Alex's handlebars and looked inside at the 'sleeping' dog.

Her eyes filled with tears. She carried the box to the side porch and put it down on the step.

"We should just sit on the steps here for a while and just be with Tony. Think about all the good times he gave us in the three short years we had him.

"I've already called your dad. He said he doesn't have any classes on Friday and so he will try to come home tomorrow night after Thursday classes."

They sat silently with Tony for thirty minutes or so.

"Alex, put the box on a shelf in the garage and make sure the doors are closed securely. We don't want any animals to get him before we bury him on Friday."

Friday morning after breakfast, Peter and Alex took a spade to the end of the clothesline and stepped a few feet further to the bank of the channel that separated the Island from the Mainland.

Peter cleared some stones away and started digging a hole three feet by two. After while Alex asked if he could dig too.

Peter was glad for the help; he knew they needed to dig a hole deep enough that racoons and foxes couldn't dig Tony up.

"Three feet ought to do enough for a dog," he remarked, noting that Alex probably didn't realize the significance of that, and he wasn't about to take this as a teaching moment.

"This digging business is hard work. Good thing Tony was only a small a dog."

When they thought they were ready they fetched Oliver and Victoria from the house. Victoria said a few words of remembrance and then recited the 23rd Psalm. Alex knew this one too and joined in with his mother. Oliver was crying too hard to speak and Peter wisely didn't either.

Victoria attempted to lower the box into the hole, but it was too deep. Alex jumped into the hole and took the box from his mother and settled it in the hole; it just fit.

"Oliver, do you want to toss some soil onto the box?"

"No!" he cried, vehemently.

"I will," said Alex and he and Victoria each took a handful of dirt and poured it over the box.

"I'll finish up here, Victoria," Peter said. "Why don't you take Oliver back up to the house?"

But Oliver didn't want to go so he and Victoria and Alex watched as Peter shoveled the excavated dirt back into the whole.

He then carried a bunch of rocks and stones from the bank of the channel and piled them on top of the dirt, to keep the animals from digging up the grave. He put one big stone at what he thought was the head of the grave and said to Alex, "tomorrow we can get a can of paint and put Tony's name on it as a marker."

"That's a good idea, Dad."

19. Goodbye Stella Bay

ALEX DIDN'T MUCH LIKE CHANGE, and he wasn't looking forward to starting all over again to find his way in a new city and a new school, teachers and classmates. But in the last three months he felt he had lost so much he had very little left to lose. So starting over in Peterborough didn't seem much worse than trying to restart his life on Amherst Island.

He had spent many hours in the Fall pondering this pending move. The three months on the busses trekking daily to Napanee ended any residual reverie of his new high school. His dreams of playing football at high school had been quashed. His best friend Hugh had moved away to Cobourg. And now they had lost Tony. Sandra had opted to go to school in Odessa, boarding Monday to Friday, so Alex didn't see her except occasionally on weekends. Even so, he felt a distance between them.
He almost welcomed the move to Peterborough.
Almost, but not quite.
It was upsetting the day the For Sale sign went up on the front lawn of 24 McDonalds Lane.
He hadn't resolved the tension and conflict between leaving familiar Stella behind and going to unknown Peterborough, between endings and new beginnings.
 Peter watched his son absent-mindedly kicking stones down McDonalds Lane one Saturday in December, a week before their move to Peterborough; he decided to join Alex to see if he wanted to chat.
"I notice you do a lot of walking these days by yourself." Peter left the thought hanging.
"Are you worried about moving to a new place?"
"Yeah, sorta." Alex mumbled in reply.
Peter left that alone for a while as they walked on down the lane.
"What do you think about while you're walking along?"
"I'm sort of saying my goodbyes.
"I think about all the places and things I did here the last three years. And won't be doing again.

"Don't get me wrong," Alex continued, "I want to go to Peterborough. I think Stella is getting to be smaller and smaller for me."

Peter wisely kept his comments to himself as they continued to amble along the lane.

"I remember how I felt when we first moved here" Alex continued, "I really liked our big old blue house, Stella Bay and the dock and the boat, but I also wished it was just for the summer and then we could go back to our old house in Kingston."

There was a pause.

"Do you think we could keep the house here and come back every summer?"

"I don't think so Alex, but I understand what you mean. It's a really lovely place, perfect in the summer. But we needed the money from the sale of this house to be able to buy the new house in Peterborough.

"And besides, soon you'll be working a summer job and you won't be able to come back here for the summer anyway."

That was a reality Alex hadn't thought about. They walked a little further.

"I guess you'll just have to focus on the new opportunity and say goodbye to this old place.

"You know Alex, this reminds me of a short skit Mark Twain used to do on the speakers' circuit. Young Mary was moving with her family from Tennessee to Missouri. And on moving day she wandered around her old property saying her goodbyes:

'Goodbye house, I'm going to Missouri.'

'Goodbye trees, I'm going to Missouri.'

'Goodbye green grass, I'm going to Missouri.'

'Goodbye God, I'm going to Missouri.'

At this point Alex looked up from his shoes and cast a questioning glance at his dad.

"Well," Peter said, "Mary didn't really mean goodbye god, it was mostly a matter of punctuation. What she meant was, 'Good! By God! I'm going to Missouri!'"

That touched Alex' funny bone and he relaxed. He was never quite sure of his father's humour but that one made sense to him.

"So, what are you saying goodbye to Alex?"

"Well, kinda like Mary, I've been saying goodbye to the Stella Bay, and these tall trees hanging over McDonald's Lane, and our house."

"You already said that, Alex. What else are you thinking about."

"Well, about Hugh and all our adventures biking all over Amherst Island.

"And well, how Sandra doesn't seem to care about me like she did before."

"Yes, well, Alex, you are a romantic male, an idealist, and when a girl gets under your skin, she leaves a permanent mark.

"You were pretty close with Sandra, and maybe you will be again one day, but now things are changing. You will always have strong memories of your time with Sandra, but you can't live in the past, you have to live in the present."

"But Dad, do you think Sandra thinks about me the way I think about her? Not knowing drives me crazy."

"I don't know Son. It seems to me your connection was mutual, so I would be very surprised if she doesn't still think of you with fondness and has questions about her own future.

"If you think you want to keep a connection with her, you need to make sure you have a serious conversation with her and say your goodbyes. Tell her that you miss the old times together and you know it will be hard to stay in touch when you move to Peterborough. Don't expect her to say the same things to you; maybe she will and maybe she won't; but don't hang your hat on that.

"Ask her if you can write to her when you move to Peterborough and will she write back. If she says yes, you have the chance of continuing a relationship with her. Of course, if she doesn't write back that's going to be a message in itself, as Marshall McLuhan might say, but I'm betting she will. If she says no, or equivocates, well, that's your answer too."

"'Equivocates'?

"and who's Marshall McLuhan?"

"Oh, yeah, equivocates, hesitates, or is non-committal or non-specific in her answer. I guess you could say, hedges."

"Oh."

"Regardless, you have to accept that she has her own life to live and you have yours. Who knows what is going to happen to the two of you in the next ten years."

Alex stopped and looked at his dad.

"What?" said Peter.

"Mom said the same thing in October when we were talking about Sandra."

The Clarences, Janey and Rebecca's parents down the lane, threw a big house party for the Jorgenson's – a going away party. The Danahers were there, and many of the neighbours, Frank Gohm and the twins, Paul Burke of the Scout Troop, and people from the District Scouting office (more to thank Victoria for being Akela for the St. Paul's Cub Pack than for the family), the vicar from St. Albans Church, even though the Jorgensons rarely went to church on Sundays, just the boys to Sunday School. Even Mr. Clarke and Mrs. MacAskill from Amherst Island Public School came. And most surprising, though it shouldn't have been, The Reverend Blair Farquharson and his wife Clara came. And Sandra.

It was a lovely party. The dining room was all decorated with ribbons and balloons. The dining table was set up with paper plates and many dishes brought by all the neighbours, and a big roasted turkey. Guests could work their way around the smorgasbord table loading their plates and retire to the living room and find a seat.

At the peak of the party Mr. Danaher got out his reflex camera and organized a group photo. "Much better quality than a little Kodak Brownie," he said.

"Oh, please send me a duplicate," pleaded Victoria.

"Of course," said Mr. Danaher.

Alex had positioned himself beside Sandra for the photo; she didn't seem to mind. He hoped he could get one too. All he had was a Class photo with her in it.

He whispered in Sandra's ear, "do you think we could go outside for a few minutes and talk without all these people around?"

"Sure Alex. I'll just get my coat and tell my mom where I'm going."

— Alex' Choice —

"Mom,' she called, "I'm going down to the dock with Alex for a few minutes."

"Okay dear, just don't get yourself the death of pneumonia."

The two of them clambered down the snow-covered stairs to Mr. Danaher's dock next door. They studied the light posts standing in the shallows of the bay.

"I guess Mr. Danaher will be making the ice rink soon," posited Sandra, making conversation.

"Yeah, I guess," said Alex, "but the ice isn't thick enough yet to start preparing the rink."

After a short silence Alex said, "remember when we used to skate round and round the ring, and then get hot chocolate?"

"Yes, I do Alex."

"And then I'd hold your hand."

"Yeah. Or maybe it was me holding your hand," she said with a gentle smile. "I'll never forget those evenings."

Alex heart glowed with emotion and delight.

"Sandra, I've been wanting to ask you a question for a year now."

"Really? What question?"

"Do you blame me for you almost getting drowned when we recovered the treasure?"

"Of course not, Alex. I was having the adventure of my life – it wasn't your fault that I got the cord wrapped around my wrist.

"And besides, you saved my life."

They both went silent for a while.

"Alex, do you remember last summer when we were swimming at Long Bay Beach, and I whispered in your ear, 'my hero'".

"Yes, I remember." Alex wanted to say, 'how could I forget' but he couldn't allow himself to be so demonstrative.

"Well, I meant it. You will always be my hero."

The silence between them then was very comfortable. 'Just like the old days' thought Alex.

"Sandra, when I move to Peterborough, may I write you letters.'

"Sure Alex, we can be pen pals. But be careful what you write; my mom will probably want to read them."

That made sense to Alex, but on one level he resented the intrusion into his private correspondence with Sandra.

"Thank you Sandra."

She looked at him for a long moment. She sensed he had something else on his mind.

"What, Alex?"

"Could I have a picture of you, Sandra. I don't have one."

"Okay, I'll send you one first chance I get to write you. But you'll have to write first so I'll know your address in Peterborough.

"And you have to send me a picture of you too," she said, laughing lightly.

Alex marveled at how easy she was around him. What had been going on the last year?

"I guess we better get back to the party."

Alex nodded.

"Alex," she said.

He turned to look at her. She reached over to him and kissed him on the lips. And smiled.

Alex had a smile on his face the rest of the evening.
Later when they got home Peter took Alex aside,
"So, what was her answer?"
Alex hesitated for a minute.
"She said she'd write.
"And she's going to send me a photo."
Peter gave him a thumbs up.

Peterborough, 1965 - 1969

– Doug Jordan –

20. Edmison Heights

THE HOUSE WAS BRAND NEW. It was everything Victoria had wanted when they first moved to Stella – a modern two-story – and landed instead in the big old 19th century frame house on McDonalds Lane.

For one thing it had two bathrooms – a full bath upstairs and a half-bath downstairs. Very modern. The old house in Stella only had one bathroom, upstairs, though Peter often joked that the outhouse by the garage was still operational for anyone who wanted to use it.

Alex wondered why it was called a half-bath when there was no bathtub at all, only a toilet and sink, but it was convenient to the main floor of the house.

But what the new house lacked was atmosphere, unless you counted a blasted construction zone, 'atmosphere'. Edmison Heights was a new subdivision in Peterborough's 'North End'. Half the houses on the half mile circle of Edmison Drive, gently wedged into the side of a hill, were newly constructed; the other half were just empty lots waiting to be filled in. The street, though paved and with curbs, was otherwise barren and forlorn, with lonely streetlamps providing the only relief, not a tree in sight, except for the stand of cedars on the side of the hill behind the neighbours' houses. This gave Victoria pause: what was a stand of cedars doing on the side of a hill? they preferred wet, almost swampy terrain? And the hill behind the Jurgenson house, currently under six inches of snow, already showed signs of run-off ruts in the barren hillside directly behind the house.

The house had a wide front porch, concrete, with a couple of pillars holding up the overhanging roof. And because the house had a higher elevation on the hillside than the ones across the street, sitting on the porch would produce a satisfying view of roofs and rolling terrain down to the river. You couldn't actually see the river as it was too far away and there were roads and houses and light industry in the way but you could imagine it. Not quite as satisfying as the towering maples and willows on McDonalds Lane, with the dock and the boat and the raft almost at their feet, but never mind, that spindly little maple planted in the front yard would be big one day.

The house had a single car garage attached and the single lane driveway was an interesting two stage lift from the street: a fairly steep grade from the curbed street, and then a level landing, about one car length in length, and then another little rise to the garage door. When the family arrived the first day the driveway was snow-covered, but Peter made a run for it. He gunned the Olds' engine, swerved and fishtailed and spun the back wheels feverishly until the rubber hit the road and the car and the clutch of terrified passengers landed on the landing.

The moving van arrived an hour or so later and parked the 43-foot trailer on the street in front of the house; the crew got out of the cab and stood for a long time studying the challenge ahead.

Peter and Alex had had the presence of mind to shovel the snow off the drive down to the pavement, except they had no shovels: they were on the moving van. But the neighbours must have been paying attention behind their curtains and pretty soon a couple of men with shovels appeared. It didn't take long to clear the snow, pushing most of it downhill, and as it was a mild December day, the residual snow had melted. The movers suggested Mr. Jorgenson park the car on the street.

Obviously, the trailer couldn't be backed up the hill; everything would have to dollied. They unloaded from the side door of the trailer, the loading ramp now worked more as a bridge across the snowy slope of the driveway. At least there was no piano.

They made a quick tour of the new house.

The living room with large picture window looked out over the front lawn with a dining room behind and kitchen beside that. The side door at the back led to the kitchen with the half-bath conveniently by the door. The basement steps lead to a semi-finished recreation room with a large fireplace. The back of the basement had a laundry tub and fixtures for a washer and dryer, very modern. There were four bedrooms upstairs and one full bathroom. The bathroom was at the top of the stairs facing the back – 'Wow, look at this,' Oliver shouted, 'there's a shaft in the bathroom and it goes all the way down to the basement. What's that for?'

— Alex' Choice —

"It's a laundry shoot so you don't have to carry your laundry all the way down to the laundry facility in the basement," explained Victoria.

"Oh, how does the laundry get back upstairs?"

"Same as always, we carry it."

"Hey Mom, there's no clothesline in the back."

"That's because we'll have an electric dryer for the clothes."

"Which room is mine?" Oliver wanted to know.

"Well, Son," Peter began, "the big bedroom at the front of the house opposite the bathroom is for your Mother and me, and the small room next to the bathroom at the back I'd like to use for my home office. You and Alex can fight over the other two."

But it was no fight at all. Oliver wanted the one at the front of the house so he could watch people going by on the street and Alex wanted the one at the back to enjoy the tranquility of the side of the hill.

Four hours later the moving van had been emptied and the movers gone, their pockets suitably lined with bonus money from considerate Peter. But the family now faced a house full of boxes and many hours of unpacking. Boxes and furniture were scattered over three floors, but no appliances. They had left their old appliances in the Stella house and had bought new ones in Peterborough for the new house: A fridge and stove and a washer and dryer – but they weren't arriving until the next day.

The movers had reassembled the beds and Victoria found the boxes with all bedding. They were too pooped to piss, as Peter would say, but at least they had a place to sleep that night.

"Okay gang," Peter announced, "we're all tired and we need something to eat. Let's go to a restaurant for some grub, get a few supplies for breakfast, and go to bed. We'll get cracking at unpacking tomorrow when we're fresh."

"Yeah, but Dad, we don't have a fridge."

"It's December Oliver, the whole outdoors is your fridge."

"Why did you buy a new house here in Edmison Heights, Dad?" Alex wanted to know.

"Well," Peter replied, "your mother had always wanted to have a new house. After the old house in Kingston and then the older house in Stella, I figured this was a good time to do it. After all, happy wife, happy life."

Alex didn't miss the wink Peter threw at Victoria.

"That's not the whole reason, Peter," Victoria gently chided.

"Yes, well, Edmison Heights is not far from the Trent University Campus so my commute will be very short."

"Hey, can we go and see the campus, and visit your office?" chimed in Oliver.

"Well, not tonight. Maybe in a couple of days once we get settled.

"But boys, there's not much to see, just a bunch of open fields beside the Otonabee River."

"Hunh?"

"Yeah, well, the university is very new and there are no buildings built yet on the future campus."

"Hunh? So where are the classrooms, and your office?"

"Well, the University has acquired three historic properties in downtown Peterborough which have been outfitted for classrooms and offices: Rubidge Hall, Catherine Parr Trail College for women, and Peter Robinson College for men.

"Who's Peter Robinson?"

"Well, Oliver, he was one of the early settlers in Peterborough and later became a member of the Legislative Assembly of Upper Canada. Many people say Peterborough is named after Peter Robinson but more likely the name was borrowed from Peterborough in England."

"Is Edmison Heights borrowed from England too?" Alex queried.

"No. Edmison was an early settler in Peterborough. He had a farm near here.

Over the next week they spent almost all of their time organizing their new house, unpacking and arranging everything. Peter's books took the longest to unpack as he still had to go to work that week. Most of the windows had no window coverings as none of the windows were the same size and shape as the 1867 house in Stella. For a while it was like living in a fishbowl. They were rather glad they had no neighbours at the back, only the hillside.

On top of all that they had to prepare for Christmas. They had time to put up a Christmas Tree, the spindliest twisted spruce

— Alex' Choice —

tree they'd ever seen; needles were falling even as they brought the tree into the house. Victoria dreaded the job of cleaning up the needles after the tree was finally banished to the back yard, January 2, later to be dragged into the stand of cedars.

Over the Christmas holidays, Peter did show the family around town. First they traveled north on Highway 28 and, just as Peter had said, came very soon upon a bend in the highway and another road veering off to the right and across a low level power dam and bridge.

"Well, kids, there's Trent University."

"Where?" exclaimed Alex, "There's just a big sign, 'Future Campus of Trent University!'"

"That's right, Son."

"All I can see is a field and a river and a big hill," Oliver chirped. "Oh, and look, there's an old broken-down ski jump off that hill."

"It's a very nice property," said Victoria, "too bad they have to take down that ski jump.

"But I can see why there is so much potential for a beautiful new campus. It has an Oxford sort of feel, or maybe Cambridge. I can see rowers on the river."

"Quite so, Victoria," replied Peter. "Trent intends to structure itself on the Oxford model, with small colleges clustered on one campus. I'm not sure about the scullers. But if this was an American University, I could see a huge football stadium built into the side of that hill, like Berkley or Michigan. Can you imagine 60,000 fans in that stadium?"

"No, I can't, Peter."

They drove to 'uptown' Peterborough and around the streets to view the three Trent buildings in different parts of town, stopping for a while at Rubidge Hall, a set of two-story buildings that looked more like row housing than a school.

"This is where my office is and most of my classes, at least for now." To say the family were a bit surprised and confused would be an understatement.

"It's nothing like the big old limestone building where you had your office at Queen's," said Alex.

'Exactly!' thought Victoria.

21. Adam Scott CVI

ADAM SCOTT COLLEGIATE & VOCATIONAL INSTITUTE was not only Alex' new high school, it was also new, only five years old when Alex entered its doors in January of 1965 to start the second semester of Grade 9. And he was certainly feeling new.

It wasn't that he felt unwelcome, he just ignored. And yet conscious of the other kids in his new class, 9C, casting furtive glances his way – who was this new kid?

Peter had driven him to school that first day even though it was barely a half-mile walk, mostly downhill. Alex was surprised his dad had done that, but Peter said it was no problem as he could easily drop Alex off on his way to work. Victoria hoped Peter had more in mind than just to drop their eldest son off at the big new school. She had to get Oliver settled in his new school, and, even though it was only a short walk to Edmison Heights Public School she couldn't be in two places at once.

Peter and Alex arrived at the large, two-story yellow glazed-brick building. There were three large elm trees in the presumably landscaped lawns and gardens at the front of the school, now buried in snow. The main entrance was an austere, formal place, not very inviting, but apparently only meant for adults and other visitors. There were no other kids around; evidently, they weren't supposed to use this door; instead, they were streaming in droves to the student entrances at the north wing and the southwest wing.

"Do you want me to walk you into the school, Alex?" Peter asked as they arrived at the front drive of Adam Scott CVI.

That was an offer Alex had hoped for but prepared to ask. He was fourteen years old now and assumed his father expected him to be self-reliant, consequently he wasn't quite sure how to answer him – he didn't want to be perceived as needy.

"Yes please. I don't know where I'm supposed to go, and I don't know where my locker is."

"Did you bring your padlock? Do you remember your combination?"

— Alex' Choice —

"Twice around to the right, 54, back counter-clockwise and around past the 54 to 3, and then back right to 35."

Peter drove his car up the angular u-shaped drive and parked in the visitors' parking area by the front entrance of the school; he walked with Alex up to the front four-panel oak doors. The main entrance was at the interior angle of two large wings going off at maybe 120 degrees, north and south. Inside there was a large atrium with well-polished stone floor pieces in large squares and laid out in regular patterns. On the opposite side of the atrium there was the gymnasium and then the cafeteria and library. Alex began to think this whole layout was one big geometry test. And he didn't know much geometry yet.

The walls were painted pale green on the lower few feet and white above, the two separated by a much darker green painted strip as if a chair-rail. Green and white were the school colours. Alex began to think green and white were Peterborough's colours. Trent University's colours were green and white and the junior hockey team…, wait, that can't be right, the Peterborough Petes Junior 'A' hockey team jerseys was a burgundy purple sort of colour with grey letters; and he'd seen in the Peterborough Examiner that the Peterborough Collegiate Institute colours were garnet and grey.

Anyway, this school was fresh and new and modern. To Alex, it looked more like a university than Rubidge Hall did.

"The office is just on the left. Mom and I met the Principal and the Vice-Principal the week before Christmas when we came to register."

They walked into the office and stood at the counter and waited to be noticed. The office was buzzing with kids and staff and phones were ringing. Alex began to feel a little anxious about being ignored but his dad was unperturbed – apparently familiar with administrative turmoil.

"May I help you?" a secretary asked.

"I'm Doctor Jorgenson, and this is my son Alex. This is his first day at Adam Scott."

Alex was a bit surprised that his father announced himself by his title and wondered why. But secretly he was proud to be a university professor's son.

"Oh, yes, we've been expecting Alex. Sorry for the chaos.

"I didn't realize you were a doctor, Doctor Jorgenson."

Alex was familiar with this confusion.

"I'm not a medical doctor, if that's what you were thinking. I'm a professor at Trent University."

"Oh goodness, that new school that's just starting up. My goodness.

"Well Professor Jorgenson, welcome to Peterborough, and Alex, welcome to Adam Scott.

"I'm sorry for all this chaos but first day after the Christmas Holiday is almost like September.

"Alex's Home Room is 9C and it is located on the second floor, in Room 213. Miss McCormick is his Home Room teacher and I think she is his English teacher as well if I'm not mistaken. She's a veteran teacher and Alex will find her very capable."

"Well, that's good Mrs.???"

"Oh, sorry, I'm Mrs. Hennessey."

"Thank you, Mrs. Hennessey," Peter said, smiling at her.

Alex thought he noticed colour rise in Mrs. Hennessey's cheeks.

"I'd take you up there myself but as you can see it's pretty chaotic here just now."

Peter thought, smiling at her, Mrs. Hennessy must like that word 'chaos'.

"Perhaps you can direct us to Alex' locker as well."

"Oh, yes, sorry. Let me see here, it's locker 2231, quite close to Room 213."

At that moment Mr. David, the principal, came out of his office and walked around the counter. He looked older than Methuselah and not particularly happy, not at all like jovial Mr. Clarke at Amherst Island Public School, but he smiled at Peter and offered his hand to shake.

'Welcome to Peterborough, Professor Jorgenson – I overheard you introduce yourself to Jenny.

'Jenny Hennessey' thought Peter, but you couldn't blame her mother for that, Jenny had married into it herself.

"And welcome to Adam Scott, young Mr. Jorgenson. I hope you have a productive and satisfying education here at Adam Scott."

— Alex' Choice —

"Yes, sir. I will."

"Has Mrs. Hennessey given you directions to your home room?"

"Yes sir. We're about to find our locker and get organized."

"Well, get a move on, bell rings at 9:00 and opening exercises will begin promptly."

Peter shook Mr. David's hand again, smiled at Jenny, a thank-you twinkle in his eye. He and Alex headed to the staircase. Room 213 was near the end of the Hall, and it only took another minute or so to find his locker. He piled his books and binders into the top shelf and hung his coat on the hook, removed his galoshes, and placed them on the bottom shelf, already rusty from five years of melted ice and snow. He looked at his dad who returned his look.

"Are you ready?" Peter asked.

"Sure, okay."

Alex grabbed a notebook and he and his dad walked through the doorway into Room 213. The general hum in the class suddenly stopped.

Miss McCormick looked up from her desk and, focusing on Alex, said, "ah, you must be Alex."

"Yes, Ma'am".

"Well, I'll be off then," Peter announced. He turned to the door as Mrs. McCormick introduced Alex to the class and directed him to his seat.

"First Row, third seat. We had a boy sitting there last term but he left at Christmas."

Alex took his seat and glanced around: chalk board on his right, windows on the far side on his left; some blonde headed girl in front of him and a sea of faces all around him. Beside him in the second row was the most stunning-looking girl he had ever seen, a sweet and perfect face, raven coloured hair softly curled at the shoulders, alabaster skin, wearing a white bouse and a light blue cardigan over. She looked a darkhaired version of Sandra.

She turned to him and offered him a big smile and her hand.

"Hi, I'm Cathy Baird. Welcome to 9C."

Alex took her hand and mumbled his name and maybe thanks.

For the rest of the class and the rest of the day Alex hardly knew what was happening.

Adam Scott Collegiate and Vocational Institute was a new school built to accommodate the growing 'North End' of Peterborough. There were ten classes of Grade 9s in 1965, about 360 kids; about the same number of Grade 10s, six classes of Grade 11s, and six Grade 12s. There were four classes of Grade 13s, about 100 students in this cadre of scholars, most of whom would be off to university. Alex wondered how many of his Grade 9 year would make it through Grade 13.

ASCVI wasn't much bigger than Napanee Collegiate, and not much newer, but somehow Adam Scott seemed more sophisticated than sleepy rural Napanee High School. And the name, Adam Scott Collegiate and Vocational *Institute*, very classy.

"Who was Adam Scott, Dad?" he asked Peter one day. "Was he another settler in Peterborough like Edmison and Peter Robinson?"

"Probably. Why don't you go and look that up in the School Library?"

Not used to being sloughed off, Alex resolved to do just that and bring back his results.

Adam Scott was the first settler in the Peterborough area and built a mill along with John Edmison on the Otonabee River in 1820. Peter Robinson arrived in the area in 1825 with some 2000 Irish immigrant families and almost overnight the town sprung up. The names Scott and Edmison might have disappeared from the annuls of history if Peterborough hadn't expanded into the north end and the Historical Society hadn't contributed those names to the districts and buildings there.

"Hey," said Alex at the dinner table as he reported his results, "this sounds just like the settlement of Amherst Island in the same time period by Irish farmers."

"I guess that's so, Alex," applauded Peter.

"Hey, this history stuff is interesting. Maybe I'll study history in university."

— Alex' Choice —

"Wow, woah, slow down," offered Victoria, the practical one, "what can you do with history except teach? I thought you wanted to be a lawyer?"

"Well, maybe I can be both."

And with that he grew quiet and soon left the table for his room.

"Well, there you go, Victoria," Peter shot back, "bursting his bubble of enthusiasm with your reality checks."

"Maybe so Peter, but I don't want you encouraging him with dreamy notions of ancient history."

The dining table grew silent and put a damper on the rest of the evening.

Oliver had no idea of what just happened, but he figured there would be no more conversations about Adam Scott.

As the year went by, and one year followed the next, Alex became more and more settled in his new surroundings. He enjoyed most of his classes, most of his teachers, and most of his school mates. He took his studies seriously and his athletics even more seriously. But mostly he kept to himself. He found he made few close friends and missed the comradery of the St. Albans Secret Society on Amherst Island.

22. Pen Pals and Preoccupation

THE FIRST FEW MONTHS IN PETERBOROUGH proved pretty lonely.

He did notice the girl in the row next to him in his Home Room. Cathy was beautiful, yet not aloof, perfectly comfortable with herself. Alex was impressed, and grateful, with how easily she engaged Alex in class. But Alex was too shy to engage her in anything that would remotely resemble an actual conversation. And strangely, he felt disloyal to Sandra if he showed interest in Cathy, even as the separation and distance yawned between himself and Sandra; if anything he felt even more besotted with her. He wondered if this pining had less to do with Sandra more to do with his reluctance to engage new friends in his new school.

Alex had tried to keep up with his friends in Amherst Island but this had proved illusory. Fuzzy, and Thursty – even Rebecca – would reply to his letters but those letters were pretty thin; he soon found he had nothing to say to them and the writing stopped. Pen pal relationships are not the same as casual in-person ones.

Even before he moved to Peterborough he wrote to Hugh McPherson in Cobourg while riding on the buses from Amherst Island to Napanee High School – he figured he had plenty of time with these long commutes. He found it challenging as his pen kept jumping lines with each bump on the road. He explained the situation to Hugh who seemed to understand and didn't mind. Alex resolved not to write such sloppy letters to Sandra.

He had told Hugh all about the daily two-hour bus and ferry rides, to and from Napanee District High School, the segregation of the different segments of the student body, his disappointment at not being able to be on the Golden Hawks football team.

Hugh commiserated with Alex but didn't hold back in telling him how he could walk to his new High School, Cobourg Collegiate, and he was on the CCI Wolves Junior Football team (mostly on the bench).

Alex had told him at length of the cave-in at the fort and Oliver's injuries caused by Old Man O'Reilly, and of the Jorgensons moving to Peterborough at Christmas time because his dad had a new job at Trent University. Hugh naturally commented that it would be 'character-building' for Alex.

And he told Hugh he was writing to Sandra. He told him he got the feeling that she was struggling to find her place boarding in Odessa and attending Ernestown High School, just as he, and maybe Hugh were. Things had changed so much since a year ago. He didn't tell Hugh of his constant worry that he was losing touch with her.

But as the months rolled by and Grade Nine passed into Grade Ten, the correspondence with Hugh became more and more irregular, and the content emptier and emptier, until finally it stopped altogether.

Sandra had given him a big hug and kiss when they said their goodbyes in December, and that moment was branded on his brain. Still Alex tried to caution himself that was just a momentary spike in an otherwise increasing distance between them over the last few months in Stella and it would only get worse from Peterborough. Yet, she had promised to write him every week.

And true to her word she replied regularly to his weekly epistles. He wrote to her home address – The Manse, St. Paul's Presbyterian Church, Stella – rather than to her boarding home address in Odessa; somehow he thought that more appropriate though imagined it would be more private if he should write to the Odessa address. He wrote her every Sunday for his dad to post on Monday, hoping Sandra would get the letter by Friday when she returned to Amherst Island for the weekend. He noticed that she usually replied on the Monday, from Odessa. The problem with this routine was their letters to each other were out of sync by a weekend, their conversation often overlapped. Sandra seemed to notice this first and asked him to stop writing weekly to allow time for the correspondence to be a more sequential exchange, but Alex chafed at having to wait two weeks to hear from her.

Her letters invariably followed a pattern in which she responded to each of the points in his letters. And then she would offer news of Amherst Island: Stella doings, her father's church activities – baptisms, wedding ceremonies, funerals – the Scout Troop at St. Paul's, the sheep farm, the Gohm twins; even news of Sean O'Reilly and Old Man O'Reilly – she had heard that the old man was down in Boston staying with some branch of the clan. She asked after Hugh, and Oliver, and Mr. & Mrs. Jorgenson. She rarely volunteered anything about herself.

Alex found himself fretting after each of her letters – they seemed so antiseptic. And how would she know about Sean O'Reilly becoming a Patrol Leader? And why did she want to know about Hugh? In replying, he would probe into her thoughts and feelings about her high school in Ernestown and her boarding family in Odessa. She always answered his questions but her minimalist style left him feeling a bit empty. He wondered if he was reading too much into this correspondence and thought about having a discussion with his father about it, but he never quite found the right opportunity. Even though he enjoyed most conversations with his dad – he usually made things relaxed and natural, except when the Professor would get off track, or make some ironic remark. He knew that he would take Alex' concerns seriously. But his apprehensions would be no further allayed.

One day in Spring after he had received a letter from Sandra, Victoria picked up on her brooding son's mood and asked about the letter. At first Alex responded non-committally but soon confessed of his misgivings about his relationship with Sandra. Victoria made short work of the question, reminding him he had plenty of time to worry about girls, and shifted the topic away from Sandra to other girls in Adam Scott.

"Are there girls in your classes you find interesting, Alex?"

"Not really," Alex replied, never mentioning the raven-haired beauty who sat next to him in Home Room and many other classes.

"Oh?"

"Yeah, they just hang around in groups of three or four giggling and glancing over at me. I think they're talking about me and don't really like me, cause I'm new."

"More likely they do like you and are just trying to draw attention to themselves."

"Really?"

"Yes, that's just the way girls are. They want you to notice them but don't want to talk directly."

Alex instantly thought of Cathy Baird. She wasn't like that.

"Do you feel awkward around girls?"

— Alex' Choice —

"Yeah, I guess."

"Well girls often feel awkward around boys too, they just handle it differently."

Alex thought this was enlightening, though hard to understand.

"Have you noticed any other girls in your class?"

"Well, not in my class, but the girl who has a locker two over from mine is forever dropping her books on the floor, because her locker is so full of other stuff, makeup and a mirror and bags."

"Hmmm," replied Victoria, "more likely she drops her books hoping you will pick them up for her."

"Why would she do that, Mom? Why can't she just pick them up herself?"

Victoria laughed, "Alex you are hopeless. She just wants you to notice her and start a conversation."

This made little sense to Alex, so he clammed up.

And he wasn't much closer to understanding his feelings about Sandra's letters.

Summer came and went and the letter writing with his two friends became less and less frequent. Hugh had said that since Cobourg wasn't that far away from Peterborough, maybe they could get together for a day if one of the dads could just drive them.

Peter said it was more like an hour's drive to Cobourg so it might be better if they made a day of it.

Eventually a date was arranged for the Jorgensons to drive down to Cobourg for a Saturday afternoon at the beach on Lake Ontario. Alex was grateful for this gesture but perceived a vague reluctance in it; the two families didn't really know each other very well. He felt the reluctance in himself too.

They met the McPhersons at their house before setting off for the beach. It was an older style yellow brick and stucco building with a mansard style roof and leaded glass windows, maybe built in the 1920s, with a small front yard, a side lane and a separate garage at the back of the house. Victoria remarked at the French doors off the large front porch that lead into the dining room. Very elegant, she said. Alex noted the McPherson's house was quite different from the Jorgenson's newly built house with a barely landscaped yard and barren hillside in the back.

Hugh took Alex up to see his bedroom in the back corner on the second floor. It had leaded glass windows back and side and most spectacularly a closet that contained a small staircase that led up to the attic. Very different from Alex bedroom in their new house in Edmison Heights.

The two families had each packed a picnic lunch and they headed off to the community beach in Cobourg. It was late August and while a sunny day, a brisk breeze blew off Lake Ontario pushing big, mildly ominous, cumulo-nimbus clouds racing east and pushing up white cap waves off the lake. The beach was pebbled, not sandy, and getting into the water was treacherous for the feet and balance. And the water was freezing cold. When the day was done and it was time for the Jorgensons to drive back to Peterborough, they said their goodbyes and piled into the car. It was a quiet drive back.

Alex wrote to Hugh and asked him to thank his parents for organizing the day at the beach. Hugh answered back with a short letter, but the life had gone out of the correspondence.

As Fall drifted into Christmas of 1966 Alex and Sandra continued to correspond but the letters were now monthly and the contents largely factual. He longed to hear her say she missed him and hoped for Xs and Os along with the salutation, but she rarely sent those. Alex worried if Sandra had a new boyfriend but he never asked her.

And he refused to stop writing.

23. Landscaping

PETER SAID IT WOULD BE CHARACTER BUILDING, and furthermore it would build up muscles and that would be desirable if Alex wanted to play football in the fall. But landscaping?

Edmison Heights lived up to its name – a sandy hill rising from the Otonabee River a half a mile to the east, part of a landscape of drumlins rolling hill and dale throughout the county, all the result of debris left-over from the gouging, scraping and retreating ice-age ten thousand years previous. There was an abandoned railway carved out of the hillside behind the house and a stand of cedar trees, north of the neighbour's house, but otherwise the hill was a clay landslide waiting to happen. When it rained little rivulets ran towards the house. Most of the water followed the contours of the landscaping left by the builder which allowed it to run between houses and down the hill to the street, leaving mud-red deposits at the curb. But some of those rivulets ran to the house so that water and mud accumulated at the concrete foundation. Victoria worried that eventually this would find its way through the cellar walls and window wells and into the basement.

"Peter," she announced, "we have to do something about the hill behind the house this summer. I think we should build some retaining walls against that hillside to keep the mud and water from running down to the house.

Peter readily agreed with her except that by 'we' he knew that really meant 'you'.

Soon after that, large loads of limestone river slabs arrived in the front driveway, along with wheelbarrows and shovels. Peter was a would-be architect and drew up some designs. Victoria said she would supervise and provide the lemonade. All that was needed was some labour. She looked at 13-year-old Oliver and 15-year-old Alex.

Over the next three weeks the boys shoveled and dug and hauled rock and gradually a wall of limestone gradually took shape. Actually, two walls with a four-foot-wide landing between the two tiers of rock. The backyard began to resemble an Incan mountain farm.

Two loads of flagstone were delivered by large dump trucks – one load on the level landing half-way up the drive, and the second load on the street at the bottom of the driveway. The boys would load the wheelbarrows with three or four large slabs and push the wheelbarrow up the driveway, along the side of the garage and into the back yard. After a week of this there was a well-warn rutted path from the driveway to the back yard.

Peter and the boys dug a vertical face into the side of the hill, about four feet high, and a second four-foot face four feet back of the first. They leveled the first tier by tossing the excess soil onto the yard below and leveled and contoured the bottom level perhaps forty feet from the house. Then prayed for no rain for just a few more weeks in the usual hot and dry July. They began to artfully place the limestone slabs along the red clay face they had dug so that the outfacing edge was reasonably squared and aligned, piling flagstone slabs, layer upon another, like a skilled bricklayer, building a wall of strength and stability, or so Peter hoped. The retaining wall began to look like the drystone walls of Amherst Island. They then backfilled the slabs and gaps with heavy gravel and the remains of the clay. In the middle of the first stone tier, about waist height, he inserted a five-step staircase of limestone slabs to the top of the first landing.

They repeated the process in constructing the second stone wall into the hill. This added another level of difficulty for the boys hauling limestone slabs to this tier.

Peter did not insert a staircase in this wall.

The walls done, the next job was to build drainage ditches on either side of the walls to take away rainfall run-off without flooding the neighbours' basements. Even so, the next major rainstorm would make short work of the coarse sand that caulked the stone wall cracks and crevices. The red clay of the yard and landing needed a cover of grass; grass seed would not establish a deep root system in time to keep the clay in place with the spring run-off, more likely to be swept away in the next major summer storm. The solution was sod. And a cedar hedge.

A tractor trailer loaded with turf and two dozen cedar saplings arrived, and a lift truck gradually removed two dozen pallets of rolled turf onto the street. You'd think three weeks of hauling and installing limestone slabs would see the hardest part of the job done, but the grass sod rolls were easily its match. Peter wondered if he would ever be able to straighten his back again. Even the lemonade lady began to feel the pain. The boys loaded the heavy rolls onto the wheelbarrow, three or four rolls at a time, and pushed the wheelbarrow up the grade of the driveway and along the now well-rutted path beside the garage to the back yard to the waiting hillside terrace and yard. Peter planted a hedgerow of five-foot cedars along the property line next to the old railway bed, and then started laying turf on the clay slope from the cedars to the second-tier wall. He then laid turf on the landing of the first tier. Finally, he laid turf over the remaining area of yard at the back of the house down to the foundation wall. After three days of heavy going the red mud of a landslide waiting to happen had been transformed into a green carpet of sculpted landscape.

Victoria admired the boys' handiwork and relaxed knowing that her plan for saving her cellar was likely to be a success. She congratulated her boys for a job well done but sagely noted that the rutted path along the side of the garage from the driveway to the back needed repair. A cement slab walkway all around to the back door would be an easy solution she suggested.

The boys faces fell with delight at the thought of this next project but a few days later another tractor trailer with pallets of cement paving stones arrived and a load of fine gravel. The wheelbarrow hauled gavel around to the back yard as Peter removed turf, leveled the surface with gravel and then raked and leveled the gravel, working his way along the back wall of the house and attached garage. He then filled the ruts made by the wheelbarrow with red clay and prepared the surface for the cement slabs. They then hauled slabs, two or three at a time – they were heavy and barely fit into the wheelbarrow; Peter then fit the slabs into a squared and measured walk. Done.

All it needed now was some shrubs and gardens to give the stark stone wall and barren walkway some relief. But that project would have to wait for next summer.

24. Body Building

THE BOYS' BODIES ACHED THE FIRST FEW DAYS OF LABOUR but being youthful, quickly recovered; Peter didn't feel quite as buoyant as the boys. When the project was finished four weeks later they were pretty sure their muscles had become stronger, even if it was hard to see the difference in the mirror. They resolved to continue to exercise their bodies.

They cut out an ad from an issue of *Superman* comics for a Joe Wieder weight training set and begged their dad if they could get it.

By the end of August the 135-pound kit of one steel barbell, two dumbbells and 110 pounds of iron plates had arrived. And an instruction booklet about what exercises you could do with the weights. But now they needed a bench and cradles to handle the barbell for standing and prone presses.

Professor Jorgenson wasn't very handy with woodworking tools – but like the blind carpenter, took out his hammer and saw a solution. Alex was mildly embarrassed that the professor hardly knew his way around a tool-belt, except that Peter always seemed to know somebody who was, like Mr. Danaher in Stella who built the boys an Olympic style three-meter diving board. This time he called on Victoria's brother in Bailieboro and explained the situation. A few days later Uncle Mel arrived in his pickup truck with a power saw, a power lathe, an electric drill and some screw nails, three pieces of 2x10 ten-foot spruce planks, a sheet of plywood and a few pieces of 2x4 and 1x3 boards.

"Okay boys, let's see what we've got here," Uncle Mel declared. And down to the basement they went where the boys had already humped the weights to the laundry room.

First, he built an upright cradle for the boys to do overhead standing presses and squats. He cut sixteen inches off two of the ten-foot 2x10s; he screwed one of the sixteen-inch pieces between the overhead floor joists, 16 inches-centred, eight feet above the concrete floor; he got out the five-foot barbell, measured it to be sure and then marked a spot on the overhead joists, four feet from the first brace, and screwed the second brace into the joists. He placed one of the eight-foot, eight-inch 2x10s against one of the braces and got Oliver to stand next to it and had him squat down to where his knees were about ninety degrees to the floor. He marked the plank with his pencil at the point where Oliver's shoulders were relative to the upright plank. He brought the two planks together and marked the second one at the same height as the first. He cut four pieces of 1x3 about 9 inches in length and screwed them on both sides of the planks where the marks had been made; he measured the top of the planks and marked the centre of the width of the plank and then one inch each side of centre. He then rigged up two sawhorses he had brought for the purpose and with his jig saw cut a two-inch-wide space down the centre of the plank almost to the level of the 1x3 cross pieces, and cut a u-shape curve at the bottom with his jig-saw. He repeated the cut on the second 2x10 plank. He then screwed the ends of the planks into the cross braces at the top by the floor joists. He then fastened some steel elbows to the bottoms of the upright planks and then screwed the bottoms of those elbows into the concrete floor. The upright cradle was now very solid and secure.

The boys were pleased now they could see the finished structure. They threaded the steel barbell through the gaps in the two planks and then loaded each end with a 25# plate and fastened the plate to the barbell with a clamp.

"Careful that one of you holds down one end of the barbell while the other is putting the plate on the other end," reminded Uncle Mel. "You don't want that heavy bar and plate falling out on your foot, and damaging your mother's concrete floor."

Victoria had listened to all this banging and cutting and had come down for a look, shook her head and went back upstairs to her kitchen.

"Okay, boys, now for the bench and cradle"

First, Uncle Mel measured Alex' leg from heel to knee. 20 inches.

"Why are you doing that Uncle Mel?" asked Oliver.

"Well son, when you're lifting a weight while lying on your back you need to have your feet firmly placed on the floor to transfer as much weight as possible from your back to your feet. This bench will be about 20 inches high, just about perfect for Alex now. Your legs are a little shorter than Alex's are, for now, but I'm sure you'll grow into it. We'll leave a couple of pieces of 2x4 for you to use as extenders, for now.

"Now what, Uncle Mel?"

"Well, now I'm going to build a box frame out of 2x4s about five feet long and eighteen inches wide, and 20 inches high, and then we'll enclose it with pieces of this 5/8ths plywood. It'll be plenty sturdy."

He proceeded to measure and cut pieces of 2x4 and then rip pieces of the plywood, just as he said, and screwed it together.

Then he asked Alex to lie down on the box and put his arms straight up above his chest. He got the barbell from the upright cradle and placed it across Alex' two hands. And measured the distance from the barbell to the floor, 40 inches.

He then cut the remaining 2x10 foot plank into two pieces, 44 inches in length. He set them against the sides at one end of the box and asked Alex to lie down on the box again and extend his arms up the sides of the planks; he marked the planks with a pencil at the place where the cradle of Alex's thumb and his hand was, about, 40 inches from the floor, 20 inches from the bench top. He marked the plank at 21 inches and then with his jig saw cut out a piece at 21 inches, then down to 20 inches and back up the centre of the plank to the top end, making a one-sided cradle.

"Oh, I see," said Alex.

Uncle Mel then screwed the 2x10 uprights into the 2x4 studs on the inside of the box by one end. Done.

"Are you going to screw the box into the concrete floor too?"

"No need, it's a pretty heavy box and when you're lying down on it you should be a good counter-weight to the weights on the bar. And you may want to move this box around from place to place."

So they put the bar on the cradle of their new homemade bench and loaded it with the two 25# plates. The bench started to rise off the floor at the base, but Uncle Mel was able to catch the bar before the bench tipped up altogether.

"Hmmm." he said, "I guess we'll need to screw the end of bench to the floor after all. But we better put it somewhere out of the way of your mom's washer and dryer.

"This bench will be a little hard. I've got a bench seat from an old pick-up. I'll cut a piece that will fit this bench and staple it to this bench next time I'm here."

And with that Alex and Oliver started their three times per week workouts in their basement gym, hoping to bulk up for their football futures.

25. Athletics

ADAM SCOTT CVI HAD A FOOTBALL FIELD AND A TRACK. And a Junior and a Senior football team. And because he could walk home after school, this was the best thing about moving to Peterborough. He had missed the 1964 football season but was determined to try out for the Jr. Lions Football team in September when he would be in Grade 10.

But in May of his Grade 9 year at ASCVI he was excited, and a little nervous, about testing himself with the Scott Track and Field team. He thought of High School track as the big leagues as compared to his experience at Amherst Island Public School – would he be up to the challenge?

The Ontario Federation of Secondary School Athletic Associations had the good sense to divide the competitions into three levels by age: Midget (up to age 14 (as of January 1)), Junior (ages 15, 16), and Senior, over 17 (but less than 19). Alex was 14 in Grade 9, and so a Midget, turning 15 August 27, and would be a Junior in Grade 10.

The competitions for qualifying for Adam Scott Lions Track & Field team was held in early May. The Peterborough District championships was to be the end of May; the winners (1st and 2nd) of that Meet would go on to the Regional Meet (COSSAA – Central Ontario Secondary School Athletic Association) in early June and the all-Ontario Championships in mid-June, before end of year final exams, barely.

Alex wanted to try out for his favourite three events: 100-yard dash, the 220 sprint, and the long jump. He knew that if he qualified for the 100-yard dash he would also likely qualify for the 440-yard relay.

Alex turned up at the Monday afternoon trials in his gym shorts, t-shirt and running shoes, hoping that he would make the team; he even had dreams of doing well in the city meet, and who knows, maybe go on to the regional meet. Afterall, he had been very successful as an elementary school sprinter. But did tiny Amherst Island Public School and the mostly rural sparsely populated Limestone District track meet measure up with a big city high school meet?

— Alex' Choice —

It was a sunny but cool and somewhat windy day, clouds scudding across the blue sky. Alex did a few easy laps around the track to warm up and plenty of stretches as Mr. Clarke had trained him, but he still felt chilled. The Phys. Ed. teacher called the aspirant Midgets to the start line. There were twelve boys, so Mr. Sawchuk indicated there would be two timed heats and the three boys with the top times in either heat would qualify for the team.

Alex was called for the first heat of six boys. They lined up in their lanes at the start line. A couple of boys dug a pair of divots in the red cinder track and settled down on one knee into a crouch. Alex dug two shallow divots too but he was only used to a standing start. Coach called, 'On Your Marks' and the boys readied themselves; 'Set', and the crouched boys rose into a stiffer position; Alex just tensed himself to take off.

Bang! The starter pistol sounded and Alex sprang into motion. Within two strides he knew he was ahead of the other five boys; even the boys with the crouch technique were slower than Alex to rise and take their first strides. So much for that technique. By forty yards Alex glanced around and realized he had a comfortable lead of 2 or 3 yards but he sensed that one of the boys was beginning to charge harder. Alex rose up onto his toes and pushed himself to top seed. By 60 yards he felt this was going to be his race. But at 60 yards he also felt a sharp pain in his hip; his hip flexor muscle had torn. He tried to continue but he just couldn't. He slowed down with a few awkward hops and limped to the finish line, last, defeated.

One of the teachers came over to him to see if he was alright and pretty quicky determined what had happened.

"You're going to need a few weeks to rest and heal that muscle," she said to him. "I'm afraid your track season is done. I'm sorry."

Alex willed himself not to cry.

He limped into the Boys' Change Room and changed into his street clothes; and limped home, sorely disappointed

September came and after a summer of building the stone wall and weight training in the basement with Oliver, Alex felt strong and ready for football season. But in the Fall of 1965 entering Grade 10, he was still feeling a bit new in this new high school and more than a little unsure of himself.

He knew the game of football – he'd been going to games at Queen's with his dad since he was nine or ten, and he watched it on tv, even listened to it on radio whenever the Ottawa Rough Riders were playing. He knew what 'first downs' were, what the line of scrimmage was, and 'offsides', 'no yards', and why there was such a thing as a rouge.

('Well, you see, Alex,' his father explained, 'football is derived from the older game of rugby and in rugby, the ball is always 'live' – is in play – unless the ball goes out of bounds or play is stopped by the referee blowing his whistle. At least, that is the case for the version of football played in Canada, the Americans have gone away from that idea and half the time it seems the ball is 'dead' in their game. In any event, in Canadian football, when the ball is kicked into the end-zone and the receiving team fails to run the ball out of the end-zone, or the ball goes out of bounds, the kicking team gets one point. It can sometimes make the difference in the outcome of the game and so shouldn't be so easily dismissed.')

But knowing how the game of football is played was very different from knowing how to play football. He knew how to hold a football, even with his smaller hands, and how to throw and catch a football, he knew how to run, fast, and zig and zag from playing tag in the school yard, and even how to plow into people from playing Red Rover at Scouts, but he didn't know how to properly block and tackle, or make spin moves, or run with a wide stance and stay balanced and use your hand to stay on your feet, or a dozen other techniques.

And in Grade 10, he had just turned 15 and was still two years younger than many of the older boys still eligible for Junior Football. And he was shorter than many of the other boys on the team. He certainly felt smaller, despite his summer of weight-training workouts and landscaping work.

But he went to practice every day and worked out hard. He loved his shoulder pads and white football pants with thigh pads and padded knees, and his green knee-socks and his cleats; he liked the way they clacked as they walked across of the hard hallway floors on the way to the change room; and he was thrilled

— Alex' Choice —

with his green and white jersey. He wasn't so thrilled about having to take off his clothes in front of the other boys and take a community shower. And even though he mostly sat on the bench during games he hauled his uniform home to his mom to wash every Friday; Victoria would scrub diligently the grass stains on the white pants and complained why they were white in the first place.

The coaches may not have noticed him in the Fall of '65 but after the Spring track meets, after Alex won the Junior 100-yard-dash in the city school championships, as well as the 220 and the long-jump, and anchored the relay, Coach Sawchuk asked, 'Are you coming out for the Junior Lions football team next year?'

And sure enough, in the Fall of his Grade 11 year, the coaches took all the boys hoping for half-back or full-back positions aside and put them through 40-yard sprints. Alex won every trial and was selected for starting half-back. The Junior Lions didn't win the District Championship but they won half their league games and all their exhibition games, and Alex scored eleven touchdowns. The team started calling him 'Flash' Jorgenson, after the comic strip character. Peter came to all of his games as did Victoria. But she worried about Alex getting hurt and was troubled to see her young man hobbling around the house the day after a game and limping to school.

But to Alex, this was the thrill of a lifetime, and he was living his dream. He felt this was an important step on his way to Queen's and playing for the Queen's Golden Gaels.

And he could hardly wait to play for the Senior Lions next year.

26. Scouts

ALEX HAD CONTINUED WITH HIS SCOUT TROOP at Saint Paul's Presbyterian Church in Amherst Island even as they anticipated their move to Peterborough at Christmas. Getting to the Friday evening meetings was complicated while Peter was commuting from Peterborough and Alex was bussing to high school in Napanee. Problem-solving Victoria solved that problem when she asked the Gohm boys if they wouldn't mind picking up Alex and driving him.

"No problem, Mrs. J., no problem at all."

The Gohm twins had turned 16 the previous January and now had their driver's licences, though they had been driving the tractor and the old pickup trucks on the farm for at least three years.

"And we can drive Oliver too; he's a Tenderfoot in the Troop now, and too young to walk!" Gary laughed at his little joke.

But once the Jorgensons had settled into a new routine in Peterborough it was time for Alex and Oliver to enlist with a local Scout Troop. Victoria chose the new St. Steven's Presbyterian Church: there was no United Church nearby and she wouldn't send them to the Baptist Church. St. Steven's was nothing like the stately and elegant St. Paul's Church on Amherst Island – didn't even have its own building yet; instead it operated out of the gym of the Edmison Heights Public School building, and so did the Cub Pack. And even though Oliver had moved up to Scouts, Victoria had become involved in the Scouting Movement and was quickly welcomed as Baloo at the St. Steven's Cub Pack.

The Scout Troop, though, operated out of the gymnasium at Adam Scott. Alex cut through the field at the end of Edmison Drive and then along Hilliard to his high school. He no longer had to worry about the walk in the dark on The Forty Foot Road, or being accosted by bullies. Nevertheless, he still found himself looking over his shoulder on the walk home, watchful for the ghosts of the O'Reillys driving by and harassing them; he still carried his big ironwood stick, and he was thankful for Oliver's company.

— Alex' Choice —

Alex had moved up to Patrol Leader at St. Paul's but he couldn't expect to usurp the patrol leaders at his new Troop at St. Stephen's. So he quietly accepted his role as First Class Scout in Fox Patrol and decided to work on earning more badges, especially the difficult qualifying badges for Queen's Scout. Oliver was invested into Squirrel Patrol.

That summer, the summer of the landscaping, the troop went camping for a week at the ancient Scout Camp along the Otonabee river, north of the new Trent University campus, or at least, where the campus would eventually be located. The camp seemed ancient because the entrance – a dirt track that turned off from the winding and pastoral River Road – was marked by a bedraggled and weathered cedar archway. The dirt track wound its way through some low-lying boggy ground, ladened with many leaning cedar trees.

"I can see why this has become a Scout Camp" opined Peter. "I suspect it was once a settler's farm but too wet to raise anything but range cows and mosquitos; it was probably bequeathed to the Scouting Association of Peterborough County for them to do what they will with it."

"Oh, don't say that Peter, I don't want my boys coming back from camp covered with bumps and bites."

"Could be worse, Victoria; at least black fly season is pretty much over."

The dirt track eventually gained a bit of a rise in elevation and opened onto a grassy knoll. There were a few hardy cedars scattered here and there, some picnic tables and firepits.

"Ah," said Peter, "this looks more like a camp."

"Where are the toilets?" ventured Oliver.

"You'll have to dig your own," said Peter.

"Yeah," said Alex, "they're called latrines."

"Oh," said Oliver, not quite understanding and definitely not believing it.

As other families arrived the Troop was just about complete. Mr. Coward, the Scout Master, checked to see that the van had been emptied of all the tents and equipment needed. He stood at alert and raised one hand in the air. After a few minutes the boys picked up the signal and stopped their chattering; the parents seemed to get the idea too.

"All right Scouts, fall in."

The boys began to move toward Mr. Coward and formed the familiar horseshoe configuration around him.

"First, you need to thank your parents for bringing you boys here for camp. I'm sure you are going to have a wonderful time, and probably they will too," he deadpanned. Peter smiled to himself, appreciating the humour in the remark.

"You boys are going to learn things about living in the out-of-doors, and how to take care of one another, things you may carry with you the rest of your lives.

"Parents, please be back here next Saturday by noon to retrieve your boys. We should have all had our breakfasts and be packed up and ready to go home.

"Now boys, once you have said your goodbyes to your parents, and thanked them for allowing you to come to this Scout Camp, you will break into your patrols and pitch your bell tents – one per patrol; they're quite large – each can sleep 10 so you will have plenty of room with just five or six of you. The first patrol to get their tent up and secure can come over to my area and you can pitch the Scout Master's tent.

"Then we'll all assemble over by the big firepit and put together the mess tent."

Oliver was looking a little defeated. Those piles of canvas looked pretty big. He didn't know anything at all about pitching a tent and he didn't know if anyone in Squirrel Patrol knew anything either. He looked forlornly at Alex who seemed eager to get started. He must have had experience with the tent business from last summer when the St. Paul's Troop camped at Frontenac Park north of Kingston.

And he wasn't wrong. Alex quietly took charge of Fox Patrol, selected a site near a big cedar tree, inspected the grounds and 30 minutes later had the big tent with ten taut guy ropes in place and one rope strung from the top of the bell tent to the cedar tree.

Fox Patrol then reported to Mr. Coward and in ten minutes had his single peak tent, with awning, up.

Squirrel Patrol was still struggling with their tent and Alex then urged his patrol to pitch in and help Squirrel Patrol get their tent finally pitched.

— Alex' Choice —

"Hey," hollered Oliver, "What's this? There's not even a floor in this tent. Are we expected to sleep on the ground?"

"That's right, Tenderfoot, and you better hope it doesn't rain this week because your tent is pitched in a little gully."

The Squirrel's Patrol Leader looked at the terrain on which his tent was sitting and realized Alex was right, but he wasn't prepared to tear it down and move it.

They all assembled near the stone fire pit and Mr. Coward paced out a large rectangular space.

"The mess tent will go here. Hound Patrol, go over to the supply depot and retrieve the large cavass tent you see there." The boys looked at each other wondering what and where the supply depot was but in looking where Mr. Coward had unloaded the van, they saw a large pile of canvas and figured that must be the Mess Tent. They raced over to it and it took all of them and some organization to carry the heap back to where Mr. Coward wanted the Mess tent pitched. With Mr. Coward's direction and some clever Scouts, they pretty soon had that tent wrestled to the ground and erected. Next, four picnic tables were humped over and placed inside the Mess Tent. Done.

"Hey, Mr. Coward," Oliver called out, "I gotta go. Where's the latrine?"

"Right, I'll show you where it's generally located. Everyone get a shovel."

Peter and Victoria had been watching all this industry with fascination, but then Peter whispered in Victoria's ear, "Time to go," and they slipped away. Peter was thinking how lovely it would be just the two of them alone for a week. Victoria was thinking how worried she was going to be all that week.

The boys each grabbed their little fold-down shovels and followed Mr. Coward behind Fox Patrol's tent and into a clearing in a small clump of cedar trees. He drew a long line with his staff in the clearing and said,

"Okay boys, start digging."

Mr. Coward was very pleased with the progress of his Troop at the summer camp and as the year advanced, he wanted to test his boys with a more ambitious excursion the following summer. He heard of a mini-Jamboree being held at the large American

Scout Camp in Poughkeepsie New York in July. He knew not all of his boys would be able to make the long trip from Peterborough to Poughkeepsie but if a dozen or so of his best boys could make it, they would likely acquit themselves well in the competitions. He sent notices home with the boys. It didn't take much persuasion to convince Peter and Victoria it was a good idea.

Peter cemented the idea with Victoria. "We can drop the boys off in Poughkeepsie and then drive on down to New York City for a week of sightseeing."

"And shopping," added Victoria.

Peter recognized this was the price of an adult weekend in New York. Victoria knew this was compensation for the hours she would have to spend at the Frick Gallery and the Symphony.

"Don't worry Victoria, the Symphony doesn't play in New York in the summer."

The drive down to Poughkeepsie was thrilling as far as Alex was concerned. They drove from Peterborough to Toronto and then along the Queen Elizabeth Way, a beautiful new four-lane expressway with a grassy meridian dotted with fruit trees, through Oakville, Burlington and over the Skyway Bridge overlooking the Hamilton Harbour. Then all along the Niagara Escarpment with miles and miles of orchards of apples and peaches, then to Fort Erie, crossing the Niagara River into the USA at Buffalo, New York. They were greeted there by a friendly border guard who asked where they all were born and where they were going.

"All in Canada sir," Peter replied. "The boys are going to a Scout Camp near Poughkeepsie and my wife and I are going to spend the week in New York City."

The guard seemed to be pleased with that answer and waived them through, wishing them a pleasant stay in America.

The drive along the wide and winding Interstate 80 was like traveling through another world, the rolling hills on one side, occasional glimpses of the Erie Canal on the other. Alex was especially amazed at the rest stops for lookouts and rest rooms, and occasionally fully equipped gas stations with full restaurants.

"We have nothing like this in Canada," thrilled Alex to his amused dad.

Alex' Choice

"You can credit that to President Franklin Delano Roosevelt, and then President Eisenhower for continuing the dream of a network of transcontinental highways."

Alex thought he might be in for another lesson in American history but Peter seemed delighted to just soak up the scenery.

Oliver was thrilled with the Onteora Scout Camp: It was hilly country in the Catskill Mountains in Southeast New York, with a canopy of tall pine trees and blankets of needle-covered grounds, and well-trodden pathways. It had cabins, not tents, it had toilets, and a wooden mess hall and kitchen – meals were prepared by regular staff members, three times a day. This was his idea of camping. Alex on the other hand was confused, if not quite disgusted. This was hardly what Lord Baden-Powell had in mind, he was sure. On the other hand, he didn't miss the bugs.

There were three American Scout Troops at the Jamboree – one from Scranton, Pennsylvania, one from Mystic, Connecticut and one from Poughkeepsie itself as host, – and the St. Steven's Scout Troop made four. The American boys were struck by the oddity of the small contingent of Canadian Scouts. The Canadians' uniforms were different from their own – a pleasant shade of grey, rather than the forest green of the Canadian uniform, and they wore caps, not peaked brimmed hats; most notably they wore long pants, not the short pants and knee socks the Canadians wore. Alex, the historian, knew the Canadian garb was very similar to their English counterparts, surely these American uniforms could not be consistent with Baden-Powell's standards. The boys only wore their dress uniforms at special ceremonies in the evening; the rest of the time they wore rugged clothes for the various camp activities. But here again the Americans were different – they had regulation Scouts utility clothes whereas the Canadian boys just wore their everyday jeans and t-shirts.

'I guess American boys are better off than Canadians,' mused Alex.

Every day there were organized activities which taught a variety of outdoor skills and tested their physical fitness. There was an obstacle course, an orienteering event, and a nature-oriented scavenger hunt. And every day there were scouting skills training events: knot tying, identifying mushrooms, and ferns, and snakes. Oliver wasn't too fond of the snakes, even garter snakes, and he was seriously anxious about water snakes, just as he worried about the turtles in the lake. If you passed the tests at the end of each activity you were awarded a badge at the evening ceremonies. If you didn't pass the test you still got an activity badge. The Canadian boys were proud to have these grey American badges sewn on their green sleeves or sashes.

Every morning started with swimming in the lake. All the boys had been assessed for their swimming skills: beginners, novices, juniors and seniors. Alex with years of swimming lessons, and Oliver not far behind him, and many hours swimming off the dock and raft at Stella Bay, were expert swimmers. On the second last day of the week there was a swim meet. Alex and Oliver acquitted the Canadian contingent very well but there was a kid from Mystic who won most of the senior medals. Alex was pleased and surprised with himself, being more of a diver than a swimmer. And a track man.

And so the stakes were high on the last day of the Jamboree with a track meet. It was a modified set of athletics events as the Scout Camp didn't have an actual track. There was a sixty-yard dash up a gently sloping hill to the big pine tree at the top. Alex won that one. There was a pie plate throwing contest, using aluminum pie plates instead of real discusses. Oliver did well in that one. There was long jump contest into a pit, which Alex also won. And a leaping contest – in lieu of a high jump the contestants had to leap and touch a pie plate hanging by a string from a branch of a pine tree which was lifted higher and higher until all contestants had been eliminated with the one leaping the highest the medal winner; a long and lanky jumper from the host team won that – he may have had a lot of practice. Giant Robert Fife of St. Steven's won the stone throw contest; and gymnastic Arthur Murray won the obstacle course. The long distance run through the forest drew no takers from Peterborough and the win went to a skinny kid from Scranton.

The Americans were generous in defeat but more than a little nonplussed with the Canadians' performance. The pride of the American hosts was to be salvaged in the final event of the meet – the 4 by 60-yard relay. The four troops lined up their teams of four sprinters at the bottom of the sloping hill, thirty yards from the big pine tree at the top; one boy from each team was to race to the top of the hill, tap the foil pan hanging from the tree with the baton, then back down the hill for the next exchange with their teammates waiting there. Oliver started off for St. Stevens and raced for dear life to the pine tree, tapped, turned and raced back down the hill to the start line to pass the baton to Robert Fife. Robert proved surprisingly swift for a bigger boy and when he exchanged the baton with Arthur Murray, three teams were almost tied for the lead but the fourth team from Mystic had fallen behind. Running downhill sounds easy but it's actually hard to keep on your feet, gravity pulling you faster than your feet can move – the Mystic boy took a tumble. Alex was waiting for Arthur at the bottom of the hill for the final exchange; the three leading teams arrived at the pine tree almost at the same time but one of the runners took a tumble on the way back down the hill. Alex had to leap out of the way of the falling sprinter and the American from Scranton pulled ahead. The two boys struggled down the hill; the Scranton Scout put on a final effort and fell as he reached the finish line, second.

The Jamboree organizers congratulated the Canadian Troop. They were awarded the Onteora Camp Trophy for winning the athletics meet, their Troop name already engraved on the little plaque on the trophy. The boys passed the trophy around amongst themselves and got to take it to their cabin for the night, but had to surrender it to the organizers in the morning to be kept in the Camp Office until the next summer.

When Peter and Victoria arrived back at camp on Saturday they were delighted, and relieved, to see some happy and very tanned faces. The boys showed little interest in their parents' adventures in New York City, and maybe mistook Victoria's relaxed smile. They showed off their medals and Peter took a picture with his Brownie camera of the boys with their trophy.

Back in Peterborough, Peter had a number of copies of the photos made for the scouts and for the Troop's fledgling archives. He wrote a story about the jamboree and submitted it to the Peterborough Examiner for publication. It was a proud day for the St. Steven's Scout Troop.

27. The Cottage

AFTER THE FIRST YEAR IN THE NEW HOUSE in Edmison Heights, the barren construction zone, and the hot summer of landscaping, Victoria began to pine for the bucolic peace of Stella Bay.

One day in June heading into their second summer, as Victoria was preparing herself and the boys with plans to keep themselves occupied, she mused aloud about having a place by a lake.

"Jeez, I don't know, Victoria, I don't think we can afford to buy a place here in the Kawartha Lakes. I hear cottages are pricey on Stony Lake."

"Maybe we could just rent a small cottage for a week or two," she replied, undeterred.

"Well, sure, that would be alright. You can do the research; I'll be happy with anything you come up with, within reason."

Victoria consulted the want ads in *The Peterborough Examiner* – cottages to let – and found a modest retreat of a dozen tiny two bed-room utility cottages on the tranquil shore of Upper Chemong Lake, aka Little Mud. Little Mud was connected by a narrows to the larger Chemong Lake, but it too was a shallow muddy lake. Birch Bend Housekeeping Cottages, the ad said, with a tiny picture of white painted cottages amongst stands of birch trees. $65 Weekly. Check-in time was Saturday at 2:00 o'clock; check-out time, Saturday morning at 11:00. She booked the place, sight-unseen, for the middle two weeks of August.

They packed up the car with their clothes and bedding and anything else they thought they needed.

"Why do we have to bring our own sheets?" Oliver exclaimed.

"Well, these are housekeeping cottages but that means you have to do your own housekeeping. The owners provide the furnishings and beds and the kitchen equipment but we have to do the rest of the upkeep ourselves. And meals. At the end of our stay the owners clean the whole cottage in preparation for the next guests.

— Alex' Choice —

Birch Bend Cottage Resort was about twelve miles north of the North End of Peterborough, but well into rustic rural country, hills and dales with struggling farms, parched rocky fields with lazy grazing cows – mostly Hereford – languidly swishing their tails to ward off flies. The cottage retreat may have had a sign hidden amongst the birch but Peter had passed it before he realized it. Eagle-eyed Oliver did notice and alerted the driver of his error.

"Hey, I think we just passed it!"

"Hey, I think you're right. I'll just drive on down the highway a bit and turn into that farm lane at the top of the hill."

He reversed course and turned into the narrow track which wound a short way into the camp, maneuvering the Oldsmobile amongst boulders and birch trees, a dozen small cottages.

They located 'The Office' – eagle-eyed Oliver noticed the sign.

"Yeah, we can all see it, Oliver," sneered Alex.

Peter and Victoria checked into the office. Mrs. Lafarge accepted Peter's cheque and directed them the short distance to their cabin.

It was a single – some of the cabins were doubles – perched on the rocks and roots of the lot, cheek by jowl with three other cottages, by the shore of the lake. The building was low elevation with an open deck over-looking the lake. Peter wondered to himself that these cottages must get flooded every spring, even though perched on cement blocks. The boys were out of the car before it had barely stopped and raced down the short path to the dock. Alex looked across the clear blue water, the bright sun jumping off the surface like diamonds. Little Mud Lake was bigger than Stella Bay; on the far shore nothing but bush.

Oliver was more attentive to the near shore. On the right side of the dock was a little sand beach, perfect for little kids to wade in and make sandcastles, On the left side was a reedy patch and then a small rocky point. Already he imaged his own little world. He peered into the water and soon noticed swarms of minnows. He guessed there would be bigger fish off the end of the dock – good thing they brought their fishing rods and tackle boxes. But there also might be turtles.

The boys returned to help unpack the car and carry things to the little cottage.

"Hey," cried Oliver, "what's that smell?"

"Now Oliver," said Victoria, "these cottages are quite old, and so they are a bit musty. And we are mostly in shade under the birch trees and that also adds an unfamiliar damp smell to your sensitive nose. It would be worse if this cottage was under full sun, we would get baked. But being mostly in shade and a breeze blowing off the lake and through the wooden screen door at the front to the windows in the back, we'll feel fresh and cool. You will have forgotten the smell in a day."

Peter could see that Victoria was trying hard to defend her decision on the cottage; it wasn't quite to the standard he had expected but he was in no position to criticize, and he backed his wife. He knew she had been brought up on a farm on Rice Lake near Bailieboro – very much like this Chemong Lake – and this was well within her experience. And for that matter, well within his own.

The front screen door opened onto a combined living room/dining room, with a kitchen counter and cupboards on one side: there was a big dining table with six old wooden chairs; two lumpy couches, a coffee table and a side table with an old lamp and a stack of old magazines, mostly fishing magazines and National Geographic; a cushioned rocking chair with a floor lamp beside it, 'perfect for evening reading', thought Peter. At the back were doors to two bedrooms: one had a double bed with a quilted cover; the other had two single beds, and quilts.

'Ha,' thought Victoria, 'here's the source of the musty smells,' and she hauled the quilts off the bed and took them outside to the rope clothesline and hung them out to air. The quilts bowed the line down of their weight till they were more or less touching the ground.

"I think it'll take more than a few hours of sun and lake breeze to rid those quilts of the musty smell, Victoria, but I see what you're trying to do.

"That line is more designed for drying towels and bathing suits than these heavy quilt blankets," Peter drily observed. "I'll look for big stick to prop up the middle."

He redirected his attention to Alex. "You've been rather quiet, Son."

"This place reminds me of Stella Bay, well not the cabin, but the dock, except there is no slope to the shore."

Peter probed some more, "and what do you think of the cabin?"

"It's better than the bell tents we had at the Otonabee Scout Camp. At least we don't have to sleep on the ground."

Peter smiled to himself, noting that Alex hadn't compared the cottage to the Onteora Scout Camp.

"I think a lot of the people who use these cottages are American tourists here for fishing."

"Hey, Dad, do you think we can get a little fishing boat like we had at Stella Bay?"

"I don't see why not," said Peter wishing now he hadn't sold the old boat when they left Stella. "There's a marina round the bend near the Narrows; I'm pretty sure we can rent something there."

On the west shore of Little Mud, opposite the Birch Bend cottage camp was the Curve Lake Indian Reserve. On their first excursion to Buckhorn to stock up on groceries they passed the entrance to the Reservation.

"I think I'd like to visit there sometime, maybe one day next week," Victoria remarked. And so the family visited the 'Trading Post' in the village on the Curve Lake Reserve; Victoria was interested in the artifacts and artwork, but Alex found it a bit unnerving, like entering a foreign country.

True to his word, the family drove over to the marina and rented a small fishing boat with a ten horse-power motor. Peter and the boys gassed it up and motored back to Birch Bend while Victoria drove the car back. Alex and Oliver were up most mornings, not always early, to go fishing, at first under the supervision of Dad who only showed moderate interest in the sport, and later, on their own – it was much as if they were back at Stella Bay. Oliver and Alex took turns driving the boat but soon Oliver and that boat became constant companions – Alex was content to spend the afternoons in the bedroom reading and listening to music, mostly The Beatles, on his tape recorder.

In 1964 Canada was struggling emotionally with what was called the Great Canadian Flag Debate. To that point Canada didn't have its own national flag, though the Canadian Red Ensign with the Union Jack in the upper left corner and the Canadian Coat of Arms in the bottom right quadrant had served the purpose for decades including in two world wars. Victoria was a British Loyalist and preferred that the Ensign be adopted as the permanent national flag but there was a lot of pressure to come up with a unique Canadian flag that distanced itself from the Union Jack/British connection, especially as Canada's Centennial was fast approaching in 1967. The Prime Minister at the time, Lester B. ('Mike') Pearson, had a design in mind but in true Canadian fashion a Parliamentary Committee was formed, contests were launched, and a number of designs came forward. The design preferred by Pearson, dubbed the Pearson Pennant, involved two narrow bands of blue on each end of the flag (to signify the Atlantic and Pacific coasts) and a sprig of three red maple leaves (maple being one of the national symbols of Canada) in the white background in the middle, the three leaves signifying the founding peoples of the nation: Indigenous, French and British.

The preferred choice of the Flag Committee was red and white with single red maple leaf in the centre. If she couldn't have the Red Ensign Victoria would rather have the Pearson Pennant than the single leaf red only pennant. To show her support during 'The Great Debate', she made her own Pearson Pennant. She cut up a white bedsheet. She dyed two panels light blue and sewed them to the ends of the white middle; she traced and cut two pieces in the form of the maple leaf sprig, dyed them red and sewed them on both sides of the white background. Peter then fastened this flag to a long wooden pole and affixed the pole to the end of Jorgenson's dock on Stella Bay. She took some kidding from the neighbours, and even some haughty jeers from Amherst Island old-timers who clearly preferred the Red Ensign, or even the Union Jack, to this cartoonish flag.

The Red Maple Leaf flag was adopted as the Flag of Canada in February of 1965. Respectful of Parliament's decision, Victoria gave up her campaign for the Pearson Pennant and no longer flew the blue flag at the Stella Bay dock but stowed it away in a box in the garage. The box moved with the Jorgensons to Peterborough and shelved in the garage but as Victoria was rummaging around for camping items she might need at the cottage, she rediscovered the flag and decided to bring it along. Peter thought this mildly foolish but he knew better than to contest it. He acquired another ten-foot pole and affixed it to the end of the dock at Birch Bend Cottages. You could see that flag from anywhere across small Mud Lake, and a beacon for boating home. American tourists often asked about the unfamiliar flag; many Canadians just shrugged, though whether out of regret for the lost flag or at Victoria's eccentricity was not clear.

The summer of the housekeeping cottage at Birch Bend Cottages had gone so well – once they were used to the depravations – Victoria was quick to renew it the following summer. Two weeks in August, just before Alex' 17th birthday and going into Grade 12.

Unlike the previous summer of misgivings and exploration of Birch Bend Cottages and Little Mud Lake, the second summer brought the comfort of familiarity. The cottage still smelled musty but it was now a welcome smell; the reedy little cove by the dock and the rocky point was still full of minnows and rock bass and perch, and Oliver was now comfortable with the resident painted turtle – he never did see a snapper and dismissed the existential threat from his mind; Alex was pleased to see that the flag pole Peter had fastened to the end of the dock was still there and was quick to fasten the blue and white pennant to it for another summer of questions.

They didn't rent a fishing boat from the marina that summer because Peter had borrowed a colleague's power boat, a nice little craft with steering wheel and all. It was slightly underpowered – only a 25-horse engine – and so had difficulty pulling someone up on water skis unless the skier was skillful, and not too heavy. Even though Peter was only a lean five feet eight inches, he never quite got the hang of hauling himself out of the water; athletic Victoria on the other hand, even though almost the same size, easily mastered the technique and skimmed all over the lake. She could take wide turns at great speed, then switch back and take little jumps over the wake of the boat; she even dropped one ski and sailed single over the turns. The boys were very impressed; Peter quietly admired his gymnastic wife. Alex and Oliver would have spent all day skiing on the lake but since two were needed in the boat, they could only go when they could persuade one of the parents to act as look-out.

Oliver had developed the interest, and the skill and the patience, for assembling model airplane kits. His bedroom was full of flying objects hanging by strings from the ceiling. Alex was not dexterous with the glue tube, or the paint brush, and this provoked his innate impatience. Oliver soon graduated from plastic model planes to balsa wood bi-wing planes complete with a tiny alcohol fueled engine installed at the front of the fuselage, just like a WWI Sopwith Camel. He attached a length of thin wire to the plane and he would fly it in circles in the yard behind the house. The Spring before they returned to the cottage Oliver watched a documentary of the Everglades swamp in Florida and was taken not with the alligators but with the fan boats. He got the idea he could build a toy one for himself out of balsa wood and an airplane engine. He went to the hobby shop in Uptown Peterborough to buy sheets of balsa and spent many hours in his bedroom drawing plans, tracing patterns on the balsa, cutting the wood with an Exacto knife, soaking and bending the balsa into shape and gluing it together; it was about twelve inches long by

— Alex' Choice —

4 inches wide, with straight sides and stern and a curved front prow – it looked more like a barge than a sleek cruiser but it was easier to make. He caulked and painted it to make it watertight. He then tested it for buoyancy in the bathtub; it floated, but tipped over and filled with water. He affixed a keel to the bottom of the boat and glued a string of lead weights along the bottom as ballast to add stability; he tested it again in the bathtub; success. He installed a prop at the back of the boat high enough to attach the little engine and keep the blades out of the water; he fueled the engine, started it up, and placed it again in the bathtub. It went backwards. He realized the engine had to be reversed in order to push the boat forward. He reinstalled the engine, and it worked. In the bathtub.

Everyone gathered at the end of the dock at Birch Bend for the little fan boat's first venture on the lake. Oliver started the tiny engine and set the boat in the water from the end of the dock, and let it go. Exciting. But it only traveled about ten feet when it hit a small wave and the water splashed over the engine, conking it out. The water had to be very calm else the tiny boat would be swamped with almost any turbulence; mornings were best for these conditions. They tried again the next morning; with calm, almost glass-smooth water the tiny boat powered over the water, but simply kept on going across the lake. Everybody cheered and laughed; Alex jumped into the motorboat and went off to retrieve the errant runabout. For the next two weeks, every calm day, off the little-boat-that-could would go, cruising across the water until it got swamped or ran out of fuel. Alex was very proud of Oliver's project; he enjoyed it almost as much as Oliver did; and admired him his talent and ingenuity.

Sandra Sgambati's family stayed at the cottage at the other side of the little stone point that separated the Jorgenson dock from the Sgambati dock. Alex wasn't sure when he first noticed her, or even whether she first noticed him. The two cottages were separated by a stand of birch and brush and Alex might have gone two weeks without any awareness of her presence. But one day he was tip-toeing his way from stone to stone to the end of the point and when he turned to look around he noticed this dark-haired girl in a pink and white bathing suit which certainly captured his attention as she waded into the water from the miniature beach at her cottage. She caught his eye but he quickly looked away, too shy to hold her glance.

Next day as he was leaving the cottage in running shoes shorts and t-shirt, about to take his daily run up the highway, she happened to be on the pathway between the two cottages and called to him:

"Hi there."

Alex stopped to see who was calling him and answered back, "Oh, hi." and waited for a minute to think what else he should say. She filled the gap.

"I notice you go running every day."

'Interesting,' thought Alex, wondering how she had noticed him but he never saw her.

"Where do you go?"

"I go out to the highway and turn towards Buckhorn. I run past the narrow causeway that separates Mud Lake from a swampy pond and on up the hill. At the top of the hill I stop and turn around. I'm not a long-distance runner and even though I think I'll keep on running down the other side of the hill and past the Curve Lake Reserve to Buckhorn I always figure I have run far enough at the top of the hill and turn around and jog back."

Right away Alex thought himself an idiot – she wouldn't want to hear all that.

But she seemed interested in continuing the conversation.

"So why do you do that running if you don't really like it?"

'How did she know he didn't really like it?' he thought. Girls seem to know how to read minds.

"Well, I play football for my high school and I want to be in shape for the try-outs next month."

"Oh, that's interesting," she continued. "What position do you play?"

'How does she know about football?' Alex wondered.

"I play half back, or maybe fullback.

"How do you know about football?" he asked.

"Oh, football is big where I come from. We have games almost every Friday night at my high school."

"Oh?" Alex replied, puzzled, "they play at night?"

"You must have lights at your football field."

— Alex' Choice —

"Oh yes, the whole town comes out for the games on Friday night."

"Really? So you have stands and everything?"

"Oh yes, we have maybe ten thousand fans come out to the games."

Alex was astounded. It sounded as big as Richardson Stadium at Queen's, but was only a high school.

"We don't even have bleachers at my school. Our games are played in the afternoon and only a few students, and a few parents, come out to our games."

"Hmmm," she said, in her turn to be puzzled.

"Where do you live?" she asked.

"Oh, just in Peterborough."

"Oh yeah? We have to drive through Peterborough on our way to this cottage.

"We come every year, but I haven't seen you before," she said in a questioning sort of way.

"We came here for the first time last summer; this is our second visit."

"Oh, yes, I did see you last year", she confessed, "your brother was playing on the point. My family has been coming here for years and years. My dad and uncle used to come here in the '30s and '40s, fishing; and I've been coming here since I was a little kid."

"Where are you from then?" Alex asked.

"I'm from Jessup, Pennsylvania. It's a little borough just outside Scranton."

"Oh," said Alex perking up, "I was at a Scout Jamboree last year in Poughkeepsie and there was a troop there from Scranton."

There was a quiet pause in the conversation.

"So, how do you know about football? You didn't answer me. Do you go to the games on Friday nights?"

"Oh yes," she said, "I'm a cheerleader."

Alex found that easy to understand; she looked like a cheerleader, if there was such a thing as looking like a cheerleader; in Alex' mind cheerleaders were short and bouncy and cute. This girl matched that stereotype exactly. She reminded him of another cheerleader, Cathy Baird

"Say, what's your name?" she asked.

"I'm Alex Jorgenson.
"What's yours?'
"Sandra, Sandra Sgambati. That's Italian."
Alex was momentarily startled. Here was another Sandra. She didn't look anything like Sandra Farquharson but she made him think about Sandra and he immediately felt a certain disloyalty. And regret. He hadn't written to Sandra in ages.
"Hey, I better get going."
"Okay, maybe tomorrow I can run with you?"
"Sure," said Alex and stepped off the porch and started through the woods to the highway. All the way up the hill and back his mind recalled and repeated the conversation with the perky Sandra Sgambati.

Next morning at 9:30, Alex stepped out the front door of the cottage onto the parch and glanced around. He was pleasantly surprised – 'why was he so skeptical?' he thought – to see Sandra jogging along the path to his cottage. She was wearing a white jumper, white t-shirt and white tennis shoes.

"Hey Sandra, good morning. Are you coming for a run with me."
"Of course. I said so didn't I?"
"Yeah, but you look like you're all dressed to play tennis."
He thought himself an idiot again for making such a remark, but Sandra just smiled and tossed the ball back to him: "Have you seen any tennis courts around here?"
They started jogging along the shoulder of the highway, Alex gauging her pace and decided to go slow enough that they could talk.
"Sandra," he asked, "do you mind me asking how old you are?"
"I don't mind.
"How old do you think I am?"
Now there Alex felt foolish again. Was she teasing him, or what?
"Geez, I don't know. I think you're probably about my age but you could be younger and just look 17, or you could be way older and in university already."
"You know I'm not in college; I told you I'm a cheerleader at my high school.

Alex' Choice

"So, you're seventeen yourself then," she volleyed.

"No, not quite, but I will be seventeen next week. I'm going into Grade 12."

"Ha, I'm sixteen too! But I just turned sixteen last month. I'm going into 11th Grade in September."

"Hey, Sandra, why do Americans say 11th grade and in Canada we say Grade 11?

"I don't know Alex. Why do Canadians say it the other way around?"

Alex thought she made a good point; they were just different, there didn't have to be a reason.

At that point a pick-up truck with three men in the cab drove by, whistled and hollered at them, "Hey, nice skirt!"

Alex was instantly on high alert, echoes of his Amherst Island episode leaping to the front of his amygdala. But the truck just whizzed on by.

"Geez, sorry about that."

"Not your fault Alex. I don't pay any attention to that."

There was a moment of silence between them until Sandra interjected,

"So, come on, slow-poke – race you to the top of the hill." And with that she took off like a dart.

Surprised at this gambit Alex hesitated and then gave chase but couldn't decide if it was a race he should try to win or let her. He decided to let her win but make a race of it, and accelerated to catch up to her. She could sense him coming and turned up her own pace and shot ahead. Doubly surprised at her speed and competitiveness, Alex began to sprint harder. As they neared the top of the hill he forgot his promise to himself and finished before her. They reached the driveway of the farm making their finish-line. Laughing and breathing hard Sandra collapsed into the grassy ditch. Alex fell in beside her. They looked at each other smiling and breathless.

"Hey, I'm getting all wet," she said.

"Yeah," said Alex, "I guess there's still dew in this long grass."

They pulled themselves to their feet and turned for home jogging gently downhill. As they reached the little causeway and only a hundred of so yards from Birch Bend Sandra challenged him again.

"Hey, race you to your cottage" and off she sprang down the highway and along the narrow lane, being careful despite her racing not to trip over exposed stones and roots. Alex kept up with her but this time let her come first.

"Well, bye Alex. Thanks for the run.

"See you this afternoon at the beach?"

For the next ten days Alex spent a lot of time with Sandra Sgambati, or at least as much as her mother would allow. Every day they raced up the highway to the farm on the hill. He took her for rides in his father's borrowed boat, they sat together for hours at a time most afternoons sitting on the rocks at the little point; they built sandcastles on the little beach by her cottage, or by the Jorgenson's.

Oliver would often join them on the point but Victoria quickly interceded.

"Oliver, you go and find something else to do, leave those two alone."

But all the while Alex kept comparing her to Sandra Farquharson. He remembered the first year with Sandra F. when they were full of fire and easy conversation and the many school projects together. Sandra S. was spunky and competitive but at the same time, conversation often lulled.

As their time together progressed, inexorably, to the last Friday Alex became more and more uncomfortable with the long gaps in their conversations and their connection began to feel strained somehow. Sandra Sgambati was not the same as Sandra Farquharson, even the increasingly distant Sandra of Amherst Island.

Sandra of Scranton agreed to be pen pals with Alex; she promised she would write to him every week and always answer his letters.

But two weeks went by and he hadn't heard from her. He wrote her a nice newsy letter telling her all about his first week back at school and football practice.

A week later he got a reply from her, but it was only half as long as his and telling not much except her cheerleader tryouts.

— Alex' Choice —

He asked her for a photo of her in her cheerleader outfit but she never sent him one.

Their letter exchanges continued but they became increasingly flimsy, until by the end of October she didn't write back to his last letter.

Alex felt let down and discouraged, and yet at the same time, somehow relieved.

He sat down and wrote a long letter to Sandra F. He told her all about his summer at the cottage, and his return to school and the mixed results of his football season, but he didn't mention Sandra Sgambati.

And he wondered about that too.

28. Girls

DESPITE HIS SUCCESS ON THE FOOTBALL FIELD, AND THE TRACK, Alex was no more self-assured dealing with girls than he was in Grade 6. He still thought of his special year with Sandra Farquharson as an aberration, and due almost entirely to the exceptional personality that was the minister's daughter. When she became less available in their Grade 8 year he felt that was more like his normal way with girls. But he missed her.

He still wrote letters to Sandra – long and descriptive narratives of the various events of his life. She always replied, though often for what seemed lengthy delays, and her letters were factual, short and perfunctory. It seemed increasingly clear to Alex she had lost that loving feeling.

There had been no time for girls during his short time at Napanee High School, especially as he spent most of his free time on the school bus to and from Amherst Island: there was nobody on the bus he was interested in, and he was sure no girls were interested in him. He wondered what it might have been like if he had been able to go to Ernestown High School.

With the move to Peterborough, he was thoroughly intimidated by the size and the newness of Adam Scott CVI, he kept largely to himself, living in his head, not in the halls.

The ever-alluring Cathy Baird was in many of his classes and still distracted but he lacked the courage to ask her out, or even engage with her except in casual chatting across the aisle.

His ten-day summer trial with Sandra Sgambati just confirmed his view. Girls were difficult to understand.

He stayed after school some Friday nights to cheer on the Midget, Junior and Senior basketball Lions, but mostly to watch the cheerleaders from the bleachers, especially Cathy. Alex didn't play basketball himself – he was too short and besides he was charged with charging too often because he played basketball like he played football, with his shoulders.

He went home after the games, he didn't stay on for the sock hop, despite entreaties from classmates, boys and girls both.

— Alex' Choice —

One gloomy afternoon in November of his Grade 12 year, football season over and he hadn't heard from either Sandra for weeks, he dragged his school bag and maybe his soul into the side door of the house. Victoria was having a cup of tea in the kitchen; there was no sign of Oliver and there wouldn't be any sign of Peter for a couple of hours.

"Alex, you're home. Do you want a cup of tea?"

Alex didn't really want a cup of tea with his mom, but also he didn't really want to retreat to his room as usual.

Victoria picked up on his gloomy mood and said, "Hey, sit down with me and have a cup of tea, with plenty of sugar. You need a pick-me-up. You look as dark as the day."

She poured him a cup of tea and placed it in front of him at the table.

"Now, tell me what's going on."

Alex tasted his tea; it was bitter despite the sugar, steeped too long in the teapot for his taste. He dumped another spoonful of sugar into his cup as Victoria grimaced, waiting. He stirred it for a long time.

"Okay, out with it," she said smiling gently.

"Nothing really." He paused. She waited.

"I guess I find these gray days of November dreary. See, I'm home at 4:30 and its already dark outside."

"Yeah, I know how you feel. Sometimes I get like that. A lot of people feel like that in November, waiting for winter. But once it actually arrives and the ground is white with snow, things get brighter.

"I bet a lot of your friends at school feel like that, and probably many of your teachers too, stressed with approaching Christmas," and she chuckled a little. "I bet you haven't even noticed."

"Nah, I thought it was only me."

"So, what was the best thing that happened to you today?"

"Well, my partner and I won playing Euchre at lunch today."

"You play euchre at lunch?"

"Yeah, most days. In the cafeteria. We hurry and eat our lunch – though I'm the slowest because I usually get a hot lunch from the line, and then we get maybe three games in. We're really fast."

163

"So who are your friends at school?
"Well, Dave Kidd, and Allan Grant, and Ken Clifford. They're all from my class."
Are any of these boys your best friend? You never bring any friends around home."
"No, they're just guys I hang out with at school and play euchre with at lunch. I haven't really had a best friend since Hugh."
"Anyone else?"
"and sometimes we let Oliver play with us."
"No girls?'
"Nah. They sit in different parts of the cafeteria."
"Any girls you're interested in?'
"Ah, Mom."
But Victoria waited.
"Well, I like Cathy Baird. She's in a lot of my classes. And Marsha Murray and Julie Dell, but they're pretty tall."
"You mean taller than you?'
"Yes."
"Sorry, I see; that can be a problem."
"But why don't you ask one of them to go to the dance on Friday nights?"
"Ah Mom, I don't know.
"They like boys who have a car. And I don't even have my driver's licence yet."
"Well that can be fixed. I bet your father would give you lessons next Spring when the roads are bare again."
There was a pause in the conversation. Victoria poured another cup of tea.
"Are you still writing to that Sandra girl in Pennsylvania?"
"No, Mom; she stopped writing, and besides, she had nothing to say."
"What about Sandra Farquharson?"
Alex face flattened. He just looked at his mom.
"I see her letters arrive here about once a month, and you still give Peter your letters to mail."
"Yeah,"
"You still miss her, don't you Alex?"
"Yeah." And then Alex started.

— Alex' Choice —

"You know Mom, I think about her almost every day. I know I shouldn't and it's three years since we left Amherst Island. I wonder what she's doing at the very moment I'm thinking about her. I wonder what she thinks about, whether she has any friends."

"Boy friends?"

"Hmmm, I don't know.

"She tells me in her letters that she is enjoying living with the family in Odessa and going to Ernestown High School, but somehow I don't think that's completely true. It must be strange living at another house and coming home on Friday night to her own family and going back on Sunday night. I'm glad I don't have to do that, but sometimes I wish I was going to Ernestown High School rather than Adam Scott."

Victoria decided to probe a little deeper on her adolescent son's feelings, taking a risk of being rebuffed.

"Do you tell her romantic things in your letters?"

To her surprise, he didn't recoil.

"No, I think about it but I'm too shy. And besides, Sandra's mother reads her mail."

"Oh, that's awkward."

"What does Sandra write to you, if you don't mind me asking?"

"Mostly she just tells me what goes on with her week – what subjects she likes, which teachers she's afraid of, things like that.

"She likes English the best, and she tells me about her English teacher all the time, a Mr. Stephens. Sometimes she writes poems, but I don't really get them."

"Oh, what are they about?

"Mostly about nature, leaves bursting open, plants pushing up through the ground, sometimes about thunder and lightning and water rushing through swollen creeks."

"Oh, that's interesting," Victoria remarked but since Alex seemed confused she thought she'd let that go.

"Yeah, poets are sometimes really hard to understand what they're getting at.

"Do you ever wish you could go and visit her in Amherst Island?"

"Yes, but I know that's not really possible."

"Yes, you're probably right; but you know, if the Professor ever has to go to Queen's for some reason maybe we could all go and visit old friends."

Alex looked at her, perked up momentarily and then let that go as unlikely.

"Maybe when I go to Queen's next year, I mean after Grade 13, maybe Sandra will be going there too."

"Do you think maybe?"

"She hasn't really said what she's thinking about after high school."

"Well, if you are still interested in each other two or three years from now, you'll likely find a way.

"In the meantime, maybe you should hang out at the sock hops Friday night and have a look around. Maybe some girl will ask *you* to dance!"

"Oh Mom."

And with that he gulped the last of his now cold tea and headed up to his room.

29. Scholastics and Conflicts

ALEX CONTINUED TO BE AN A LEVEL STUDENT but he began to recognize there were other kids at least as smart as he was, maybe smarter. And without being completely aware of it, he was beginning to feel stressed thinking he didn't have enough time to do all the things he wanted to do, or felt he needed to do.

He had started a stamp collection when he was in Grade 8 at Amherst Island Public School. He'd save his allowance and order more stamps from the mail-order service every month, treasuring especially the colourful and irregular-shaped stamps from San Marino and Monaco. He didn't really care when his dad pointed out that most of those colourful stamps were printed by these tiny little countries for the sole purpose of generating revenue from philatelists. He had two stamp albums – one for world stamps and one for just Canada – and all the equipment a serious philatelist might need: a catalogue for identifying stamps, a magnifying glass for examining the stamps, tweezers for handling them, cellophane hinges for mounting the stamps in his albums, cellophane envelopes for storing sets and especially 'valuable stamps', a bottle of carbon tetrachloride and a petri dish for soaking and removing stamps from their envelopes. He was proud of his collection.

Victoria used to tear off the corners of envelopes and save the stamps from mail that came to the house, or passed from the neighbours. She was happy for Alex' hobby because she had had her own stamp collection when she was a girl in high school in the 1930s. Alex asked if she still had her collection – it might be valuable now – but she said she left it at her father's house when she left home and wasn't sure what happened to it. She thought maybe her older brother had claimed it and gave it to his son, and that had become a sore point between them. Most of the stamps she salvaged now were Canadian, naturally, but occasionally stamps from letters arriving from the United Kingdom, the United States of America, and postcards from travelers in European countries, and Australia. Alex would examine all these finds but discarded most as duplicates of ones he already had. Eventually he began to notice his desk drawer was full of saved envelops and he hadn't examined them for ages; in fact he hadn't looked at his collection for more than a year. So one day in Grade Eleven he packed up his albums and paraphernalia in a box and shoved the box into his closet.

Alex became Troop Leader of his Scout Troop in September of 1966 and a Queen Scout by May of that Grade 11 year, his final year of Scouts. He was turning 17 in August and would have to go up to Rangers in the Fall, and he didn't really relish the idea. He was going into Grade 12 and he wanted to devote all his time and energy to sports – Senior Football in the fall, Track and Field in the Spring, and a winter of weight training in the basement with his brother. He was, however, active on the Boys Athletic Association however.

He felt himself getting stronger and stronger, but not much taller; still, he enjoyed crashing into other players when he carried the ball. He didn't really think about it: he just lowered his shoulder and lunged at the other player, expecting to run over him; sometimes he would just absorb the hit and then spin out of the tackler's grasp and run for a few more yards before he was gang tackled by a swarm of defenders who had cornered him. It became a point of pride for him that when somebody tried to tackle him the other guy felt it harder than Alex did. Even when he was hit hard, he always bounced back up, never letting the other guys know he was hurt from the hit. He was alarmed at the pain in his shoulder one day when he tackled a bigger boy and his shoulder struck the other's thigh pad at full speed; the doctor thought he had suffered a subluxation of the shoulder and a pinched nerve but a week later that didn't deter him from returning as a determined runner when his arm had healed.

In the spring of his Grade 11 year Alex was already training for Track season, with brother Oliver, now in Grade 9. They practiced every afternoon after school – sprints and starts from starting blocks, and wind sprints for fitness; they ran the half-mile Edmison Drive loop every night before bed. They were ready: Alex was a Junior, Oliver was a Midget.

But they weren't really ready. One evening at the dinner table, Peter said, "if you boys are going to be serious track athletes you're going to need proper shoes."

— Alex' Choice —

So the next day the three of them drove 'Downtown' to the local sporting goods store and got fitted for track shoes. Alex got a sleek pair of red Pumas, with four long spikes on the balls of the shoes – long spikes were for sprinters and jumpers, short spikes were for long distance runners; Oliver got a pair of blue Adidas. They both would have preferred green to match the Adam Scott school colours but green wasn't available. Alex was amazed at how light-weight the shoes were. They looked fast just resting in his hand. He could hardly wait to get them on the track.

"Now boys, you're going to have to practice with these shoes before race day to get used to them otherwise you're going to trip over those spikes."

"Okay Dad," the two of them chimed in chorus.

The next day at practice they were the envy of the other boys. Alex suddenly became aware that many of the boys, and all of the girls, only had running shoes; he felt a little embarrassed that he had this privilege when the other athletes didn't have the money for such a luxury.

And sure enough, Oliver took a tumble two steps out of the starting blocks and skinned his hands and knees on the red brick gravel track.

Alex had emerged as a star halfback in Grade Eleven, scoring eleven touchdowns that season. But now he was going up to Senior Lions and he felt he was starting all over again. Kindly Mr. Sawchuk was no longer his coach; Mr. Ward, the Senior Lions coach, was miserable. He was from the old school in which the coaching style seemed to be to intimidate his charges and challenge them to perform by abusing them verbally.

Alex wasn't alone in feeling this abuse on the Senior team – half the team had been his mates as Junior Lions – but they all felt young compared to the veterans now in Grade 13.

Alex made starting half-back and he did score eight touchdowns, even though the Senior Lions only won half their games, and lost again to the hated Garnet and Gray of PCI.

But he remembered his Grade 10 Latin teacher's advice – 'if you are disciplined and diligent, write out your declensions and conjugations every day, you will learn you can master anything you put your mind to'.

May and June brought another Track Season; now he was competing as a Senior and many of his competitors were serious athletes, some of whom were also members of the Peterborough Track Club. Alex won the 100-yard dash at his school meet but it was a close call with Joe Burns, an Indian kid from Curve Lake. Alex also won the long jump and the 220 but he had the feeling it was a good thing Joe had entered the 440 and triple jump instead. Alex won all his events at the Peterborough District track meet but it was a different story at the Central Ontario regional meet: He got a blue ribbon (2nd) in the hundred and yellow (3rd) in Long Jump and 220. Joe got reds in all his events.

They teamed up in the 4x110 relay with Joe leading off and Alex finishing. They won the District meet handily and they might have got the red ribbon in COSSA except the Scott team was disqualified because the second runner had passed the baton to the Scott third outside the passing zone. Alex was disappointed but he knew how that felt from his experience in Grade 7.

Except for Physics he enjoyed his Grade 12 academic year and he got good marks. He had the same Latin teacher as the previous two years and worked hard at his declensions, memorizing vocabulary and remembering which gender each noun was to ensure the adjectives would agree; he was rewarded with high 80s. He liked English and Algebra but wasn't fond of French for some reason; his favourite subject was History. He still didn't have much confidence around girls but this was shaping up to be his happiest year in high school.

30. Eleanor

AND NOW IT WAS GRADE 13, A SIGNIFICANT STEP UP in academic demands. It was the qualifying year for anyone who had plans for university. Of the 142 kids in Grade 12, only 100 went on to Grade 13. And the teachers were blunt about the chances of those kids getting their Secondary School Honours Diploma unless they worked very hard.

It was striking to Alex the number of kids in his Grade 13 year who had been active in school extra-curricular programs in Grade 12 but had abandoned those activities in Grade 13: nobody on the Student Council, none on the Ascovian yearbook team, nor the UN Club. Alex had dropped out from being the Boys Athletic Association rep but he did play for the Senior Lions football team still pursuing his dream to play for the Queen's Golden Gaels.

To graduate with an Honours Secondary School Diploma a student needed to pass nine courses with an overall average of 60%. He was equally good at maths and sciences as his arts courses.

He wanted to be a lawyer so he figured he should take Latin (Grammar and Latin Literature) and History. And besides he liked Latin and History and had good marks in them. He took Algebra, Geometry and Trigonometry, English Grammar and Literature and Chemistry. He no longer had his Latin teacher from the previous years but now Mrs. Elliott, the head of the department and head of Guidance. He wasn't thrilled.

As the Fall semester drew to a close, football season well behind him and the dreary days of November wearing him down, Alex contracted the flu. But he had to sit his term exams and then Mrs. Elliott insisted he retake the Scholastic Aptitude Test. He was tired, aching and having difficulty concentrating on the exam.

The Christmas Holidays finally arrived and Alex spent the whole of them in bed, and the whole of Christmas Day in delirium. His flu had become pneumonia.

By New Year's Eve he was feeling better; still weak, but better. A friend from his class invited him to a neighbourhood party. He asked his mother if it was okay and Victoria accepted he was well-enough to go, but had to be home soon after midnight.

"Are you sure that's a good idea, Victoria?" Peter queried.

"Yes, I think so Peter, and besides, maybe he'll meet a nice girl at the party."

Peter raised an eyebrow but didn't disagree.

SOON AFTER SCHOOL RESUMED IN JANUARY Mrs. Elliott called Victoria to make an appointment, she wanted to go over Alex results.

"I'm sorry Mrs. Jorgenson, but I've got to tell you Alex' results were not what we should have expected for someone who hopes to go to university. In fact, these SAT scores are quite low."

"I don't understand, Mrs. Elliott. Alex has always had good marks in school; he works hard at his studies and he is very conscientious."

"That might account for him getting through Grade 12, but Grade 13 is a wholly different thing."

"Hold on there, Mrs. Elliott; he didn't just 'get through', he did well."

"Well, I have also reviewed his marks on his December report card and they have definitely slipped from last year. His English marks are below what is expected for succeeding in university and he's not doing at all well in my Latin classes. In fact, the only classes he seems to be doing well in are Chemistry and History."

"I noticed that on his report card," Victoria affirmed. "He always did well in Mr. Hooper's Latin class – marks in the 80s and 90s."

Mrs. Elliott didn't comment but Victoria got the distinct impression she wasn't impressed with Mr. Hooper.

Victoria could feel her ire rising. "And I know he really likes Chemistry and History, and his teachers.

"But really Mrs. Elliott, what is going on in your Latin Classes that his marks are so low?"

"Well, Mrs. Jorgenson, Grade 13 Latin Grammar and Literature is much more demanding than Grade 12 Latin."

"You do realize Mrs. Elliott that Alex played Senior Lions football all Fall – he even dislocated his shoulder – and I know football takes a lot out of him."

Mrs. Elliott seemed unimpressed with Alex' achievements on the gridiron.

"Maybe so but that's no excuse for getting poor grades in Grade 13. Studies have to be his priority.

"And that doesn't explain his poor SAT grades."

"Do you realize Mrs. Elliott, Alex was ill last December? He had the flu and probably shouldn't have been in school, never mind write that SAT exam again the last week. He had pneumonia all through Christmas.

"I still don't understand how the Guidance Office lost his results and he had to retake the exam. I wonder what his results were last time. I'm sure we would have heard from you last year if you had doubts about Alex' ability to go to university."

Stung by this evident criticism of Mrs. Elliott's department, she huffed "I understand, Mrs. Jorgenson, that you may be upset, but this is where things stand.

"Of course Alex will continue for the year and likely will even earn his Honours Secondary Diploma but I think you should start thinking about what his career path will be next year. I don't think he will qualify for university with marks like these."

Victoria gave Mrs. Elliott a look that bordered on a glare, and pushed back her chair, rising to leave.

"We'll just see how the year turns out, Mrs. Elliott, and we will consider our options then. I think you will be surprised."

Victoria turned her back on Mrs. Elliott and opened the door. She didn't offer her hand to shake.

When Victoria reported all this to Peter that evening, out of earshot of Alex, Peter shared Victoria's annoyance but much more phlegmatically, as was his disposition.

"I was never much impressed with Mrs. Elliott," he said, "much too severe and judgmental.

"I think you did well, Victoria, to keep your cool. We'll just give Alex as much encouragement as he needs and we shall wait for results come next June.

"I'm betting he will prove Mrs. Elliott wrong. I'm sure he will earn admittance to Trent, maybe even Queen's!"

As January gradually gave over to brighter, if colder days, Alex gained his energy back. Football season was over and he had no other distractions. He was able to give all his attention to his studies, though he and Oliver continued to work out in their makeshift weight room in the basement three times a week.

His nightly routine after supper, still at 5:00 o'clock, (Peter was often home on time now that he only had a ten minute drive from campus), was to go to his room at 6:00 and work steadily until 9:00, finishing his homework assignments and going back over his notes from class. He paid especial attention to his Latin courses, particularly Latin Literature.

Victoria had told him of her discussions with Mrs. Elliott though Alex sensed that there had been more to that conversation than Victoria let on. He told his mom that he really didn't feel well when he wrote the SAT exam; he said he was sweating and many times he felt the desk was tilting toward the floor.

Victoria was alarmed, "Oh my gawd Alex, I wish I'd known you were that sick. You were probably already running a fever and delirious like you were Christmas Day."

"Yes Mom, but Mrs. Elliott is also right. The courses are much harder this year, and I'm not enjoying English Literature much – especially that King Lear play – and Latin Literature is very hard."

So he spent an hour every night pouring over the Latin texts, his English/Latin dictionary by his elbow on his desk.

At 9:00 he'd leave his desk and sprawl on his bed re-reading his history text and making notes. He really liked American History. He memorized all the Presidents and Vice Presidents – Washington, Jefferson, Adams, Jackson, 'Tippecanoe and Tyler too'. He liked the Canadian Prime Ministers – except William Lyon Mackenzie King – but it was hard to get excited about the Statute of Westminster, even though it was supposed to be a key milestone towards Canada's sovereignty; American history seemed more momentous to him. He also spent time on his Chemistry studies – memorized the elements and symbols in the periodic table and all their valances; he would solve all the extra chemistry equation questions at the end of each chapter: he loved the logic of it and how the left side always had to balance with the right side; it was like algebra, even Latin in a way, with adjectives having to agree with noun declensions.

And every second week he would write a letter to Sandra Farquharson.

It wasn't all homework and studies though. There was also Eleanor.

He knew Eleanor Tysdale slightly from some of his classes, and he found himself at ease talking to her at the New Year's Eve party.

Eleanor was a chestnut-haired beauty, perhaps not movie star looks but appealing in some mysterious way, her green eyes smirking knowingly, a round face, wide mouth, pouty lips, lightly freckled face. She was medium height for a girl, slightly shorter than Alex with a shapely silhouette and well-filled sweaters. Alex began to notice her and wondered why he hadn't before.

But one day in early January, she surprised him in geometry spare whispering questions in his ear.

"Are you going to the basketball games this Friday night?"

He didn't answer right away, not sure what to say.

"What's the matter, cat got your tongue?" she persisted.

Was it just his imagination or did she linger on that word tongue? Impossible, girls weren't like that.

"Yeah, I guess," he mumbled.

"You know there's a sock hop after. A deejay plays all the latest hits; sometimes there's a real band. It's fun."

"Yeah, I know" he replied whispering, his head sideways to get a glimpse of Eleanor.

"Okay, good. I wasn't sure you knew. I've never seen you there."

"Yeah, I don't go out on Friday nights much. Never felt I had a good reason."

"Well, now you have a good reason. See you on Friday."

And with that she had the good sense to leave him alone. Alex found it hard to concentrate on his studies for the rest of the spare, going over and over the same questions.

The conversation stayed with him all that evening too, distracting him from his studies. And worrying. He wasn't confident about the sock hop after. There would be dancing and he didn't know how to dance. Would he be expected to dance with Eleanor?, or others too? And was she a good dancer? If she expected him to swing – was that what it was when you danced to rock and roll music? – he would die of embarrassment.

He talked to his euchre mates the next day and they laughed and teased him.

But Dave Kidd said, it's no big deal, Alex. You don't have to do all those fancy jive steps. Everybody does the twist these days and just shake and move around to the beat.

"Hey, I'll go with you Friday night. I'll be your wingman."

That made Alex feel better. He didn't know exactly what a wingman was but he needed some moral support from a teammate. He knew this wasn't the same as football; Dave, and Allan were his friends, but were they his mates?

Still unsure of himself he decided to talk to his mom.

"I think I'll go to the basketball games Friday night," he began.

Victoria perked up right away.

"That's wonderful, Alex. I think you should be getting out more often. You can't stay in your room studying all the time."

She waited, noting the worry on Alex' face.

"Why so glum?"

"There's a sock hop after the basketball games, but I don't know how to dance."

"Oh dear," she responded, smiling encouragingly.

"Why don't we try a few things here to get you started."

With that she got Alex to help her push the dining room table to the wall and put a Johnny Mathis record on the hi-fi set.

"Mom, they won't be playing any Johnny Mathis songs at the dance."

"Never mind Alex, we need to start with the basics.

"Here, put your left arm around my waist, like this," she said, taking his arm and placing it at the small of her back; Alex felt very uncomfortable holding his mom like that. Then she took his right hand in her left.

"This is the waltz. It's the easiest and you'll need to know this if there is any slow dancing. It's really just a three-step box: forward, side, together; back, side, together; listen to the beats of the music: 1,2,3; 1,2,3."

"How will Eleanor know what to do?"

— Alex' Choice —

"Eleanor is it?" Victoria perked up at the name. "She'll know. Her steps are opposite to yours, but she'll follow your lead."

Alex was doubtful but took his mom's word for it. She was a girl after all and she must have had some experience.

"Okay, let's try that again. Forward – see, you step forward with your left, but I step back with my right – side – see, your right foot goes forward but to the right, my left foot goes back but to the side to match your foot – together – you bring your left foot sideways to meet your right, but I move my left foot to join my right? See?

"Now, reverse: your right foot goes back, and I follow, your left foot goes back but to the side, your right foot closes to your left and now you've completed the box. Got it?

"Forward, side, together; back, side, tougher; 1,2,3; 1,2,3."

"But do we just stay in the same place all the time?"

"No, you can change direction by moving your lead foot in another direction, and travel wherever the music takes you, but still counting 1, 2, 3. You're supposed to put some pressure on her back and gently guide her in the direction you want her to go." Victoria took his hand and put it firmly on her hip and gripped his left hand more firmly. If you want to turn her to the right, you put pressure on her hand and step with your right foot steering her in the right direction; but of course it's her left; if you want to turn left, you just put pressure on her hip and sort of steer her to the left.

This was all too confusing to Alex and felt altogether too intimate, but he trusted his mother who seemed to think this the most natural thing in the world.

Victoria changed the record for something with a faster beat.

"Next we'll try the basics of the foxtrot, though I doubt many kids your age actually do the foxtrot."

After a few rounds of slow, fast, slow, Victoria said,

"Now, let's try a few jive steps."

"Jive?" said Alex.

"Yes, Jive, or whatever it's called these days. Swing? Hip hop?"

She showed him how to twirl the girl, and step around behind her, and generally do the two-step.

The more they practiced the less awkward Alex felt dancing with his mom, and the more assured he became.

"Was Dad a good dancer?"

"No Alex, he was not. He was just like you, too shy to reveal he wasn't good at it. He doesn't seem to have rhythm, even though he was good at sports. He's more of a comedian than a dancer."

She chuckled and Alex joined her in the joke.

"Okay, maybe that's enough for now," Victoria said. "But just like your football moves, you have to practice them a lot to have them become automatic. But the only place you can practice is on the dance floor.

"And don't be shy. And don't pretend you can dance when you're actually still learning, you can't fake dancing. Just tell the girl the truth, she'll understand; she might be just as inexperienced as you; if she's mean about it, you don't want to be with her anyway. If Eleanor is an accomplished dancer just ask her to show you a few things. I'm sure she will be happy to teach you."

Alex wasn't so sure but at least he had a better idea of what he needed to do on the dance floor.

Friday night came and Alex left the house for school around 6:30 to be on time for the Junior Lions game at 7:00.

"Have a nice time Alex," his mother said, encouragingly. Peter looked up from his newspaper, "What time do you expect to be home, Alex?"

"I don't know Dad. I think the sock hop ends at 11:00."

"Well, you might go out for food after, but try to be home by midnight.

"Do you have any money?"

"Yeah, I've got five bucks."

"You might need more than that if you end up taking a girl with you after. Here's a ten."

Victoria smiled at Peter, gratefully.

"Thanks Dad," and out the door he went.

It was a cold February night but Alex didn't feel it on his walk to the school. His mind was full of anticipation and worry about the evening ahead.

— Alex' Choice —

Dave Kidd was already seated in the bleachers when Alex arrived; he hailed him to sit with him and a few other friends.

Shortly thereafter Eleanor arrived with a couple of girlfriends and the three of them sat in the row in front of Alex and his friends, but off to the left a little way. Alex wondered what would happen next. The gap of several feet could be several miles. He had no idea what he should say to her, or even acknowledge she was there.

But the ever-confident Eleanor turned to him and said, "Hi Alex. Nice to see you out tonight."

"Do you think the Lions will win?"

Alex was amazed at her asking that question, opening the door for a conversation. How did she know how to do that?

"I don't know Eleanor. I don't know how strong our Junior team is, but our Seniors may have a chance. At least it's not PCVS we're playing tonight."

Eleanor smiled at him benignly and Alex blushed realizing he sounded just like Professor Jorgenson explaining something.

The Junior game went smoothly, and the home team won handily.

As the Senior Lions and the St. Peters team were warming up, Alex was surprised that Eleanor had persuaded her friends to move up one row next the boys. She sat beside Alex, giving him a relaxed smile.

"Now we can talk without having to shout at each other."

"Yeah, I guess you're right."

Before the game began the Senior Lions Cheerleaders took to the floor.

Alex' eyes were full of Cathy Baird leading the team. They finished their routine; Cathy caught Alex' eye and waved at him. Alex smiled and waved back furtively.

Eleanor didn't miss a thing.

"Hey, I think you are sweet on her. She's very pretty."

"Yeah, I guess. But we're not anything. She's been in my Home Room since Grade 9 so that's how I know her."

"Are you staying for the sock hop after? Maybe you can dance with her."

Alex was shocked with this idea. He didn't know how to reply.

The Senior Lions lost in an exciting and close game. Alex was very conscious of the energetic girl cheering wildly beside him. But he was also very conscious of that beautiful cheerleader cheering in a structured disciplined way on the floor.

"Are you staying for the sock hop?" Eleanor asked as she and the other girls climbed down from the bleachers to take their ritualistic trip to the girls' washroom. Alex nodded, but mildly anxious.

When the girls got back the deejay had set up his kit and music was already blasting across the gym floor. The girls removed their shoes and were on the floor in their white bobby socks, twisting and jiving.

Dave Kidd got up off the bleachers and joined the girls on the floor, the four of them sort of dancing in a pack.

After a bit, Eleanor came over to Alex still sitting on the bleachers and said, "Okay Flash, take off your shoes and come on down to dance."

"Why did you call me Flash?"

"Don't be silly, everybody knows that's you nickname from football."

Alex knew his mates called him Flash which both pleased him and embarrassed him; but he didn't know the whole school referred to him as Flash. He got that moniker the previous year and it ended up in the Ascovian Yearbook, but Alex figured nobody read the yearbook.

Eleanor pointed at his shoes and held out her hand imperiously. Alex removed his loafers and took her hand as he climbed down from the bleachers. She led him out on the floor and started to move her body in a rhythmic and enticing way.

"Come on Alex, just do what I'm doing."

He found himself concentrating hard on her feet until she told him to stop looking at the floor but look at her face. He did as he was told and she smiled at him.

Soon another song was playing, and then another. Alex became more and more relaxed on the floor, even though he felt his arms and feet were completely out of sync. He began to look around the whole gym at all the other kids squirming and jiving on the floor. And then he realized he was looking for something in particular.

— Alex' Choice —

"Are you looking for Cathy?" Eleanor shouted to Alex against the loud music.

Alex blushed, embarrassed that he should be caught in his indiscretion.

She laughed. "I think she went home. She doesn't usually stay for the dance after."

Alex felt a pang of disappointment, and confusion. Here was this attractive and enthusiastic girl in front of him and he was thinking of someone else. He was enjoying dance yet annoyed with himself for not having come to these Friday evening dances before now, even last year in Grade 12. Why had he left it till Grade XIII? Maybe he would have had a chance with Cathy if he wasn't so shy.

Eleven o'clock came before he even thought of the time. Now what?

Dave said, "Why don't we go to A&W Drive-In for burgers? I could sure use a Papa Burger and a root beer now."

"Do you have a car, Dave?" asked Eleanor excitedly.

"Yeah. You and Alex can come with me and MaryAnne."

They piled into the car, as dozens of kids swarmed the parking lot or otherwise made their way home walking in groups of threes and fours. Some mysterious signal between the girls seemed to confirm who sat where – Maryanne sat in the front seat with the driver, Eleanor in the back with Alex. They weren't in the car two minutes before Eleanor hitched herself closer to Alex, peeled off her glove and felt for his hand.

Dave parked his car in the angled spots as the server came over to the car to take their order.

The foursome ordered hamburgers and drinks – root beer, and floats, and milkshakes, Alex ordered onion rings, Eleanor said she'd share her French fries with him – and it was time to pay. Alex, grateful to his dad for the extra money, offered to pay for Eleanor but she said, "hey, no need. I have money."

Afterward Dave dropped Maryanne off at home and then Eleanor. She turned to give Alex a quick kiss on the cheek and then out of the car with a wink. Then finally Alex home.

"Hey Alex, that was a good time. I think Eleanor is really keen on you. We should try this again next week."

"Yeah Dave, I think you and MaryAnne got along pretty well too. Thanks for the ride."

He let himself into the house quietly to find Victoria still up, reading in the living room.

"Glad to see you are home safe and sound Alex. Did you have a nice time? How was the dancing?"

"Yeah Mom, it was okay.

"You were right about one thing, Mom, Eleanor was a very good teacher."

Victoria's eyebrow twitched slightly, wondering for a second what Eleanor had actually taught her novice dater, but quickly let that go.

Alex got ready for bed but lay in it for a long while, going over the evening in his head: the engaging Eleanor, the elusive Cathy. Then suddenly Sandra Farquharson burst on his mind and he began to dwell on her. She would be back at home on Amherst Island, no Friday night sock hops for her. She would be in her bed sleeping at this hour. He tried to push Sandra out of his mind and go back to the excitement of his time with Eleanor, but she wouldn't go. He really missed her even though he hadn't seen her for more than four years. Finally, he gave up trying to fall asleep, got out of bed, and wrote Sandra a long letter.

Next morning, Victoria saw the envelop addressed to Sandra Farquharson lying on the side table by the front door for Peter to mail on Monday.

"You had your light on late last night Alex," she said, rhetorically.

"Yeah, I couldn't get to sleep."

"Everything okay?"

"Yeah, I guess my mind was a bit busy from the evening."

Victoria thought she wouldn't ask about the letter to Sandra.

Alex went to all the Lions home games and sock hops for the rest of the winter, and was delighted to spend the evening with Eleanor at the sock hop, and then A&W after.

When the basketball season was over, the four of them continued to double date, Saturday night at the movies and Chinese food afterwards. Eleanor always paid her own way, much to Alex relief. She told him she was a cashier at Dominion Store.

He enjoyed their outings and he welcomed her reaching for his hand in the movies and sitting close to him in the backseat of the car but he didn't think of Eleanor as his girlfriend; he didn't actually know what to think.

He wrote to Sandra frequently; he didn't tell Sandra about Eleanor.

31. Driver's Test

HE WAS CERTAINLY ENJOYING HIS SOCIAL TIME WITH ELEANOR – she was confident and outgoing, and rather uninhibited. She always took the initiative to hold Alex hand, and play footsies with him in the movie theatre or under the table at the restaurant. Alex didn't mind, but still felt he was a novice at all this romance business. He was also conscious of needing to keep his mind on his studies.

They had fun double-dating with Dave Kidd and MaryAnne – grateful that Dave had a car – but Eleanor gave Alex signs that she didn't really like Dave, and while she was friendly with MaryAnne, they weren't close.

As the school year was coming to a close Eleanor said to Alex one day, "Hey, when are you going to get your driver's licence? Don't you think it would be nice for us to go out, just the two of us?"

Alex hadn't really thought of that; he stumbled for an answer.

"I've been thinking of that Eleanor; I think maybe in the summer, after exams are over."

Next day he reminded Victoria that she had said Peter would give him driving lessons.

"Of course, Alex. You should ask him at supper table tonight."

Peter readily agreed,

"You already know road safety from your years riding your bike, but a car is different and you need a Driver's Permit before you can drive a car.

So next day Alex went down to the Licence Bureau and got a copy of the Rules of the Road and immediately started to study. By Friday he was back to the Licence Office to take his knowledge exam and qualify for his Learner's Permit. Saturday was his first lesson.

"Now Son, you already know how to ride a bike and drive a motorboat, but a car is not the same."

Alex prepared himself for long lecture from the Professor but he was very motivated.

Alex' Choice

"First, you need to know the dimensions of your vehicle. Perception is different once you're behind the wheel of a car."

So before Peter gave Alex the keys, they took a walk around the car. Starting at the driver's side front bumper.

"Notice where the headlight is on the car, then look up to see the steering wheel inside the car.

"Now, here on the passenger side front bumper, consider where it is from the driver's seat.

"As we walk the length of the car consider how far it is to the back taillight from the front headlight."

Alex paid close attention. Suddenly he realized he'd never thought of the dimensions of the car before.

"Now Alex, as we walk along the back bumper, notice how far it is from the driver's seat.

"And here we are at the driver's side taillight. From the driver's seat this is almost impossible to see. Now if a car was alongside you in this position, you wouldn't be able to see it either. This is called the blind spot and is the cause of many accidents.

"Now, you sit in the driver's seat."

Alex climbed into the driver's seat and stroked the steering wheel with a mixture of pride, confusion and anxiousness.

"Now son, look at the driver's side front fender where the headlight is.

"Now the passenger side."

"Gee, Dad I can't see the bumper from here!"

That's right son, you can't but when you're driving you have to *know* where it is if you don't want to bump into other objects in your way, like the garage door frame, another car, a kid!"

"Oh!"

"Now look out the back window. What do you see?"

"Gee Dad, it's not easy to turn my head all the way around to see out the back."

"Right. So stretch yourself. Now what do you see?"

"Nothing."

"That's right. That's why we walked around the car, so you could get in your head what is there, and where, even though you can't actually see it.

"Now look in the rear-view mirror. What do you see?"

"I see the driveway and across the street."

"Yes, good, but you can't actually see immediately behind the car, can you?"

"No."

"That's why you have to look with your eyes, not rely only on your mirror."

Peter got out of the car and walked around to stand by the bumper on the driver's side.

"Look in your side mirror. What do you see?"

Alex was amazed; he couldn't see his father even though he knew he was standing there. "Nothing."

Peter took a step to his left.

"Do you see me now?"

"Yes."

"Keep looking in the mirror and tell me when you can no longer see me."

Peter took a few steps further to the left until Alex shouted, "Now!"

"Now turn your head to the left and look behind you. What do you see."

'Now I see you!"

"Keep looking while I walk back to the car."

Alex craned his neck to follow his father but eventually he couldn't turn his head any further and Peter disappeared from view.

"Wow, that's amazing. How will I ever know if something is there? Geeze Dad, how can you drive safely when you can't even see everything that's around the car?"

"That's right Alex. That's why you have to be looking around constantly using your rear-view mirror, side-view mirror and your neck, scanning for what else might be on the road.

"Also, as we shall see when we get going, you have to look at the road and the traffic and anticipate what might happen next. You can't just follow the guy in front of you, you have to keep an eye on everything that's going on all around you."

Peter got in the passenger seat and asked Alex to start the car. Alex looked down to the ignition slot, inserted the key and began to turn it.

— Alex' Choice —

"Woah, Wait. Foot on the brake, check that the transmission is in Park, look around, then turn the key."

This was turning out to be much more intricate than Alex had imagined. He appreciated now how important it was to take things seriously when driving.

Alex backed the car carefully down the driveway and turned the car into the street. He nearly hit the parked car on the opposite side of the street. Suddenly he saw it as he glanced in the mirror and jammed his foot on the brake.

He looked at his father, sheepishly; Peter kept calm, and didn't say anything. Alex said it for him, "Now I see what you mean by looking around and in your mirrors all the time.

Alex made it down the street and around the block several times, only driving over the corner curb with his right rear wheel once.

"Good thing that wasn't somebody's bike, or foot," Peter deadpanned.

That was enough for one day but over the ensuing six weeks Alex got more and more practice time with Peter, and a couple of times with his mother.

"I think you're just about ready for your driver's test son," Peter said one day. You still need to work on your parallel parking, but I think you'll do alright.

"Let's go down to the Licence Bureau tomorrow and make an appointment for your road test."

They made their appointment for two weeks, the earliest they could make it.

But when test day came, Peter noticed some fluid dripping under the car in the driveway. He opened the hood and inspected the engine compartment. He didn't know much about cars but he figured he could do a basic diagnosis of the problem. Ha, the brake fluid reservoir was practically empty. That must be why the brakes were feeling a bit spongy lately. He figured it might be too dangerous to drive the car to the garage so he phoned for a tow.

The Chevy dealer sent around their wrecker and hooked Peter's Olds to the hook.

"Good thing you called, Professor Jorgenson. This car has leaked all its brake fluid. We'll tow it into the garage and get it all fixed up for you, probably it will be ready by tomorrow."

"I'll need a loaner for the day, and overnight" Peter said.

"Okay, get in with me and I'll take you with me to the garage."

Peter returned an hour or so later, in time for Alex to go to the Department of Transport Licence Bureau for his driver's test, driving a new Chevrolet Corvair.

Peter gave the keys to Alex and wished him luck.

"It's a nice new car Alex but it's smaller than the Olds and so you'll need to recalibrate your perception of the car's dimensions."

Alex mentally shook his head to his father's language.

"And one other thing, it doesn't have power steering and brakes so you'll have to use more force to turn the wheel and applying the brakes.

Peter took a seat in the bureau waiting room while Alex was greeted by Mr. Turner, the Examination Officer, clipboard in hand. Mr. Turner got into the passenger seat while Alex walked around the back of the car taking stock as his father had instructed. He inserted the key in the ignition, put his foot on the brake, checked his mirrors and his views and turned the key. He then engaged the transmission – 'Reverse' – to back out of the parking space; and pressed the gas pedal. The car jumped; he jammed on the brakes.

Peter winced. Alex, surprised and embarrassed, explained the situation to Mr. Turner: "This isn't our usual car – it's in the garage for a brake problem. The gas pedal on this car is much lighter than what I'm used to.

Mr. Turner nodded in understanding but was still all business.

Alex then changed gears to 'Drive' and drove off the DoT lot, turning right onto the street, pulling hard on the stiff steering wheel and taking the turn quite wide. The examiner made notes on his clipboard. Alex came to the first stop sign on the test route and applied the brakes. The pedal was stiff and Alex could tell he would likely overrun the stop line so he pressed harder on the brakes, causing Mr. Turner to lurch forward in the passenger seat.

— Alex' Choice —

Mr. Turner said nothing as he put another mark on the paper on the clipboard.

Thirty minutes later Alex turned into the parking area of the Licence Bureau.

The Examiner removed the pink copy of the exam results and gave it to Alex.

"I'm sorry Alex, I can't pass you, based on today's test. You do not have good control of this vehicle. You are too late in stopping and your turns are too wide, especially your right turns. And you made a mess of your parallel parking."

Alex was almost in tears as Peter approached them. Mr. Turner eyed Peter and returned to Alex.

"I realize you were not familiar with this car and you certainly struggled with the manual steering and braking but that can't be used as an excuse.

"I recommend you make another appointment for a few weeks' from now and bring you dad's usual vehicle next time for the test."

He smiled at Alex.

"Don't be upset. Lots of people fail their driver's test the first time. That's why we get danger pay."

Peter smiled at this little joke, but Alex was not amused.

What was he going to say to Eleanor?

32. Grade XIII Finals

GRADE XIII WAS ALEX' FINAL YEAR OF HIGH SCHOOL. It was also a year of change, endings and new beginnings. He was being stretched academically and he was growing in social confidence. It was also his last year of high school athletics.

By mid-May Alex had been keenly feeling the pressure of the looming final exams. These were significant for many reasons – not only would they determine his future but they were unlike any exams he had taken so far. Grade XIII finals were 'Departmentals' and every Grade Thirteen student had heard the stories of how difficult they were. They were composed by the provincial Department of Education, and the exams were sent back to Toronto to be marked by teachers from other schools anonymously. Not only that, the exams were written in the gymnasium instead of a regular classroom, invigilated by two or three teachers pacing the room.

Alex used all his available time preparing for these final exams, studying and working on his assignments. But he still wanted to compete in the May and June High School Track and Field meets. The trouble was, he didn't have the time to go to practice each day after school. Instead, he limited his training to one circuit around the block with Oliver at bedtime.

He tried out for his three favourite events but noticed right away he didn't feel as strong and as fit as the year before. And that Joe Burns fellow in Grade 12 would have been a serious threat except the coach made sure the two boys didn't compete against each in the same events.

The District Meet was held at Kenner Collegiate in the South End. The Adam Scott team traveled to Kenner by school bus but parents and student spectators had to find their own way. Professor Jorgenson was at a conference out of town, but Victoria rarely missed one of her son's competitions. It was a sunny day, but the meet started at 9:00 o'clock and the air was still chilly from a cool spring night. As Alex warmed up in his green and white Adam Scott warm-up pants and sweatshirt, jogging and stretching on the grassy sections on the far side of the track, he was surprised to see Eleanor walking with Victoria towards him. Was he actually surprised? In fact, he largely expected to see Miss Enthusiasm there, and he was happy to see her.

"So Flash," she said with a wink, "how do you think you'll do today?"

"Hard to say Eleanor," he replied, confident but with a hint of doubt. "Most of the other competitors I recognize from last year and I beat them then. But I'm not feeling so fit this year, not enough practice."

They lounged by the fence chatting and laughing while Alex awaited his first event, the 100-yard dash. Victoria kept a discreet distance.

First came the Novice heats, then the Juniors; finally the Seniors' heats were called. Alex pulled himself up from his seat against the fence beside Eleanor. She bounced up too, as Alex struggled to pulled off his warm-up pants over his spikes. "Here," she cried, reaching for his pants, let me help with those. She bundled up his suit then she gave him a kiss. "Good luck, Alex," she said, smiling at him, sparkles in her eyes.

Victoria wondered at this display of familiarity but decided she was just being old-fashioned.

"Come on Eleanor," she said, "let's get a seat near the finish line."

Alex made his way to the start of the 100-yard dash at the top of the straight on the bleachers side of the field. He looked down the track to the finish line, psyching himself. And then he noticed Eleanor waving excitedly to him.

Alex adjusted the starting blocks in his lane – lane 5, an excellent lane as he could see the other sprinters either side. The starter called, 'On your marks', and the boys all took their positions in their bocks, adjusted their feet, and settled.

'Get set' and the boys raised their hips from the crouch and transferred their weight forward to their hands. The umpire held the starting pistol over his head, holding the boys in their start positions for a second, and,

Bang.

Alex leaped out of his position and found his stride in ten yards and his top speed by thirty yards. By seventy yards he felt he had a comfortable lead, but he also felt his right hip-flexor muscle tightening a little. 'Oh no,' he thought, 'not that again.' But he had a comfortable lead, so he relaxed his pace and coasted to the finish line, first.

He watched the second heat from the infield and noticed there was a kid from Crestwood who won his heat handily.

Alex came over to the bleachers to retrieve his warm-up clothes from Eleanor. Victoria had noticed Alex slowing in the race and, 'was he favouring his right leg a bit?' she wondered.

"Are you alright Alex?" She asked, careful not to project too much maternal concern.

"Yeah, Mom, I'm okay. Maybe a bit stiff in my hip-flexor."

"Well young man, I brought some heat liniment with me just in case. You put this on."

Alex looked at Eleanor slightly alarmed but nevertheless took a big dab of liniment and put his hand down his shorts and rubbed it on his hip-flexor muscle.

"Be careful Alex not to get any on your other parts."

Alex glared at his mother while Eleanor blushed, a mixture of smirk and abashment.

They waited for the girls 100-yard dash heats to finish, and then the Midget and Junior Boys finals.

The Senior Boys finals were called and Alex set his blocks; he was in lane 3. All eight lanes were assigned for the finals.

"Runners take your marks."

"Set."

And the gun sounded.

Alex, leaped from his blocks but the gun sounded twice more indicating one of the runners had made a false start. Alex thought it was the kid in Lane 6, from Crestwood.

The umpire called all the boys back to the start line.

"Runners, take your marks,"

"Set,"

And once again, bang. Alex burst from his blocks and this time there was no double bang. Alex sensed the runner in lane 6 was slow to start this time. Alex was in the lead at 30 yards and held it by 70 yards, but by 90 yards the kid in lane 6 was closing. As the two hit the finish line Alex thrust his chest out and broke the tape first.

– Alex' Choice –

Eleanor and Victoria were cheering wildly for Alex' triumph, holding each other as they jumped up and down on the bleachers; Victoria looked at Eleanor and smiled at her, but noticed a sort of wild excitement in Eleanor's eye.

They climbed down off the bleachers to get a closer look at Alex accepting his red ribbon.

"How's the hip, Alex?" Victoria asked.

"It's fine Mom."

"Well, give yourself plenty of time to relax that muscle, tenderly relax it – a hard stretch may do more harm than good – and tell your coach."

After checking with his coach, he found his Mom and Eleanor having lunch by the fence.

"So, what did your coach say?"

"He said I should scratch from the Long Jump event and save my leg for the 220. So that's what I did. My heats should go off at about 2:30.

He applied more liniment and settled on the ground.

Victoria stopped him.

"Don't lay on that cold grass until I get you a blanket from the car."

She returned with the blanket, placing it against the fence. Alex and Eleanor sat down and wrapped the blanket around their legs. Victoria smiled at their easy comfort with one another; she returned to the bleachers to watch Oliver in his high jump event.

The 220 was almost a repeat of the 100-yard dash. Alex won his heat but in the final he tired by the finish of this grueling sprint and the Crestwood kid beat him by a couple of yards. Alex wasn't happy to lose but he knew his fitness level was the reason. At least his hip flexor held together.

A week later it was the Regional Championships – the Central Ontario Secondary School Athletic Association Finals in which all the winners (first, second and third place finishers in each event) in the various District Championships competed. First and second place winners at COSSAA would then go on to the All-Ontario (OFSAA) Finals. The COSSAA finals the previous year were in Lindsay but this year were being held in Cobourg at the Cobourg District High School. Alex wondered whether he would see Hugh there.

Victoria offered Eleanor a ride to Cobourg but Mrs. Tysdale wouldn't let her go; she had to stay home to study as the Grade XIII Final Exams were fast approaching. Alex was stressed himself over these pending exams and his usual enthusiasm for the track meets was definitely diminished. He brought his Latin note books to work on while he waited between heats. He didn't feel the usual excitement and the stomach butterflies somehow felt different; it felt more like a chore that had to be done than the thrill of competition. And he worried that he might not do well.

The Senior Boys 100-yard heats were called. There were two heats of six runners each, the top three from each of the four Districts. The top three from each heat would go on to the finals plus the two next best times.

Alex dug into his blocks and was off with his usual burst; tore down the track, giving just about everything he had against this stiff competition. He lunged for the tape finishing second but had the distinct impression that the third-place runner had let up before the tape. He was pleased that his hip-flexor held up.

He walked back up the track to the start line to retrieve his gym bag and warm-up suit, lost in thought. In the melee of kids sorting themselves out he heard someone call his name.

He looked up to see his old friend Hugh running over to him.

"My God, Alex, it's good to see you. I kinda wondered if you were still doing track."

"Hey Hugh. Good to see you. Are you in this meet too?" ('Stupid question' he thought, 'why else would Hugh be there, and wearing a warm-up suit?')

"Yeah, I'm in the next heat."

"Well you better get ready. Let's talk after your heat."

Alex changed out of his track shoes to his runners, packed up his gear, and trotted down to the finish line to see how Hugh did.

The starter pistol went off and Hugh charged down the track in the thick of the pack. A black kid from Port Hope easily won the heat, the Crestwood kid second, as Hugh finished third. He'd be in the finals later against Alex.

"So, Alex, how did you do in your heat?"

"Second by a whisker, but the guy who finished third was coasting.

— Alex' Choice —

"So, Hugh, how've you been? What's it like here at Cobourg?"

"It's alright Alex. Took me a while to get used to it. But I made some friends and, you know me, I'm used to moving."

"But you've been here five years now."

"Yeah, my dad hasn't been transferred again. Maybe he's staying put at this branch."

"Hey Hugh, I didn't realize you were doing track? I didn't see you the last two years at COSSA."

"Yeah, well, in Grade 11 I got mono and was off school for six weeks in the spring. And last year I got suspended."

"Suspended! What for?"

"Ah, crazy stuff. A couple of the guys and me were drinking at the back of the bus. Coach caught us and we were suspended and sent home for five days. My dad was some mad."

"Geez Loueeze, Hugh. You're always trying something. Remember when we took our bikes across the ferry to Amherstview. I was lucky my dad didn't punish me for that."

"Hey Alex, it's not your dad you have to worry about, it's Old Man O'Leary!" Hugh started to laugh. "He sure had it in for you over that treasure business. Whatever happened to him?"

"I don't know, Hugh. Sandra said he went to live on Wolff Island and then went down to Boston, distant relatives or something. Don't know where he is now. Dead maybe."

"Hey, do you still see Sandra?"

"No. Not since I left Amherst Island five years ago. But we're still pen pals."

"Really? You still stuck on her?"

"Geez, Hugh."

Hugh looked at Alex and figured there must still be something there that Alex wasn't telling him but he decided to leave that one alone.

"So, do you have a girlfriend in Peterborough?"

"Yeah, sort of. I don't know. I really like her and I'm pretty sure she likes me, but…"

"Hey, is she here?"

"No, but my mom is. She invited Eleanor…"

"So her name is Eleanor, eh?"

195

"But she couldn't come because Grade XIII final exams are coming,"

"Well, do you make out with her?"

"Geez Hugh, that's sort of private."

Hugh punched Alex on the shoulder, "You're just the same Alex, all serious and proper."

Alex was silent for a moment, not wanting this conversation to continue in that direction.

"What are you thinking of doing next year, Hugh?"

"I'm hoping to go to Queen's. How about you?"

"Yeah, that's what I want to do too."

"You still thinking about playing football for the Golden Gaels?"

"Yeah, I hope so."

"Well, Alex, maybe we can meet up when we get there."

"Okay, Hugh, I'll write you when I know what's happening. But you have to write back!

"We better get warmed up for the 100 finals; they'll be called soon.

"Good luck Hugh, but I hope I beat you, as usual."

"Not on your life. You'll be breathing my exhaust."

Hugh smacked Alex good-naturedly and the boys separated to join their own teammates.

Alex could feel the familiar tension rising in his core as the start of the race approached. He took a few deep breaths to calm his nerves; he knew he needed to be relaxed to give his best performance. But he didn't feel relaxed, nor did he feel confident. Alex pulled off his green and white warm-up sweats, struggling for a minute to unhook his spikes from the fabric.

The eight sprinters were called to the start line. Alex caught Hugh's eye; Hugh threw him a wink.

'Runners take your marks.'

Alex was in Lane 3, Hugh in Lane 8 – not a good lane, the black kid from Port Hope took Lane 5, Crestwood was in 2, the tall kid from Trenton who came third in Alex' heat was in 6.

The boys settled in their blocks.

'Set.'

The crowd was quiet, everyone filled with tension.

Bang.

— Alex' Choice —

And the boys were off. Alex got a good jump but he could feel the whole line were away smoothly.

By 30 yards, the black kid in lane 5 and the 'sleeper' in 6 had a slight lead; Alex and Hugh and Crestwood just behind. By 70 yards lane 5 and 6 had widened their lead by another yard or so. Alex pressed to catch them; Crestwood keeping pace. By 90 yards Alex sensed that he wasn't going to catch the leaders, and in concentrating on them he didn't see Crestwood on his left lunging for the finish line.

Alex finished fourth, Hugh fifth. They wouldn't be going to OFSSA next week.

Alex was deflated but Hugh was his effervescent self.

"I guess we're not the fasted kids on the block anymore, eh Alex?" Hugh declared, clapping Alex on the back.

Alex didn't answer. He was not as quick to recover as Hugh.

Hugh pressed on. "Are you going in the 220 too?"

"Yeah? You?"

"Na, I just made it for the 100. But I'll be cheering you on for the 220."

An hour later the Senior Boys were called for the 220 heats. Most of the runners from the 100 were entered in the 220 as well.

Alex felt his energy was fading and wondered if he had enough in the tank to run two more grueling races. He decided his strategy.

The first heat was called to the blocks; Alex was in this heat. Qualifying for the finals was the same as for the 100 – the first three finishers in each heat qualified and the two best times from the remainders. Alex was pretty sure the two best guys from the 100, and maybe one or two other runners who had saved themselves for the 220, would hold back in the heats, just fast enough to qualify for the finals. Well, let them.

The start judge called them to their marks; set; and the gun.

Alex was off like a shot out of a gun. He reached top speed before the bend in the track and leaned into it bursting into first place at the top of the straight. He poured it on and held his pace all the way to the finish line breaking the tape handily. He was pleased with himself but he sensed it was a hollow victory.

An hour later it was the 220 finals. He was assigned lane 4, the middle of the track.

The gun went off and so was Alex but even before he completed the bend he knew he hadn't enough juice left to do his best. He didn't give up but resigned himself to watching four or five other boys begin to pull away from him. He was sixth, gasping at the finish line.

Hugh ran up to him after the finish as Alex bent over, his hands on his knees breathing heard and trying to recover. Victoria joined the two of them.

"Are you okay Alex? That was a very hard race."

Alex didn't answer. He was not in a talking mood.

"Your friend Hugh found me in the stands. We cheered hard for you."

Hugh remarked, "it's very tough for kids in Grade Thirteen to do well at this late season meet."

"We're very proud of you."

Alex smiled wanly at the two of them. They chatted for a little while longer until Alex said he was ready to go home.

Hugh asked, "aren't you staying to watch the relay races?"

"I don't think so. Adam Scott doesn't have an entry and I don't really want to wait around waiting for the school bus home."

Then turning to his mom, asked, "how did Oliver do in the high jump."

"I think he's ready to go home too, Alex. He came fourth so he's not going to OFSAA either.

"I'll ask your coach if you can come home with me rather than wait for the bus to take you back to Peterborough."

"Goodbye, Mrs. Jorgenson."

"Goodbye, Hugh."

"Goodbye Alex. See you at Queen's."

THE FINAL EXAMS WERE UPON THE GRADE THIRTEENERS, the dreaded 'Departmentals', written under close scrutiny in the gymnasium. Two weeks of three-hour exams, one in the morning, and one in the afternoon each day. Alex was apprehensive but he figured he was as prepared as he would ever be. He felt more self-assured than he did for COSSAA.

He had nine exams to write. Mercifully Latin Grammar and Literature were held on the same day, as was English Grammar

Alex' Choice

and Literature; the three math exams were each on separate days, and luckily, so were Chemistry and History.

Entering the examination hall/gymnasium was mildly intimidating. The gymnasium was filled with rows and rows of student tables and chairs with a teacher's desk arranged at the front, a portable chalk board rolled in with the name of the course and the time allocated: 9:00 – 12:00, or 1:30 – 4:30. For some courses there were 120 students writing all at once, some of them night school adults. Alex found a table and seated himself, and waited for the proctor to distribute the exam booklets; it reminded him of getting set at the start of his races on the track. Once the proctor announced that they could begin Alex became completely immersed in his task at hand.

Each day Victoria asked how the exam had gone, despite Peter having recommended she back off.

Alex felt he had done well in Chemistry and History, and, he thought, Geometry, but he was not so sure about Trigonometry and Algebra. He had never quite got the point of Trigonometry but thought he had done well enough on the exam. He had had high marks in Algebra all year but when he got home from the exam he reported to his mom that the exam was hard.

"That's okay son," said Peter, "sometimes they set an exam that is too tough and then they adjust the marks on a bell curve."

Alex didn't know what that meant but took his dad's word for it."

The day of his Latin exams Victoria was especially apprehensive for her son. After her meeting with Mrs. Elliott, she had worried about this course. Alex' marks had gone up in April, but only marginally.

"I think they went pretty well Mom," Alex reported.

And then they waited.

Three weeks later he got a letter in the mail with his final grades: 88 in History; 86 in Chemistry; 85 in Geometry; 78 in Trigonometry; 77 and 73 in English Grammar and Literature. 65 in Algebra.

"Ouch," he said, "I must have really flubbed that exam because my mid-terms were in the high 70s. Mr. Armstrong will be disappointed."

"What about Latin?" Victoria blurted; she couldn't suppress her curiosity.

"80 and 82 Mom."

"Wow, you must have aced that final exam!"

"So, what is your overall average?"

"79.7."

The number landed with a thud. Alex was going to be only a few marks off, but he would not have an overall average of 80, the threshold for an Ontario Scholar designation. Alex looked at his parents, disconcerted. Somehow, he felt he had let his parents down, and himself too.

"Nevermind, Son," said Peter, soothingly, careful not to patronize his earnest son, "these are excellent results. With marks like these I'm sure you will get admission to Trent, even Queen's."

A few weeks later he got letters from Trent and from Queen's. He was admitted in Arts and Science to both, but a scholarship to Trent. There was no hesitation. He was going to Queen's.

A few weeks later Victoria chanced to meet Mrs. Elliott in the grocery store. They acknowledged each other as only two sparring cats can.

"I'm sure, Mrs. Elliott, you are aware of Alex' final results?"

"Yes, Mrs. Jorgenson, you must be very proud of Alex."

"Yes. Mrs. Elliott, especially his marks in Latin."

Victoria smiled at Mrs. Elliott, "And he is going to Queen's in September."

"Oh," said Mrs. Elliott, properly chastened.

Victoria turned her back and walked away.

"Now that you've finished high school Alex, and you're going to be 19 this summer, time for you to get a summer job and earn some money for school next year."

"Sure Mom," Alex said, with a nervous jump in his stomach, "But I don't know what jobs I can do."

"Never mind, I've found you one already. I was in Farmboy the other day and I asked the owner – I actually know him from my nursing student days in Peterborough – if they needed any summer help. I told him you had just graduated from Grade

— Alex' Choice —

Thirteen and would be going to Queen's in the fall and you could use a job. He said he can always use stock clerks.

"You start on Monday."

"Gee, Mom, but Farmboy is way down on Lansdowne Street in the South End. How am I going to get to work?"

"Your dad said he could drive you. His schedule is pretty flexible in the summer."

It was with a mixture of relief and resentment that he had a summer job – why did his parents make these arrangements without consulting him? – excitement, doubt and anxiety. He didn't know a shallot from an onion, but he figured he'd learn.

He told Eleanor that evening of his good fortune. He knew she already had a job as a cashier in Dominion Store.

"That's great Alex.

"But when are you going to get your driver's licence?"

Alex was taken aback until he saw her wink at him.

Alex called the Licence Bureau the very next day and made an appointment for a second try for his driver's permit. The examiner advised that the next opening was not until the end of July – summer was a very busy time in Peterborough as examiners took their vacations and many youngsters were trying their exams now that school was out. The examiner suggested Alex try the Lindsay office as they might not be as busy, being a smaller town. Lindsay had an opening for the following Monday so Alex booked it and asked his dad at supper if that was okay.

"No problem Alex, I'll drive you over to Lindsay Monday but first we should take a few refresher sessions.

"At least this time you'll be able to drive the Olds."

Alex had no problem with the exam and was issued a temporary permit. He could take Eleanor out that night!

Peter tossed him the keys, "Here you go Son."

Victoria was somewhat apprehensive – her little boy was not 12-years old anymore.

"Where are you going Alex?"

"Just to Dairy Queen for an ice cream cone, Mom."

"Okay Alex, but please be home by 10:00."

The summer passed quickly. He worked an irregular schedule and this interfered with any plans the family might have had for a week at the Birch Bend Cottages. Alex and Eleanor made full use the Olds: the movies, picnics at the Indian River Conservation Reserve, the Drive-In Movie Theater out Hwy 28 north of the Trent campus, swimming in the Otonabee River near the Scout Camp, and necking sessions at Armour Heights.

Peter remarked at the footprints on the car ceiling.

"Now Peter!" admonished Victoria.

Alex had wanted to go to Queen's since he was 11 years old. He wanted to play football for the Queen's Golden Gaels; and he wanted to be in Kingston, to be closer to Sandra. He had assumed she would be going to Queen's too.

He wrote to her as soon as he had his results, and asked her what courses she planned to take next year at Queen's.

He was very surprised when Sandra had decided to go to Nursing School at the Wellesley Hospital in Toronto.

Eleanor opted for the University of Toronto, in Physiotherapy.

KINGSTON, 1969 – 1973

– Doug Jordan –

33. The Road to Queen's

THE DRIVE ALONG HIGHWAY 401 SEEMED INTERMINABLE, and then the long S bend descending the limestone escarpment to cross the Collins Creek and marshes at the outskirts of Kingston was like a descent into purgatory.

Alex was surprised at his trepidation and sense of foreboding. He had been contemplating going to Queen's University since Grade 5 or 6; he knew the campus well, having visited his dad's office there many times; and he knew Kingston well, having lived in Kingston as a little kid and then on nearby Amherst Island. He had just turned 19 ten days previously and he was feeling rather grown up. Living away from home was what he wanted, the logical next step to becoming an adult, almost on his own. So why was he feeling so apprehensive now?

Sunday morning the week after Labour Day, they had packed the trunk of Peter's Oldsmobile with suitcases and boxes of all the things they thought Alex would need living at the men's residences at Queen's. Even that expression, men's residences, created mixed feelings in Alex' mind. He must be a man now, not a boy, but he didn't feel like he was a man yet. He was leaving home for the first time, and he was ready, but he didn't feel ready. He was beginning to think this was a mistake; maybe it might have been better if he had decided to go to Trent after all and continue to live at home.

Car loaded, the family took their places in their usual seats. Oliver had the option of accompanying the family or staying home; he surprised Alex by saying yes to Kingston. Victoria had asked if Eleanor wanted to join them on the trip but Eleanor was off to enroll at the University of Toronto the same day. She and Alex had said their goodbyes to each other on Saturday night. They went to a movie at the Capitol Theatre but sat in silence all through it, their thoughts more on the morrow than on the screen, clutching hands more in desperation than affection. They parked at Armour Heights afterwards, one of a dozen other cars checking the view over the city. They made out frantically but weren't able to stave off curfew hour despite their efforts to shut out the inevitable goodbyes. Eleanor was crying as she opened the side-door of her parent's house, and a last furtive glance at Alex in the driveway. Alex found himself more than a little upset as he drove the family Oldsmobile home.

Peter asked if Alex would like to drive to Kingston, but Alex declined. He was in no mood to concentrate on his driving, brooding instead about this major step in his life.

Peter took the most direct route he could, choosing to get his son to Kingston as quickly as possible and not extend the anguish longer than necessary by taking the scenic back roads. There would be other times for that. He drove down Hwy 28 from Peterborough to Port Hope, and then turned east on the 401 expressway to Kingston. As they passed by Cobourg Alex wondered if Hugh was on the road to Queen's at that time too. At least he had that to look forward to when he got settled in Leonard Hall.

After Cobourg they passed signs for Brighton, then Trenton and Belleville, their final destination drawing ineluctably closer. Then Napanee. Thoughts of his short time at Napanee District High School flooded his mind, though not with much fondness.

Next came the exit for Millhaven and the ferry to Amherst Island, then Odessa and the Road to Amherstview. Alex' mind shifted to thoughts of Sandra; imagined her parents packing her up to go to Toronto. Peter caught a glimpse of Alex in his mirror peering out the window at the passing exit.

"Did you want to detour to Millhaven for a quick tour of Amherst Island, Son?" Peter's eyes twinkled in the mirror but found no humour in his son's gloomy visage.

Startled, Alex quickly said, "No, Dad. No time for that now.

"Maybe I can visit the island one weekend when I'm at Queen's."

Victoria glanced at her husband. They both had an idea what was on Alex' mind.

And then they reached the long sweeping descent into Kingston. Alex' apprehension and excitement increased. It seemed to Peter Victoria's aspect had darkened some too. Even Dr. Jorgenson felt the significance of this turning point in his son's life, and by extension his own. He was determined not to make light of it, but equally, he didn't want this parting to be sorrowful.

— Alex' Choice —

Too soon they came to the Division Street Exit and turned off the expressway. The drive through Kingston's outskirts, light industrial sectors, through residential areas, past car dealerships, and corner stores, seemed interminable. When they reached the intersection with Princess Street they knew they were only a few blocks from Queen's campus. They turned right on Union Street. The street was crawling with students and families and cars. All in the Olds but Peter scanned the street taking in the sight of the old familiar buildings that lined the street. Peter was vigilantly avoiding pedestrians.

"There's your old office building, Dad!" hollered Oliver, excitedly.

"Well, no, Oliver, that's Miller Hall, for mining engineering. The Old Arts Building where my office was is a few blocks south of here. These old limestone buildings all look the same."

"Did you want me to drive by it?"

"Is that really necessary Peter?" Victoria offered, "I'm sure Alex just wants to get to his residence and get unpacked."

"No, that's okay Mom," said Alex, "we can drive by if Oliver wants."

Peter turned south from Union Street onto University Avenue, with its boulevard of towering and leafy elm trees. They came to the lane at Kingston Hall – the 'New Arts' Building – but it was barricaded to vehicle traffic.

"I guess we can't get there today, Oliver. Maybe another time."

Instead, he turned right onto Queen's Crescent, past Ban Righ Hall, then the circular golden physics building, Stirling Hall, on the left, and the giant women's residence, Victoria Hall, on the right.

"Hey Mom, there's your building," laughed Oliver.

And then it was Leonard Hall.

Peter drove past the entrance of Leonard Hall looking for a place to park the car so as to be able to unload its cargo. But there were dozens of other families all seeking the same end. He drove around the block a few times until a spot finally opened up.

They unloaded the car and carried bags and boxes into the lobby of Leonard Hall. The lobby was swarming with families and nervous frosh all waiting their turn to use the elevator. Alex had been assigned a single room on 2nd Floor East, looking south over the quad and out to Lake Ontario. They used the stairs.

"This is a very nice room, Alex. You have a desk and chair and overhead lamp, and bookcase for your books; oh, and a nice bulletin board."

Oliver jumped on the single bed and stretched out. "Hey, this is a bit hard."

Just then a young man's head appeared at the open door.

"Hello", he said, "you must be Alex.

"I'm Norm Vanstone, the Floor Senior on this wing. My room is at the end of the hall, just a few doors down from you."

Peter extended his hand. "Hello, I'm Doctor Jorgenson. This is Victoria, Alex' mother,

"and this is Oliver."

Oliver quickly changed from his prone position to sitting on the side of the bed.

"Well, nice to meet you all."

"What is your role as Floor Senior, Norm?" asked Peter.

"There's a Floor Senior on each floor in both wings of the Residence; all of us are upper classmen – I'm going in to third year Physics, and this is also my third year in Leonard Hall. Our job is to make sure everyone on his floor feels welcome, gets along and pays attention to the Residence regulations so everybody can devote their time to their studies.

"There are eight single rooms and four doubles in each wing, sixteen men altogether per wing."

"Whew, that's a lot of testosterone," Peter remarked. Victoria threw him an admonishing look.

"Warden Edwards," Norm continued, "is Proctor for Leonard Hall; he has his own rooms on the first floor with his wife. She's the only woman in the Men's Residence, except for the cafeteria staff of course.

"Warden Edwards expects good behaviour here in Leonard Hall so that students can study without disturbance. But it's not all work though. The idea is that residents are able to make friends and have social activities to fully enjoy their experience at Queen's.

"Have you had a chance to tour around the residence yet? We're lucky that the cafeteria for the Men's Residences is located

— Alex' Choice —

on the lower ground floor of Leonard Hall; the men in the other residences have to walk across the quad to get here which isn't pleasant in January when the wind and sleet is blowing in from the Lake. There's breakfast, lunch and dinner each day except Sunday when there's only brunch from 10:00 till 2:00. There's also bread and butter and such left out in the evening for snack. Guys often bring fruit and bread back to their rooms after dinner.

"And there's the tv room in the basement level and the lounge, plus the pay phones. There's a residence library on the first floor – some guys especially in the double rooms prefer to study away from their roommate."

"So, that's about it. If you have any more questions just bang on my door or look for me around the halls. I've got more incoming residents to greet today."

Norm waved goodbye and returned to his room.

Peter remarked, "He seems a pleasant enough fellow, though a bit serious."

Victoria helped Alex unpack his things, underwear and pyjamas for his dresser, shirts and pants hung in the closet. Alex unpacked his books and papers and put them on his bookshelves. He pinned a calendar to the bulletin board as well as the framed photograph of Sandra.

"Did you leave the Sandra Dee poster at home?" Peter quipped.

Peter glanced at Victoria with the unspoken question. Victoria scowled gently in reply and directed the question to Alex.

"Don't you have a photo of Eleanor, Alex?"

"No Mom, she never gave me one."

Finished unpacking, the family took a tour of the whole residence. It was pretty much as Norm had described it. Alex was most impressed with the cafeteria, so much bigger than the one at Adam Scott, a great modern hall with a long rail for trays to parade past the staff dispensing food.

"I think we should get something to eat before we get on the road for Peterborough," Peter announced. "What do you say we visit The Fontainebleau for a nice lunch."

"Oh, that would be nice, Peter," Victoria said. "You remember Oliver, we went to that fancy restaurant once when we lived on Amherst Island."

"Yeah, and Alex took Sandra to see Lawrence of Arabia at the movies."

Victoria glanced at Alex but there was no reaction to Oliver's remark.

"What do you say, Alex?"

"Sure, all right," Alex replied, glumly.

They drove downtown Princess Street, parked the car and took the steep stairs to the second-floor restaurant, formally laid out with little table lamps and linen tablecloths.

Lunch was a quiet affair, everyone feeling the weight of the passing minutes before they had to leave Alex and go home to Peterborough.

They drove back to Leonard Hall and said their goodbyes on the sidewalk. Victoria kissed her son on the cheek; Peter shook hands with him. Victoria's eyes filled with tears as she settled herself into the front seat; Peter kept his eyes front not wanting to betray his own emotions. Oliver was oblivious until the car pulled away from the curb; he looked out the rear window to see Alex standing at the sidewalk waving forlornly. Oliver waved back, suddenly realizing things would never be the same.

34. Orientation

FROSH WEEK WAS FIVE DAYS devoted to administrative and social activities aimed at helping the incoming freshmen get oriented and integrated into life at Queen's. Queen's University didn't allow fraternities and sororities and depended on the men's and women's residences to provide a certain amount of social cohesion for the first-year students. But not all new students were able to be accommodated in the residences and few upper classmen and women; instead they had to find accommodation in the many apartments and houses in the blocks near and around the campus. To inculcate school spirit the University oriented student identity around their graduating year. Alex was registered as Arts '73, the year expected to complete his four-year Bachelor of Arts degree. The other classes were Eng. '73, Meds '75 (Premeds plus Medicine was six years), and Commerce '73. The classes one year ahead of the Frosh were responsible for organizing the social events for the week: open house in the coffee shop and cafeteria in The Students Union Building; a giant scavenger hunt that sent teams of three or four all over Kingston looking for obscure items. Alex had lived in Kingston the first eleven years of his life and he figured he knew the town pretty well. It didn't occur to him this event was designed to get students from out-of-town familiar with the host city. The week culminated in a Golden Gaels Football exhibition game at Richardson Stadium and a big dance in the gym in the evening.

On the Tuesday of Frosh Week, Alex opened a Kingston bank account. He soon discovered all the national banks had branches in downtown Kingston, none on campus; all were an eight- or ten- block-walk from the campus. His bank in Peterborough was the Toronto-Dominion Bank so he naturally opened a TD account in Kingston. That decided, he transferred his earnings from his summer job and deposited a cheque from his dad; he ordered a book of cheques. One of these was needed for the next day to pay his fees and purchase books and supplies.

The Second-Year class reps also provided scholastic mentoring for the incoming class. Reps were paired with small groups of first-year men and women to help them select their courses, organize their class schedule and get them fully registered with Administration. This was an important function for Arts Frosh who had a lot of decisions to make in choosing courses from a thick syllabus of courses. Freshmen Arts had to decide their major course of study, with whatever implications that might have for their long-term career preferences, and for their upper year courses requiring earlier year pre-requisites. For Frosh in the other faculties – Engineering, Commerce and Meds – it was a lot simpler… they had few choices and the only challenge was to find the buildings and classrooms where their courses would be taught.

Courses selected, the next step was buying the required textbooks. Alex found the melee of kids who flooded into of the Clark Hall bookstore intimidating. He also felt a strange paradox of feelings about his purchases: pride in his new collection of thick and dense textbooks and other readings, and binders and supplies, mixed with alarm at the cost of the collection, well over $230. His big bank account the day before had shrunk drastically almost overnight.

The pre-game party began early Saturday morning, though it was evident that some students had partied all night. Alex was surprised at the stock of beer and booze that had magically appeared in the rooms; they had an early lunch in the cafeteria and marched *en masse* the few short blocks to the North gate at venerable Richardson Stadium. The game took on a whole new meaning for Alex because now he sat on the students' side of the stadium with his Freshman Arts class, not on the Alumni and Faculty side as he had when his dad had taken him to games as a kid.

And it became a dawning crisis in his mind that the football team was on the field and he was sitting in the stands. He now realized that he should have checked out the team a lot earlier.

Monday morning brought the first day of classes and that afternoon he resolved to seek out the Golden Gaels football coach. He had been thinking about that all Frosh Week, but was feeling swept away with all the demands and newness of his first week; at least, that's what he told himself.

— Alex' Choice —

He couldn't shake the feeling that he was nervous about trying out for the Gaels, that old feeling of doubt and fear crowding his mind. He knew all week there was some sort of activity going on at Richardson Stadium on Union Street but he couldn't bring himself to investigate further. He had a lot to do that frosh week; but he couldn't deny it to himself – he was procrastinating.

As he entered the gates to Richardson Stadium he saw several dozen men in football gear already on the field. He asked someone where he could find Coach Tindall and was directed to offices near the Men's locker room under the main stands.

Frank Tindall was a grizzled old veteran coach of the Queen's Golden Gaels football team, already a living legend. Alex was extremely nervous to approach this patriarch, but Mr. Tindal warmly greeted him.

"What can I do for you son?"

"I'd like to try out for the football team, sir."

"Oh?"

"What's your name, son?"

"Alex Jorgenson, sir."

Coach Tindal looked him over and then said, "Are you any relation to Dr. Peter Jorgenson? He was a professor of psychology here at Queen's a few years ago. Great supporter of Queen's football."

"Yessir, he's, my father."

Coach Tindall studied him for a while longer.

"What position do you play, Alex?"

"I'm a halfback sir."

"Oh, that makes sense, you're not really big enough to be a lineman, or even a fullback. You must be fast."

"I guess so sir."

"Where did you play football last year, son?"

"I played for the Adam Scott Senior Lions, sir. In Peterborough,"

"Who was your coach?"

"My coach was Charlie Ward, sir."

"Well, I never heard from Coach Ward last June when we were canvasing high schools for players. Did Mr. Ward not tell

213

you you needed to get in touch with Queen's Football way last spring?"

"No sir."

"Well son, you should have been here two weeks ago."

"I didn't know sir." Alex face was pale and he could feel his heart racing. Why didn't Mr. Ward tell him about this, or even his dad? He sensed that things were coming apart.

"I'm sorry son, all the boys have been at camp now for two weeks. The roster is full, the starters have been picked and the cuts made. Our first league game is Saturday.

"I'm afraid it's too late for you to join the team this year.

"Tell you what, there's a winter try-out camp in February in the gym. You sign up for that and we'll see about next year."

"Yessir, I'll do that." But Alex was shattered.

His walk back to Leonard Hall was a very slow march.

Alex soon settled into a routine at Queen's. He had five first year courses: Introduction to Politics, Economics 010, Sociology 080, Economic Geography 040, and English 010. Because of his interest in history, he tilted towards the social sciences, though curiously he didn't take a history course. Even though he loved chemistry and science in general, he figured he struggled too much with Algebra and Trig to entertain seriously a degree in Natural Science. He had some notion he might like to be a lawyer and economics and politics seemed more apt to him. His parents didn't object – though Victoria wondered why he wasn't taking psychology like his dad. Peter always said it didn't really matter what sort of degree one took, so long as one found it interesting and provoked critical thinking.

He was up at 7:00 and down for breakfast in the Leonard Hall cafeteria by 7:45, and walking to his first class at Dunning Hall – Political Science, 9:00 a.m., Mondays, Wednesdays and Fridays,. This was followed by lectures at 10:00 and 11:00 scattered around campus; sometimes the ten minutes between classes cut it close. He'd be back at Leonard Hall for lunch and spend the afternoon, most days, studying and reading in his room. Tuesdays and Thursdays he had only two courses, each two ninety-minute classes – Economic Geography mornings at Ontario Hall and afternoons, English at The New Arts Building.

— Alex' Choice —

He made few friends; his only companions were a couple of guys who lived on his floor. There were a few other Adam Scott graduates in the Residences but he wasn't close to any of them.

He did meet up with Hugh in Frosh Week. They were delighted to see each other again and they spent a couple of hours lounging on the sunny lawns along University Avenue, chatting about their plans and commenting on the women parading up and down the boulevard in groups of three or five. They promised each other they would make plans to do things together, but Hugh was Commerce '73, not Arts – he thought maybe he would go into banking like his father – and a packed course curriculum, so fewer opportunities for socializing than they expected. The Commerce Faculty was very much smaller than the Arts faculty with small classes of less than 100 students, mostly held in small classrooms in Dunning Hall, and while Alex' Poli/Sci class was held in the large lecture theatre in Dunning, Corry Auditorium, the rest of his classes were scattered around the campus.

Hugh roomed in Morris Hall of the Men's Residences, and even though Leonard Hall was less than 100 yards removed, somehow, to Alex, Morris Hall seemed distant and foreign at the far end of the Quad closest to the cold shores of Lake Ontario. It had the reputation of the Party Hall in the Men's Residences. They met up for breakfast and dinner from time to time, more by accident than by plan; there were no telephones in the rooms of the Residences and so ease of communications was seriously hampered. Alex had walked down to Morris Hall a few times to call on Hugh but each time Hugh had been somewhere else and Alex walked back to Leonard Hall feeling somehow defeated.

Hugh went home to Cobourg most weekends. It was convenient for him because it was only an hour and a half by train. Hugh left plenty of hints he had a honey in Cobourg.

It was not so convenient for Alex to get back to Peterborough. He could take the train to Cobourg, or maybe Port Hope, but someone from home would have to come and pick him up and drive him to Peterborough, and return Sundays. Alex' best option was to take a taxi from Queen's to the 401 interchange at Division Street and hitchhike to Port Hope then on to Peterborough on Hwy 28.

Alex wrote a long letter to Eleanor, telling her all about his first week at Queen's – though not of his distress of his disappointment about the Golden Gaels football team; he told her he missed her and reminisced about their summer romance. He asked how her first week at the U. of T. went. But he didn't mail the letter. He didn't have her address in Toronto and he was unsure about mailing it to her parents' house. Instead he phoned the Tysdale residence in Peterborough and asked Mrs. Tysdale for Eleanor's phone number in Toronto. He saved quarters for the payphone in the basement of Leonard Hall and on a Tuesday evening, placed the call. Five minutes and his stock of coins passed quickly but long enough for him to get her mailing address. She told him she would be home for their graduation and was looking forward to seeing him. She said she had a new dress.

He wrote a similar letter to Sandra. They had been exchanging letters for five years and so he had no compunction about mailing it to the Manse at St. Paul's on Amherst Island. He confessed to her his disappointment in not being on the Golden Gaels football team. He asked her when she would be home to visit her family.

35. Graduation Weekend.

AT THE END OF SEPTEMBER ADAM SCOTT Collegiate and Vocational Institute held its Graduation Ceremonies for the graduating classes of the previous June. The event was scheduled for Friday evening, with a dance after. Alex skipped his Friday classes to get an early start hitchhiking home to Peterborough.

It was an exciting time for the returning graduating class of 1965. So much had changed since only four months ago with kids scattered into the next phases of their lives, young adults eager for new experiences, or maybe a little nervous.

Alex was dressed in his new sports jacket and slacks, white shirt and a sharp tie borrowed from his dad. His mother complimented her smart-looking son. Alex was hoping Eleanor would think so too.

Alex had proven himself a strong student through his high school years, but Grade XIII had been challenging for him. He may have finished first graduating Grade 8 from tiny Amherst Island Public School but being first from 100 kids in Grade XIII at Adam Scott CVI, Peterborough, was another matter. He had found there were lots of kids smarter than him. He was competitive, and worked hard but there was always someone ahead of him. He wasn't sure where he stood in the overall class but he was a bit chagrinned he didn't win the History Prize – it went to the Valedictorian (who also won the prize in Latin!) – nor in Chemistry, it went to the second scholar in the class. Seemed unfair somehow; it felt a lot like his track and field career – a lot of second place ribbons. But overall, he was proud of his achievement and happy that his parents were happy with him.

He was looking forward to the dance afterwards. He had already got a glimpse of Eleanor during the graduation ceremonies. She was wearing a white jacket over a very striking crimson dress, knee length with full skirt and a lowcut bodice. She threw him a beaming smile; he hoped his mouth was not still gaping as he smiled back at her.

After the ceremony Peter tossed the car keys to Alex.

"It's a nice evening. Your mother and I can walk home but you might need the car after the dance."

"Thanks Dad."

The gym was cleared away of chairs and quickly converted into a dance hall; a fine local rock and roll band filled the air with sound.

Eleanor practically leaped on Alex, wrapped her arms around his neck and pressed her body into his, forcing a big hug on him. Surprised and a bit confused, Alex put his arms around her waist but looked nervously around to see if others were watching. They were.

Eleanor dragged him onto the dance floor and even though it was a fast tune she chose to wrap her arms around his neck once more and oblige him to hold her close in that classic clutch mode, two arms around her waist.

She whispered loudly in his ear to be heard over the band, "I've really missed you, Alex."

"Me too," Alex felt obliged to reply, and he meant it, but he felt too exposed; and rather rushed. Besides, he wanted to visit with some of his other classmates and football team mates as well.

After the third straight turn on the dance floor Alex pulled Eleanor over to the side tables and said, "It's okay with me if you visit with some of your old friends. I want to talk to a few people from our class too."

Eleanor nodded in agreement but there was a small hurt smile on her face as she did so.

He walked over to the Valedictorian and congratulated him on his triumph. John was gracious in his thanks, but then Alex couldn't resist asking him what his mark in history was.

"Ninety," John replied. "What did you get?"

"Eighty-eight," replied Alex.

"Wow, you might have beat me for the history prize if you hadn't answered that essay question critiquing William Lyon McKenzie King's time as Prime Minister."

"Yeah, maybe, but I think I was right, and I made a good argument." John smiled good-naturedly and Alex returned the smile.

"See on campus sometime John," he said, but they weren't close friends and it wasn't likely they'd get together much.

Next up was Peter Fletcher, the Chemistry Prize winner with a mark of 89.

— Alex' Choice —

"Gee, Alex, if you got 86 you must have come second because everyone I've talked to found the chemistry exam hard."

The Offensive Guard from the Senior Lions football team and a couple of other Lions swarmed him, clapping him on his back.

"Hey, Alex, are you playing for Queen's this year?" Reg enthused.

Glumly Alex replied, no, he wasn't, and his tone signaled he didn't want to talk about it.

"Geez Flash, that's too bad. Queen's has certainly missed out."

Just then, Cathy Baird tapped Alex on the shoulder.

"Hey Alex, dance with me?" she asked, more of a gentle command than a question.

Alex eyes opened wide as Cathy took his hand and walked him on to the dance floor. It was a slow dance so Alex carefully placed his right hand on Cathy's waist and held her right hand in his left, she put her hand on his shoulder; as they took a few waltz-like steps around the floor, she cocked her head and gave him an appreciative smile.

"Where did you learn to do the waltz, Alex?"

"My mom taught me."

"That's nice."

"You know Alex, you've been in my home room every year. I'm going to miss seeing you in class."

Alex was astounded to hear her report this. He never imagined she had paid any attention.

"Where are you going to school this year, Cathy?" He already knew the answer but he was looking for a conversation starter.

"I'm at Western, taking psychology."

"Oh," but Alex didn't know what to say next.

"Just like your father," she continued with a laugh.

"What are you doing after the dance, Alex? Want to go with me and some friends downtown for Chinese Food?"

"Gee, I don't know Cathy. I'm sort of with Eleanor, and she might want to do something else."

Cathy looked over to the side tables and caught Eleanor's eye firing daggers her way.

"Oh, I see," Cathy replied, "maybe another time." But they both knew there probably would never be another time.

"You better go and rescue her Alex, before she gets too upset."

The music ended and they held each other's eye for a minute.

"See you, Cathy." He turned from her and walked over to Eleanor waiting for him at the table. She reached for Alex hand and marched him right back on the dance floor.

"So, are you going to be seeing Cathy now?" she said, a bit accusatorily.

"No, I don't think so Eleanor. I think that was a goodbye from our five years as classmates."

Eleanor relaxed and stepped closer to Alex, nuzzled his neck with her lips.

Alex said, "She asked if we'd like to join her and her friends for Chinese food afterwards."

"I'd rather go to Armour Heights, Alex."

She turned in his arms deliberately brushing her breasts against his arm.

He became very conscious of the nearness of her. She pulled her hips against his as the dance became slow. Alarmingly, he could feel his member growing involuntarily in his pants. No doubt she could feel it too.

"Maybe we should leave now," she said in a low husky voice.

Alex felt a mixture of excitement and reluctance but nodded.

He took her hand and escorted her from the gym to the parking lot. As they reached his dad's car, he walked her around to the passenger side door, opened it to let her in. She turned to him and pulled him close, kissed him with intensity; she opened her lips and probed his for his tongue.

Alex returned the kiss but at the same time was feeling nervous that others might see them.

He released her, and settled her into the seat. He couldn't help noticing the ample cleavage she was revealing. She caught his eye and smiled.

Alex got into the driver's seat as Eleanor shifted along the bench seat to be close to him. She pressed her hip against his, her head on his shoulder and her hand on his thigh. They made the ten-minute drive to Armour Heights in silence, their minds filled with thoughts of what might lie ahead. This was a place they knew well from their summer of dating but somehow the passion now was a lot hotter. Maybe it was the month of absence.

Parked at a private spot at the lookout, Alex turned to her, unsure of what he should do next. Their summer make-out sessions were more mechanical than emotional, as if they were rehearsing for some future life experience. This felt different somehow. Eleanor seemed much more certain of what she wanted. She faced Alex and put her hand around his neck and pulled his lips to hers; they began necking in that familiar way, but her tongue was way more active than he remembered from the summer. He liked it but was a bit unnerved. She kicked off her shoes and pushed up her billowing skirts, then threw one leg across Alex hips. He held her hip with his left hand and soon was stroking up and down her side, feeling her ribs through the fabric of her dress, and the skin of her back.

His hand lurked at the bottom of her breast, she made no move to stop him. His hand moved up to cup her breast feeling the lace of her dress. But Eleanor took Alex' hand in hers and slipped it inside her dress to hold her bare breast. Alex was on high alert now. He palmed her breast and felt her nipple harden as they kissed and necked with increasing heat.

He felt her hand on his thigh move, stroking and petting the bulge of him in his pants.

Now she had both hands at his pants and tried to grasp his fly and pull the zipper down.

Alex was fully aroused, but increasingly alarmed now.

He removed his hand from her breast and pulled himself back from her just enough to bring himself out of reach of her hands.

"What's wrong Alex? Don't you want me?"

"You know I do, Eleanor, but I think we need to slow down a bit."

She withdrew from him and proceeded to rearrange the top of her dress. Alex did up his fly.

Eleanor was plainly upset and frustrated.

"Okay, I guess you better take me home."

"Sorry Eleanor."

Alex hardly slept a wink that night and when he did finally relax it was almost dawn; he slept in till noon.

"What's going on with Alex, do you think Peter?"

"I think he had a pretty full evening Victoria and I'm sure he's exhausted."

Alex called Eleanor that afternoon and asked if she wanted to go out with him that evening; her voice was a bit clipped; she said she thought she should spend the evening visiting with her family. Alex wasn't quite sure where things now stood.

"See you at Thanksgiving then, Eleanor?'

"Sure. Alex, that will be great."

Peter drove Alex to Cobourg Sunday afternoon for him to catch the train back to Kingston. On the way home Victoria said to her husband, "Peter, do you think it's time for you to have a talk with Alex about sexuality. He seems pretty involved with Eleanor, and I'm not sure what is going on with Sandra."

"I already had 'the talk' with Alex when he was twelve Victoria," he replied with a twinkle.

"You know perfectly well Professor of Psychology that talk may have been efficacious when he was 12 but he's 19 now."

"Efficacious?" Peter chucked, "now that's a pretty big word, talking about sex."

"Peter, I'm serious.

"Do you think Alex is sexually active now?"

"I don't know Victoria, probably not. But Eleanor seems a sexy, confident young woman, and Sandra used to be rather precocious though I don't know what's the state of the union now, pardon the pun."

He waited for Victoria to respond but nothing was forthcoming.

"Okay, I'll talk to him about oxytocin and commitment, and respecting the girls and his own self-worth."

"And contraception!"

"Yes, and contraception."

Back in Kingston Alex wrote Eleanor a long letter, telling her how exciting it was to be with her and looking forward to seeing her in two weeks, but he also hinted that he thought they

Alex' Choice

might have gotten a bit carried away and maybe they needed to slow down.

Still struggling with the meaning of Eleanor in his life he suddenly felt compelled to write Sandra and asked her whether she would be home on Amherst Island next weekend. He would really like to see her. He said he could take a taxi from Leonard Hall to the ferry at Millhaven and he could walk up to her house.

He received a reply three days later from Sandra.

'I'm excited to see you Saturday. Plan on staying for dinner.'

They spent a sunny Fall day on the island, biking the backroads, throwing stones into the lake, walking amongst the maples and oaks of the cemetery, luxuriating in the Fall colours.

Dinner was an informal affair at the Farquharson's kitchen table, pot roast and vegetables, tea biscuits, apple pie for dessert.

Sandra stood with him on the back porch as her father got the car out of the garage. She kissed him goodnight.

"I had a lovely day, Alex," she said, smiling warmly.

The Reverend Farquharson drove him back to the ferry at 10:00. "Will we be seeing you again, Alex?"

"I hope so sir."

Alex took the ferry across to the mainland, studying the black water of the channel at night. He caught the waiting taxi back to Leonard Hall. His head was full of wonder at this magical day. It was just like old times, he and Sandra so naturally comfortable with each other.

"I suppose you will be home in Peterborough Thanksgiving Weekend," she had said.

"Yes Sandra, but I don't go home every weekend, it's too much trouble travelling, so only once a month. Maybe next time you come back to Amherst Island we can do this again."

"Sure Alex. I don't come home every weekend either. How about the second weekend after Thanksgiving. Maybe I could come into Kingston and we could go to the Queen's game."

"Great idea Sandra."

And so began Alex' double life. Once a month home to Peterborough to see his family and the alluring Eleanor, and once a month to heavenly Amherst Island to spend time with the divine Miss Farquharson.

36. First Year Queen's

Alex thumbed his way home for Thanksgiving weekend. Hitch-hiking always seemed so forlorn to Alex, standing on the side of the busy highway with his thumb out, of a hot or dreary Friday afternoon. Good thing his classes were over by noon on Fridays but he still had to go back to his Residence, get some lunch and pack a bag for the weekend; by the time his taxi had reached his drop-off at the 401 it was past 2:00 p.m. and he still faced 3 or 4 hours of travel time before he got home, if he was lucky. He drew little comfort from the dozens of other students using the same means to escape Kingston on the weekends. He often waited 40 minutes or more before a car or truck would stop to pick him up. There was a sort of informal queue of student hobos strung out along the expressway, waiting their turn to be picked up by some generous and thoughtful driver. Alex soon learned you didn't doddle when a car pulled over; he also noticed that the few girls who hitch-hiked didn't have to wait as long as the fellows.

Some students had home-made signs announcing their destination: Oshawa, Pickering, Toronto. Alex never got around to making his own sign, Peterborough – he figured it unlikely that anyone driving along the 401 west actually had Peterborough as their final destination. He'd often have to make two or three stops before he could be let out at Port Hope and then hitch a ride north on Highway 28 to Peterborough. But even when he reached the city limits, he still had to make it across town to the North End. Sometimes the driver was going right through Peterborough on 28 on his way to one of the Kawartha Lakes north of the city. He would be dropped off at the corner of Water Street and Marina Blvd and he could easily walk the rest of the way home from there. At other times the driver was continuing on Highway 7 to Lindsay so he would be dropped off at the western outskirts of Peterborough. He'd look for a phone booth and call home for Peter to come and pick him up; he always kept a few quarters in his pocket for the pay phone. The usual 2½ hour drive from Kingston to Peterborough often took as long as five hours.

— Alex' Choice —

Victoria fretted about Alex' mode of travel each time he made the trip, but Peter assured her there was nothing to worry about; he had hitch-hiked himself many times in his undergraduate days. It was character building, he said. Victoria scowled.

Traffic Friday of Thanksgiving Weekend was heavy on the 401 but this meant the rides were more frequent. He was home in Peterborough in time for the Jorgenson's usual supper hour, 5:00 o'clock.

As they sat around the supper table everyone was eager to hear Alex's stories of his first weeks at Queen's.

"Have you been to any Queen's football games, Alex?," Oliver wanted to know.

"Yeah, sure, Oliver, I don't miss a game. A bunch of the guys on my floor start celebrating around 10:00, and then we go to lunch at the caff and then walk over to Richardson Stadium."

"Celebrating? Alex? At 10 in the morning? The game doesn't start till 1:00." Oliver quizzed, puzzled.

"Well, you know, getting ready for the game."

"And do you and your friends throw up on the neighbourhood lawns?" Peter deadpanned.

"Peter!"

"I know, Victoria," Peter acknowledged, a big smile on his face, "but that used to really annoy you when we lived in Kingston."

Alex scowled but ignored his father's question.

"The stadium is packed, Oliver, and so we want to get there in good time to get a decent seat. You know how it is; Dad used to take us to games when we lived on Amherst Island, only it's different now because I'm a student and we all sit on the east side, not the faculty and alumni side when we were kids. There's maybe eight thousand students on the east side and another three or four thousand fans on the west side."

"Yeah, I remember," said Oliver.

Alex continued, "and when Queen's scores a touchdown the whole student body stands up and sings the 'Oil Thigh' anthem and do the can-can dance."

"Yeah, I remember," chirped Oliver.

225

"Those wood and metal bleachers shake and wave under the massed movement. It's amazing, though some of the girls scream and cry and climb down from the stands."

"And what version of the anthem do you sing?" Peter asked mischievously.

"What do you mean, Dad?"

"You know what I mean Alex. I may have been a faculty fogey, but I was also a Queen's undergrad once too.

"How do the words go again?"

"Ah Dad."

"Yeah Dad, sing the anthem," Oliver chirped.

"Okay, Alex, let's do it together."

"Sure Dad, but we're not going to do the dance."

So the two of them started to sing, pounding the table rhythmically with their fists. Victoria was alarmed. Oliver was excited.

Queen's College colours we are wearing once again,
Soiled as they are by the battle and the rain,
Yet another victory to wipe away the stain!
So, Boys, go in and win!

[Chorus:]

Oil thigh na Banrighinn a'Banrighinn gu brath!
Oil thigh na Banrighinn a'Banrighinn gu brath!
Oil thigh na Banrighinn a'Banrighinn gu brath!
Cha-gheill! Cha-gheill! Cha-gheill!

"What are those curious words, Dad?" Oliver wanted to know.

"They're Gaelic, Oliver. They mean: 'The university of the wife of the King forever'."

"That doesn't make any sense, Dad?"

— Alex' Choice —

"Well, actually it does, Oliver. Queen's was founded by Queen Victoria in 1841. Its full name is 'Queen's University, Kington', because there's also a 'Queen's University, Belfast'."

"In Ireland? Is that why it's Gaelic?"

"Well, no, Oliver, it's actually Scottish because it was first sponsored by the Presbyterian Church as a Theology College.

Oliver tired of this history lesson; Alex started to worry this would become another of the Professor's long lectures. As interesting and amusing as they often were, Alex had other plans for the evening.

Peter could read the tea leaves and left off his history lesson. But he wasn't quite ready to put aside his impishness.

"The students usually do a chant at the end of the anthem: 'What's the sport of Kings? Queens! Queens! Queens! Oil thigh na banrighinn, Cha-gheill! Cha-gheil! Cha-gheill; Oil thigh na banrighinn, Cha-gheill! Cha-gheil! Cha-gheill!'"

Victoria rolled her eyes, simultaneously amused and reproving of her husband's hijinks.

"So, Alex, shall we do the alternate words?" Peter invited.

Alex looked askance at his father, reluctant to continue but Peter was in full throat:

"Oil her thighs and ba…"

"Now, Peter, that's enough," interjected Victoria.

"Let's tidy up this kitchen and let Alex go visit Eleanor."

Alex borrowed his dad's car and drove over to the Tysdale's house. He sat with Eleanor and her parents in the living room, exchanging pleasantries, but since he and Eleanor appeared not to have any plans, Mrs. Tysdale asked if they'd like to play cards.

Eleanor raised her eyes in minor panic begging Alex to say something to get them out of this.

"I like playing euchre," Alex remarked. Eleanor stared at him in disbelief.

"Excellent," exclaimed Mrs. Tysdale, "Euchre is Mr. Tysdale and my favourite game. We play it with friends every other Friday night but as this is Thanksgiving weekend, we're not playing with them tonight.'

She bounced up from the salon chair and walked over to the hall closet.

"Okay, it'll only take a minute to set up the card table and chairs in the living room.

Alex teamed with Eleanor; Mr. and Mrs. Tysdale were long-time euchre partners. It quickly became apparent that Mr. Tysdale was a serious and deliberate player, but Mrs. Tysdale was very fast. Eleanor was cautious and less experienced. Mrs. Tysdale smiled at how fast Alex played his cards and scooped his tricks. He also moved quickly to gather up the cards after the fourth trick when one side had a trick and the other had won three. Mr. Tysdale preferred to play out the whole hand. Eleanor was never sure what was actually happening. She recovered her mood but longed to play footsies under the table with Alex, except her father's long legs were in the way.

After the rubber match, Mrs. Tysdale declared, "well Mr. Tysdale, I think it's time to go to roost and leave these kids some time to visit without having to entertain us old folks."

"Yes Mother," Mr. Tysdale acquiesced, "quite right."

"Eleanor, be sure to offer Alex some nice goodies."

They packed up the cards, broke down the card table and chairs, and put them away; the parents went off to bed.

Eleanor took Alex by the hand and guided him to the couch.

"That was so embarrassing," she exclaimed.

"No it wasn't, Eleanor. I thought it was kinda fun. Your mom is a fast player."

"Yes, she is. She's very competitive. She's good at everything she plays, bowling, scrabble, you name it."

"You're pretty fast too, Eleanor, except maybe in euchre."

She looked at him, somewhat askance.

"I mean, you are full of energy and take the initiative all the time."

Eleanor was quiet for a minute, not quite sure where this conversation was going.

Alex sensed the mood had shifted and wanted to recover it. He leaned in to kiss her and she warmly returned his kisses. But she didn't make any advances with her tongue.

Alex pulled away gently and said, "maybe it's time I went home. It's been a long day, hitchhiking from Kingston and all.

"Can I call on you tomorrow, Eleanor."

— Alex' Choice —

"Sure Alex, I have no other plans but on Sunday we are driving to Barrie to have Thanksgiving dinner with my mom's sister and my grandma and then they are driving me back to Toronto the next day."

"Oh," said Alex, taken a bit by surprise, but also, oddly relieved he didn't have to think up more plans for them for the weekend."

"The weather is supposed to be nice tomorrow, what do you say we go for a walk in Burnham Woods and then maybe you could come to dinner at my house?"

"That would be nice, Alex."

She kissed him warmly good night at the back door. Alex walked slowly to the car and drove slowly home, thinking, puzzled.

Saturday passed pleasantly. He and Eleanor walked the tree-covered paths of Burnham Woods along with dozens of other couples and families out to enjoy the warmth of a fading Fall day. Eleanor was neatly dressed in white – white runners, white slacks, white pullover that didn't disguise her figure; auburn hair and rosy skin, she was picture perfect for a luminescent Fall day. They held hands, engaged in a leaf fight, and laughed at the squirrels racing around the tree trunks guarding their territories from one another.

They had dinner in the dining room – roast beef. Peter and Victoria at the head and foot of the dining table. Oliver on one side against the buffet and hutch, Alex seated beside Eleanor who was toward Peter's end of the table.

"Turkey tomorrow night," remarked Victoria, "there's only so much turkey The Professor can tolerate."

Eleanor carried on polite conversation with Dr. and Mrs. Jorgenson, while discreetly holding Alex' hand under the table, and rubbing her leg against his. She also demonstrated that she had a healthy appetite for beef and Yorkshire pudding, and red wine; apple pie after. Oliver was well behaved – Victoria had refreshed his dining room manners for when they had guests.

They spent a gentle evening chatting in the living room while Peter enjoyed a glass of Sambuca.

"Would you like one, Eleanor? Alex shouldn't as he has to drive you home."

Eleanor accepted enthusiastically, looked Peter in the eye and clinked glasses with him. Victoria furrowed her brow slightly.

The evening passed convivially, Eleanor and Peter bantering throughout over a second glass of sambuca.

By 10:00 Eleanor began to give signs she was ready to leave. Flushed and glowing, Eleanor said her goodbyes to Alex' parents and took Alex' arm as he escorted her to the car. Alex settled her into the front passenger seat and she promptly scooched across the bench seat, awaiting Alex to get in the driver's side. She placed her hand on his thigh, but Alex didn't respond.

"Are you going to take me to Armour Heights now Alex?"

Always surprised by Eleanor's forwardness, Alex paused before answering.

"I don't know Eleanor. You have to get up early tomorrow with your family and drive to Barrie. Maybe I should just take you home."

Eleanor removed her hand from Alex' leg and pulled away from the middle of the bench seat.

Silence hung between them all the way home. He parked in her driveway. After another minute of silence, Eleanor shifted her body towards him and gave him a long meaningful kiss. She looked him in the eye, beseechingly, and said, "Oh, Alex, what am I going to do with you?"

Not knowing what she meant by that, Alex said nothing. Eleanor pulled away from him and opened the door, got out and climbed the walkway and porch stairs to the house. She turned to look back at him, sadly smiled at him, and went inside.

Thanksgiving Dinner Sunday was a family affair at the Jorgensons. The boys stuffed themselves with turkey and stuffing, mashed potatoes and gravy, peas and squash, until they could hardly move. Peter and Victoria shared a bottle of Pinot Noir, and included the boys, almost adults now. Yet they still found room for pumpkin pie and whipped cream. Peter was more measured in his consumption, claiming allergies to turkey and sage, and pumpkin spices. 'No wonder he's still so slim,' thought Victoria admiringly.

— Alex' Choice —

Peter drove Alex to Cobourg Monday for him to take the train back to Kingston. Alex settled into his studies in earnest following Thanksgiving weekend but Eleanor remained on his mind. He was in turmoil by feelings for her — attracted by the energy and raw sexuality of her, and at the same time, a bit intimidated by it too.

He wrote her a long letter trying to explain himself. She replied with understanding and asked him to meet her the following weekend in Peterborough.

A week later he hitch-hiked home on Friday afternoon and was soon out the door after dinner to see her. They visited for a while with her parents and then went for a Dairy Queen ice cream cone and a trip to Armour Hill. But there was awkwardness between them, the conversation Alex planned to have didn't happen.

He spent Saturday morning helping his mom with chores and the afternoon watching football on TV with his dad and Oliver. Dinner time came slowly but by 7:00 he borrowed Peter's car again and headed to Eleanor's house.

She greeted him enthusiastically at the door.

"Bye Mom, Alex and I are off to the movies and maybe something after. She winked at Alex, grabbed his hand and was out the door and climbing into the front seat before Alex could even get the door for her. She shifted over to the middle of the bench seat and held Alex' hand. They stood in line at the Paramount theatre waiting to buy tickets for the show. Seated in the dark she quickly reached for Alex' hand and pulled it into her lap. She pressed her leg against him; Alex was surprised when he felt her stockinged foot slipping off his loafers and peeling down his sock, teasing his foot.

They were slow to leave the theatre, groping under the seats for a missing loafer. They went to King Chow Chinese Restaurant for egg rolls, feelings of warmth filling them.

"Eleanor, what I said in my letter this week, I'm sorry if you were upset last time."

"Shhh, Alex," she said, "I know. We don't have to talk about it. I want us to have a close relationship but with you in Kingston and me in Toronto it's hard. It's like we have to start over every weekend.

"Please, let's go to Armour Heights."

Alex wasn't sure this was a satisfactory conclusion to what he had been thinking but his excitement to be with her pushed those doubts out of his mind.

They made out passionately till well past midnight, their hands very active and their loins aching, but they had come to know when to put on the brakes.

Sunday, they drove around the countryside comfortable again with each other.

Two weeks later he was back in Peterborough. He arrived home late Friday afternoon, kissed his mom, dropped his bag, and borrowed his dad's car to visit Eleanor for the evening. It was a repeat of the pattern from the previous weekend home: tension Friday Night, passionate make-out session Saturday, bitter-sweet separation Sunday.

"Now Alex," Victoria announced the second time this happened, "this is not a hotel. This is your family. You can't just come home, drop your bags and out the door again without even a 'how-do-you-do!' I've even held dinner for you instead of our usual 5:00 o'clock. Sit down here and have dinner with us. Then you can go and see Eleanor."

The frantic Fall continued apace: classes Monday to Friday, home to Peterborough every two or three weeks, alternate weekends visiting Sandra on Amherst Island. The whole time Alex felt continually conflicted. The ever-alluring Eleanor left his body wanting more of her, but Sandra was in his head.

By December and the looming mid-term exams, trips home were put on pause. The December mid-term exams were held in the grand auditorium of Grant Hall, or in the gymnasium. Alex could now see the value of the Grade XIII departmental exams in the Adam Scott gym – he was prepared for this formality and wasn't intimidated, much. His final exam was Friday the 19th. He visited Sandra on Amherst Island the next day. He gave her a set of cultured pearl earrings for Christmas. The Reverend and Mrs. Farquharson exchanged glances.

The next day he took the train to Port Hope; Peter met him there and drove Alex home for the holidays. Small talk and a comfortable silence carried them along.

— Alex' Choice —

The Christmas break passed swiftly. The Tysdales were in Florida for the week. The Jorgensons basked in the gentle joy of their family traditions at home. Victoria was grateful to have her son home for the holidays. She remarked that at least this year Alex didn't have pneumonia. Alex wrote long letters to Sandra.

Everybody helped with clean-up after the Christmas feast; Victoria washed and the boys dried the pile of plates and pots.

Chores done, Victoria and Oliver repaired to the living room to watch television.

Peter said, "Alex, why don't you join me in my study and we'll have some sambuca. You missed out last Thanksgiving when Eleanor was here."

Alex was a bit puzzled at this invite; Victoria glanced over at Peter with a question on her mind.

Alex and Peter settled into their leather chairs, glasses of warmed sambuca in hand.

"I like to crunch on the coffee beans at the end." said Peter.

Alex tried that but didn't like the gritty texture in his teeth.

"Another?" asked Peter.

"Okay Dad, sure, but no coffee beans in mine," said Alex.

After a moment of comfortable silence, Peter surprised Alex with, "How are things with you and Eleanor?"

"What do you mean Dad?" replied Alex guardedly. Is this why his father had asked him to join him in the study?

"I mean, you spend a lot of time with her and I get the feeling she's really interested in you. She seems a young woman who knows what she wants."

"Yeah, I guess" replied Alex.

"Really, Alex, I shall remind you that I was 19 once and had my challenges trying to figure out what women want – still trying actually – and I want to offer you any advice I can."

There was a gentle pause in the conversation as they savoured their sambuca, Alex worrying his next remark.

"Yeah, well, I like Eleanor, but I get confused by her sometimes. I have a hard time knowing what is expected of me. But you're a psychologist, Dad. What do you think?"

Peter shrugged. He remarked,

"And did I understand your mother right that you're seeing Sandra again?"

"Yeah, I've visited her a few times on Amherst Island, and last week before I came home."

"So you've got two girlfriends. You dog you," Peter quipped good-naturedly.

"It's not like that, Dad. Sandra and I are just friends."

Peter raised an eye-brow, but said only,

"That can be confusing. Especially since most women won't tell you exactly what they are thinking about."

"Yeah."

Another pause.

"I'm pretty sure I know what Eleanor wants, but I don't know what Sandra wants."

"Oh?"

"Yeah, Eleanor wants to be a physiotherapist, and travel in Europe, and I don't know what else. And she wants to get married."

"To you?"

"I guess."

"And what do you want?"

"I don't know Dad. I suppose I'll get married, but not yet anyway."

"To Eleanor?"

"I don't know Dad."

"Are you having sex with Eleanor now?"

"Geez, Dad!"

"Well, are you? It's important that you take precautions if you are, or are planning on it."

Alex studied his shoes.

"The thing is, Alex, when you're making out with a girl, and it's getting hot and heavy, sometimes it's pretty hard to stop. And if you don't have a condom with you, that can lead to trouble."

"But isn't it the girl's responsibility to put on the brakes?"

"Well, maybe, Son. Lord knows girls are told all the time to be careful; 'wait until marriage', they're told. They've all heard the warnings about not getting pregnant; but you know, Alex, boys have responsibility too. And, generally speaking, girls want sex just as much as most guys. So when the passions are up, she may not be able to stop any more than you."

"Yeah. I get it. Sometimes I worry Eleanor is too much for me. Sometimes when we're making out on Armour Hill, she gets really physical. And I seem to be the one who has to slow things down."

Peter listened carefully, and perhaps a little wistfully, remembering when he was nineteen, not so long ago.

"I'd like to go further," Alex continued, "but I remember what you told me back when I was twelve and we had the talk,"

"Oh?"

"Yeah, you said that as boys and girls get older their bodies may be more in charge than their minds but it's important that as guys, we need to respect the girl's feelings and circumstances."

"That's right son. It takes two to tango and both of you have to be thinking how much you mean to each other. There's way more to relationships between a man and a woman than just the desire to have sex. That desire can become very compelling, and rational decision-making goes out the window.

"But it's more than that."

"You mean like, pregnancy, and STDs?"

"Yes Son, that too, but there are other consequences than those risks.

"In fact, when you have sex with someone, chemical changes take place in your brain caused by the hormone oxytocin. Not only does your brain tell you, 'wow, I want more of that' but it also tells you you want more of that with that girl, you want to possess her – not just her body, but her whole person – and take care of her. Sex is the thing that cause healthy people, emotionally healthy people, to bond with one another and want to be a couple and likely have children. Hormones drive reproduction in animals, but in humans, generally, it's what also causes couples to want stay together and raise babies together. We're really not much different from cardinals and beavers – they mate for life and share in the raising of their offspring. Lions are different – the males seem to have missed that oxytocin hit.

"Some people call that need for bonding, love – and there can be real pain and suffering when love ends; you have to take responsibility for that possibility too, for yourself and for the girl.

"Yeah, I get it. I find myself thinking about that stuff when I'm making out with Eleanor, but I don't think she's thinking about that at all."

"I'm not surprised Alex. She seems like she's a passionate young woman. Is she taking contraception pills, Son?"

"I don't know, Dad. I don't think so."

"So if you decide to have sex with her, you better be prepared."

"Yeah, I thought about that, but it's very hard.

"I went into a pharmacy after Graduation weekend to investigate, you know, buying rubbers, but they keep them behind the pharmacist's counter, and I was too shy to ask the pharmacist and so I didn't get any."

"I understand. Even as an old married man I find it uncomfortable to ask for condoms from the pharmacist. It's just like buying liquor at the liquor store – you can't just pick out the bottle you want from the shelf, you have to go to the counter with your order paper. It's all so controlling. But don't get me started.

"So what do you say we go and find a pharmacy that's open tomorrow and we'll get you a package."

"Okay, Dad."

"What size will you be needing?" Peter asked, straight-faced.

"Geez, they come in different sizes?"

"No Son, I was just teasing you. They're like balloons that expand to fit; there's only one size but people joke about that all the time."

Back in Kingston Alex examined his box of condoms. He took two out and fitted them into a compartment in his wallet.

As soon as he got back to Kingston he called Sandra in Toronto to ask about her Christmas and to see when she would be back in Amherst Island. It was a rare thrill to be able to speak with her on the telephone. Like Alex, she hadn't a phone in her room in Residence but there was a community phone on each floor; she couldn't call Alex in Leonard Hall since there were only the pay phones in the basement. Alex couldn't call her 'collect' as he did his parents so saved quarters in order to make the long-distance call from the pay phones. They might have talked for hours but in ten minutes he'd run out of quarters and had to hang up.

Alex continued to exchange letters with Eleanor but their correspondence seemed banal; her letters lacked the enthusiasm she brought in person, though, he had to admit, he was guarded in his own letters. Alex suspected Eleanor was dating other guys in Toronto but that didn't really trouble him.

Alex felt a renewed warmth in his relationship with Sandra. He saw her almost every other weekend, usually on Amherst Island, though occasionally Sandra would come into Kingston to see him for the day; since women weren't allowed in the Men's Residences, and they were too young to visit bars and lounges, they had to amuse themselves in other places – strolling on Princess Street, visiting the Agnes Etherington Art Gallery, and coffee shops. They watched matinees in the downtown movie theaters. Alex always reached for her hand and she always gave it to him. She never played footsies with him in the dark but there were times when holding hands turned to squeezing and stroking of palms and fingers, raising Alex' heart rate; he sensed Sandra breathing harder too.

One cold weekend in February, The Reverend Farquharson surprised the two of them with an invitation for Alex to stay overnight.

"It's bloody cold out there tonight, Alex, I don't envy you taking the freezing ferry over to the mainland tonight and hoping the taxi comes to pick you up on time.

"Why don't you stay the night here and go back to Kingston tomorrow. You can use the spare bedroom. I'm sure we can find you a toothbrush and you can wear a pair of my pyjamas, though they're likely two sizes too big for you" he said with a hearty laugh.

Blair Farquharson was a massive man, six feet tall but barrel chest, and girth, strong harms and a thick neck, a true highlander but with an Edinburgh education. Evidently Sandra took after her mother's slender build.

Sandra looked at her father in amazement and then at Alex to gauge his reaction. He had evidently lost his voice but his look told her he was mildly apprehensive; at the same time his lack of speech didn't mean no.

Mr. Farquharson saw it too, "Don't be shy Alex, we won't bite, will we Clara?, though I can't be sure about Sandra."

Sandra blushed and Mrs. Farquharson shot her husband a censorial glance.

Recovering, Sandra remarked, "you realize Alex if you stay over, you'll have to go to church with us tomorrow."

So it was decided, he would stay over. After dinner they settled in the parlor chatting, Alex on the couch with Sandra, Mr. Farquharson in his reading chair, side table and lamp near to hand, Clara in her own chair, with her knitting. Blair declared he might have a wee dram of Glenlivet and asked Alex if he'd like a snifter too. Alex took a peek at Sandra for guidance but then had the good sense to accept.

"Are you going to have some too, Sandra?" Alex asked.

"Dear me, no," she said, "I hate the stuff."

By 10:00 it was evident it was bedtime at the Farquharson household.

"I'll be up early Alex to rehearse my sermon for tomorrow's service. Breakfast is at 8:00; service at 10:00."

"Come with me Alex," said Mrs. Farquharson, "I'll find a pair of pyjamas for you, and a toothbrush, and we can make up your bed."

The parents had the main bedroom on the ground floor. There were two bedrooms upstairs; one was Sandra's, as Alex well knew from his Scouting years at St. Paul's Church peering at the manse hoping for a glimpse of her, the other was the guest bedroom, the two rooms separated by a hall-way and a bathroom.

"Now kids," Clara said, "straight to bed and to sleep, we have an early morning tomorrow." She looked sternly at Sandra.

Sandra was first to use the bathroom and then retired to her room, leaving her door half open.

Alex had changed into Blair's voluminous pyjamas and when he'd finished brushing his teeth and turned off the bathroom light, Sandra called to him in a raised whispered voice,

"Alex, come here for a sec."

Alex stuck his head in her door and looked around. This was her sanctuary, a place he'd longed to see over all those years standing in the parking lot of the church.

"Sit down on my bed, Silly. I want to talk with you.

Alex' Choice

"You know, you don't have to go to church tomorrow if you don't want to. But I'll have to go."

"I want to come with you," Alex replied.

"If you come with Mom and me you know it will be all over the island by noon."

"Oh, I hadn't thought of that," said Alex. "Will that be a bother to you?"

"No, not at all. Will it be a bother for you."

"No, Sandra. I would like it if people thought we were, you know, together."

Sandra smiled.

And so they talked. And talked. You'd think for two people who had known each other since Grade Seven they would have said everything they needed to say, and yet they were still talking at 2:00 in the morning. Finally Clara called upstairs, "Sandra, you and Alex stop your talking and get to your beds!"

Alex smiled and shrugged and got up to leave. Sandra smiled back, grasped his shirt and pulled him to her. She gave him a big warm kiss and then let him go.

"Good night, Alex."

"Good night, Sandra."

Alex settled in the guest bed and thought about the kiss and the nearness of Sandra in the next bedroom. He could hardly believe this was real.

He soon fell asleep, very content.

In February the Golden Gaels Football Club called for all aspiring players to a day of tryouts at the Bews Gym. Alex answered the call but his self-doubt dominated his thoughts. Going through football drills in the gym was a foreign concept to him. He yearned for the familiar world of his high school grid iron in Fall.

But he willed himself to show up at the gym, changed into shorts, t-shirt and running shoes and submit himself to examination. The gym was crowded with young men big and small, tall and slim, line-men, receivers, safeties and running backs. He was surprised and disappointed Coach Tindall wasn't present for the drill. Drills were supervised by current players. Others had clipboards and took notes.

Alex participated in all the drills – shorts sprints, vertical jumps, receiving, turns and spins, it didn't feel right on the slippery gym floor in running shoes. and even though he felt he had done as well as any other half-backs, he didn't feel the competitive drive; he felt he was just going through the motions. And maybe it showed.

The day ended anti-climatically with the coaches encouraging all the young men to work on their fitness over the summer and to watch for a letter in their mailboxes.

Alex never got a letter.

By Reading Week in February Alex faced a new challenge: where was he going to live in the Fall? Norm Vanstone took Alex aside one day and asked him what his plans were for accommodations next year. Alex said he wasn't sure but he thought he would apply for another year in Residence, even though he knew only a few men in second year or higher were accepted.

Norm surprised him when he suggested that in his opinion, Alex would make a good Floor Senior. He encouraged him to apply.

"You're quiet and serious but you also get around the floor and the other boys seem to pay attention to you. You seem to have natural leadership; we don't really want Floor Seniors who are too flamboyant. Warden Edwards doesn't want Leonard Hall to become Party Central. That's what's happened at Morris Hall."

Alex smiled at this information since he had a good idea his friend Hugh was part of that reputation.

"Okay Norm. I'll put in my application with that intent."

"Good, and I'll recommend you to Warden Edwards."

Alex' application was approved and so his living quarters worries for the next year were put to rest. Moreover, Warden Edwards said Alex would become Floor Senior of 2nd East, because Norm Vanstone was staying on for a fourth year in the Men's Residences, but moving up to the fourth floor with the best view in the Residences. Alex could hardly believe his good fortune, and wasn't sure he deserved it.

— Alex' Choice —

Alex sat his final exams with the usual anxiety but no longer intimidated by the formal examination hall; and he was pretty confident he would be moving on. The Head of the Political Science Department took him aside and wanted to know what Alex' intentions were for second year.

"I'd like to major in Poli-Sci, sir."

"Good," said Professor Mackay. "We will be glad to have you."

As his first year at Queen's ended and home to Peterborough for another summer, he had only a couple more concerns – what was he going to do about Sandra, and Eleanor; and what was he going to do for a summer job?

37. Canada Bread

ALEX DIDN'T HAVE TO WORRY LONG about a summer job. Victoria had seen an ad in *The Peterborough Examiner* and had called the Depot Manager of Canada Bread about it. He said they needed a driver for the summer to cover for regular drivers taking summer vacations; they had a replacement driver from the previous summer lined up but he had taken another job, leaving them in the lurch. Victoria told him Alex would be home from University on Friday and that he had worked at Farmboy the previous summer. The Depot Manager phoned Tony Strano and got a glowing report. When Alex showed up for his interview on Monday morning, the Manager looked him up and down, asked him if he had his driver's licence, and then asked,

"Can you start tomorrow?"

"Ah, Yessir, I guess."

"Okay, be here at 6:30 a.m."

The Canada Bread Depot was in Peterborough's 'East City', across the Otonabee River, not too far from where the Jorgensons lived in Edmison Heights in the 'North End' but too far to walk. This was compounded by the fact Alex had to be to work for 6:30 a.m. when the rest of the household was still barely moving. Peter agreed to take him to the depot for the next day but that still left a problem for how Alex would get home since the day was not at all a regular-hours job. He could take a city bus but it would be a long commute with two transfers. Or he could ride his bike.

On Tuesday Alex arrived at the Depot at 6:30; the manager introduced him to one of the veteran drivers.

"This is Lloyd Harrison. He's going to show you the ropes. You're going to be doing his route for the summer; you'll cover for him when he goes two weeks fishing end of May; after that he'll be covering for the other regular drivers' while they go on their vacations.

There were a dozen other van-like trucks parked throughout the large, enclosed warehouse. Trays of bread and pastries were stacked against the walls next to each truck.

— Alex' Choice —

"Pay attention, Preppie," Lloyd instructed, "and watch while I load the truck."

Lloyd rolled his stacks of trays over to his truck and started loading them into the back and racking them on the tracks designed to keep the trays in place.

Truck loaded, Lloyd tossed the keys to Alex, and said, "Okay, time for breakfast. You may as well drive, I'll navigate."

He got into the passenger side of the truck. Alex' eyes opened wide at this unexpected plan, but remembering his dad's lessons, took a long look at the size of the van, climbed into the driver's seat, checked his mirrors and the seat, gauging the distance of the pedals for his legs to reach.

'Woah,' he thought in a bit of a panic, 'this truck has an extra pedal!'

He put his foot on the brake as he'd been taught and turned the key. The engine tried to turn over and the truck lurched ahead a foot.

"Woah," said Lloyd, "you got to push in the clutch first."

"Oh, yeah," said Alex, guessing that must be what the other pedal was. An image of the Amherst Island school bus jumped into his mind.

He depressed the clutch some and turned the key. The starter turned over and the engine started; he let the clutch out, but too fast; the truck lurched and the engine stalled.

Lloyd looked at Alex, a question on his face but only said,

"Yeah, these old clutches can be a bit tetchy. Let the clutch out slowly." Alex concentrated on the clutch but the truck started hopping ahead.

"Quick, depress the clutch again," Lloyd squawked. "Foot on the brake."

Alex was pleased that the engine didn't stall this time, but he was alarmed and embarrassed that he was failing in Lloyd's eyes. He figured he was going to lose this job his first day.

"Hey, kid, don't you know how to drive a truck?"

"No sir. I never drove a truck before."

"Didn't the manager ask you if you drove truck?"

"No sir, he only asked if I had my driver's licence."

"Well, Jesus, I guess now I have to teach you how to drive as well as to learn the routes."

Lloyd shrugged in consternation.

"Okay, let's get started. Can't spend all day in this here depot.

"Okay, slowly let the clutch come back up to the top and feel the engine engage the transmission."

Alex tried to do what he was told but he must have let the clutch out too slowly this time and the truck promptly stalled again.

Alex started the truck again and let out the clutch, repeating the jerk and stall routine. The guys still loading their trucks in the depot had stopped what they were doing to watch.

"Wait a minute, Alex. You never drove a truck before, but surely you drove standard?"

"No sir, I've only driven my dad's Oldsmobile and it's automatic."

"Unbelievable," muttered Lloyd.

"Okay, Alex, let's make sure you're in the right gear.

"Depress the clutch again so we can manipulate the gearbox."

Alex watched as Lloyd moved the long-handled lever on the floor.

"As I thought, you were in third gear, not first. You'll never get this truck moving from stop in third gear.

"Look, the gears follow an H pattern."

Lloyd took the shifter and found the middle neutral place.

"See, this is neutral," he said as he waggled the lever.

He moved the lever forward. "Up to the left is first gear." He moved the lever down, "down to the left is second gear;" he continued moving the lever as he spoke: "then up to the right-middle is third, and down to the right is fourth; up to the far right is 5th. Then down and jogging a bit to the right is reverse.

"Here, you take the shifter and find first gear.

"Now down to second.

"Okay, Alex, start the engine and try again."

'Good', thought Alex. He let out the clutch and the truck lurched forward and promptly stalled.

"You're still in second gear, Alex. Put it in first and try again, just a little faster letting out the clutch, and at the same time depress the throttle a little at the same rate."

Alex' Choice

"Throttle?"

"Jesus Alex, do you know nothing about cars?"

"Sorry sir."

"Throttle, gas pedal."

"Oh."

Alex started the engine again, made sure he was in first gear, gave the engine some gas, and let out the clutch. The engine roared and the tires chirped on the concrete floor. He quickly shoved in the clutch and let off the gas pedal. But didn't stall the engine.

"Okay, Alex, too much gas pedal. You gotta ease out the clutch and gently depress the gas pedal at the same time.

Looking at his gear box and then his pedals, he tried again; and he got the sequence just right and the truck pulled smoothly ahead.

"Whoa! Stop!" yelled Lloyd. "Watch where you're driving. You almost hit the garage door frame."

"Sorry. Lloyd. Maybe I'm just not cut out to be a truck driver."

"No, Son, I'll make a driver of you yet.

"Now back up and we'll try to get out of this depot without hitting anything."

Alex looked at him and suppressed the feeling of panic now flooding his mind: back up?!

He looked at his shifter handle, waggled it in neutral and then brought it down to the right. He heard a satisfying clunk. He checked his two side-view mirrors, depressed the clutch, started the engine, pressed the gas pedal a little and released the clutch slowly; the truck reversed smoothly and slowly.

"Far enough Alex, now forward."

He found first gear, gave the engine a little gas and slowly and coaxingly released the clutch. The truck moved forward slowly without jumping and Alex drove the truck out of the garage. He didn't hear the applause coming from the garage behind him.

He drove a little way across the depot yard to the street exit. He depressed the clutch and put his foot on the brake, stopped his truck. He looked both ways, and engaged the engine again, turning the steering wheel to turn right onto the street, the truck lurched only slightly. At least the back wheel didn't go over the curb.

"Okay," said Lloyd, "now second gear."

Alex put in the clutch but didn't take his foot off the gas, the engine raced; he pulled the shifter down into second gear and let out the clutch. The truck lunged forward. Surprised, Alex slammed on the brakes; the engine stalled.

"You see what happened there Alex," Lloyd asked. "You have to let your foot off the gas when you change gears and then give it enough gas again once you've engaged the next gear.

"Okay, let's get going and not block all this traffic. We're already late for breakfast."

Alex managed to get the truck the few blocks to Hunter Street and located the diner, easily enough with the sight of 5 other Canada Bread trucks parked on the street nearby. He found an open space which he was able to drive into without having to negotiate a parallel parking routine.

"Good start, Alex," said Lloyd, without irony. "Now, for a fried egg sandwich to last us 'til lunchtime."

Lloyd drove the rest of the day; Alex was to pay attention to landmarks and turns, and customer stops. The whole route was noted in the logbook but it would have been hard to follow those instructions if you'd never driven the circuit before.

Tuesdays and Thursdays were Lloyd's country route: Hwy #7 East, stopping at various farms along the way, through Norwood, stopping at the old Norwood Hotel, a few stops in Havelock, then almost to Marmora where they stopped at a roadside restaurant for lunch. Lloyd knew everybody at every stop they made, and everybody else they drove by.

It was almost 12:30. Alex was already tired and wondered how long this day was going to be. They were on the road again at 1:00 and headed north from Havelock to Warsaw, stopping at farms along the way and delivering trays of bread and one of assorted pastries at the general store. Lloyd removed expired items from the store and took orders for delivery Thursday. Each stop meant a visit and conversation with each customer if they were home, or with the dog – the inevitable German Shepherd tied to the porch post – if they weren't.

— Alex' Choice —

He told Alex which farms were blessed with sweet water and which were cursed with sulfurous wells.

"I've been driving this route for almost twenty years, Alex, and besides, I live in Havelock."

That amazed Alex: it meant Lloyd would leave his house every day 5:30, drive 25 miles to the depot, load his truck and drive back out to Havelock to do his route.

From Warsaw, they headed north along County 4 to Crowes Landing stopping at farms and the General Store. Lloyd advised that deliveries in May were lean but by the end of June and all through the summer the store would take many trays of bread and pastries to serve all the cottagers. After McCracken's Landing they turned west along the south shores of Stony Lake on Birchview Road and finally 22 miles back to the depot. It was almost 7:30. Lloyd looked at his exhausted protégé and commented,

"I know Alex, Tuesdays and Thursdays are pretty long days. And in summer with the stores and the cottagers, they're likely going to be even longer. But you know, it makes for a great summer."

Lloyd showed him how to deposit his receipts for the day and fill in his order book for his load for Thursday when they would do this route again. They were finally done by 9:00.

"See you tomorrow, Alex. Tomorrow will be easier, it's only a city route, mostly in the North End of Peterborough."

Alex called his dad to pick him up.

"Hard day Alex?"

Alex regarded the question as rhetorical and didn't answer.

Peter was up with Alex next morning and drove him to the depot for 6:30 a.m.

Lloyd was already there and had the truck just about loaded. He tossed Alex the keys.

"Okay, time for breakfast."

Alex started the truck and drove to the diner with hardly any hiccups. True to Lloyd's word they were finished their route by 3:30 and back to the depot, unloaded their truck and placed their order book for Friday, and home. Peter picked him up around 4:30.

"How was your day today, Son?"

"Better," replied Alex and was soon telling his dad everything he'd experienced the last two days.

Peter smiled and nodded, and kept his comments to himself. His son was getting an education.

Thursday and Friday were repeats of Tuesday and Wednesday. Friday evening Alex arrived home to find a two-toned cream and brown VW bus parked on the road in front of the house.

"Hey, that's a cool looking bus," Alex commented. "I wonder who owns it."

"You do," Peter remarked.

Next morning, Saturday, Alex drove his VW bus to the depot, backed into a spot next to the other drivers' vehicles. He was grateful to Lloyd for teaching him how to drive standard; he handled his VW bus like a veteran. This feeling of accomplishment lasted only a few minutes:

"Hey rookie," called the other drivers, good-naturedly, "nice wheels."

Saturday was only a half-day city route, but scattered across the north and west end, different from the Monday, Wednesday, Friday route. These were weekly customers, mostly retired and widowed people who didn't need much bread but did need to talk. The education of Alex Jorgenson continued.

Summer vacation gave relief from studies, and a chance to earn some money for the next year of schooling, but he never worked so hard in his life. The work week was nominally 44 hours – five eight-hour days but not including lunch, and a four-hour half-day Saturday morning. In reality, his Tuesday and Thursdays' rural route were fourteen-hour days; his weekday city route were ten-hour days, and Saturdays were only seven. In all, his actual work week was about 65 hours. He was paid $65 per week, plus commission, which averaged about $20 per week. He learned not to bother calculating his actual hourly rate of pay, but it was less than minimum wage. For the summer he made about $1350 and this just about covered his tuition and Residence fees. In reality, Peter paid those fees and Alex' earnings became his spending money to last him the academic year.

Alex' Choice

His summer in Peterborough also meant he was absent from Sandra. Student Nursing was a twelve-months-a-year training program so she was in Toronto all summer, home at Amherst Island some weekends. He wasn't able to make it to Kingston because of his work schedule and she wouldn't be available in Toronto. They had no opportunity to see one another from May to September. He was tempted to ask her if she could come to Peterborough for a weekend but really didn't think that was feasible so never actually broached the subject with her. They contented themselves with weekly letter writing.

But Eleanor *was* in Peterborough for the summer.

Alex called on Eleanor the week after his training week at Canada Bread. She had a summer job as a cashier at Dominion Stores and they saw each other frequently all through the summer: swimming in the Otonabee River at their favourite swimming hole; driving in his VW Bus around the Kawartha Lakes of a Sunday afternoon. She even spent a day touring with him in his bread truck on his country route.

He couldn't help being fascinated with Eleanor's voluptuous figure and radiant skin, in her bikinis and bathing suits. He noticed that other men couldn't keep their eyes off her either. No doubt she was aware of this attention, but she made it plain that she was with Alex. And Alex liked that she was with him.

They went to drive-in movies in his VW bus but barely watched the movies; their hands were very busy but both somehow realized they needed to keep control of their physical relationship. Alex knew what held him back; he wasn't sure what was going on in Eleanor's mind.

And he wrote to Sandra almost every week.

38. Second Year Queen's

SEPTEMBER FINALLY ARRIVED and Alex was back at Queen's for his second year, and second year at Leonard Hall. And what a difference a year makes. He still didn't like the long S turn on the 401 as they approached Kingston but unpacking at Leonard Hall and saying goodbye to his parents was not the angst-filled event of the previous year. Oliver didn't come this year. And why should he? – he was eighteen himself now, had his driver's licence and Alex' VW bus. He was in his last year high school and planned to make the most of it. He figured he would be in University the following September himself – it was pretty much expected of the Jorgenson boys – but he didn't intend to go to Queen's. Maybe McMaster in Hamilton.

As a Floor Senior Alex had the larger room at the end of the hall. He brought from home a daybed that would double as a couch, and a coffee table. He had built a floor standing speaker with the help of his uncle Mel and he had a small amplifier and turntable. He didn't plan on turning his room into a party room – what would Warden Edwards think of his Floor Senior then – but he did have in mind quiet social gatherings in his room of members of his floor and the odd evening of euchre. And he had begun buying classical music records to go along with his Beatles collection. His first album: Tchaikovsky's famous marches.

He had 18 undergraduates on his floor including himself, five of whom were second year men as Alex, and 13 Frosh. His best friend the previous year, Charlie Horton, from Thunder Bay, had moved into a rental house with a troop of Pre-Meds students but another friend from Leonard Hall had returned and asked to be assigned to 2nd Floor East, Alex' Floor. Jon Page, of Point Clair, Quebec, settled in, two doors down from Alex and became a constant companion. He and two others from the floor became regulars around Alex' coffee table.

But Jon didn't play euchre. He said euchre was unsophisticated and declared it was high time Alex learned how to play an adults' game – Contract Bridge. Some argued Bridge was the most important thing they learned at University; some said it was the only thing they learned at University.

— Alex' Choice —

Alex hadn't seen much of his friend Hugh McPherson in First Year, even though Morris Hall was close by Leonard Hall. In Second Year, Hugh moved out of Residence and into a rental house with some other guys from Cobourg.

Hugh chided Alex for playing it safe and staying in Residence but reckoned as how looking out for the well-being of 17 other guys probably carried a lot of responsibility.

"Hey Alex," he said, "it's like you're still running the St. Albans Secret Society and Leonard Hall is your fort."

By second year Alex knew his way around campus but primarily frequented the familiar buildings where most of his classes were held – Dunning Hall and the Arts Building; the engineering buildings were foreign territory. He enjoyed the coffee house at the Student's Union, the grandeur of the Douglas Library Reading Room, and the smell of sweat in the ancient Weight Room in the basement of the Bews Gymnasium. Alex was always welcome to come and party at Hugh's place but he preferred the comfortable confines of Leonard Hall.

Even though he wasn't training for football any longer, he had formed the habit of weight training three times a week, and now that he had access to all this gear in the Gym, he may as well use it. Ancient though it may have been, it was still orders of magnitude better than the makeshift weight apparatus in the Jorgenson's basement. His dream of being a Queen's Golden Gael halfback may have faded, but he hadn't given up on building muscles.

It also suited Alex that the weight room was almost abandoned most of the time so he could focus on his workout without having to engage others. Still, it was useful to learn from other experienced weight trainers in lifting technique. And it was smart to have a spotter when pressing heavy weights on the bench or standing press. He was proud of the increasing loads he could lift though he was still a lightweight compared to some of the giant linemen on the Queen's Football team. He was not tall but his grip, arms and shoulders were powerful, as were his legs. He always surprised bigger guys that he could beat any member on his floor at Leonard Hall in hand or arm wrestling, but they didn't realize half of the strength comes from the legs, and technique.

One Friday afternoon in February he was the only person in the gym. Undeterred he loaded up the bench press free weight bar with 235 pounds of plates. He lay on the bench and hitched his way under the cradle. He took three deep breaths to oxygenate his muscles then lifted the loaded heavy bar off the cradle with an oomph. He then carried the bar down to his chest and, taking another deep breath, heaved it back up to the straight arm position. He took another deep breath and completed another lift cycle. By the fifth lift he was finding his arms pretty tired and shaky; he struggled to get the bar back up to the top of his reach. Nevertheless, he brought the load down to his chest for one last rep. He pushed hard but he couldn't raise the bar more than a few inches off his chest. He needed to rest for a minute to recover his strength, the bar balanced across his chest his arms stabilizing it. He took three more big breaths and tried to lift the weight off his chest and back onto the cradle. He couldn't do it.

He began to feel a bit panicky, trapped under the weight of the bar across his chest; he wished now he had a spotter as you always should when lifting heavy weights to assist in getting the weight back in its cradle. He called out to the next room to get someone's attention, but he already knew there was no one there to hear his call. There was nothing else for it but to try to crawl his way out from under the bar. He tried lifting it just enough to get it over his head but he couldn't even make it that high and he ran the risk of dropping the bar on his face. He wondered if he could tilt the bar to one side and squirm out from under the bar. He turned his head to the right and began to push the bar to one side until the right-end plates levered the left end up and gradually slid to the floor. He inched his head under the bar and crept his way down the bench; now he could turn and sit up, his feet on the floor, his ribs bruised and right ear only slightly worse for wear. The bar now rested against the bench. He removed the heavy plates from the ends of the bar one by one and put them back on the rack; he then put the naked bar back in its place on the cradle. He'd given himself a scare but he'd learned his lesson.

That wasn't his only scare from weight training. Often he'd walk from his last class in the afternoon to the gym for a workout, and some of those days with only an apple for lunch on the run. Being young and invulnerable he didn't think to drink much water or electrolyte replacement. After his workout he'd walk the short block to the general store on Division Street at Earl and wolfed down a Crispy Crunch chocolate bar and a Pepsi. One day as he waited at the cash register to pay, feeling a little light-headed, and probably looking worse, the Chinese woman behind the counter said:

"You very pale. You alright?"

"I'm fine," Alex replied, but at that moment, he saw tiny lightening bolts in his eyes and his knees began to buckle. He reached for the counter for support.

"Okay, mister, I get you chair.

"You sit down here," the Chinese lady commanded.

Alex was thoroughly embarrassed but accepted to sit.

Within a minute or two the sugar from his treats had reached his brain and he was feeling better. He rose from his chair.

"I'm going to go now," he said, "thanks for the rest."

"You okay to walk now?" she said, alarm still in her voice.

She looked him over, "Okay, your face not so pale now.

"You take care yourself."

Ever after that Alex would stop into the general store after his workout and the lady at the counter would check him over.

"You okay today mister?"

"Yes ma'am," Alex would smile and nod to her. He never knew her name, nor she his.

The Bews Trophy intramural sports competition was another device, like frosh week, that the university encouraged to create esprit de corps among the student body. Each class year in each faculty was an organizational unit. Each class elected representatives to the larger student government – the Queen's Alma Mater Society. AMS for short. An organization committee from each class would reach out to class members and encourage them to participate in various social and community events. Alex often wondered whether he should get involved with student affairs but his natural reluctance inhibited him from stepping up. And he had his duties as a Floor Senior and a member of the Floor Seniors' Council at Leonard Hall. Maybe that was enough.

The Bews Trophy focused on sporting events. It was awarded to the class that had accumulated the most points in the set of such events throughout the year, for winning and participating, so as not be monopolized by jocks and jockettes. Events for the most part were co-educational to give women a chance to play. Varsity athletes were ineligible to participate. There were many events and tournaments: badminton, cross-country running, track and field, flag football, hockey and skiing, to name a few. The Phys. Ed. Classes had a clear advantage, as did the larger engineering classes, 98% comprised of men; even the growing Commerce Classes dominated many events. The small Meds School classes were clearly disadvantaged but gamely fielded teams. The Arts faculty, even though the largest set of classes at Queen's, had never won the Bews Trophy.

But in Alex' second year, the organizing committee of Arts '73 had a plan. Bews Trophy Points were awarded for winning (and placing and showing) in each event, but they were also awarded according to how many members of each class participated in each event. Arts '73 may not have the athletes to win many events but they could certainly field large contingents for each event, and maybe earn some second and third place results as well.

Alex eyes lit up when he heard there was a flag football tournament, and a track and field competition; flag football may not have had quite the caché as the varsity Golden Gaels but it gave Alex that thrill of competition he had been missing. He amazed his teammates and classmates, and maybe himself, with his speed and agility avoiding 'tacklers' trying to snatch the flags flying from his waistband. His team won the whole tournament. He scored many touchdowns. He had the most fun beating Hugh's Commerce '73 team.

He brought his track spikes to Kingston after his Thanksgiving Weekend in Peterborough. He was entered in the 100-yard dash in the Bews Track meet. He coaxed Hugh into entering as well for Commerce '73.

"Ah, I don't know Alex, it doesn't feel like track season to me."

"It's late October and it's getting pretty cool. And I don't have time to train."

"Neither do I, Hugh, but we've been playing flag football; we can still run."

– Alex' Choice –

The Bews Track Meet was held at The Royal Military College sports field because Queen's didn't have a track. Donning his red Pumas, Alex felt the old adrenalin that always marked the tension of a race. He won his heat handily, and the next two, and then it was the finals. He looked for Hugh but he wasn't at the start line; he must have lost in a previous heat.

Alex was very conscious of his tight hip flexor muscle, the cool of the gray Fall air, the fact this was his fourth heat in a day, and worried whether he might injure himself.

He needn't have worried. He won his race in a time of 10.1 seconds, the best time of his life, though hardly a threat to Harry Jerome's record. 'Maybe I'm getting stronger with age,' he wondered.

Alex wasn't the only one alert to his time. The head of the Queen's Track Club was following the participants at this intramural meet.

"That was a pretty good time," he remarked.

Alex replied, "yeah, I even surprised myself. I haven't raced since Grade Thirteen, and that was eighteen months ago. I'm really not in shape."

"Why don't you come out for the track team? We train every Tuesday and Thursday afternoons at RMC while the weather is still decent, then we'll work out in the gym over the winter. Next year we'll have a running track at the new Jock Harty Arena.

Alex urged himself to join the track team but his heart wasn't in it. He agreed with Hugh's sentiment: cool Fall afternoons with the sun disappearing by 5:00 just didn't feel like track season. He conjured up a dozen reasons why this wasn't the sport for him anymore: he'd never competed in an indoor meet, and outdoor season couldn't really begin until May, long after the school year was over, and by then he had his summer job. In the back of his mind, he also worried that he would run into some serious competition at the university level – memories of his final high school meet undermined his confidence. Still, he thought, maybe he would work out over the summer with the Peterborough Track Club and prepare for track season the following September at Queen's.

255

39. Sean O'Reilly

As Alex walked off the RMC field, he heard someone call his name: "Hey, Alex, how are you doing?"

Alex looked more closely at the young man dressed in a Royal Military College Cadet uniform walking towards him.

"Wow, Sean O'Reilly, is that you? I didn't recognize you in uniform."

"Yeah, and it's been six years since you left Amherst Island."

"And you were going to Regiopolis in Kingston so I would hardly have seen you anyway, except for Scouts."

"Where are you living now?"

"I'm a Floor Senior in Leonard Hall."

"That figures. You always seem to be in charge of something or other.

"Are you still seeing that pretty girl from the church?"

"You mean Sandra Farquharson. Yeah, now that I'm back in Kingston I go over to Amherst Island sometimes and visit her. She's in Nursing in Toronto so I don't see her very often."

"Hey, Alex, are you in a hurry to get back to Queen's? Why don't you come over to the Cadets Mess with me and we can get a beer and catch up."

"You can drink at your mess? But we're underage!"

"Yeah, but we have our own rules in the Armed Forces."

So Alex joined Sean at the Mess for a long visit. Some of what Sean told him of Amherst Island doings he had already heard from Sandra or her parents, but he learned a lot more about Sean's own family. His father had really cleaned up the farm – rebuilt the barn and all the fences; they had thirty head of Holsteins and were selling all the milk he could produce. They had renovated the cabin that his Uncle Nelson had lived in until he was banished from the homestead, and it was now rented out as a B&B place – his mother was very happy to play hostess and entertain guests, even if just to see another woman on the farm from time to time. Alex laughed at this,

"I never thought of that. With a husband, you and Shamus, and your uncle Nelson, I guess she was the only female."

"So, what happened to Shamus?"

"Well, not so great. He dropped out of high school and bumped around Kingston for a while. He got tangled up with Uncle Nelson and had a few scrapes with the law. I told him he better get straightened out and stay away from that crazy old man. I told him to join the army. So now he's at St. Jean in basic training."

"And what about your Uncle Nelson?"

"You mean, Old Man O'Reilly," Sean said with a laugh. "We know that's what everybody calls him.

"He's never going to be up to anything but no good. After dad kicked him off the farm, he bummed around Kingston and Wolff Island for a while but then disappeared for a few years. Congregated with a bunch of hoods in Boston we understand.

"He's back in Kingston now, lives in a rooming house out Montreal Street near the Train Station. I see him every once in a while when I'm downtown to the bank, but I try to stay clear of him. He mostly drinks; sells weed to Queen's students, or panhandles on Princess Street."

Alex grimaced. He knew lots of students tried drugs but he was nervous about that. And he thought those students should be nervous of dealers such as Nelson O'Reilly.

"And Alex, he still holds a grudge against you. He's forever whining about the treasure he says you stole from him in Stella Bay. He never acknowledges you gave all the proceeds back to my dad. You made a big difference in our lives, but that crazy old coot doesn't see it that way.

"You should try to avoid him if you can, Alex."

Despite his playful summer with Eleanor Alex only visited home every six weeks or so in his second year at Queen's – Thanksgiving, a weekend in November, Christmas break, Reading Week in February – but he spent almost every other Saturday with Sandra, on Amherst Island or in Kingston. His correspondence with Eleanor became more and more mechanical, their weekend visits almost perfunctory. Despite the powerful attractive force of the alluring and ardent Eleanor his eagerness to see her had waned, and she felt the increasing detachment. Not so his visits to Amherst Island.

Reading Week in February at home gave him respite, drawing comfort from the familiar surroundings and the gentle maternal ministrations. He spent the time telling of happenings at Queen's the previous couple of weeks, his studies, the food at the cafeteria.

"You don't appear to be losing any weight, Alex," Victoria commented ironically, a consternated turn of the eye.

"Now Victoria," intervened Peter, "sophomores on cafeteria food result in ten or twenty extra pounds.

"Are you going to the gym Alex?"

"Yes Dad, there's a weight room in the basement and I'm there three times a week, Monday, Wednesday and Fridays, except of course when I'm hitchhiking here."

"We don't see much of Eleanor these days Alex. Is she home this weekend?"

"No Mom," Alex shrugged, "she's pretty busy in Toronto. Her Reading Week is next week; she's going to Fort Lauderdale. Maybe I'll see her at Easter."

"And Sandra?"

"Yeah Mom, I see her whenever she can get home for the weekend. I visit her mostly on Amherst Island, spend the day with her and have dinner with her parents."

Victoria didn't ask any more questions. She was vaguely relieved that her son's relationship seemed to have cooled with the vibrant vamp Eleanor. And she somehow felt he was safe with Sandra.

But Alex was less settled about this situation. He couldn't help being drawn to Eleanor's assertiveness both socially and sexually. He admired her self-confidence, and she was exciting to be around. But somehow, he didn't feel the connectedness he had with Sandra. Surely, she was seeing other men in Toronto. Yet he wasn't greatly troubled by this.

The demure Miss Farquharson, warm and welcoming, made him feel comfortable and relaxed whenever they were together. But she had chosen to go to Toronto for some reason besides just nursing. He was more troubled by this.

40. Cashway Lumber

ALEX HAD LEARNED A LOT ABOUT WORKING LIFE in his summer as a delivery driver for Canada Bread. But the hours were long and the pay modest. He hated to think what his hourly wage would be if he stopped to actually calculate it. He liked the breadman job – once he had mastered his truck driving skills and his trade routes – but he figured a job with better hours and better pay mattered more. That meant having to find one, and that was more daunting than spending another summer behind the wheel of a truck. He really had no idea how to go about job hunting besides perusing the want ads, and he dreaded having to make calls; still, he didn't want to suffer the embarrassment again of his mother finding a job for him. So he accepted the Canada Bread offer to drive the wholesale truck and open up the summer season serving stores and marinas in cottage country. He was flattered that they wanted him back. And driving the big 5-ton double axel truck was a testimony to how far he had come in learning how to drive professionally. When he showed up at the depot that first of May the regular crew welcomed him back: 'Hey, rookie, we hear you're driving the big rig this summer'. But he told the depot manager that this was only to be temporary until he found another better-paying job.

He began checking the 'Help Wanted' ads in *The Peterborough Examiner* but nothing suitable came up. He didn't want another summer of landscaping – he'd had enough of that building the retaining walls in the Jorgenson's backyard. Often he'd follow-up on an ad only to find the job had already been filled. Eleanor suggested he apply to Loblaws where she now worked and be a stockboy, but he thought better of it.

As it turned out, he got a lead, not through a help wanted ad, nor through his mother, but via his brother Oliver. Oliver knew a guy from Adam Scott whose dad owned a construction company; Steve Peconi didn't work for his dad but did work weekends at a building supply company; he said they were looking for an extra summer crew member.

Alex stopped by Cashway Lumber the next day and asked for the store manager. He told the manager he'd heard from Steve

Peconi about a possible summer job. The manager asked about his previous experience and seemed impressed that he had driven truck for Canada Bread, especially the rural route to the camps and cottages around Stony Lake.

"Lots of cottage building going on up there in cottage country," the manager said. "You're going to see a lot of those construction types and do-it-yourselfers here.

"Can you drive lift-truck, young man?"

"No sir, but I'm sure I can learn."

"I'm sure you can too. If you can drive a truck, you can drive a tractor.

"Can you work Saturdays?"

"Yes sir?'

"When can you start?"

"Next week sir, I need to give notice to Canada Bread so they can find another driver for the summer wholesale run I'm doing."

"Okay. You'll need to buy safety boots with steel soles, and you should probably buy work gloves.

"Fill in this application form and leave it with the cashier at the counter. You can start Monday."

"Okay, great."

Alex moved to get out of his chair and leave.

"Did you want to ask me about your hours and pay?"

"Oh, right."

"The store is open Monday to Wednesday, 7:30 to 6:00, Thursday and Friday till 9:00. Saturday from 7:30 to 5:00.

"We'll work out a schedule for you, but you'll have to work Saturdays and either Thursdays or Fridays till 9:00. It's a 40-hour work week and we pay $2.25 per hour. Any overtime is at time and a half. Okay?

"That's great sir," Alex quickly replied, trying to curb his enthusiasm.

"I'll call the yard foreman so he can meet you and take a walk around the yard and the warehouse. He'll meet with you Monday to start your training.

"Ah, here's Glen now.

"See you Monday."

— Alex' Choice —

Cashway Lumber was an Ontario-wide chain of lumber and building supply stores. The Peterborough store/yard was located in the North End of Peterborough on the east side of the Otonabee River on Parkhill Road. A railway spur terminated there which was very convenient for receiving large shipments of lumber; convenient if the lumber was baled in large bundles loaded on flat-bed cars, allowing easy lifting by forklift and tractored into the yard, not so easy if the lumber had to be off-loaded from box cars and re-piled by hand.

The yard was gated and fenced, which hardly prevented minor pilfering but most of the stock in the yard was stands of lumber – 2x4, 2x6, 2x8, 2x10, and 2x12 spruce in 8-, 10-, 12-, 14- and 16-foot lengths, three or four loads high – and pallets of asphalt shingles, and any other stock that could stand to be stored outdoors. There was a large warehouse where the fine dressed pine, plywood, paneling and drywall, moulding and plumbing was kept. There was a large overhang that extended from the warehouse where pallets of rough plywood were kept. When the yard was in good shape and the customers were scarce, the Yard Boys would perch themselves on the stockpiles and while away the time, especially on those torrid July and August days when the sunlight bounced off the piles of lumber and the temperature soared well into the 90s Fahrenheit. There was a dark weathered 8 by 8 post that held up the overhang of the storage shed and on it was marked in pen, or carved with a knife, the record high temperatures over the years, well into the low 100s.

Glen, the yard foreman, did most of the chores involving the forklift, partly because it was potentially dangerous, and costly if the driver dumped a load, and partly because he enjoyed it, and rank had its privileges. Cashway had a contractor with a flatbed truck who delivered cottage lot loads all around the countryside. Cashway had building plans and associated supply sheets for a number of cottage designs. A customer could order the entire package for delivery at his site anywhere in the Kawartha district. The driver was an Indian from Curve Lake Reserve; Alex swore Stan looked a lot like Joe Burns; Stan said he didn't know him, but then, Stan had very little to say at the best of times.

Alex proved himself a diligent worker – he hated being idle and he would take up chores during slow times that nobody else deemed very satisfying; he sorted and organized the moulding cases, restacked the panels and pine in the warehouse, sorted out all the plumbing pipes and fixtures, copper and ABS. It wasn't long before Glen gave Alex a lesson on the lift-truck.

"I hear you drove a bread truck last summer" he said, introducing the topic.

"Yeah, I was a real novice at the beginning – I hadn't driven standard before and I kept stalling the old rust bucket – but by the end of the summer I could get that truck moving from third gear."

"Well with this forklift tractor you'll never stall it, the gears are so low. But your left leg might get tired. You coax your load with the clutch, gently letting it out as you maneuver your load."

The lift truck was a reconfigured standard farm tractor with large drive wheels and small front wheels. The trick though was that the fork was installed at the back of the tractor and the driver's seat, gearbox and steering wheel reversed to face backwards. This way you could see your load easily but you had to learn to steer the opposite way. Glen let Alex practice on pallets of shingles, compact and stable. Then he graduated to strapped packages of plywood and paneling. Next, it was a deck of 2x4 by 8-ft studs. Unwieldy bundles of 2x12 16-ft joists were still Glen's territory because those very long boards were quite unstable if you didn't find the mid-point accurately.

One Monday well into the Summer, Stan was preparing a cottage load for delivery way north of Apsley at Chandos Lake and he was in a hurry to get out of the yard to deliver it on time later that afternoon. Monday was Glen's day off. The 2x12 16-foot floor joists were to be loaded first on one side of the flatbed, and the 2x8 12-foot ceiling joists on the other side.

"Okay, College Boy," Stan hollered to Alex, "I need your help with this load. Get the forklift and fetch me 14 pieces of 2 by 12 sixteens and load 'em on the flatbed and then 20 pieces of 2 by 8 twelves.

"When you're done that you can put the rest of the load of plywood and shingles together. I'll get all the small stuff organized."

Alex knew what to do but he hadn't handled those long lengths before.

— Alex' Choice —

He drove the tractor to the 2x12 16s stand and piled 14 pieces onto the forks, carefully centred, and gently drove his load over to the truck. Gingerly he lifted the load to the side of the flatbed but lining it up proved tricky because those sixteen footers extended four feet past the end of the 12-foot flatbed. He sighed with relief when he had settled his load onto 4x4 cross pieces on the truck-bed. He returned to the lumber piles to the 2x8 12s, selected twenty pieces and loaded them onto the forks; he drove them over to the truck and settled them onto the other side of the flatbed. Piece of cake. Next came the dozens of pieces of 1x8 16-foot Colorlok siding. This proved much trickier as the 1-inch heavy siding was very floppy and the treated side slippery. He laid loading laths across the 2x12 joists and settled his load of Colorlok siding down on the flatbed, gingerly pulling his forks out so as not to disturb the load. Next came two full bundles of 2x4 studs and then 4x8 sheets of tongue and grove $5/8^{ths}$ floor plywood and $3/8^{ths}$ particle board panels for the roof, then three pallets of asphalt shingles. And that would be enough for one day. They would be doing a second load in a few weeks' time of plumbing and electrical and interior paneling. Stan inspected the load and strapped it secure on the flat bed, giving Alex a simple nod of the head.

Alex was very pleased with himself and his confidence in his driving skills soared.

It wasn't long after that when he decided to restack the dressed pine in the warehouse. Dressed pine was mostly used in interior work, as flooring, or wall covering, and sometimes for shelving and even cabinet making. The clean white wood with sweeping wave patterns and the occasional knot was attractive, and expensive. The pine was stored in the warehouse, locked at night because it was prone to warping and weathering, and maybe theft, if stored outside. The one-inch boards came in widths of 6, 8 and 10 inches, and lengths of 8, 10, 12 and 16 feet. It was stored in heavy racks with shorter lengths on the ground floor for convenience of shipping, (because these lengths were the most popular) and the longer lengths on the third and fourth rack, 15 feet above the floor. The lift truck could barely reach the top rack, its forks at the full height of its lift.

The yard had just received a new load of pine in a boxcar on the railway siding beside the yard. The boxcar was filled with various lengths and widths of dressed pine boards and had to be unloaded piece by piece, not in bound bundles that could be lifted off a flatbed by lift truck. Alex and a day-worker spent three sweltering days pulling boards out of the boxcar and stacking them in sorted piles alongside the boxcar. At the end of the day Alex would move the stack into the yard for safe-keeping until he was able to stow them away in the racks in the warehouse.

The following week he figured it was time to organize the stock in the warehouse. It was a slow day; he was alone in the warehouse because the other crew members sat on the plywood piles under the eaves waiting to serve customers. Alex drove the lift truck into the yard to retrieve the first stack of new pine stock then trundled it into the warehouse; next he maneuvered the various loads of existing stock off the rack and piled the old stock on top of the new stacks of the same dimensions. The 8- and 10-foot lengths stowed on the floor and first rack were no problem, but the 12-footer pile lifted onto the second rack, ten feet above the floor, was much trickier. The forks had to reach into the centre of the stack of the 12-foot lengths to stay balanced, but even so, the big load swayed disconcertedly. Alex was full concentration on this delicate task.

Last was the 16-foot length stack. He got the existing stack of a dozen boards down without much difficulty but those 16-foot lengths nevertheless flapped perceptively like wings of a jetliner in turbulence. He transferred the dozen boards of old stock on top of the new stack of 16-footers. Now his stack was 32 inches high. He worked his forks carefully into the centre of the long and heavy load, lifted the load six inches off the concrete floor to be sure it was balanced; next he positioned his tractor and load at the centre of the rack where this load was to go. He drove very slowly but even so he felt the load wave slightly up one end and down at the other. Steering was surprisingly light, and that was because the heavy load cantilevered the small steering wheels at the back of the tractor so as to barely touch the floor.

He began to lift his load, slowly and steadily, but with each upward movement he could feel the ends of his load swaying, slightly. Eventually he had his load to the full height of the lift truck's reach, eight feet above his head, fifteen feet off the floor. He was beginning to sweat. He let out the clutch very slowly and gently and moved the truck inch by inch towards the rack and his load into position over the rack cross pieces. He braked gently but the load started to sway even more, side to side. Looking up at his load he could see the struts of the lift waying from side to side with the load. It was precarious indeed. He was scared now that the load could tip one way or the other and the tractor with it. How did he get himself into this dangerous situation?

He waited. Gradually the load stopped swaying and the tractor steady again. Very gently he let out his clutch again and nudged his load further into the rack until he could see it was in position. Then very slowly he released the hydraulic and the forks brought the heavy load of pine down on the cradle beams in the rack. Free of his load he carefully backed the forklift out and when clear brought the forks back down to the ground.

He sat there in his tractor for at least five minutes in relief.

Just then Glen came into the warehouse and saw Alex resting on the seat of his idling tractor. He studied the racks and then took in the big load of pine on the top rack.

"How the hell did you get that load up there?!" he said, displeasure and alarm in his voice.

"Were you in here alone?"

Alex nodded.

"Never do that again. That was very dangerous. You cud'uv got yourself killed."

"Yes sir."

Glen walked away shaking his head. But Alex got the feeling there was a hint of admiration in Glen's attitude, even if it was a reckless thing to have done.

OLIVER HAD BECOME A MEMBER of the Peterborough Legion Track & Field Club. He had finished his high school career that June and had done well in the COSSA Track meet in the 220-yard dash. The PTC Coach had recruited Oliver and Joe Burns following the meet. Oliver was planning on going to McMaster University in September and had half a notion he might like to be on Mac's track team, so he figured working out over the summer with the Track Club would be a good idea. Practice was twice a week at Kenner Collegiate's track in the 'South End'; he had to drive from the 'North End' to get there but the Jorgenson VW bus was still in service.

"Hey, Alex," Oliver said after a few outings, "you should come with us to practice. It would be good for you if you're thinking of racing for Queen's next year."

Alex had largely put thoughts of a track career out of his mind, but he felt something of a challenge in Oliver's invitation.

"I don't know Oliver, I'm in terrible shape and I'm pretty tired after a day at the lumber yard to be doing wind-sprints twice a week at Kenner."

But the following Tuesday was his day off, so he decided to give it a go.

It had been a hot July day and the temperature was still in the mid-80s at 5:30 when he and Oliver drove to Kenner for practice.

Coach welcomed Alex to the Club.

"I hear you're a sprinter like your brother," Coach queried.

"Yeah, but I'm faster," Alex said with a smile, catching a glare from Oliver. "Well, maybe not in the 220."

Practiced started first with a warm-up – four times around the track at a light jog. Alex grimaced at the thought of it – he knew this was just the beginning of what was likely to be a grueling work-out – but he mentally psyched himself and started off at a gentle pace. Oliver and Joe's gentle pace was somewhat more vigourous than Alex's; Alex was content to keep pace with the high jumpers and shot-putters who were in no hurry to put in their four laps.

Alex was breathing pretty heavily at the end of the warmup but a whole series of stretching routines helped him get back to normal breathing.

For the next hour or so the athletes practiced technique: the high jumpers in their pit practicing take-off and twists, the milers doing many laps around the track, shot-putters their spins, the sprinters in their blocks.

Towards the end of practice Coach got the sprinters together to do a bit of time trials. Alex and Oliver, Joe and a couple of others lined up in their blocks at the start line. Coach had no gun but started them off with a hand signal. Alex was slow out of his

Alex' Choice

blocks and was startled to see Joe leap ahead and already flying down the track. The competitive urge surged in Alex and he accelerated away quickly. He and Oliver were close but Alex had his eye on Joe's back. He raised himself onto his toes, a technique that had worked so well for him in past races. He was closing fast on Burns who seemed to be gliding along effortlessly. By sixty yards Alex was almost abreast of Joe. Joe got a glimpse of Alex out of the corner of his eye, found another gear and pulled away from Alex who was beginning to tighten up and losing speed; Joe won the race handily, Oliver squeezed past Alex at the finish line.

"Pretty good time, Alex, for first time back," said Coach, but Alex wasn't assuaged.

Excellence in athletics was more than just DNA and technique, it also required peak fitness; 220-windsprints were the routine favoured by Coach. He lined up all his athletes at the midpoint of the home straight and started them all off at a fast pace for half the track, 220 yards, then the athletes would walk the second half of the loop to catch their breath, returning to the start line; then all the athletes would do another loop of the track – race 220 yards and walk 220. Oliver and Joe were well ahead of the rest of the other athletes; Alex attempted to keep pace for the first set but was already flagging going into the second round. By the fourth loop he was gasping for breath even as he walked the 220 section, and just as he began to sprint the fifth loop his calf muscle cramped. He stopped and bent over to massage out the sharp spasm in his calf but as he did so, his other calf cramped. He twisted his torso to reach this new assault when all the muscles in his abdomen began to spasm. Then his fingers began to tingle and soon his hands were cramping. He felt his face and cheeks tingling and his eyes close. He fell to the ground crying in pain. His eyes contracted to narrow slits and all he could see were flashes of light. He thought he was going to die.

Oliver did too. He and Joe raced over to Alex apparently convulsing on the ground.

"Geez, we gotta get him to the hospital," screamed Oliver. "Help me get him to the van, Joe" he yelled, panic enveloping both boys; all the other athletes abandoned their wind-sprints and gathered around writhing Alex dying in the infield.

Coach arrived with a small paper bag. He elbowed his way through the group of fearful onlookers.

"He's not going to die," Coach said firmly, "he's just hyperventilating. It looks worse than it is.

"Here Alex, breathe into this bag."

Alex' eyes were shut; he had stopped screaming, and his body had stopped jerking, but his breath was still fast, the muscles in his legs knotted; he didn't respond to Coach's instruction.

"Here boys, sit him up while I put the bag over his mouth and nose.

"Now breathe in and out of the bag, Alex."

Alex was still breathing hard but not quite so fast.

Coach said, "Try to slow your breathing, Alex. Take a longer breath through the bag, try to hold it, then out into the bag, then in again.

"Good."

Alex' breathing began to return to normal. Coach removed the bag. Alex' fingers and stomach muscles relaxed, feeling returned to his fingers and as he opened his eyes; he could see people again though they seemed out of focus.

Coached massaged his still cramping calf muscles.

"Straighten your leg Alex."

Coach then grasped Alex foot and bent it forward towards Alex' shin, stretching the calf muscle. The cramping stopped.

Oliver was still alarmed.

"Do we need to take him to the hospital?"

"No, I shouldn't think so. He's young and healthy. I don't think there's anything physiologically wrong with him; he's just over-extended himself and hyperventilated."

"What's with the paper bag, Coach?"

"When somebody hyperventilates, they are breathing too fast and upsetting the normal balance of oxygen to carbon dioxide in the bloodstream. Too much oxygen relative to CO_2 makes the muscles go into spasm. Breathing into a bag and re-up-taking the spent breath, the lungs take in more carbon dioxide and the balance is restored in the blood stream and then the spasming muscles can relax again."

— Alex' Choice —

Eventually the excitement died down and Alex recovered well enough to get up and walk, but he was exhausted. It was a dramatic end to track practice that night.

And as it turned out, that was the last time Alex stepped on a track.

The closest Alex came to hyperventilating again came from a heavy necking session with Eleanor, a year later, but that was a breathlessness of another sort.

41. Civic Holiday

WITH THE AUGUST LONG WEEKEND APPROACHING, Alex decided to visit Sandra on Amherst Island. He hadn't seen her since April and he needed more than letter-writing.

He hadn't seen much of Eleanor that summer, either. Her aunt in Barrie had found her a summer job as a receptionist in a physiotherapy clinic. Fond memories of the previous summer kindled some mild yearning but he didn't take any initiative to reach out to her.

She came home to Peterborough Dominion Day weekend to visit her folks. They went to the movies on Saturday night and swimming at their favourite swimming hole on the Otonabee on Sunday afternoon before she was driven back to Barrie Sunday evening. She didn't play footsies with him in the theatre, and they didn't play beach blanket bingo on Sunday afternoon. Alex had the distinct impression she might have a boyfriend in Toronto, or somewhere. He didn't ask.

By the end of July he was feeling pretty dry. And it was Sandra on his mind. He knew Sandra was going to be home Civic Holiday weekend. He asked if he could visit with her on Amherst Island.

'Of course, Silly' she had replied, 'I'm always glad to see you, and my parents too.'

He had to work Saturday but he had the Tuesday off and that would allow plenty of time for him to drive to Amherst Island and back and not be rushed. Civic Holiday is celebrated the first Monday of August in Ontario and many other provinces in Canada. It may have been intended as a day to commemorate citizens' appreciation of their municipal services and responsibilities but more likely it was an excuse to enjoy a midsummer holiday in a country with few warm days in the year to celebrate.

Victoria was reluctant to let him go but Peter reminded her Alex was almost 21 years old and he had to be free to make his own plans. Alex persuaded Oliver to let him have the VW bus for the weekend.

Alex' Choice

"Sure Alex, it's your bus anyway, even though Dad says you have to share it with me."

Alex packed up the bus on Friday evening and was ready to go as soon as he got home from Cashway Saturday afternoon. He took the back way to Kingston, partly to savour the summer evening and partly because it might be faster via Campbellford, Tweed, Napanee; it wasn't. He took Hwy 2 to Odessa and finally to the Millhaven crossing to Amherst Island. He arrived at the Manse with the setting sun around 9:00 pm.

Sandra practically leaped into Alex' arms when she greeted him at the door. Alex was delighted though a little surprised at her show of playfulness; he blushed and glanced around to see the Reverend Farquharson and Mrs. Farquharson's reactions to this display.

He needn't have worried. Reverend Farquharson grasped Alex' hand vigourously. Clara Farquharson stepped in and gave him a motherly hug.

"Gee Alex," said Clara, "we thought we wouldn't see you till tomorrow afternoon. You must be eager to go to church with us tomorrow."

Blair slapped his thigh and let out a hearty laugh. "I'm sure that's so, Clara. Right Alex?, isn't that so?"

Alex blushed but couldn't help but smile at Mr. Farquharson's good humour and welcome.

"Well, anyway," Clara continued, "your room is ready for you. I've got your bed all made up and your toothbrush is by the sink beside Sandra's."

"I don't suppose you've eaten, Alex. I have some cold roast beef and potato salad.

The Farquharsons visited with Alex around the kitchen table while he filled himself with the leftovers.

It was early to bed that evening for all of them. Alex sat with Sandra on the side of her bed, holding hands and chatting easily, but soon gave way to eyes getting smaller, in need of sleep.

Sunday was a beautiful sunny day – perfect for a midsummer holiday. Alex and Sandra were excused from attending the summer church service, preparing instead for a day at the beach. They packed a picnic lunch, donned their swimming suits under their clothes and bicycled over to Long Point Bay beach; they laid out their towels and built sandcastles by the shore. Alex was amazed to see Sandra in a rather revealing bikini, not her usual chaste one-piecer. He studied her slim body, narrow hips, flat stomach, and perfectly proportioned breasts riding effortlessly on her chest. He was enchanted, but at the same time puzzled: Why was he attracted to Sandra's lithe and athletic figure, so different from Eleanor's voluptuous body?

Covered in sand from their construction work, Sandra leaped up and challenged Alex to chase her into the water. He demurred, conscious of the arousal in his swim trunks. Surprised at his reluctance, she studied him, her eyes resting on his trunks for a minute; she smiled and nodded, then turned and ran for the water. Alex soon joined her, running to deep-enough water to screen himself from her, and hoping the cooler water would also cool his fervor. They frolicked and splashed waist-deep until Sandra plunged into deeper water inviting Alex to chase her. She turned and leaped on him, wrapping her legs around his waist, then landing a quick kiss on his lips. His excitement didn't abate; she unwrapped her legs from his waist, and slid off him, her pubis rubbing against his protuberance as she landed on her feet. Her eyes twinkled as she glanced at Alex face, knowingly.

"I'm hungry," she said. "Let's have some lunch." She laughed and raced back to their towels on the beach. Alex took his time walking back to the shallows.

They relished the egg salad sandwiches and lemonade Mrs. Farquharson had prepared for them. They lay back on their towels soaking up the warm rays of the sun, and the glow from their comfort.

They read, and chatted and dozed all afternoon, Alex' body tensing and relaxing with the ebb and flow of his emotions.

They pedaled home in time for Sunday dinner. The Farquharsons had their Sunday dinner in the evening rather than the traditional noon dinner on Amherst Island because, as the minister giving Sunday Service, there wasn't time to prepare a major meal at noon.

Dinner was roasted chicken with all the fixings. Sandra smiled at Alex' appetite and then her mother, appreciating the extra effort Clara had made to welcome and perhaps impress Sandra's young suiter.

— Alex' Choice —

After dinner, the foursome retired to the front porch; the Reverend Farquharson directed his attention to Alex.

"Will ye have a wee dram of Drambuie with me, Alex?"

"Yes sir," replied Alex, "I don't mind if I do. I've never had Drambuie before. But I do have sambuca with my dad from time to time."

"Auch," said Blair Farquharson, "that Italian stuff. This is better. Sweeter."

He glanced at Sandra with a questioning nod.

"No thanks, Father, I don't need any encouragement."

Clara raised an eyebrow, and returned to her knitting.

The evening passed gently as they watched the summer sun set across the fields of Amherst Island.

"I guess early to bed tonight folks. We need to be up in good time tomorrow if Sandra is to get to the train station on time."

Alex hadn't thought of that but of course – just because he had Tuesday off, didn't mean Sandra did.

"I can drive her to Napanee to catch the train, sir. Save you the bother."

"Okay Alex. Is that old VW bus safe?" he laughed.

With that, everyone made motions to go to roost.

"Now kids," said Mrs. Farquharson, "you've had a long day together so no talking till all hours tonight."

Sandra lifted her eyebrows in a smile at her mother. Alex wondered at a possible hidden meaning in that mother/daughter exchange. Women and their codes.

Alex and Sandra climbed the stairs to the second-floor bedrooms almost like a married couple.

They brushed their teeth together in the bathroom and when they had finished, Alex turned to kiss Sandra good night.

"Come and sleep with me in my bed, Alex," she whispered.

"Really, are you sure?"

Sandra gave him a wink holding her finger to her lips; she took him by the hand and lead him into her bedroom.

She had a narrow double bed, 48 inches, roomy for one, cozy for two.

She pulled back the comforter and pitched it on the floor – too heavy for this hot August night; she pulled back the blanket and sheet and climbed into her bed, she shifted her body towards the wall, then pulled the sheet up to her chin.

This was mildly confusing to Alex, so he just stood there.

Sandra grabbed the corner of the blanket but remained under the sheet.

"Here," she whispered, "you get on top of the sheet and pull the cover over you."

He did what he was told, and lay down beside her, put his hands behind his head and stared at the ceiling.

Sandra rolled on her side, facing him. "Come here, Silly, you have to hug me."

He turned to face her and awkwardly threw an arm around her waist but the whole thing seemed very antiseptic to him. Not at all what he had expected.

"But I thought we were going to, you know, make out, Sandra?" he said, confused, almost pleading.

"We are, but if you thought we were going to have sex, Alexander, you are mistaken. Not until we are married."

Alex was surprised by her use of his full name, and that word 'married', and not without some pleasure. She said it as if with certainty, but for Alex, nothing seemed certain in this world.

"This is called bundling, Alex. It's an old Scottish tradition. When a couple are courting, they can sleep together but they have to leave the sheets and blankets separating them."

She smiled and laughed quietly at Alex' confusion.

He rolled towards her; she took his face in her hands and kissed him affectionately.

The tenderness soon turned to passion. Alex found his hand stroking her sheet-covered back and her bum. She pressed her chest against his and stroked his back. He was very aware of her firm breasts pressing against him. She slipped her hand up under his pyjama top to feel the bare skin of his back. She felt the hardness of him against her stomach as they pressed into one another.

He tried to put his hand inside the sheet barricade so he could feel her skin but his weight on the sheet gave no quarter and she made no move to remove it.

Their mouths hungrily consumed one another, gentle cries uttered from her lips as they pressed their bodies harder against each another. She could feel his erection through his pyjamas and the sheet, pressing against her pubis; then he pressed more urgently and she could feel him hold his breath, his body rigid against hers. She whispered, "it's okay Alex." Then felt him shudder, and then relax.

They relaxed into each other's arms and soon fell fast asleep.

Alex awoke with dawn's early light and for a moment wondered where he was. The memory of the night came flooding back. He gazed at the sleeping beauty and carefully extricated himself from her arms.

He went to the toilet and then returned to his own bed, climbed into the sheets and instantly fell asleep again.

The next thing he heard was Sandra laughing, "rise and shine sleepy head.

"Breakfast is almost ready."

She stood there in her flimsy two-piece pyjamas, the morning light shining through them, hiding very little. She turned and flounced out of the room.

Alex shortly came down with his suitcase packed but his hair still ruffled.

"Good morning, Alex. You look well rested," Clara said with a gentle smile.

"Yes ma'am."

They packed the VW bus and made the 10:00 o'clock ferry. The forty-minute drive to the Napanee train station passed too quickly.

They weren't ready to part.

"Why don't I just drive you to Toronto, Sandra?"

"Oh, Alex, would you? It'll be a waste of a train ticket but I'd love to stay with you longer."

They arrived at the Nurses' Residence around 3:00, starving hungry. They settled for rotisserie chicken dinner at the nearby Swiss Chalet restaurant but that didn't satisfy all their appetites.

He kissed her goodbye on the sidewalk in front to the Nurses Residence. She climbed the residence steps and watched as Alex got into his VW bus and pulled away from the curb.

She wondered when she would be able to see him again, but she hoped it would be soon.

Alex pulled into the driveway of the Jorgenson's house at 7:30.

"You're home early Son," said Peter, inquiringly.

"Yes Dad. Sandra had to get back to Toronto today so I drove her and then drove home."

"Are you hungry Alex?" Victoria called. "I have some leftover chicken."

"No thanks Mom, I've had enough chicken this weekend."

But he knew he needed more.

42. Portsmouth Tavern

THERE MAY HAVE BEEN GRUBBIER DRINKING HOLES IN KINGSTON, but facing across the harbour to the massive stone walls of the Kingston Penitentiary made it most intimidating. By 1971 the Tavern in Portsmouth Village was 100 years old, maybe older, a two-and-a-half-story stone building with gable-windowed roof, white stucco with black Tudor-style planking; low-slung, low-ceilinged, home to town drunks and ex-cons, and a few underaged Queen's students.

Drinking age in Ontario was 21, which meant most undergraduate Queen's students had to find other ways to explore emerging Bacchanalian behaviour. Alcohol and the opposite sex were not permitted in the Residences so enterprising undergraduates found other venues: smuggled girls were not possible so smuggled booze into student residences was the most usual form of entertainment. Aided by Wardens who looked the other way, smuggling a mickey of rye was one thing, but hauling 2-4 cases of beer was enterprising indeed. Students living in off-campus student housing with absentee slumlords provided an easier party option, though still needing an older agent to buy their hooch. Counterfeit IDs as passports to Kingston watering holes were for the truly daring, yet as common as the Saturday edition of the *Kingston Whig-Standard*.

For the more adventuresome socialites – under-aged or otherwise – Lakeview Manor, so-called because it overlooked Lake Ontario, a large and rambling white clapboard manor building, with green trim gables and window frames, just down the road from Portsmouth Tavern, was the venue of choice. It was the most popular spot with kids from Queen's – weekend bands, a dancefloor, and pitchers of beer, enhanced the appeal. Kingston Police dropped by occasionally just to keep everybody on their toes.

The King George Inn in downtown Kingston on the waterfront was strictly for grad students, and wealthy sophisticates from Toronto. Nobody went to the main Kingston hotels except on Prom nights.

The home for the truly desperate crowd was Montreal House, a crumbling hotel, close to the railway station. Most Queen's students dared not go there unless on a dare. For reasons known only to themselves, Hugh and his roommates frequented it, presumably as an alternate to the Portsmouth Tavern; the beer was cheap, 10 cents a glass. And they didn't have to worry about ID. Nevertheless, it was a place too far for Alex.

While Lakeview Manor was the beacon for hundreds of socially inclined undergraduates, Alex was rarely amongst them. When he was underaged he worried that he would suffer the embarrassment of being refused service and lose face. Or worse, he would be arrested when the place was raided by Kingston's finest. But in reality, he didn't really enjoy the social pressure of going to the bars and feeling obliged to flirt and engage with women. He was uncomfortable with small talk, and besides it was useless trying to be heard over the crowds and the bands.

In his first two years at Queen's, being underaged, Alex largely limited his partying to Leonard Hall, and then mostly on Golden Gaels gamedays in the Fall. Many kids, frosh mostly, fresh from the confines of mom and pop, went crazy with their new-found freedom. They got themselves plastered nightly, failed most of their mid-terms and ended up not returning for the winter term. When Alex became a Floor Senior in second year, he found it tricky to strike a balance between counseling other residents and leaving them to find their own way in life. At a minimum though, the party people had to be schooled to respect the needs of the other residents in Leonard Hall. Sundays to Wednesdays were relatively quiet on his floor; Thursdays seemed to be party evening; Friday, many residents went home for the weekend; Saturdays were dead.

Though now in year 3 at Queen's and just turned 21, legal drinking age, Alex rarely bought booze or frequented bars, embarrassed to still have to produce valid ID. He may have been somewhat disinclined to go out much but he found himself accepting invitations from Hugh and the boys to join them some Saturday afternoons at Portsmouth Tavern. They'd draw quizzical looks from the owner behind the bar, or his wife – whoever was on duty that day – as the establishment didn't get many students and were doubtful of their intentions. But sociable Hugh would sit for a while at the bar chatting up the proprietors and in so doing gave them to understand he and the boys were not ne'er-do-wells, just there to spend a quiet afternoon. The other patrons would look up from their pints but soon paid the boys no mind.

The boys would spend the afternoon studying the other patrons, wondering what their stories were, but those patrons, huddled in their ones and twos, rarely talked to preppy Queen's undergrads. In consequence, the boys would invent stories for them, often imagined murders and broken marriages. Only a few frequenters were women, likely wives and girlfriends of the men, or waiting to visit their men in the pen, perhaps themselves likely ex-cons, or so imagined the boys. It was not an establishment for the light-hearted set. Certainly, it wasn't a place Alex would take Sandra.

The boys would while away a lazy Saturday afternoon solving the problems of the world: Under what circumstances would capital punishment be justified? Should abortion be legalized? Maybe Quebec should be allowed to secede from Canada, but can parts of Quebec also be allowed to secede from Quebec? Should the USA withdraw from Vietnam and let the dominoes fall where they may? Was Descartes right about existence? Is there a soul?

Eventually Hugh would tire of these mental gymnastics and take a walk around the village. Alex kept his old friend company, joining him in throwing stones into the harbour.

"It's not the same as when we skipped stones across the water at Amherst Island, is it Alex?" Hugh declared, philosophically.

"I guess everything changes."

"Well, not much changes on Amherst Island, Hugh; we change."

They continued to throw stones into the harbour.

"You been back there Alex?"

"Yeah, I've been over to visit Sandra a few times when she's home from Toronto to see her parents."

"Oh.

"You still getting it on with that girl in Peterborough?"

"Na, not so much. She's at U of T and we have trouble coordinating our visits home.

"Besides, I think she's got a boyfriend in Toronto."

The pair stared at the dark water of the harbour.

"What about you Hugh? You've got that girl in Cobourg…"

"Yeah, she wants to get married after I graduate. I'm pretty much assured a job in the Bank of Montreal and she wants a bungalow and a couple of kids.

"You know Alex, I sometimes think my life will be over once I leave here. Maybe that's why I do crazy things sometimes."

"Like drinking at Montreal House?"

"Yeah. Sometimes I look at those losers and wonder if that's my future too."

"Geez, Hugh, that's morose!"

"Well, anyway, …" Hugh's voice tailed off.

"You've been friends with Sandra for a long time. Are you going to marry her?"

"I don't know Hugh; I think about that, but then I think about Eleanor. And I still don't know what I'm going to do for a career."

"I thought you wanted to be a lawyer?"

"I thought so too, but now I'm not so sure. I don't really know what lawyers actually do, and I don't think I'm the Perry Mason type.

"And I don't want to be a psychologist like my dad."

"Yeah, but you could be a philosopher. You're the one who always asks those deep questions, 'What's the meaning of life?' for Gawd's sake. Or maybe an author?!"

"I don't think so Hugh. I don't think I'm smart enough for that.

"Have you noticed, Hugh, we're no longer the smartest kids in the class?"

Hugh laughed, "Yeah, not since Grade 8 at Amherst Island Public School!

"Maybe you should take an MBA after your BA, Alex."

"Na, I don't want to be an accountant, or a banker." He nudged Hugh in the ribs.

"Yeah but, you could become a titan of industry!" Hugh laughed.

They got lost in their own thoughts for a while until Hugh said, "maybe we should go back in. It's getting chilly out here, and it's not just the temperature.

"Say Alex, if you ever bring Sandra into town, let me know. I'd like to see her again."

A few weeks later Sandra did arrange to come into Kingston one Saturday afternoon but she had to be back on the Island that evening. Since they had both turned 21 that summer they had more than coffee shops as a place to meet. Alex thought he'd show her Lakeview Manor. She took a taxi from Millhaven Landing to Portsmouth Village to meet Alex at the Manor at 2:00. But the place was completely dead at that time of day. Things didn't really get started until 8:00 p.m.

They toyed with their coffees, feeling awkward with the emptiness of the place and not having another option.

"We can walk to campus from here, Sandra, or …"

"It's okay, let's just walk."

They left the Manor and walked along Yonge Street to King Street, the heart of the old village.

"Hey, Alex," she said as they passed the Tavern, "isn't this the place where you and Hugh hang out?"

"Yes, Sandra, but I don't think it's a place you would want to frequent."

"Why not Alex? If it's a place you and Hugh go to, I'm not shy about going in there with you."

She stepped up to the entrance and pulled the heavy door towards her, then stepped into the dark lounge. Every eye lifted to see her standing in the doorway as she waited for her eyes to adjust to the dim light. She turned to Alex to urge him to follow her in.

As Alex entered he looked reflexively to the window table where he and the boys usually sat. He wasn't really surprised to see them there, but he wasn't sure he was pleased.

Hugh called out to him, but before Alex could answer, Sandra was already making her way over to Hugh's table. He stood to greet her and she instantly moved into his arms for a hug. Hugh introduced his roommates, Roger and Bert.

"What'll you have to drink? Gin and tonic?" Hugh asked.

"No Hugh, I can drink beer with you boys."

With that Roger found two more chairs and held one for Sandra.

Within minutes she had the whole troop relaxed as she cast her light and smiles on each of the boys.

The proprietor's wife served them, inspecting Sandra closely. She visibly relaxed and spread a protective arm around Sandra's shoulder.

"These are pretty good boys, dear, but if they step out of line just give me a shout." She winked and returned to the bar.

The five of them spent an animated afternoon, chatting, playing darts.

By 5:00 the proprietor's wife asked if anyone was hungry.

"Lamb shanks the special tonight; it's a favourite. And of course, there's always shepherd's pie, and fish and chips."

"Wow," said Sandra, "this feels like a real English pub. Not at all like I expected from your letters Alex."

Slightly chagrinned Alex studied his beer glass as Sandra with a happy glow on nudged his knee with hers under the table.

By 7:30 she announced, "I better get a move on if I'm going to catch the 8:00 o'clock ferry."

The taxi arrived and the boys all tumbled out on to the street to wish her goodbye.

"I had a really lovely time, boys; we should do this again." She smiled and beamed at them.

"You coming, Alex?"

"Ah, I guess so," Alex said, clumsily.

He held the cab door to the back seat. Sandra got in and scooted over on the seat pulling Alex' hand to lure him in too."

The boys all looked at one another and back to Sandra,

"See you later, Sandra.

"You too Alex!"

The cab door closed and the driver pulled away.

The boys looked at one another again.

"Lucky beggar," said Roger.

Alex didn't come back to the tavern that night.

43. The Incident at the Bank

THE JORGENSON FAMILY DID THEIR BANKING at the Toronto-Dominion Bank so naturally enough Alex did his banking there too. The branch closest to campus was on the corner of Montreal Street and Princess Street. Each September he transferred his summer job earnings from his branch in Peterborough to his Kingston branch and drew the balance down as the weeks went by over the school year to cover his miscellaneous expenses. He was grateful that the major school expenses were footed by his dad, but he was chuffed at contributing and managing his own affairs.

Alex had opened his account at this Princess Street branch in his first year at Queen's. Now it was his third year and he was well familiar with the weekly walk downtown to the bank.

It was a middling long walk from Leonard Hall, through campus to Division Street, turning right along Clergy Street following the bend to Princess Street and then southeast two more bocks to Montreal Street. For variety's sake he walked past the Court House to Sydenham and then along Brock Street past the Hotel Dieu Hospital to Montreal Street and finally the bank. But it wasn't a walk he welcomed; more, mildly, dreaded. His solitary walk felt lonely. He also resented the time lost. He often found himself deep in thought, calculating his expected expenses and anticipating his declining bank balance; he always fretted that he would run out of money before the end of the year and he would hate to have to ask his dad for more money. He wondered if other kids had money worries and envied the classmates who seemed to have endless funds.

There was usually a panhandler sitting on the street corner of Princess and Montreal Streets, especially Thursdays and Fridays when working people deposited their pay cheques and students made withdrawals for the weekend. Alex didn't pay much attention to the bedraggled old man with his hat out and his head down, but he did notice the dog, a large German Shepherd sleeping on a loosely bundled blanket beside the panhandler. The well-fed dog reminded Alex of Max, the Thurston's dog chained to a tree on McDonald's Lane in Stella, nine years earlier.

One fine late October afternoon Alex neared the end of his weekly walk to the bank, passing by the Hotel Dieu, and entered from the side door of the bank on the Montreal Street side. As Alex waited in line for a teller he became aware of a ruckus on the street, and a dog barking urgently. He turned his head to look. There was a little old lady clutching her handbag to her chest from a grubby old man apparently grasping at it while a German Shepherd danced and barked around the melee. The old man looked vaguely familiar – the panhandler from the corner? Without giving it another thought Alex left the queue and raced out the side door of the bank to confront the man. The assailant had the old lady's handbag in both hands now but the woman clung determinedly to the strap, while the dog on hind legs bounced against her back barking enthusiastically; perhaps he thought it was a game. Alex grabbed the handbag, pulled it out of the old man's hands and in doing so the old man fell backwards onto the street.

And then he recognized the old man: Nelson O'Reilly of long-go Amherst Island. Nelson was clearly the worse for wear now ten years on and evidently having lived rough.

Nelson pulled himself up from between parked cars in a rage and lunged at Alex on the sidewalk but Alex stepped deftly out of the way so that Old Man O'Reilly plunged into empty air and crashed into the plate glass window of the bank. Nelson turned himself around and took another lunge at Alex, flailing wildly. Like a boxer, Alex stepped aside and Nelson crashed into the parked car, semi-prone over the trunk. Alex grasped the old man's arms and held them behind his back. Nelson squirmed and thrashed, trying to get free but Alex was too strong for him. The dog turned his attention from the old lady and latched onto Alex' arm. Alex shook him off and as the dog was about to take another leap at him, Alex instinctively put out his hand as a stop sign and yelled, 'Max! Down!' The dog instantly stopped and lay down on the sidewalk.

A small crowd had gathered at that point; Alex called for someone to call the police.

"Already done," someone from the bank replied, "on their way." Nelson began to look for his escape, trying to wriggle free of Alex' grasp but just then a patrol car pulled up.

— Alex' Choice —

"Okay, Nelson," said the police officer, assessing the situation quickly, obviously familiar with the ne'er-do-well panhandler, "I guess we'll have to take you to the station to sort this one out."

As they poured Nelson into the back seat of the cruiser the old reprobate glared at Alex with murder in his eye,

"I know you, kid,' hollered Nelson, "you're that smarty pants professor's son. You're the one who stole the treasure of Stella Bay from me. I'm not forgetting what you done."

"That's enough, Nelson," said the police officer.

"You better watch out sonny, I'm a-gonna get you yet."

The officer asked Alex and the old lady their names and what had happened. After they had given their short version of events, the officer said, "it looks like he can be charged with assault and attempted robbery."

The old lady said she was grateful that Alex had intervened and saved her bag, but since no real harm was done, she didn't think she would proceed with charges.

"What about you Alex? You going to press charges?"

"I don't think so sir. I just wanted to help this lady here."

"What did Nelson mean by you stealing his treasure from Stella Bay?"

Alex gave the police officer a quick summary of discovering a long-hidden chest in Stella Bay that went back to smuggling days in the 1930s and Nelson claimed it was his, but an inquiry determined it was rightfully the property of the discoverer – Alex – and Nelson had no claim.

"We'll hold Nelson in jail for 24 hours but if you don't press charges by then we'll have to release him."

"What's going to happen to his dog?" Alex inquired.

"We've already called the SPCA. They'll keep him overnight or until Nelson claims him."

"By the way, why did you call the dog Max? Did you know that was his name?"

"No, I didn't know him, but I knew another German Shepherd named Max and I just guessed many big dogs are called Max. And anyway, it just came out."

"Well, that was quick thinking. Good thing the dog was well trained. I can't imagine Nelson was responsible for that."

That night Alex decided to get in touch with Sean O'Reilly and let him know what happened.

"Geez, I'm sorry Alex. I told you he was back in town and up to no good. I'm sorry you had to run into him.

"But now, he'll be holding an even bigger grudge against you.

"Maybe you should press charges and they might put him away for a few years. Serve him right."

"Na, I don't need the headache of a trial and all. And I don't think the old lady wants to get involved.

"I'll just have to make sure I avoid him."

A week later, Old Man O'Reilly was seated at his usual spot on the corner of Princess and Montreal. And for weeks Alex avoided the Princess Street entrance to the bank, using the side door on Montreal Street. Nelson never looked up from his hat in his lap; but Max noticed Alex, and thumped his blanket with his tail in an involuntary greeting.

44. The Heart Attack

NOBODY EXPECTED IT. How could anybody expect it? He was only 49 and seemed the picture of health. The doctor said it may have been a congenital thing.

The Reverend Blair Farquharson had been working in the Church graveyard with Duncan the groundskeeper that cold Saturday afternoon in early December doing maintenance on the plots – clearing brush from tombstones buried under years of overgrown grass and roots, straightening to a more erect position those leaning stones that yielded to a long-handled spade as a lever. There wasn't a lot of snow on Amherst Island – the damp winds blowing off the lake took most of it away – but the ground was freezing up.

They had come upon one head stone that had fallen completely over. The two of them attempted to prise the heavy stone seized into the ground, straining to move it with their shovels, trying to lift it back to vertical. As they strained at their spades Blair felt a pain in his chest and down his arm. He must have strained something. They continued to work that stone but now he felt his eyes narrowing, his head light, his body very tired.

"I've got to sit down a moment, Duncan," he said, but as he began to sit on a nearby headstone he keeled over on his side. This was serious.

Duncan spoke to Blair and tried to sit the big man upright but Mr. Farquharson wasn't able to hold himself erect. His chest was aching.

"I think I'm having a heart attack," he whispered hoarsely.

The groundskeeper realized he might be right and ran to the manse to call the Amherst Island Emergency Volunteers.

"What's up, Duncan?" Clara asked, alarmed at the look on his face.

"It's Reverend Farquharson," he said, glancing across the parking lot to the cemetery.

Clara understood instantly, dropped her spoon and ran to Blair.

Frank Gohm took the call.

"Duncan, get blankets and try to keep the minister warm."

Frank called the ferry and instructed them to return immediately to the Island terminus and wait there. He raced his car over to the Emergency Response depot, only yards from St. Paul's Church, and set the general alarm siren calling the volunteers from all over the Island. He then drove the emergency response vehicle to the church.

Determined Reverend Farquharson had already lurched his way to the manse under the supporting arm of the groundskeeper. Clara was in a controlled panic.

Just as the community alarm was sounding, Sandra and Alex arrived at the manse, having walked from the ferry from their shopping excursion in Kingston. They entered the house by the kitchen door. Instantly Sandra sensed something was wrong and hurried to the front room to find her father lying on the couch, and her mother with tears running down her cheeks trying to minister to her husband's distress.

Sandra sat on the edge of the couch, looked into father's pale face and dilated eyes. His breath was shallow and rapid. She felt for his pulse.

Blair turned his gaze to Sandra and in a forced whisper, "Take care of your mother."

"Okay, Dad. You just get better."

Alex stood in the kitchen feeling completely useless, an interloper in this family crisis.

Frank arrived a few minutes later; he could see there was no-one in the graveyard so he backed the van close to the manse and rushed inside with his emergency kit.

Frank loosened Blair's clothes. He felt his pulse – weak and fast.

Frank put an oxygen mask up to Blair's face, but even with Alex' help he and the caretaker couldn't lift Blair's bulk from the couch onto the stretcher; all they could do was wait for the rest of his crew members to arrive to get him into the van.

An eternity of ten minutes passed before two more crew arrived; the four men, including the groundskeeper, strained to carry the heavy burden to the emergency vehicle. They fitted the gurney into the back of the van; Clara climbed in beside Blair.

Alex' Choice

"I'm sorry, Sandra," Frank said, "you'll have to squeeze in the front seat with John O'Reilly if you want to go the hospital with your Mom."

The van sped to the ferry dock, siren blaring, just as the ferry had arrived and the necessary few vehicles on board backed off to make room for the emergency vehicle. The ramp closed and the ferry made the 30-minute return trip to the Millhaven side. It would be another 20 minutes for the vehicle to get to Emergency at Kingston General Hospital, already on standby for the incoming patient.

Alex sat on the steps of the manse with Duncan. He felt completely flustered and impotent.

"This is truly tragic," Duncan said, shaking his head.

Alex could hardly keep from crying,

"I don't know what to do. Should I stay here and wait, or should I go back home?"

"They could be a long time at the hospital, Alex. You should probably go back to your place. I can lock up here and keep watch for when the ladies get back."

Alex packed up his things, still in turmoil for wanting to be there for Sandra but knowing there was nothing he could do. He walked back to the ferry with a very heavy heart.

He phoned his parents, collect, from the basement payphones in Leonard Hall. He told his parents what had happened and asked them what he ought to do.

"Shall I go to the hospital?" Alex asked.

"Alex, of course, you need to be there for Sandra," his mom said.

"Now Victoria," Peter interjected, on the extension in his office, "let's not get too far ahead of ourselves. We don't even know for sure what Reverend Farquharson's condition is, though it sounds very serious.

"Alex, this is a bit tricky. I know you have strong feelings for Sandra, and it seems she cares for you, but this is now a very personal family matter and they probably won't be able to include you in events.

"I agree with your mother, you need to support Sandra but not at the hospital; go back to Amherst Island tomorrow but stay in the background.

"Thanks Dad," Alex replied, but he already knew what he had to do.

Next day he took an Amy's Taxi to Millhaven and the ferry across to Stella; walked up to the Manse. There were many cars in the parking lot and the lights were on in the church. Was there a Sunday Service after all? Was The Reverend Farquharson recovered enough to conduct the service?

He climbed the steps to the side door of the manse and knocked.

Sandra appeared at the door. She looked terrible, her face tight, her eyes red. She stared at Alex, blankly, and stepped back holding the door open for him to enter.

She closed the door and turned to Alex again.

"Oh Alex," she choked out the words, "He's gone."

Alex looked to her, held out his arms to her; she leaned into him, her face on his chest. He held her as the sobs came, wracking her slight body. Alex' eyes were wet with tears too. They clung to each other for a long time until Sandra had recovered herself somewhat.

She stepped out of his embrace. "I've got to go back to Mom. She's in the front room. You can come."

She took his hand and lead him into the salon.

Mrs. Farquharson extended her hand to him, waving her fingers to take hers. Alex took her hand and she pulled him to her. He sat beside her on the couch.

"I'm so sorry Mrs. Farquharson. This is so tragic. This should not have happened. He was such a good man."

"Yes Alex, he was.

"I'm glad you are here.

"Blair really liked you. He would want you here to comfort Sandra.

"It was a severe myocardial infarction, the doctors said. Severe damage to the heart muscle. There was nothing they could do. They'll know better after the autopsy. There is a history of heart disease in his family. I do hope Sandra is not affected.

"Any heart disease in your family Alex?"

"None that I know of Mrs. Farquharson."

"Oh, that's good." She looked at Sandra.

They spent the rest of the day just sitting and chatting. Alex made tea.

By late afternoon the vigil at the church had dispersed.

Ladies arrived at 5:00 o'clock with a baked ham and scallop potatoes and trays of sweets.

Alex sat dinner with Sandra and her mother and then helped tidy up.

"I better be getting back to campus," he said. "I have classes tomorrow and I'm sure you won't want me hanging around."

He didn't sleep a wink that night, or so it seemed, his mind constantly shifting from Sandra to The Reverend Farquharson.

The next day Clara's sister and other relatives arrived from Norwood. The funeral was Wednesday. The minister from the St. Andrews Presbyterian Church in Tweed, Reverend Blair's old ministry, presided. Over a thousand people crowded into St. Paul's and out the doors and onto the lawn and driveway, despite the biting cold. Alex attended the service, but he did not sit with Sandra and her mother. He knew it was not his place.

The Reverend Blair Farquharson was interred in the St. Paul's Cemetery, very near the fallen tombstone he had tried to resurrect. Only close family made the dreadful walk to the grave to witness the interment.

Alex milled around the reception area hoping Sandra could pull away from guests and grievers to speak with him. Eventually she found her way across the room to him. She was like an automaton, mechanically going through the motions of mourning. He put his sandwich plate aside and held her hands in his, and held her eyes with his.

"I've got to go Sandra. And you have enough to do with all these mourners.

"I'll see you soon."

But he did not see her soon.

45. Distance

SANDRA'S VISITS HOME BECAME MORE ERRATIC. She was in her third-year nursing and this meant she was an intern nurse taking shifts in the hospital. She didn't get many weekends off so when she did get a chance to come home to see her mom it was often mid-week. And she didn't tell Alex she was home.

When Sandra and Alex did manage a time together, it was strained. Alex felt the distance, and emptiness, that somehow had come between them.

He consulted his father who explained some of the emotional and mental processes Sandra must be dealing with since the death of her father.

In addition, not only had Sandra and her mother lost a father and a husband, Clara was also obliged to move out of the manse once the church had placed a new minister in St. Paul's. Clara wasn't sure where she wanted to be. She had friends in Montreal but she didn't have strong ties with them. She had family in Norwood and had enjoyed her time living in Tweed during Reverend Farquharson's second congregational assignment but had no particular reason to go back to those communities. They had lived on Amherst Island now for nine years and this seemed more like home than anywhere. But now she needed a job and there were none on rural Amherst Island. She decided she would move to Kingston.

Christmas came and went and Alex wasn't invited to visit Amherst Island. He sent her a card and a poinsettia but other than a short thank you card, he didn't hear back.

Sandra became so depressed and despondent she wanted to quit her Nursing training. Her mother needed her; she felt she should move back to Amherst Island to be with her. But Clara insisted Sandra complete her training. The head of the nursing school also recognized the risk of losing her to grief; she invited Sandra to her office for tea, and long chats, encouraging her to stay on. She arranged for Sandra to have light duties, at least until Sandra found her feet again.

Sandra decided to finish her training and look for a nursing job at one of the Kingston hospitals when she graduated in May.

— Alex' Choice —

Alex rarely saw her now, even her letters were spare. Despite his father's advice to be patient, Alex became more and more anxious and frustrated with Sandra's distance. He worried she was losing interest in him and dating other guys in Toronto, desperately searching for someone to fill some unfillable void in her life. Alex surmised he couldn't satisfy her need.

He didn't know how it had happened, but Alex believed he was in love with her. And he knew he was being unreasonably possessive; he had no right to presume to claim her. He'd known Sandra since they were twelve and he knew he had always been very fond of her, but, he thought, more as a pal than a girlfriend; evidently it was more than that now, at least to Alex. He wanted to be with her all the time. But how had this happened? He and Sandra were affectionate with one another but not overtly sexual; well, except for that time bundling. His father had never explained this sort of yearning to him.

In late March, with final exams looming and Alex feeling more and more isolated from Sandra, he was desperate to see her. He needed to declare himself to her. He phoned the Farquharson house, Saturday, in hopes Sandra would be home for the weekend but Carla said she was not. He asked Mrs. Farquharson if he could visit with her and went to Amherst Island.

"What shall I do, Mrs. Farquharson. I'm in love with Sandra and I feel I am losing her."

"I don't think you are losing her Alex, she is very fond of you, I'm sure. She just needs some time and space to sort things out for herself.

"You know Alex, Sandra went to school in Toronto because she felt she needed to have some experience of a bigger place, to explore and learn about herself; that probably included dating. I know how she must feel. I grew up in Norwood but I went to McGill University in Montreal. That's where I met Blair, though I dated other young men. You know, Alex, Sandra never really dated anybody when she was at Ernestown High School. Being a minister's daughter, and even boarding with another minister family, is hard. She never really had any boyfriends after you moved, or even any dates.

"When she went to Toronto she started seeing other boys, and I thought that was perfectly natural but Blair was worried. He and I were talking about you – it was a month before he died – he said, 'I don't know what's going on in Sandra's head but if she's not careful she's going to lose that boy'.

"He was very fond of you Alex.

"You need to patient and give her some time."

But Alex couldn't stop his mind from worrying the problem. Tuesday evening he phoned the nurses residence at the Wellesley Hospital to talk to her. A friend of Sandra came to the phone, "I'm sorry Alex, she's not in". But she didn't say where she was.

Alex fretted and worried the whole night and in the morning he decided to take the bus to Toronto.

He read passages from Kahlil Gibran, *The Profit*, but his mind drifted in and out of the pages, returning again and again to what he should do once he arrived in Toronto. He couldn't sort out the problem and he didn't find any solutions in that poet-philosopher's musings. As the miles rolled by along Hwy 401, he knew this was a mistake but there was no going back now – he had to see her.

He arrived at the bus depot on College Street around 3:00 o'clock. He knew it was too early to expect Sandra to be off shift so he decided instead to find a hotel where he could spend the night. He looked east two blocks to see the chic and modern Westbury Hotel on the corner of Yonge and College. He walked in the imposing golden doors to the palatial lobby, knapsack over his shoulder; he approached the Check-in Counter.

"Do you have a reservation, sir?" the clerk asked, an eyebrow slightly raised.

"No, I just need a room for tonight, and maybe tomorrow night."

"I'm sorry sir, we have no vacancies for tonight."

Alex found that hard to believe – it was a Tuesday and the hotel didn't seem to be busy, the lobby was almost empty – and he wondered if he was getting steered out of the hotel.

He found the courage to press his case: "Surely you can find a room for one night, I know hotels always keep a few rooms in reserve."

"I think you'll find that is only in the movies, sir."

Alex' Choice

Alex was irritated by this insolence but felt his impotence and lack of experience. He looked pleadingly at the clerk.

"I'm sorry," the clerk relented, "I can't authorize something like that. But I'll speak to the Manager."

The clerk left the check-in counter through a door behind him. Alex could hear fragments of his conversation with someone and after a minute a young professional manager arrived at the desk. Alex explained that he had just arrived by bus from Kingston to see his girlfriend. The young manager made a quick assessment and gave Alex a kindly smile."

"I understand perfectly well your situation, sir. But may I suggest a rooming house we have an arrangement with. Mrs. Sullivan's place is just around the corner on McGill Street. Why don't I give her a call to see if she can accommodate you.

Alex felt downcast on top of everything else he was feeling. He realized he had little choice, and in truth he knew he couldn't really afford to stay at this fancy hotel.

He walked a few blocks east from Yonge Street, his anxiety growing as he searched the hidden world of the back streets of downtown Toronto, the rows and rows of ancient abodes, until he found Mrs. Sullivan's rooming house.

Mrs. Sullivan did have a vacancy, and after looking him up and down, signed him in for the night, $23, cash. "But young man," she said, "no drinking in the rooms and no girls."

Alex couldn't imagine inviting Sandra back to this foreboding place with the tyrannical landlady, but now he didn't know where he would go with her.

Mrs. Sullivan gave him supper – chili on toast – and listened to his story. She softened considerably, recognizing the misery of young love even though she was long past her own bouts with it.

"I'm sorry Alex, but I can't help you in this. Rules are rules and I have five or six other guests to think about.

Alex knew that dinner at the Nursing Residence would be over by 6:00 p.m. so he decided to walk over to the residence, arriving around 6:30.

He had to check at the Security/Reception Desk by the front door next to the lobby. The matron checked her logbook.

"I'm sorry sir, she booked out about 15 minutes ago.

"But I can call up to the floor and see if someone knows what time she may be expected back.

A few minutes later a student nurse arrived at the front desk.

"Hello, Alex, I'm Jane Evans. I'm a good friend of Sandra's.

"We've heard a lot about you."

Alex' perked up at this unexpected fragment of information but didn't respond.

"She wasn't expecting to see you here tonight, was she?" Jane asked, rhetorically, knowing full well Sandra was not.

"No," Alex replied, "I didn't tell her I was coming."

"Well, I'm really sorry Alex, but she's not here."

She paused for a few minutes and decided she should report the obvious. "She's on a date."

Jane could see the crest-fallen look on his face, and replied quickly, "but she has to be in by 11:00 o'clock curfew.

"Why don't you come back around 10:30 and maybe you'll catch her."

He found a diner nearby and settled into a booth with a coffee and his notebook. He wrote a long letter to Sandra which he thought he would give to her that evening. And he thought about what he should do about his life – and what would he do if Sandra wasn't in it.

He arrived at the nursing residence around 10:30. Sandra still wasn't back but Jane and Linda came down to entertain him in the front lounge until Sandra should arrive.

She walked through the front door ten minutes later. She was shocked to see Alex and her girlfriends chatting in the lounge. Alex turned to her, a look of desperation on his face. She walked briskly across to where they were sitting.

"Alex," she said, her voice ringing with alarm, "what are you doing here?"

"I just had to see you, Sandra. I'm going crazy not knowing what is going on."

"Don't be ridiculous Alex. There's nothing going on."

"I can't see you now. It's almost 11:00 o'clock and you have to go.

"I'm not working tomorrow. Why don't you come back tomorrow morning and we can go to a coffee shop and talk?"

— Alex' Choice —

She was clearly upset and was on the verge of tears as Alex gathered himself to leave.

"I'm sorry, Sandra."

He didn't sleep well that night, a strange bed, a strange house, and an unrelieved problem.

In the morning, he asked Mrs. Sullivan if he could stay another night. He arrived at the Nurses Residence round 10:30 and they walked to the same diner Alex had spent the previous evening.

They talked through lunch; they both ordered club sandwiches but neither of them had much appetite. Alex told her he was sorry for causing so much turmoil but he couldn't help himself. He said he loved her.

She sat looking at Alex for a long time, not responding. He held her eyes and let the silence between them be.

"I don't know about that Alex. You are my best friend. Surely you realise I'm trying to sort out a lot of things in my life. I want you there somehow but I'm not sure how that will work. I have to take care of my mom now that Dad's gone."

Her eyes welled with tears. Alex' eyes were wet too. He made a move to come around to Sandra's side of the table, but she put her slender hand up, her look told him to stay put.

"I don't know what I want with my life. I just want to go to parties and dances, coffee houses in Yorkville and all the things I never got to do on Amherst Island."

"I understand Sandra, but the thought of you dating other boys here in Toronto drives me crazy."

"You are crazy, Alexander," she said with a wan smile. "You don't own me, and I will lose respect for you if you try to control me."

She started to cry.

Despite her previous warning, Alex came around to her side of the table to sit beside her on the booth bench.

She put her head on his shoulder, crying. "I miss my dad," she said.

After a time of gentle weeping, she looked at him, "Alex, please don't be jealous, you just have to give me time."

"Yeah, that's what your mother said."

"My mother? When were you talking to my mother?"

"I went to visit her on Saturday. I wanted her advice."

"And did she tell you to come and see me in Toronto?!"

"No, she didn't Sandra. That was all my idea."

"Well, don't ever do that again!"

"No, I won't."

After a long pause, both of them deep in their thoughts about this conversation, Sandra turned to him and said,

"Alex, you know I'm graduating at the end of May."

"Yes, Sandra."

"I would like you to come to my graduation ceremony. Please, would you come? My mom only has a few friends without Dad and I'd like you there. You can ask your parents to come too if you like."

"Are you sure you want me there, Sandra?"

"Yes, I'm sure. There's nobody else I would want there."

A moment passed in silence with their thoughts,

"But you need to know I've been invited to a bunch of proms and graduation parties between now and then with people at the U of T, and I need to go."

He studied her earnest face, and understood he had to let her do what she needed to do.

He walked her back to the residence; their hands brushed and Alex grasped hers gently in his, she didn't withdraw. They departed at the front steps of the Residence, both exhausted from their difficult conversation.

Alex walked back to the Rooming House, heavy in thought and in heart. He said hello to Mrs. Sullivan who asked him how his meeting went. He allowed it went okay but as he dragged himself off to his room, her heart wrenched for his pain.

He lay down on the bed and fell fast asleep.

He woke at 6:00, disoriented, but the smell of Mrs. Sullivan 'famous' Irish Stew brought him around. He tucked into a bowl of it, filling his stomach and warming his troubled mind.

"May I use the phone in the hall, Mrs. Sullivan?"

"Yes, if it's not long distance. Just leave a quarter beside the phone."

He dialed Eleanor's phone number. She answered on the second ring. Alex smiled to himself.

"Where are you, Alex?" she exclaimed.

"I'm in Toronto."

"Where?!"

"I'm in a rooming house on McGill Street."

"Oh my gawd Alex, that's only a few blocks from my apartment. Can I see you?"

"Sure, Eleanor. Where can I meet you?"

"Why don't you come over to the Student's Union at the Double Blue Lounge, we can have a beer and talk."

They settled into a quiet booth. Eleanor listened attentively to Alex stumbling through his story. She could read the confusion and anguish in his eyes and his voice even though he tried to disguise the most of it. She frowned at the mention of Sandra's name.

"You've been struggling with Sandra for years, Alex. Maybe you should just let her go."

Alex didn't answer that but could feel the weight of the last two days lift. The conversation moved on and before he knew it, Eleanor had her shoe off and was playing footsies with him under the table.

"Can you come back to Toronto next weekend Alex? I'd love to see you again. There's all kinds of end-of-school parties and dances going on. It would be fun."

"I don't know Eleanor; I've got exams coming up in a couple of weeks and term papers due; I sure didn't make much progress on them this week."

"Well get to work on them and get yourself back here. It'll be your reward."

"Can I call you tomorrow when I get back to Kingston and let you know?"

"Sure Alex, you've got my number," and she gave him a wink.

He walked back to Mrs. Sullivan's Rooming House feeling a whole lot lighter. Mrs. Sullivan was waiting for him in the sitting room. "

"Have a nice evening, Alex?" she enquired gently.

"Yes ma'am.

"Mrs. Sullivan, can I rent a room for next weekend? I'm invited to a prom."

"Sure Alex, the room you're in now is available."

She smiled to herself as he walked down the hall to his room.

The next week passed quicky as Alex worked feverishly to finish his three big assignments. He turned them into his professors Friday morning and was on the bus back to Toronto that afternoon, suitcase in one hand, suit bag in the other. He was excited by the prospect of seeing Eleanor and the glamour of a Formal in a big Toronto hotel. He wondered what she would be wearing to the Formal on Saturday.

He didn't write to Sandra that week. He accepted that she needed space from him, and he was beginning to see that he needed space from her too.

He checked in with Mrs. Sullivan.

"Come in the kitchen with me, Alex," she said, familiarly, "we'll have a cup of tea."

"You seem a lot more light-hearted than you were last week, young man," she smiled at him, not nearly as severe as Alex had thought the previous time.

"Will you be needing some supper tonight?"

"No, Mrs. Sullivan," he replied, "I'm seeing Eleanor for a bite at the diner around the corner. We need to make final arrangements for the Formal tomorrow night."

Alex spent Saturday studying in his room at Mrs. Sullivan's Boarding House waiting for the hours to pass while Eleanor was getting her hair done and her nails and makeup.

He changed into his suit and Sunday best and made his way to Eleanor's apartment for pre-party cocktails with her roommates before they walked to the nearby Chelsea Hotel for the prom.

Alex was all eyes as Eleanor entered the living room. The two other young men, the roommates' dates, also got an eyeful. She was wearing the same low cut crimson gown she had worn to her high school graduation prom three years previous, and with her voluminous auburn hair piled high on her head, exposing a long neck accentuated by a pearl drop necklace that reached down her chest drawing the eye to her cleavage. Her now full womanly figure flowed over the top of her dress which accentuated her waist and hips; with her fiery hair and clear white skin, she was a vision of Venus herself.

Alex' Choice

The three roommates and their dates nursed their Southern Comfort Manhattans, chatted lightheartedly and feeling very sophisticated. But it was time to carry on to the hotel for dinner and the dance. They had planned to walk the few blocks to the hotel but even with a shawl, Eleanor was too exposed to manage the distance even though the late March temperature was unseasonably balmy. The other girls, elegantly gowned and wearing high heels uncertainly, weren't eager for the walk either. They called a couple of cabs; the two roommates and their dates shared one cab; Alex and Eleanor had the other to themselves.

Once settled in the back seat Eleanor nuzzled into him.

"Oh, Alex," she breathed, "I'm so glad you were able to come with me to this Formal. I wouldn't be going if it wasn't for you."

Alex vaguely wondered why she hadn't had a date with someone else but quickly swept that thought out of his mind, distracted by the look and the scent of her.

The ballroom of the Hotel held five hundred attendees. Dinner and drinks in this elegant place made Alex feel very grown up indeed. Dinner over and tables rearranged, the dance began. Alex was mesmerized by Eleanor's every move. He didn't even worry about his dance steps. Before Alex realized it, it was midnight.

He was supposed to be back at Mrs. Sullivan's Rooming House by 11:00 but for this special night she had given him a key to the front door. Still, he didn't want to abuse the privilege.

He begged forgiveness and persuaded Eleanor it was time to leave.

Reluctantly she agreed.

"I wish you had taken a room at the hotel Alex. We could have spent the night."

Once again Alex was amazed at her forwardness, and now wished he had taken steps.

"I didn't think I would be able to do that Eleanor, and besides, I don't have the money."

"It's okay Alex. I understand. I just want to be with you longer."

They got into a cab for the short ride back to her apartment. She laid her head on his shoulder and when they arrived clung to him as they climbed the stairs to her apartment. She invited him in. They were the first ones home. She dropped her shawl to the floor and stepped into Alex' arms pressing him against the door, her mouth reaching for his.

She stepped away from him, then turned and backed into him again. Alex plainly understood she was inviting him to put his arms around her, and his hand inside her dress. As he pushed inside the cup of her dress he felt the gentle weight of her ample breast; he kneaded the erect nipple with his thumb. She reached behind herself and groped for his now urgent manhood in his pants.

"Oh, Alex," she murmured, "I want you."

But just then they heard a key in the lock of the door and stepped out of the way.

"Oh," said her roommate, "did we interrupt something?"

"No," Alex rasped, "I was just saying goodnight to Eleanor. I've got to be getting back to my room."

Flushed and frustrated, Eleanor stepped into him again and gave him a kiss on the cheek.

"Will I see you tomorrow, Alex?"

"I don't know Eleanor, I need to get back to Kingston.

"Early breakfast?"

"I don't think so Alex. A girl needs her beauty sleep."

She offered him an ironic smile, as Alex opened the door and left.

He had another sleepless night, no doubt from the excitement of the evening, and maybe too much Southern Comfort, but mostly from the unresolved tension in his loins.

He wrote Eleanor a long letter on his ride back to Kingston on the bus. He told her he'd had a wonderful time and he looked forward to seeing her often in the summer.

But he couldn't escape thinking about Sandra. The following weekend was Easter Sunday, April 2. He decided to visit her and her mother on Amherst Island. He had promised her he would go to her graduation ceremony in May and he wanted to make sure these plans were still go.

— Alex' Choice —

"Oh Alex," cried Mrs. Farquharson, "it is so kind of you to join me to watch our girl graduate. With Blair gone it will be a big comfort to me that you be there."

Sandra nodded in agreement. She seemed to regard it as given that Alex would be there. He felt he was being treated as part of the family now, but somehow that wasn't satisfactory.

"Are your parents going to come too, Alex?" Clara continued. I am so fond of your mother, so courageous living with all you boys."

"Yes, I think so Mrs. Farquharson. I told them they were invited and they said they would be glad to come. I'll be in Peterborough working at Cashway again this summer but I'm sure I can get the day off and the three of us will drive down to Toronto for the day."

"Oh, that will be lovely, Alex," Mrs. Farquharson replied.

"We'll be staying over at the Chelsea Hotel for the night and taking the train back to Kingston the next day.

"You know that I'm moving to Kingston the first of May? I've found a little house in Cataraqui and I'm starting a job in June."

"Oh, that's wonderful, Mrs. Farquharson.

"I wish I could help you move but I'll be in Peterborough by then. My last exam is April 21."

"It's alright Alex. I have a moving company coming and all the boys from the Emergency Response Team are helping."

Sandra's Graduation Day was May 18th. It was a beautiful spring day, sunny and bright, the last of the daffodils sprinkling the lawn. Peter backed his new Oldsmobile out the garage; Alex held the door for his mother and then got in the back seat. They arrived at Hart House in plenty of time for the afternoon ceremony at 2:00. The Wellesley Hospital did not have a theatre big enough to accommodate a crowd of 60 graduating women and their families and guests, so the Hospital rented the Hart House Theatre at the University of Toronto for the event.

"Gee," Peter commented, "I haven't been back here since grad school, but it hasn't changed a bit."

"You're pretty quiet, Alex," he continued, "something on your mind."

"Yeah, I was thinking what an important day this is, and how Sandra's life is changing. And I was thinking I'd be graduating myself this time next year."

He didn't say so but he had also cast his mind to Eleanor who would be so familiar with Hart House.

"Quite so," said Victoria, somewhat pensively, "they grow up so fast." She looked at Peter, evidently reflecting on the passing of the years himself. Peter was more a sentimentalist than his pragmatic wife and Victoria's moment of wistfulness surprised him. He knew this was a moment to savour.

They soon found their seats next to Clara Farquharson and her sister in the impressive old theatre with its vaulted ceiling and red plush seats.

Soon a company of young women in white – crisp white traditional bibs and aprons, white shoes and stockings, and white peaked caps – came marching down the centre aisle. Sandra's guests strained to find her in the sea of clones, and there she was in the middle of the pack, looking serious, focused and serene. The company trooped to the reserved front rows and were seated, alphabetically. As the ceremony progressed and the graduates were called to the stage, one by one, Peter crept near the front with his camera to capture the moment.

After the ceremony the party repaired to the lawns where tea and sandwiches were laden on white linen clothed tables. Peter looked for something stronger but nothing was on offer.

Sandra joined her family and agreed to a round of photographs and accolades.

She was more relaxed now; she greeted her aunt, and thanked Victoria and Peter for coming, smiled warmly at Alex and laughed at Peter's jokes. Eventually she found herself by Alex' side. Victoria studied the young couple and smiled to herself, remembering her own graduation, not so many years ago, and speculating about these sweet babies and what the future might hold for them.

As the garden party reached its natural wind-down Peter announced it was time to hit the road and go back to Peterborough.

— Alex' Choice —

They said their goodbyes. Alex held Sandra's hands in his, uncertain what to do, but she leaned into him and kissed him tenderly on the cheek.

"See you around Alex. Come and visit us in Kingston when you can."

Alex was quiet the whole way home.

46. The Summer of '72

AT THE END OF THIRD YEAR Alex returned to Peterborough for his second tour of duty at Cashway Lumber.

No longer the rookie, having mastered how to operate a lift-truck without dumping his load, the foreman trusted him with any job in the yard. He had a talent for organizing and arranging inventory throughout the lumberyard; he even relished the tedious task of sorting mouldings and hardware. By August the manager had moved him to work the customer order desk when things got very busy on Thursday nights, Fridays and Saturdays. Those were the busiest days of the week and dozens of would-be handymen bought supplies to take to their summer cottages for repairs or builds.

He enjoyed this job, being mostly outdoors, the physicality of the work, the satisfaction from organizing the stores, the growing responsibility he was afforded. He even enjoyed working with customers; well, most of them; some of the tradesmen and veteran builders had little patience with a Summer Student who couldn't possibly know much about construction. But the novices, and especially the young women, were grateful for Alex' knowledge and help. When they entered the warehouse full of fresh pine lumber and fir plywood they invariably commented on the smell of the place: 'doesn't it smell wonderful in here', they'd say, to which Alex would respond, 'yes ma'am', even though, habituated to it, he no longer noticed the fresh fragrance.

His days were full and he rarely thought about his love life. But every few Sundays he wrote to Sandra, still needing to check in on her; she faithfully replied by Friday, but Alex could read nothing into her words. She was still working at Wellesley but she was expecting to get a job at KGH and move back to Kingston in September to keep company with her mom.

Alex phoned Eleanor as soon she was home in Peterborough for the Summer. She hadn't gone back to the Barrie Physiotherapy job, but instead cashiered once again at the Dominion Store in the North End of Peterborough. They hadn't

— Alex' Choice —

seen each other since the March Prom in Toronto but after an hour on the phone Alex' apprehension dissipated.

"Was that Eleanor you were talking with, Alex?" his mom asked.

"Yes Mom. We're going to the movies tomorrow night."

"So you're back together now? We haven't heard you talk about her for a while."

"I don't know Mom. We're just going to hang out for the Summer."

Alex picked Eleanor up at her parents' house the next day. Mrs. Tysdale was delighted to see him, asked about his year at Queen's and what he was doing for the Summer.

"Maybe we can get in a few evenings of euchre," she suggested guilelessly.

They drove downtown to the Paramount Theatre. Eleanor's bounce and enthusiasm was on full display. It was contagious. Alex reached for her hand in the theatre; she grabbed his hand hard and squeezed and kneaded it in hers. She slipped off her shoe and with her toe worked his sock down his calf and tried to poke inside to his foot. Alex could barely concentrate on the action on the screen.

Afterward they drove to the A&W drive-in for a hamburger and root beer, laughing and chatting. Finished, Alex gently suggested they go up to Armour Heights, but Eleanor demurred.

"Why don't we go home to my house. I'm sure my parents will be in bed by now."

They parked in the driveway, quietly entered the sleeping house through the kitchen, and settled on the living room couch. They took no time getting into their familiar kissing and petting. After a while Eleanor unraveled herself from him, took his hand, and pulled him with her to lie on the carpeted floor.

Their eager bodies pressed against one another, their hands busy. Alex massaged her breast under her sweater. Excitement mounting and wanting more he moved his hand along her abdomen, his usual restraint somehow vanished, and began to let it travel perilously close to her pantied mound. Both were breathing hard.

But she stopped him, took his hand and moved it back to her hip. She turned on her side to face towards him and pressed her hips into his. She felt his swollen groin against her pelvis, felt him pressing against her pubis. She reached for his head, pulled his face closer to hers, her tongue desperately exploring his mouth. She felt him rhythmically grinding against her pubis; she returned the pressure. He stopped; she held her breath as she sensed him holding his and she felt him release against her, feeling her own contractions too.

She gazed into his eyes. "I love you, Alex."

Alex mumbled something similar in reply.

Their energies spent, they began to unwind themselves from each other.

"I guess I better be going home."

She nodded, silently agreeing.

They made their way to the door and said their tender goodnights. Eleanor kissed him deeply at the door and let him go into the night. Alex drove home in a daze.

With both being in Peterborough for the Summer Alex saw Eleanor frequently: they went to the drive-in theatre, the drive-in burger joints, the movie theatres, parks and picnics. They made out heavily when they could be alone. Eleanor's libido was strong; Alex was a healthy young male and could hardly resist responding to her; they explored each other's bodies as much as two people could while still keeping most of their clothes on. Still, Alex he was a bit embarrassed about their exertions on the Tysdale's living room floor; he felt he had to slow things down.

They arranged a camping weekend at Serpent Mounds Provincial Park. To preserve the fiction of chastity they went with two friends of Eleanor's. Alex and Eleanor had separate tents but after campfire, chatting and fondling in the dark, it was time for bed. They washed their faces and brushed their teeth in a bowl at the picnic table then followed their flashlights to the outhouse to pee before bed. Holding hands on the way back they arrived at Alex' tent but hesitated to separate.

"Wait, Alex," she whispered, "I'll get my pillow from my tent."

In two minutes, she was back wearing pyjamas and climbing into Alex' tent. He unzipped his sleeping bag and spread it out for two, then covered themselves with the blanket he'd brought to protect against August night chills.

They snuggled under the blanket, turned on their sides to face each other. They kissed tenderly, not quite believing they were together in the tent. The kissing became more intense. Soon Alex had his hand on Eleanor's round and ample breast, kneading the nipple through the fabric of her pyjamas. She reached her hand down to Alex' pyjama bottoms and quickly found his erection. She stroked it eagerly through the fabric but in minutes she reached for the drawstring of his pyjamas, frantically fumbling to undo the knot. Alex didn't resist. She tried to pull his pyjama bottoms down but Alex had to help with that; she sat upright to pull her top over her head and then quickly removed her bottoms. She lay down, naked on the sleeping bag.

"Come on Alex, you too."

Alex quickly pulled his pjs off and as soon as he had, Eleanor pulled him on top of her. Kissing hungrily she opened her legs to receive him. He fumbled to find his way into her and she had to guide him. Penetrated, she muffled her cry.

"Wait, Eleanor, I have to get a condom."

He pulled out and crawled over her searching for his pants and his wallet. He found the condoms, tore open a packet and threaded the tight latex over his member. She inspected him and stroked his covered tool. She lay back down on the sleeping bag pulling Alex on top of her once again, still strong with emotion but more deliberate now. He found his way back inside her and within minutes his passion was spent.

After a minute he moved to get off of her but she pulled him back down to her in a tight and gentle embrace.

"Oh, Alex," she whispered, "I love you."

Alex was taken aback as those words rattled around in his brain a few moments.

"I love you too Eleanor," he replied in a low, husky voice, and in that moment he meant it, but his father's words echoing in his brain, 'what is love?'.

Their two camping companions were not surprised to see Eleanor emerge from Alex' tent the next morning.

"Sleep well last night Eleanor?" one of them remarked.

Eleanor responded with a Mona Lisa smile.

It was a joyful day of camping chores and swimming and reading. After campfire there was no pretense, Eleanor went straight to Alex' tent for the night. Their lovemaking continued as the night before, Alex stopping mid-way to put on a condom.

"I really wish you didn't have to use those things, Alex. Stopping while you put one on ruins our rhythm. And I want to feel you without that plastic barrier."

In the dawn's early light, Eleanor was ready to resume their lovemaking from the night before. She began kissing him and soon was reaching inside his pyjamas for his erection.

But Alex stopped her.

"I'm sorry Eleanor. I only had two condoms in my wallet."

"Don't worry about it Alex. I won't get pregnant. My period is coming in a few days, so I'm safe."

She pulled him to her again, stroking and squeezing his member. He reached down to find her folds, and felt all the more urgent at the wetness of her.

She opened her legs for him as he clambered on top of her, searching for the way into her once again.

"Wait she said, "let me get my pillow."

She put her pillow under her bum and lower back, bent her knees and tilted her hips up to meet him. He entered her easily, amazed at this innovation and how deep inside her he reached. They both shuddered with their release.

Afterwards, Eleanor laying on her side, one arm around Alex chest, her head on his shoulder, Alex murmured in her ear, "That was amazing Eleanor".

"I love you," he whispered, but Eleanor was asleep.

After their camping weekend, for the rest of the summer they found it difficult to create the right circumstances to be carnal with each other. Her parents' living room risked discovery; the backseat of the VW bus or his dad's big car was awkward and clumsy. They took a big risk of discovery while on a picnic at the Indian River Conservation Area. And they took another sort of risk with contraception. Eleanor eschewed the condoms except at the peak of her cycle.

"We can use the rhythm method for birth control, Alex. My periods are very regular and I can tell when I'm ovulating. You

Alex' Choice

can use condoms during the middle of my cycle but I'd like you to go bareback the rest of the times."

Alex wasn't so sure about this. He understood now what his dad was trying to tell him during the chat about how hard it is to put on the brakes when you are in the heat of the moment. How can he be sure she is calculating her safe times correctly.

"I think maybe you should go on the pill, Eleanor."

"I know Alex, but I have to go to our family doctor to get a prescription and I'm too shy to ask him. And I couldn't possibly tell my parents. What if the doctor tells my mom about me on birth control?"

"He wouldn't do that Eleanor. But I know what you mean. I find it very awkward to buy condoms at the pharmacy."

"Where did you get the ones you have?"

"My dad."

Eleanor opened her eye wide in surprise. "You talk to your dad about this stuff? That's amazing."

"Have you told him that we are having sex?"

"Yes. But he guessed that already."

"Oh my gawd, how am I going to look at him the next time I'm at your house?

"And your mom too? Does she know?"

"Probably."

"I'll die of embarrassment."

"No you won't, Eleanor. You are too self-confident and self-assured to shrink from my parents; more than me."

September came all too soon. Eleanor went back to Toronto for her fourth year, Alex to Kingston for his last year at Queen's.

47. Roommates

THREE YEARS LIVING AT LEONARD HALL WAS ENOUGH. Time to take that next step in being almost on his own – his own apartment. Well, at least an apartment shared with a few roommates. And he had just the solution. His best friend Hugh was looking for a fourth to share digs with a couple of his friends from Cobourg.

218A Alfred Street was the middle unit of an ancient rowhouse complex of three adjoining units, upper and lower apartments, only a few blocks north of Union Street. This was the third year Hugh and his Cobourg colleagues had rented the ground floor unit.

"Geez Hugh," Alex had exclaimed when he first visited Hugh at his new rental quarters in Second Year, "when my family used to live in Kingston, before we moved to Amherst Island, our house was just across the park from you on Albert Street."

The lower-level apartment was quite large: A sitting room at the front, a bedroom next the hall on the way to the kitchen – probably the dining room in its earlier life – two more bedrooms at the back and a bathroom. One of the back bedrooms was large and bunked two. Hugh's friends, Roger and Bert from Cobourg, shared the double room, while Hugh had the single. Alex inherited the converted dining room. He brought a single bed from home as well as a dresser and desk and chair. He moved his fold-a-bed/couch from Leonard Hall as well as his coffee table.

He installed his now upgraded hi-fi system, turntable and a pair of large floor-standing speakers his Uncle Mel had helped him make, and his beginning LP record collection, in the front room. He bought 1x12 ten-foot pine plank, cut in two, from the Kingston Branch of Cashway Lumber and a box of bricks, and from that built a shelving system on which to mount his turntable and stereo amplifier and store his records. The roommates were impressed at this definite upgrade in their furnishings. People in the apartment upstairs and next door were alarmed at the arrival of the big speakers and the prospect of 218A becoming a party place but they needn't to have worried – Bert was a serious student and a classical music buff, and Roger was rarely at home.

Alex' Choice

The boys had developed the protocol that each roommate took turns preparing the main meal every evening and tidy up on a rotating cycle. Dinner was at 6:00 whether guys were there or not. Each was responsible for his own breakfast, invariably cereal or toast, on the run. Bert introduced Alex to muesli and yoghurt. They were on their own for lunch, usually on campus. They were remarkably successful at keeping the place presentable, especially when Eleanor came to town.

Eleanor started to visit Alex in Kingston, traveling by train or bus from Toronto every couple of weeks. Having his own room in the shared house allowed them a certain amount of privacy. Eleanor had no qualms in sleeping with Alex in his single bed, though the running joke was she slept on his fold-out couch.

Eleanor got along famously with the other boys, her natural gregariousness making it easy. She was completely comfortable parading around the apartment in her baby doll pyjamas leaving little to the imagination of the three other roommates. Alex wasn't so comfortable with this display but he had to smile to himself noting how the boys spent a lot more time in the parlour when Eleanor was there.

But the boys also liked Sandra and wondered without asking where Alex' relationship with her stood.

Even though Sandra now lived in Kingston with her mother, Alex saw her less often than he did Eleanor. Sandra worked shifts at Kingston General Hospital, with few weekends off. When she worked evenings and nights there was no time to see Alex, so he only saw her once or twice a month on her days off. Most often he would take a taxi to Cataraqui and take tea with mother and daughter. In many ways it seemed like an echo of his visit to Amherst Island. Sometimes he and Sandra would take in a movie. This proved a bit awkward for Alex as he more than a few times saw the same movie twice – once with Sandra and then again with Eleanor, or vice versa.

Sandra always warmly greeted him when he arrived at the tiny Cataraqui house. Clara too. He would spend pleasant afternoons over tea, sometimes supper, then spend the evening, the three of them watching tv. There was something easy and comforting in this homey routine. Sandra never seemed to seek out opportunities to be alone with Alex. He no longer stayed overnight – her mom's little two-bedroom house was a bit claustral for that – and he wasn't eager to expose her to his apartment and his roommates, and the echoes of Eleanor. Still, it puzzled him that Sandra never asked about his apartment, merely inquired about his roommates; she never joined them at Portsmouth Tavern.

Alex was mindful of his father's advice, that grief can last a long time, and can leave lasting effects. He resolved to be patient with her. Their relationship extended gentle, not cool exactly but detached, almost platonic. So when Eleanor showed up, weekends, Alex' healthy young male libido showed up too. Eleanor's easy willingness and passion simply pushed Sandra from Alex' mind, only to return on Mondays.

Eleanor invited Alex to her Graduation Prom in March.

He rented a tux and took a bus to Toronto.

Eleanor welcomed him to her apartment with expectant open arms wearing only underwear.

"You're here early," she said with a wink and a smile.

Alex was pleasantly shocked and appreciative at the sight of her, the separation of her slim thighs, the curve of her ample breasts swelling up over the cups of her bra.

"Where are your roommates?" he inquired.

"They knew you were coming and went home for the weekend so we could have the place to ourselves.

She watched his eyes studying her. She glanced down to his pants and could see the bulge that had grown there. She stepped into him, kissed him eagerly, then searched his mouth for his tongue.

"Let me hang up your coat, Alex. You can take off your shoes."

She took him by the hand and led him to her bedroom.

Within minutes of passionate kissing, Eleanor had her hand down his pants. In reply Alex slipped his hand inside her panties his practiced fingers feeling for her now wet folds.

She undid his belt and pulled his pants and underwear off him, then, removing her own panties, pulled him to her bed.

"Wait Eleanor, I have to get a condom." She let him go as he rummaged around in his suitcase and found a rubber. She took the packet from him and tore it open, then rolled it down his thoroughly erect member. They fell passionately into her bed.

They roused themselves an hour later, now hungry for food. Eleanor had made a tuna casserole and while it warmed in the oven they chatted over the kitchen table wearing only their underpants. Alex was beside himself in amazement at how relaxed she was with him; and yet, he felt mildly uncomfortable.

She put on a housecoat while they ate their dinner; they watched a movie on tv but Eleanor wasn't really interested in it. What she was interested in was Alex' arms and legs. She took off her housecoat and leaned her breasts across his chest, kissing his neck and ears.

Alex gave up on the movie, turned off the tv and returned to her lying on the couch. He kneeled beside her and began kissing her, then moved his lips to her breast, nuzzling and kissing them, then sucking. She grasped his erection with her hand pulled his pants down over it. She rolled on her side to take him into her mouth. This was the first time she had done this. He reached for her swollen mound.

"I want you inside me now Alex," she said with a husky whisper.

"Wait Eleanor." He went to get another condom, ripped open the packet and rolled it on himself. She had removed her panties, lay back on the couch waiting for him, one leg over the back of the couch; she pulled him on top of her. Within minutes she was crying out in her passion.

"Let's go to bed now Alex."

"I need a shower first Eleanor."

"No Alex, we can take one together in the morning. I'm very tired now."

She lead him to the bed; she laid on her side, her back to him for him to spoon her. Soon they were fast asleep.

They awoke early the next morning, his morning erection poking her back.

"Are you ready again, cowboy?"

"Eleanor, you are amazing. Yes, sure, but first I've got to go to the toilet."

He went to the bathroom and before he had even started brushing his teeth she came in and sat on the toilet.

"My turn," she said. He looked at her in embarrassment and amazement.

They stood beside each other at the sink brushing their teeth looking at each other's naked torsos in the mirror. He could hardly concentrate on his brushing as he watched her breasts jiggle with each movement of her arm.

He rummaged once again in his toilet kit for his package of condoms. She helped him put it on. She led him back to the bedroom, positioned a pillow under her hips and beckoned him to come to her. They found each other in the bed, their lovemaking this time was much slower and deliberate. Alex was in heaven, in amazement, but at the same time, worried that this was his last condom.

They showered together; Alex' mind was beyond consciousness at the feel of her soap-lathered breasts, as she washed his manhood.

They had a busy day ahead of them: he cracked open his books while she went to her appointment at the beauty salon for her hair-do and manicure.

He dressed in his rented tux and waited for Eleanor to emerge from her bedroom, excited to see what sort of gown she would be wearing.

She didn't disappoint. A long Lincoln-green velvet gown setting off her auburn hair strikingly. The front of the gown was deeply cut exposing much of her rounded globes, wide shoulder straps and long sleeves, backless, plunging almost to her bum.

Wide-eyed and speechless, Alex scanned the whole of her.

"Like it?" she asked, coquettishly.

"Yeah, it's beautiful.

"It reminds me of that gorgeous red dress you wore before."

"And do you remember what happened afterwards at Armour Heights?"

"Don't remind me, Eleanor."

"And you made us stop."

Eleanor laughed. "But now you're happy to make me!"
"Eleanor, you are just terrible."
"Yes, but do you love me?"
Alex smiled appreciatively but he didn't answer her.

They went to the prom at 'Hart House'; first, dinner with champagne, then the ball with a formal band, and much more champagne. By midnight they were ready to go home and to bed.

As soon as they were in the back of the cab Eleanor was pulling herself close to him. Surreptitiously, so the driver couldn't see them, though no doubt he wasn't fooled, she put Alex hand inside her coat and then inside her dress to feel her breast. The boldness of her both excited and alarmed him.

As soon as they were inside her apartment she was kissing him again, ardently.

"Give me your tongue" she said.

She pulled off his overcoat and dropped it on the floor, then his tux jacket, and his suspenders, undid his pants and pulled down the fly, and then pulled his pants to the floor.

"Come to the bed, darling."

She turned and began peeling off her dress as Alex struggled to get his pants over his still laced dress shoes. Finally out of all the equipment, he followed her trail of clothes to the bedroom.

She was already in the bed the sheet up to her chin.

"Come here honey, I'm ready for you."

Alex pulled down his underpants, looping them over his erection. He lay down beside her and she pulled him to her.

"I want you in me now, Alex."

He entered her but then stopped.

"Eleanor, I don't have any more condoms."

"That's alright honey, I'm safe now."

With relief, but a small nagging doubt, he entered her again; they soon finished with a mighty lurch.

Next morning she made him bacon and eggs. He had the sense of them living a fantasy, as if they were on honeymoon.

On the bus back to Kingston he thought of nothing but the enchanting voluptuous Eleanor.

So why was he having these nagging doubts?

48. Montreal House

FOR REASONS PERHAPS ONLY KNOWN TO HUGH, Montreal House was his favourite drinking hole, saving perhaps the Portsmouth Tavern. It was rather a long way from downtown Kingston, out Montreal Street, across from the train station. The boys had to take a taxi to get there; the Amy's Taxi driver always gave them an incredulous look when they gave their destination.

Montreal House was a rundown hotel, originally built to accommodate visitors arriving in Kingston by train. But by 1973 it was occupied almost exclusively by troubled transients.

The neighbourhood was as dilapidated as the hotel, with broken warehouses, and rusted broken fences, and tired houses – tiny bungalows and slumping two-stories, with peeling paint and shudders hanging by one hinge, weeds high in the yards. Down the street a short way from the hotel was another large building that could have been the Montreal House's twin – three stories, sagging roof-line, wrapped in false red-brick tar-paper siding, some of it loose and flailing in the wind. Maybe once a hotel too, but now abandoned.

Montreal House may have been a hotel still, but it survived as a tavern, its patrons, the down and out of the area, supplemented by traveling vagrants. Hugh said this was one of the reasons he liked to go there – to observe the fauna of another world, away from that of spoiled Queen's men. It was the same reason he liked the Portsmouth Tavern – the chance to observe ex-cons staring at the thick stone walls of the Kingston Penitentiary across the harbour from the tavern. This side of Hugh always came as a surprise to Alex, making him wonder he didn't really know his friend as well as he had thought, a closet anthropologist, not a budding B. Comm. banker.

The Montreal House only charged 10¢ a glass for beer – those tall slim glasses opening as a tulip at the top – a buck for a pitcher; the glasses held only six ounces of beer and the boys argued they had to drink a lot of them, with the thin pale lager that passed for beer, to get drunk.

The tavern had two entrances, as required by Ontario liquor laws, a main entrance and a separate side entrance, labeled

'Ladies and Escorts'. Alex couldn't imagine bringing ladies to this desperate establishment but the tavern nevertheless had its female clientele, toothless and ragged, some more fearsome even than the male patrons. He wondered which door these ladies used to gain entry to the 'lounge'.

He also wondered, idly, and a little apprehensively, whether he might bump into Nelson O'Reilly here.

It was the last Friday of March but an early spring evening in Kingston when Hugh announced they all needed a break from their studies, final exams be damned. The other musketeers needed little persuading, all for one and so on.

It was already dark when they arrived at the Montreal House, but the tavern seemed even darker, and made darker still with clouds of cigarette smoke; low black painted ceiling, walls painted red, but so many years ago, and now coated with decades of cigarette smoke that it was hard to distinguish the red walls from the black ceiling. And dimly lit – it was as if the manager knew the patrons preferred to nurse their beers in obscurity. To Alex this just added a sense of despair and foreboding but to Hugh it was all part of his study of species. At least he agreed they could sit by a window to keep sight on the comings and goings outside.

Men huddled in their ones and twos on the opposite wall and in the corners. Women cackled at the bar, often directing their barbs at the boys by the window but desisted when they got no reaction from them.

But one night a ragged unshaven patron, slouched over his beer in the far corner, did take notice of the women's remarks directed at the boys.

Nelson pulled himself up from his chair and stumbled across the room where the boys were sitting. He stopped in front of Alex.

"I knows you, ya little shit. Yur the punk kid who stole my treasure."

Alex looked at Nelson, alarmed, his prior apprehension now realized. Nelson glared at Alex menacingly; Alex studied his glass, trying to ignore the old man. Hugh and the boys watched with various degrees of consternation. But the old man persisted.

He jabbed his finger into Alex' collar bone. And again. On the third jab, Alex grabbed Nelson's hand and wrested it aside.

"Leave me alone," he said as forcefully as he dared without adding to the antagonism or drawing attention to the situation.

It was too much. Nelson took a swing at Alex. As Alex drew out of the way, he toppled over backwards on his chair.

Nelson leaped, or fell, on top of Alex, swinging wildly.

Alex lifted the scrawny old man off of him, a bench-press a lot lighter than his usual barbell lift. Hugh and the boys jumped out of their chairs and pulled the swinging and kicking Nelson away from Alex.

A few of the other patrons scuttered around to watch, as did the shrews from the bar.

"Fight, fight!"

The bartender was soon at the melee and pulled Nelson and the boys apart.

"Alright Nelson, that's enough. Those boys weren't causing you any trouble; you better just leave. Go home and sleep it off."

As Alex got to his feet Nelson took another swing at him; the bartender cranked Nelson's arm behind his back and moved him to the door.

"Now you get on out of here, and don't come back tonight."

Nelson turned a murderous eye on Alex and shook his fist. "I'll git you yet, you swine."

"Sorry about that, boys," the barkeep said. Here's a pitcher on the house."

The tavern soon settled down to its usual gloomy mood.

"Wow, that was exciting, Alex," Hugh exclaimed. "He sure hates you."

Alex wasn't amused. He was ready to go home but it was early yet and Hugh and the boys were enjoying themselves, Alex' episode with Nelson adding to the lore of the place.

He picked his way across the tavern to the men's room to take a leak. He could feel all eyes on him. Especially the harpies sitting at the bar.

This might have been an interesting social experiment for Hugh but for Alex, he had never felt so out of place in his life, worse even than the first time he stopped at Mrs. Sullivan's Rooming House in the back streets of downtown Toronto.

49. The Rooming House

No-one knew how it started but a crowd had already begun forming when someone stopped in at the Montreal House and casually announced the old rooming house down the street was on fire. A few patrons lifted their heads but nobody lifted their asses off their chairs to go see what was happening, except Hugh and the boys.

Down the street the four of them raced, Hugh leading the way, his crazy friend Roger Racette right behind him; Bert and Alex followed along less keenly, more out of academic curiosity than excitement.

When Alex and Bert arrived, they looked through the small crowd of onlookers who had collected at the opposite curb but Hugh and Roger were nowhere to be seen.

"A couple a damn fools went inta de building," someone said.

Bert looked at Alex, "do you think?"

"Likely," replied Alex.

Just then Roger and Hugh appeared at the side door with their arms full of articles – a lamp, some clothes, a battered jewelry box. They dumped their loads in the yard, and turned as if to go back into the building. It was mostly junk, but Hugh said "there's lots more stuff in there. Everybody said that flop house had been abandoned but seems people are living there, or something. We're going back in."

"You're crazy, Hugh" Alex yelled and grabbed his sleeve. But Hugh had a wild look in his eyes from too many glasses of cheap beer and excitement.

He pulled away and plunged back into the increasingly smoke-filled house, Roger right behind him.

Roger shortly came back out, coughing from smoke and rubbing his eyes.

Hugh came out a short while later carrying more stuff.

"That's enough Hugh," Alex implored, "don't go back in there."

"Yeah, but there's a dog tied to the kitchen counter."

And with that he went back into the house.

The passing minutes seemed like ages – Hugh still hadn't emerged from the now smoke-filled house. The boys paced nervously on the street as cars slowed to gawk, some stopping to join the other spectators on the other side of the street.

Alex couldn't wait any longer; he had to rescue his friend, and maybe that dog.

More anxious moments passed until Alex finally emerged from the house dragging Hugh with him; Hugh had one arm slung over Alex' shoulders as Alex held him up. Hugh's face and hands were black with soot, he croaked between coughs, "we've got to get the dog."

"The dog's chained to a hook on the wall. We need an ax," said Alex.

By then the firetrucks had arrived and were getting their hoses hooked up.

Alex grabbed an axe hanging on the ladder truck and headed back into the house.

"Where you going, kid?" yelled one of the firemen, but Alex had already plunged through the door and into the smoke-filled house.

Fighting through the smoke and the heat, eyes watering, he found the big furry dog lying unconscious on the kitchen floor. His leash was fastened to a steel eye-ring screwed into the counter. Alex couldn't get the leash unfastened at the wall hook nor at the dog's collar as the dog had pulled and stretched the leash to such an extent that the knots were too tight. He tried to unscrew the eye bolt but it wouldn't budge. He took out his Scout pocketknife and tried to cut through the nylon leash but it was too thick and heavy.

Gasping for air now Alex reached around in the dark and smoke-filled room for the fireman's ax he had brought with him but dropped on the floor when he had tried to undo the knots.

He found the ax and feeling along the counter he located the steel ring again.

He stood with the ax and took a swing at the ring but missed. His eyes were stinging and watering and he was coughing heavily now. He raised the ax over his head once more and brought it down. He heard the satisfying clang of metal on metal and he knew he had struck the steel ring. He tried once more and this time felt the ring come away from the counter. He bent down, feeling for the leash; he tried to urge the dog onto his feet but he wasn't moving. Alex dropped the axe and lifted the dog.

Minutes later Alex emerged from the smoke-filled house carrying his heavy burden, motionless in his arms. The crowd across the street let out a loud cheer.

Alex put the dog down on the ground; he now had a good look at him. He looked a lot like Max, Nelson's German Shepherd.

"Okay kid, that's enough," the fireman hollered.

"Yeah, but I think there's someone else in the house, I heard what seemed like hollering coming from upstairs."

They turned to the house, flames now bursting through the roof and licking the eaves.

And there in the window, curtains aflame in the burning room was a grizzled old man.

Alex instantly recognized him as Old Man O'Reilly. Alex looked in horror as Nelson banged his head and hands against the glass, breaking the window, but that wasn't going to get him out of the house: the window was barred to keep out intruders.

With the breaking window a blast of air rushed into the overheated house and the room burst into raging flames.

Nelson screamed in fear and pain and at that moment the ceiling of the second story bedroom came crashing down, taking Nelson with it into the flames.

50. The Emergency Room

AN AMBULANCE RUSHED HUGH AND ALEX TO THE HOTEL DIEU Hospital. They were treated for minor burns and smoke inhalation but were required to stay overnight for observation and perhaps released the next day.

The story reached Amherst Island in record time by that mysterious communications grapevine that carried news of disaster, this time no doubt by the fraternity of fire fighters, and soon had found its way back to the Farquharson's in Kingston.

"Oh my god, Mom, Alex is hurt. I have to go and see him."

Sandra caught the next bus and was downtown to Hotel Dieu Hospital within another hour.

She found the boys in Emergency. Alex had only minor burns to his hands and singed hair; Hugh was in worse condition second degree burns to his hands and ears, his hair and eyebrows were almost gone; both were wearing oxygen masks but their breathing was steady.

Sandra kneeled by Alex' side. Her eyes were full of tears.

"Oh, Alex, what have you done?"

Alex turned his head to her, pulled off his oxygen mask.

"I'm alright Sandra, just a little difficulty breathing. I think Hugh is in worse shape."

Sandra took his face in her hands and kissed him hard on the mouth.

"Oh Alex, what will I ever do if I should lose you too?"

Alex studied her face, tears running down her cheeks; he was chewing over her words, unsure of what she meant.

"You're not going to lose me, Sandra."

"I will if you keep running into burning buildings, and diving into deep water trying to save people."

"Hmmm," he murmured, "like Stella Bay."

Alex tried to laugh but could only manage a squawk and then started to cough.

"It's no laughing matter," she said with a beginning smile, and raising her hand to give him a pretend smack on his face.

"Don't ever do something like that again, Alexander."

She leaned in to give him another kiss.

Alex' Choice

"I wish I could get a nurse to treat me like that," said a croupy voice behind them.

They turned to look at a now conscious Hugh in the next bed.

Sandra looked at Hugh with relief and a laugh: "And that goes for you too Mister. No more running into burning buildings!

"My goodness, you two stink of smoke. You're both going to need a hot bath and a change of clothes if you're ever going to get that smell off you.'

"Sorry nurse," Hugh croaked, "my hands are bandaged. You're going to have to give me a sponge bath, all over."

Sandra threw him a look of feigned offence. "Seems you're beginning to feel better already, Mister," Sandra said.

The three of them started to laugh and cough in relief.

"I suppose I better let my parents know what's happened," said Alex.

"Already done. Mom telephoned them as soon as we heard. She said she'd call them back when she had more information about your condition. Now that I've seen you, I'll let them know you're fine, or at least, no worse than before.

"And as for you, Hugh McPherson, Roger called your parents and they're likely already on the road from Cobourg."

Shortly a duty nurse came by to check the boys' vitals.

"You boys seem okay, but you smell like polecats."

The three of them started to laugh, and cough.

"What's so funny?" the nurse said.

"I just finished saying the same thing – they need a bath."

"I see," she said. "They're to be admitted overnight so we'll have to remove their clothes and give them a sponge bath to get some of that smoke and grime off. We'll get them gowned and wheel them up to 2nd Floor Meds.

"We can bag their clothes so you can take them home to the laundry."

"I'll take them," said Sandra, then laughing, "but they can do their own laundry when they get home!"

"But nurse," cried Hugh, "my hands!"

"I'm sure your hands will be healed in no time," Sandra replied. "You'll be able to do your laundry."

"But nurse," Hugh continued, "will I be able to play piano?"

"I don't see why not."

"That's good. I never could before."

"My God Hugh, that's a terrible old joke," Sandra, admonished, smiling and shaking her head. "I'm pretty sure you're on your way to a full recovery."

"Either that," Alex chimed in, "or he's suffered more brain damage."

Sandra returned to serious mode, "I guess I better get out of these ladies' way while they clean you boys up.

"Nurse, I'll be in the waiting room. You can give me the bag of their dirty clothes and I'll take care of them. I'll swing back tomorrow with some clean duds so they can be discharged."

Not long after the nurse brought out the bag of dirty clothes.

"The boys will be going up to Meds 2 in a few minutes if you want to say goodbye to them."

"Yes, I do."

She followed the nurse back into the emergency arena just as the orderlies were pushing the beds out of the curtained areas.

"Well, my goodness don't you two look dashing in your hospital finery," she offered with a smirk.

"Geez, Sandra," said Alex, "these gowns are pretty breezy. I'll get exposure of my manhood."

"It's not that cold in here, Alex," Sandra smirked.

"If you can find his manhood," hooted Hugh.

"Okay, away with you.

"I'll see you boys tomorrow."

It was too late in the evening to take the bus home so she hailed a cab at the taxi stand.

When she got home her mom was in bed but got up to check on things with Sandra. She grabbed the bag of dirty, smokey clothes and took them right away to the washing machine. Hugh's jacket was singed beyond washing and was consigned to the trash.

Sandra called Bert and Roger to bring them up to speed.

Clara said she should call Mr. & Mrs. Jorgenson as they had said to call no matter what the time.

Sandra was nervous about calling them, not just because it was now well after midnight but because of the uncertainty she felt had crept into the relationship.

But she called.

— Alex' Choice —

Victoria answered on the second ring.

"Hello, Mrs. Jorgenson, it's Sandra."

"Oh, my dear girl, thank you for checking on our Alex.

"And there's Peter on the other line in his office."

"Yes, Ma'am, and Sir," Sandra replied. "I had to see him as soon as I heard.

"I can tell you that he is fine. He coughs a lot from the smoke inhalation but that will clear in a few days. He's been admitted overnight for observation but don't worry, he is fine.

"He was on oxygen when I arrived at Emergency, but I think he won't need that by tomorrow. He has no burns. They took away all his clothes because they are drenched in smoke and grit. Mom's got them in the laundry now. I'll go to his apartment tomorrow and take him fresh clothes."

"My goodness, that is so kind of you Sandra."

Sandra was beginning to feel the emotion of it all. She began to cry.

"Sandra, Honey, are you all right?"

"Yes Ma'am. It's just that Alex saved my life once, and he was there when my dad died; I can't imagine not being there for him."

"We know, dear," Victoria replied.

"How is Hugh?" asked Peter, shifting topics slightly.

"Hugh's okay too. He has burned hands and singed hair, but he'll likely be discharged tomorrow too. He may need to wear bandages on his hands for few days, and a toque for his bandaged ears. I hope Alex is prepared to play nursemaid for a while." They all laughed.

"I think Hugh's parents came up from Cobourg last night. It's only an hour and a half drive. Maybe I'll see them tomorrow."

"Do you think we should come see Alex?"

"No, I don't think so. As I said, I'm sure he's fine and there's nothing for you to do. I can take care of him if he needs anything."

"Well, that's lovely, dear.

"Thank you so much."

"Goodbye, Sandra, Thank you," Peter added.

Sandra set out for the Hotel Dieu around 10:00 the next morning; she knew, as a nurse, rounds would be just about over and if all was well the boys would be discharged that morning.

But first she stopped by the boys' apartment on Alfred Street to get some clothes for Alex and Hugh.

Bert greeted her at the door, gave her a familiar hug and a bemused look.

"I'm here to pick up some clothes for the boys," she said. Sandra had never been to the apartment before; maybe that's what Bert was thinking about, Sandra wondered.

She glanced around the salon taking notice of the old used couch, the makeshift student shelves and large floor-standing red cloth-faced speakers.

Bert led her down the hall and opened the door to Alex' room. The bed was made, and the room was tidy. Sandra wasn't surprised.

"There's his dresser, and his closet is over there. I guess you can find some clothes for him. I'll leave you to it."

Sandra sat at his desk and surveyed the room more closely, imagining Alex living in this room. She studied his desk calendar. She noticed the previous weekend marked 'Toronto'. Out of idle curiosity she pulled out a few drawers. She discovered a photo of Alex in a tux, his arm around the waist of a beautiful girl with auburn hair and a gorgeous green gown. She felt a sharp pang of shock and surprise.

She closed the desk drawers feeling remorse for her snooping and turned her attention to the dresser. It felt odd to be rummaging around in his underwear and socks picking out items. She found a fresh pair of jeans in one drawer and a heavy sweater in another. His red leather Queen's jacket was hanging in his closet. 'He'll need that,' she thought, knowing his light spring windbreaker was in her mother's washing machine.

"I'm done here, Bert. But maybe I should take some clothes for Hugh as well."

"No need, Sandra. Mr. McPherson said he and his wife were going to Simpson-Sears to buy him some things."

"Okay, then, I'm off."

She had found a small suitcase and stuffed Alex' change of clothes in it, but she wore his leather jacket over her own clothes.

— Alex' Choice —

She arrived at Meds 2 and soon found the boys' room, a two bed ward, ever the roommates. She wasn't surprised to see Hugh's parents already there, hovering over his bedside, but the worry had dissipated.

Mrs. McPherson glanced up at Sandra and exclaimed, "Oh, you must be, Sandra. My goodness you're all grown up. Seems like yesterday you three were in Grade 7 together in Stella. How long has it been?"

"Ten years," answered Mr. McPherson, laconically.

"Yes sir," Sandra affirmed, "I arrived in Stella in 1962."

"And we left in '64," replied Mrs. McPherson. "And here we are in '73. My how time flies."

"Now Martha, Miss Farquharson didn't come here to visit with us. I'm sure she came to minister to Alex."

"And Hugh too, sir," Sandra declared. Mr. McPherson smiled.

"You should have seen the two of them last night," she continued. "What a fright, all covered in ashes and soot. The hospital sponge bath got some of it off but they both need a good hot bath, though Hugh's going to need some help with that."

"But I only take showers, not baths," said Hugh.

"Well," replied Sandra, "with those hands you're going to need someone to get into the shower with you and scrub you down. Who do you think's going to do that?"

"You?" remarked Hugh, good-naturedly.

"Not bloody likely!" Sandra exclaimed.

"Who's going to wash Alex?"

She didn't answer right away. "His hands are fine; he can scrub himself."

Mr. McPherson suppressed his chuckle.

"I guess we need to get these boys discharged. We're going to take Hugh back to the hotel with us and get him into that bath.

"What about you, Alex?"

"I donno. I guess I'll just go back to my apartment."

"Well, no, you're not, Mr. Jorgenson," Sandra interjected, "you're coming home with me. Mom insists that we should take care of you for a few days, make sure you get some good food into you."

Mr. McPherson nodded, sagely.

51. The Choice

THE BOYS WERE SOON RECOVERED and back to their rental house, and back to school. The Fire Officials reported that they were both fools to have gone into a burning building but it was understandable that Hugh felt compelled to rescue the dog, and Alex to go in after to rescue Hugh. No one mentioned that Hugh had already been in the building for clandestine reasons and the boys were glad to leave the whole story untold.

Alex had spent two delightful days at the Farquharson's recovering from his 'ordeal'. He would have been fine on his own, but he didn't mind the attention he got, mostly from Clara.

First thing she did was to point him to the bathroom.

"Shower or bath, Alex?"

"I prefer a shower, Mrs. Farquharson."

"Well, you'll find everything you need there. I hope you don't mind using our shampoo – it's not too girly.

"Here are your clothes all laundered from Friday night. Just toss those clothes out in the hall and I'll launder them. They'll be smelling of smoke after you've been wearing them."

Alex caught Sandra's eye just as he was about to close the bathroom door. She had a look of mild consternation. Alex reflected on that look, and the fact Sandra had been quiet all the way home in the taxi and had quickly surrendered her care of Alex to her mother.

Showered and refreshed, he emerged from the bathroom to the smell of something good wafting down the hall from the kitchen.

"I hope you like beef barley soup, Alex. It was Blair's favourite. And I've got cheese sandwiches on the grill. And home-made pickles."

Sandra smiled at all this fuss and joined in.

"Now Mother, let's not spoil the boy too much."

They sat around the kitchen table, enjoying the company and the gentle conviviality.

"What shall we do about Max?" Alex mused.

"Who's Max?" queried Clara.

— Alex' Choice —

"Max is Nelson's German Shepherd I rescued from the fire. One of the firemen rushed him off to the pound and called in an emergency vet. I don't know what happened. I just hope he's alright."

"So what will happen to him now, Alex?' Sandra queried.

"I don't know Sandra. Probably they'll put him up for adoption but if there are no takers, after a while they will euthanize him."

"Oh, that would be terrible, after you risked your life to rescue him,"

"Yes, and he's a really nice dog. I used to see him all the time at my bank with Nelson at that corner panhandling. He knows me from the incident at the bank last September."

Alex proceeded to tell the story of his encounter with Nelson and his attempted purse-snatching of an older lady.

"Maybe you should keep him Alex," Sandra suggested.

"Gee, I don't know Sandra. I have to go home to Peterborough for my summer job and then next year I hope to be in Grad School, so I don't think I can take care of him. I suppose my mom would take him; she still misses our beagle, Tony."

"Grad school, Alex?" quizzed Sandra.

"Yeah, I think I'll be coming back here for an MBA."

"Really Alex?" Sandra interjected. "I didn't know you were thinking of coming back to Queen's next year. That sounds wonderful."

"Well, that's not final yet. And even if I do get into the Business School, I still have to find an apartment and I don't know about keeping a dog.

"So you see, I don't think I've got room for a dog in my life just now, especially a big German Shepherd.

"Maybe I should ask the O'Reillys if they would take him. After all, he was Nelson O'Reilly's dog.

"Or maybe Mr. Thurston would like to have another German Shepherd to guard his house in Stella."

"Or maybe he could guard my house," Carla mused.

"Mom? What are you saying?" Sandra exclaimed.

"Well, I could use a companion. And it would be nice to have someone here when you're working nights. We have a nice, fenced yard that the dog could patrol.

"And Alex could see his dog whenever he wanted to visit."

They left the conversation there but the next week, Carla had brought Max home.

The last week of term ended without incident. Hugh's hands were bandaged for ten days but he was still able to hold a pencil and attend classes, finishing up his year. Alex had some major essays to submit in English, Politics and History so he had to spend many hours in the Douglas Library researching and writing and little time for anything else.

He wrote a brief letter to Eleanor telling her of the fire incident. He didn't refer to their passionate Prom weekend or offer any sweet nothings. He didn't have the time to see her in Toronto nor visit his family in Peterborough. Besides, Eleanor was also locked down in her final weeks of term.

But he did find time to visit with Sandra, and Max.

Mostly he dropped in late afternoons when Sandra had finished her day shift, or was up from sleeping following her night shift; he'd have tea with her and Mrs. Farquharson. They were gentle afternoons; Sandra was quietly attentive and tender. Max slept at Alex' feet.

He sat his final exams in April. He bid Sandra and her mother goodbye and told them he would be in touch.

"Of course you will, Silly; we've been pen pals for nine years!"

And then home to Peterborough to await his results.

Alex started his third tour at Cashway Lumber in Peterborough almost immediately. Spring was a very busy time in cottage country and they were very glad to have him back, now working most of the time on the order counter.

By mid-May, two weeks after they had both been home after final exams, Alex had still not reconnected with Eleanor. She phoned Alex Sunday evening and told him she had to speak with him. There was something alarming in her voice, or maybe it was Alex' own guilt for having been distancing himself from her.

The next afternoon they drove out to their favourite spot by the dark and narrow channel of the Otonabee River, quiet in May, and so peaceful, and private.

Alex' Choice

Alex parked the VW bus overlooking the river. They studied the dark waters and the cedars on the opposite shore; an awkward silence hung between them. Eleanor turned to Alex, and studied his face; her look was serious, a glimmer of worry in her eye.

"Alex," she said, "I'm pregnant."

Alex was stunned. He had been worried that Eleanor was unhappy with him but he hadn't expected this.

"Geez, Eleanor, how did this happen. I thought we were being careful."

"I know Alex but I guess that last time in March I told you I was safe but I must have been closer to ovulation than I thought."

Many thoughts raced through Alex mind. He had strong yet conflicted feelings for Eleanor; he cared for her, but he wasn't ready to get married, and become a father. He was graduating in less than a month and he had applied to go to Grad School in September. He didn't have a job and had no idea about finding one, or even a place to live. He also knew Eleanor had wanted to practice physiotherapy for a few years before she settled down. They had never talked about getting married, or having a family.

He figured his parents would be terribly disappointed in him. And what would Eleanor's folks think?

"What are we going to do Eleanor?" he blurted, his lip trembling.

She didn't answer.

"I suppose we should get married," he continued.

"Yes, Alex, that might be nice. I could tell my parents today. And we could organize a wedding right away. We could live in my parents' house at first and Mom can help me with the baby."

They mulled this over for a few minutes.

"But Alex, I don't want to force you to marry me.

"I found out for sure I was pregnant ten days ago. I've had some time to think about this and you just found out now. I'm sorry.

"If you don't want to get married, I could still go ahead and have this baby on my own. I could put him up for adoption."

"Wait, how do you know it's a boy?"

"I don't, of course. I just think it would be a boy."

"Oh."

"Or, I could have an abortion."

"Really? But's that illegal."

"Yes, I know, but I talked to my doctor, and he said something could be arranged.

"He also said, once this pregnancy is resolved he was going to put me on birth control pills.

"He said, 'If you knew you were going to be sexually active, why didn't you come to me before now?'

"I told him I was afraid to because he would tell my mom.

"You were right Alex. I should have gone to see him."

"It's too late now," Alex said ruefully, but not accusatorily.

"So what are we going to do now?" he said.

"I guess you're going to have to think about this for a few days, but we need to make a decision soon."

Alex stared at the far bank of the river, his mind jammed with jumbled thoughts.

Later that evening Alex decided he needed to speak with his father. It was Monday and so Victoria would be out for her Cub Pack meeting. He couldn't wait. He asked his dad if they could have a chat. In his study. Peter raised an eyebrow and they moved into Peter's home office.

Alex told him all about Eleanor's announcement. Peter listened very carefully to his son's story, with no interruptions or questions. When Alex was done, he said, "Well Son, this is an important moment in your life, but I should tell you it's not the first time something like this has happened to young people, or even older people.

"May I ask you a few questions, Alex?"

"Sure Dad."

"What do you think your responsibilities are to Eleanor?" Peter asked.

"I'm very fond of her, Dad. She's fun to be with, she's exciting and ambitious; she has plans and dreams for her life.

"I think I should marry her, Dad. I should take care of her and her baby."

"It's your baby too, Son.'

Alex grimaced.

"Of course, you have responsibilities for this pregnancy, just as Eleanor has. But you also have responsibilities for your own life, and for Eleanor's. Both of you have hopes and dreams, forging a career and living your lives as fully as you can. Marrying and having a family may be part of those dreams but this pregnancy has hijacked those plans. It's a difficult moral and ethical problem you both face, balancing a duty you have to this zygote, versus a duty you have to your own future happiness.

"There may be other solutions to this problem."

"Yeah, Eleanor has already thought about that. She said if I didn't want to marry her, she could have the baby anyway, or give him up for adoption. She also said she could have an abortion."

"Yes, Alex, I think she's right, those are her other options.

"You are part of this problem, but the choice is hers as to what she wants to do about this.

"If she decides to keep the baby then you will of course have obligations to support her. Your mother and I can support you in that until you get yourself established in your career, so put that aside for the moment. But to help you decide, I need you to answer a few more questions."

"Sir?"

"Do you love her, Son?"

"I don't know Dad. I don't know what I think."

"That's alright, Alex; love is a very complicated thing, a word used in too many ways and often loosely. When you are young and driven by hormones it's very hard to tell what is love and what is lust.

"Obviously, Eleanor can raise your desire for her; and she is a very lusty young woman, I can see that easily myself, she exudes sexuality.

"Have you ever told her you love her?"

"Yeah, mostly just after we've had sex. I have strong feelings of warmth, and even gratitude."

"Yes, that is a very common feeling following loving sex.

"And has she told you she loves you?"

"Oh yes, many times. She's not exactly casual about it but the words come easily to her it seems, and especially when we are making out and she is ready for intercourse. That's when she tells me."

"Well, that's a very common thing for women. It's almost as if they give themselves permission to take the next step because they believe they love the man and hope he loves her in return."

Alex took a minute to absorb this new wisdom.

"But you don't think you love her."

"No, I guess not, not really; in fact, I often feel a little frightened about her, her passion; but I think I can learn to love her, Dad,"

"Yes, Son, probably you can. And you can also come to resent her.

"Let me ask you another question: Do you love Sandra?"

Alex was surprised at this question. He hadn't expected Peter to bring Sandra into this conversation. He just looked at his dad with confusion written all over his face.

"I see you are unprepared for that question, but I want you to answer it anyway. What's the first thought that comes into your mind: do you love Sandra?"

"Yes Dad," Alex replied, his lip trembling, his eyes filling with tears.

"Your mother and I have known you have had a strong bond with Sandra for years. There have been many obstacles and yet you are still closely connected with her.

"Have you had sex with Sandra?"

"No Dad. We've made out a lot and we both seem to have strong urges, but we never take it all the way. She always puts on the brakes. I respect her too much to pressure her, and I think she respects herself too much to compromise herself if she doesn't feel completely ready."

"Yeah, I understand that, raised as a minister's daughter in a strict Presbyterian home."

"Maybe, but I think it's more than that."

"Does this mean you don't respect Eleanor?"

"That's not right Dad. Of course I respect Eleanor. But it's different. Eleanor is eager – she mostly pushes me into it. Sandra is somehow more, I don't know, chaste."

"So, you love Sandra, even though you haven't had sex with her."

"Yes, I guess I do."

"Have you told her you love her?"

Alex' Choice

"Yes, back a year ago when her father died and I thought I was losing her. I went through a crazy time and beseeched her."

"You mean that time you took the bus to Toronto to see her?"

"How do you know about that?"

"You should know better than to tell your brother your secrets," he said, smiling at Alex.

"But you never said anything."

"Well Son, some things should be just left alone."

"Does mom know?"

"No, I don't think so; and I told Oliver to keep that to himself.

"But your mom is worried about you. She can sense that you are in a dilemma over Eleanor and Sandra. I told her not to interfere, that you had to work these things out for yourself and if you wanted advice, you would ask for it.

"And I'm not going to tell her about our conversation here. That will be up to you."

They let that thought rest for a while.

"So when you went to Toronto to see Sandra," Peter continued, "that probably wasn't real love, Alex, that was possessiveness, and fear, mixed with desperation."

"Yeah, I guess. She told me never to do that again."

"Has she ever told you she loves you?"

"Yes, after the fire when she visited me in the hospital. She was crying and holding me close. That's when she told me."

"And what did you say?"

"I didn't say anything. I was crying too but I didn't know what to think. I thought I was committed to Eleanor.

"But that was two months ago, and since then I've been thinking all the time about Sandra and neglecting Eleanor."

"Ah, and now Eleanor has reached out to you and tells you she is pregnant.

"Why don't we leave this a few days for you to think on a bit more. This is one of the biggest decisions you will have to make in your life, so you need to give it a lot of hard thought. Not only as it affects your own future but Eleanor's as well. However, if she is pregnant we need to move fairly quickly to consider all your options, you and Eleanor both."

337

The next day early Peter went to his office at Trent and called Eleanor at home. She hadn't left for work yet as he hoped. And she answered the phone.

"Eleanor," he said, "It's Peter Jorgenson."

Eleanor was on full alert now.

"Yes sir?"

"Alex has told me what you told him. He doesn't know I'm calling you."

"Eleanor," he said, gently, "I want you to know that Mrs. Jorgenson and I are very fond of you and we would want what's best for you both. You must be aware this situation will affect the two of you for the rest of your lives. The two of you need to make some important decisions, but the final choice must be yours.

"Have you told your parents, yet? You shouldn't have to do this alone."

"No sir, I haven't told my parents. I don't know how."

"If you are willing to discuss this with me, I'd be glad to guide you."

"Okay, sir, I'd like that. I feel so trapped."

"There's no need to feel you have to do this all by yourself.

"Can you come and meet me at my office. It will be very private there. I meet with students all the time."

"Yes sir. I can come today – it's my day off."

"Well, come as soon as you can.'

"Where's your office, sir?"

Eleanor arrived at Professor Jorgenson's office 30 minutes later. She was smartly dressed in a green plaid pleated skirt, crisp white blouse and green blazer, and woolen tam. She looked the perfect image of a Trent University student, not University of Toronto. How clever, thought Peter Jorgenson.

"Thank you for coming downtown to meet with me, Eleanor. I know this is very unusual and you must be nervous, but please, just try to relax."

"It's okay Mr. Jorgenson."

"When Alex told me of your situation – and I mean your and Alex' situation – we talked about the consequences for your whole lives because of it."

Eleanor nodded.

— Alex' Choice —

"He says he likes you very much; he finds you exciting and he admires your self-confidence and assertiveness.

"But then I asked him if he loves you.

"He said, he didn't know."

Eleanor looked downcast at this.

"Do you love Alex, Eleanor."

"Yes, I do, Mr. Jorgenson. I want to be with him all the time. And I am so excited when I am with him."

"I can see that, Eleanor. You are a very passionate young woman, and I understand what Alex means when he says you are assertive, you go after whatever it is you want.

"I don't mean that as a bad thing Eleanor. Women today are learning they have to take care of their own needs and wants."

"Yes sir. I know that. My mother has drummed that into me since I was little, that I need to have a career that I can fall back on."

"Alex says he will marry you and take care of you if that's what you want."

"No, Mr. Jorgenson, I don't want Alex to marry me because he thinks he has to."

"What do you want, Eleanor?"

"I just want him to love me."

She was beginning to cry now. Peter offered her the box of tissue he always kept in his office.

"You realize Alex has long had another girl in his life."

"Yes, Mr. Jorgenson. He's told me a little about Sandra from Amherst Island." She looked a little glum.

"And I know she went to see him in hospital when he was injured in the fire.

"And that's when he began to go silent."

Eleanor was crying harder now.

Peter waited, then said, "and what else, Eleanor?"

She looked up at Peter, her eyes full of tears,

"I'm not pregnant, Mr. Jorgenson.

"I just told Alex that in hopes he would love me and we could be together again."

Peter gave her time to compose herself.

"You know Eleanor, if he committed to you under these false pretenses, what do you think would happen?"

"He would be very disappointed in me. Probably he would grow to hate me."

"Maybe, Eleanor. And you know then, that is not a good basis for a long-term relationship, never mind a marriage."

"Yes, I know, sir. I'm very sorry I caused all this trouble."

"But better we fix it now than later, Eleanor.

"I know you must be in a lot of pain, and I'm very sorry for that. I'm sure Alex never meant to cause you this pain."

"So why did he keep on seeing Sandra and still fucking me?"

Then quickly, "I'm sorry sir, that was vulgar."

"You had every right to say that. You were having sex with Alex and you loved him. He wasn't being completely honest with you and you felt betrayed."

"He never really talks about her, but he's said enough that I know she is still a big part of his life."

"I think so Eleanor, but I also think he's quite unsure of her.

"Still, tricking him into marrying you would likely make things worse."

"Yes, I see that now.

"So, what should I do?"

"You need to call Alex and continue your conversation. He intends to call you once he's decided what he thinks is best for the two of you, but I think it best if you call him first.

"I don't know what he will decide about his relationship with you, or with Sandra, but if he decides he wants to be with you it must be because he truly loves you."

She smiled at him.

"I understand sir. I know that's right.

"Will you be telling Alex about our conversation?"

"No, Eleanor. Our conversation is confidential. What you choose to tell him is up to you."

The meeting ended. Eleanor rose and put out her hand to shake Peter's. He took it and shook it warmly, but feeling this was quite inadequate. He wanted to hug her, knew she needed a hug, but it was not appropriate. He gave a mental shrug and noted the conflicting aspects of social expectations.

That night she called Alex and asked him to meet her.

"I know you may not be ready, but I need to see you again."

"Okay, Eleanor, how about tomorrow evening? We could drive down to Cleary Park and watch the fountain in Little Lake."

"I'd like that, Alex. I don't want to go back to our swimming hole again."

He picked her up at 7:00 and they drove to the municipal park. They found a private bench away from strollers and settled there. She sat close to him and reached for his hand. Alex grasped hers tenderly and began to speak. She put a finger to his lips and said, "shhh, don't say anything. I need to speak first."

He turned to face her, very unsure what would happen next.

"Alex, I lied to you when I said I'm pregnant."

Alex opened his eyes wide in amazement.

"I just told you that because I was afraid I was losing you.

"I know now that was a mistake.

"It would be an empty relationship built on a lie. You would find out anyway and then you would hate me.

"I would hate myself if that happened."

Alex studied her for a long while. He didn't say anything, only thinking all the implications of what she had just told him.

"Are you mad at me Alex?"

"No, Eleanor, I'm not angry with you.

"I'm very grateful you told me this.

"I wasn't ready to marry you Eleanor, but I would have if you wanted me to."

"I do want you to marry me Alex, but not this way. I know now that if you want to marry me it's because you truly love me.

"But I think you love that Sandra girl."

Alex looked at Eleanor for the longest time, studying her comely face, the wonderful times of their lovemaking flashing across his mind. He pushed those thoughts out of his mind. It was becoming clearer what he wanted to do now.

"I'm not sure what the future holds for me, Eleanor, but thank you for letting me go free. I will always love you for that."

He kissed her tenderly, she accepted passively. They got up from the bench and walked to the car.

They didn't hold hands.

52. Graduation Day

IT WAS A FINE SUNNY MORNING THE FIRST FRIDAY IN JUNE. Alex stood on the corner of University and Union contemplating the day ahead, and the days that had led up to this one.

Alex' graduation ceremony for Arts and Science 1973 was at 11:00 a.m. at the new Jock Harty Arena. The ancient and majestic Grant Hall had grown too small to accommodate 600 graduates and their families. The graduands had to be at the Student Union to collect their gowns and mortar boards at least an hour beforehand and at the Arena by 10:30.

Alex had driven down to Kingston with his parents the night before. They spent the night at the downtown Holiday Inn and after breakfast, dropping Alex at the Union, Peter and Victoria drove to Cataraqui to pick up Sandra and Clara Farquharson. Victoria was delighted when she heard that Sandra and Clara were to be Alex' guests. She had quietly asked Peter what was the situation with Eleanor and suffered mixed feelings when he told her he thought that relationship was over.

Alex had hardly slept the night before, his mind full of excitement and anticipation of everything that was to happen that day. He could hardly believe that Sandra would be there too. His heart fluttered a bit at the thought of her.

As he viewed the familiar buildings from the corner of Union and University, he reached reflexively into his pocket, feeling for the ring he knew was there.

In the week after his fateful meeting with Eleanor his mind was in constant churn as he considered his future, the harm he had caused Eleanor, and his uncertainty about Sandra. It was two weeks until graduation and he had so many unresolved questions about his future: would he be going to Grad School next September? If so, where was he going to live, and if not, what should he do about a job? He began to think he'd be spending the next year still working at the Cashway Lumber Yard. But mostly he thought about Sandra.

On his next day off, he went to downtown Peterborough to deposit his pay cheque in the Toronto-Dominion Bank. Across

— Alex' Choice —

the street was Peterborough Credit Jewelers. He crossed the street and went in. He studied the rings in the glass covered cabinet.

A middle-aged sales lady with greying hair and a maternal manner, said, "Do you have marriage in mind young man?"

Alex was shaken out of his thoughts at her voice, startled to hear the word marriage out loud.

"Um, yes, I guess so," Alex mumbled dumbly.

"Well, you've come to the right place if you are interested in a quality wedding set at a good price."

Alex nodded, his vague thinking becoming more focused.

He pointed through the glass, "How much is this set?"

The sales lady unlocked the display case and put the ring set – engagement ring and matching wedding ring – on the counter in front of Alex.

"Well young man, that depends on a number of things: you can buy the engagement ring alone or you can buy the set of rings. The engagement ring here is $400, but that depends on what size of centre stone you select. The ring set is $600 if you buy them both together now, but $650 if you buy them separately."

"Oh, that's a lot of money."

"Yes it is, young man, but the rule of thumb is that the engagement ring should be about one month's salary."

"Oh. But I'm still a university student and my summer job doesn't pay very much."

"What's your name, young man?"

"It's Alex Jorgenson."

"What are you studying at University, Alex?"

"Politics, Ma'am. I'm graduating Queen's in two weeks, and I hope to enroll in the School of Business in September."

"Well, Congratulations!

"And the young lady?"

"She's a Nurse at KGH in Kingston."

"Oh, lovely. But she won't be able to wear her rings at work, you know. If she should ever break a thermometer the mercury would ruin the gold rings. But we could make a stainless-steel ring for her."

Alex looked at her, startled. He hadn't thought of that; he wondered how Sandra would feel, not being able to wear her rings.

"I like this one," Alex declared, slipping the rings on his little finger. "I like the little wings with tiny diamonds that sort of interlink. It has a different look than the other sets."

"Yes it does, Alex. Do you think your girlfriend will like it?"

A small involuntary shudder tricked Alex' mind at the word 'girlfriend'. He knew he loved Sandra but he always thought of her as someone he had always loved, not his 'girlfriend'.

"I think so," he said. "She likes things that are just a bit out of the ordinary. I think we are similar that way.

"But can I put a different stone in the centre other than a diamond? She really likes green. I was wondering if I could put an emerald instead of a diamond."

"Well, diamonds are traditional, but I don't see why not. It would certainly stand out."

"I'd like to take this one. But I don't have $400 just now."

"Well, Alex, that is something we can work out. I don't have any loose emeralds in the store but I can order some for delivery in a couple of days. I'll need a deposit if I should order one and have it mounted in this setting in place of the diamond."

"How much deposit do you need?" Alex asked, nervously.

"A 40% deposit will allow me to hold it for you and order the stones."

"Okay," said Alex. "Will you take a cheque?"

"Yes indeed.

"And I will hold the wedding ring for you and let you have the set for $600. I can have the ring ready for you next Monday."

So Alex wrote a cheque for $160 dollars. It would just about empty his bank account and now he worried how he would raise the balance of the payment.

On Thursday at work, he took Steve Peconi aside and asked him if he could borrow $240 to cover the balance.

"Sure thing Alex. What's up?"

"I want to buy an engagement ring."

"Wow. No shit."

"If you can give me the money tomorrow or Saturday, I can go back to the jeweler's and pick up the ring. I'll pay you back by the middle of July."

"Okay. I can do that. Glad to help a man about to give his life away," Steve smiled.

— Alex' Choice —

"But please don't tell anyone, Steve."

"Sure thing, Alex. Mum's the word."

Alex went back to the Jewelry store the next Monday. Mrs. Holden was there to greet him.

"Well Alex, I think you're going to really like the stone we installed in the ring.

"It's a lovely pale emerald, lighter than most emeralds but we think it looks happier than the darker emeralds. All emeralds have flaws in them, and this stone has one also. Only a jeweler would notice it but this flawed stone allows us to insert a bigger emerald in the ring than the diamond that was there."

And with that she opened the ring box and showed him the ring.

"Oh my goodness, it's beautiful," exclaimed Alex. "It's everything I had hoped for Sandra."

"Sandra, is it?

"Well, Alex, if she truly loves you, she will love this ring. You have wonderful taste."

He wore the black robes over his suit, carried his mortar board hat in his hand and red and gold stole over his arm. He studied Dunning Hall across the diagonal of University and Union. He peered south on University Avenue towards Grant Hall. He always enjoyed this view of the gently sloping downhill street, the centre boulevard with tall draping elms, leafy now in June throwing shade all down the avenue. He took a long look at Douglas Library and conjured up the image of the expansive stately reading room on the third floor and the many hours he had spent there. The ancient and ugly Ontario Hall with its heavy stone steps and oak doors – he always thought this building dour. Across the street to little Richardson Hall, the nerve centre of the University. And finally to Grant Hall with its classic clock tower.

As he walked towards the Arena he melded with hundreds of graduands all heading the same direction, their journey at Queen's almost over, four fast years having raced into the past.

The graduands congregated in Bews Gym, next door to the Arena, to get instructions from the proctor: 'you are arranged in alphabetic order, you will parade single file, down the centre isle of the Arena, eyes front – not searching the stands for family; you wear the mortar boards and carry the hoods. Then you sit in the front rows of the hall in the order you paraded in; when instructed you will line up, ten at a time, to the left of the stage. As each graduand's name is called, you will climb the steps of the stage, cross to the centre, face the Dean of Arts and the Chancellor, and kneel. Remove the mortar board and pass the stole to the Dean who will put it over the graduand's head and arrange it. The Chancellor will take the mortar board and touch each shoulder with the edge of the mortar board, place it on the graduand's head, and hand you your parchment; then announce, 'rise, Bachelor of Arts'. Rise and exit stage right, returning in order to your original seat. Do not gesticulate to the assembly.

Alex could already feel the emotion of the moment ahead.

The ceremony proceeded quickly, God Save the Queen, and the Lord's Prayer. Honourary Degrees were awarded to the year's nominees and a valedictory address was given urging the new graduates to honour themselves and their alma mater in their lives ahead. Then the parade of graduands.

Before he knew it, Alex was exuenting the Hall and waiting for his parents on the lawns. He saw Sandra first and his heart took a little leap: the slim figure dressed in a lime green summer dress, white lace collar and white buttons down the front, a matching belt cinching her tiny waist, the skirt several inches above her knees as was the fashion. She took his breath away.

Victoria and Clara didn't miss the look of admiration that Alex sent her way. Peter nodded at two young people, their whole lives ahead of them, but how would it unroll? They posed for many photographs, a very contented party.

The University had laid on tea and sandwiches but Peter opted for a luncheon for the five of them at Aunt Lucey's Restaurant. Alex struggled throughout lunch trying to figure out how he could organize some private time with Sandra.

After lunch Peter took a trip to the men's room and Alex followed him.

"Dad, would you mind if I stayed over this weekend in Kingston. I haven't seen Sandra in months and I haven't had much private time with her today."

"I understand Son. Where will you stay tonight then? And how do you plan on getting home?

"I can sleep on the Farquharson's couch. I've done that many times before.

"And I thought I would take the train to Cobourg on Sunday. Could you pick me up there?"

"Sure Son, that's okay.

"You probably need some money. Here's a hundred bucks."

"Gee, thanks, Dad," Alex said, full of gratitude for his dad's understanding.

Saturday was another beautiful June day. Clara had welcomed Alex home the previous afternoon, organized a light supper and watched tv with the kids before heading off to bed, leaving Alex and Sandra some time to themselves. Alex had been on pins and needles all day waiting for the chance to be with Sandra, rehearsing in his mind what he wanted to say to her. Sandra had been warm and comfortable throughout the day, happy to have been part of Alex' special day, but quietly at a distance. They sat together on the couch, gently holding hands. Alex searched his mind for how he would put the question he longed to put to Sandra. He wanted it to be in a romantic place, not on Clara's couch.

"What do you say we go for a picnic tomorrow, just you and me. We could pack a lunch and go someplace quiet."

"I'd love that, Alex. But we don't have a car. Where can we go by bus for a picnic?"

"I have an idea, Sandra. We can get a taxi to take us to Kingston Mills. It's not far and we can watch the boats go through the locks.

"We can get the driver to stop at Kentucky Fried Chicken to pick up some take-out; all we'd need is a blanket."

"That sounds like fun, Alex. You are full of ideas, aren't you?"

Alex thought to himself, 'she has no idea what else I have in mind'.

So next morning he called Amy's Taxi to pick them up around 10:30 and drop them at the locks at Kingston Mills, to return to get them at 4:00. It was a lovely warm late Spring day. Sandra brought an old woolen blanket from home, and a towel.

"What's the towel for, Sandra?" Alex asked.

Sandra pulled up her shirt to reveal her bikini top underneath.

"I might go swimming," she said coquettishly.

"But I don't have any trunks," said Alex.

"That's okay, Alex. You can watch. Or," she winked, "you could come in your underwear!"

"Not likely, Sandra; that place is too public."

They found a picnic table not far from the locks that opened on to Colonel By Lake. They ate their cold fried chicken and coleslaw, and watched the boat traffic. Alex felt growing excitement, waiting for the right time to talk to Sandra, highly aware of the ring box in his pocket. He laid out the blanket on the grass by the picnic table but Sandra wanted to go for a swim. She took off her shorts and removed her blouse and headed for the mooring wall by the lake. She dangled a toe in the water.

"Oh, that's pretty cold!" she exclaimed.

"Of course, Sandra, it's only the 2nd of June." Alex retorted.

"Oh well," she said, "I can't stop now." And with that she plunged into the water. She swam out to the deeper water a-ways and then swam back to the edge. She splashed water at Alex.

"It's not too bad once you get in." she cried.

"Liar!" Alex retorted, smiling.

She swam back out to the deeper water one more time and then returned; she climbed out of the water, as Alex held the towel for her, but noticing her goose-bumped skin, and erect nipples under her bikini top. She toweled her short hair and then wrapped the towel around her shoulders.

"My god, Sandra, you're chilled," he exclaimed.

"Yes, but you can keep me warm until the sun does its job."

He wrapped his arm around her shoulders and led her to the blanket. They settled there as Alex continued to hug her close to give her his warmth.

Once she had stopped shivering, he started.

"You know Sandra, this feels just like when we used to meet at the fort at St. Albans."

"Yes Alex, that was so much fun."

"We've been friends for, gee, ten years now."

"I know Alex. It's like we've always been together. Kinda like brother and sister."

Alex' Choice

"Gee, I don't think so Sandra. Do brothers and sisters make out and bundle?" he laughed, but slightly alarmed.

"That's not what I meant, Alex. What I mean is, it's like you have always been part of my life. Well, mostly."

"Correct, Sandra.

"And I can't imagine not having you in the *rest* of my life."

Sandra suddenly sensed this conversation was going in a direction she hadn't considered. She turned her face to him, suddenly serious, and seeing the earnest look on Alex' face.

"What do you mean by that Alex?"

"What I'm saying is, we've been together for half our lives already, and I want us to be together for the rest of our lives, too."

Their eyes locked in silent study.

"Sandra, will you marry me?"

Sandra was speechless, she looked at Alex for a long time.

He reached in his pocket and brought out the ring box. Sandra looked down to the box, realizing what it must contain.

"Alex, don't open the box. I need to think first, I need to talk about this. I don't know what to say.

"We've never really talked about marriage before now. We've never talked about what we want in life. Do you want kids? How many? Where should we live?

"How will I care for Mom?

"So many questions."

"Sandra, I love you. We can sort out all those questions."

Sandra remained silent.

"Do you love me, Sandra?"

"I think I've loved you since the first day I saw you," she answered. "I think I've always loved you. I've always thought it was natural as rain that we would be married one day.

"But Alex, now I'm not so sure."

"What do you mean, you're not sure?"

"Alex, I'm not sure you really love me. Maybe I'm just a habit for you."

"That's not true Sandra. You've always been there in my mind. When I moved to Peterborough I yearned for you. And when I came to Queen's I hoped you would be going to Queen's too so I could see you more often but you surprised me when you went to Toronto for Nursing instead.

"And when I thought I was losing you, I thought I was going crazy."

"You mean that time you came down to Toronto to see me without telling me?"

"Yes."

"You were crazy." She smiled at him.

"But Alex, I've always sensed there was another girl in your life."

Alex felt alarm rising in him now. But he didn't know what to say.

"And, I'm sorry Alex, I saw the picture of you with another girl in an evening gown. You had your arm around her waist, and you looked very happy. She is beautiful."

"You saw that picture of Eleanor and me at her Prom?"

"Eleanor, is that her name? Yes, when I was getting a change of clothes for you from your apartment when you were in the hospital with smoke inhalation, I guess I snooped in your desk drawer. I'm sorry."

"I didn't mean to snoop, I was just sitting at your desk, imagining how it was for you in your apartment, studying. I lay down on your bed and looked at the ceiling, imagining you looking at that ceiling. It just seemed so natural for me, trying to be in the same space as you lived in.

"And I was so worried about you hurt in the hospital.

"And I thought of when I almost drowned at Stella Bay.

"But that other girl, Alex. You never told me about her."

"I know Sandra. I should have, I guess. I just wasn't sure what she meant to me and if you would be upset."

"Tell me about her, please."

"She was in my class in Grade XIII in Peterborough. We dated the last few months of Grade Thirteen; you know, basketball games, and sock hops and A&W. But then she went to U. of T., and I went to Queen's, and I thought it was over. Except we got together again at our High School Graduation Ceremony. And it was off and on again all through university, especially in summer when we were both home in Peterborough from university.

"But then when your father died you became distant from me and I ended up spending more time with Eleanor. I went to her Graduation Prom in March. That's when the photo was taken."

"So where do things stand with her now? Did you go to her Graduation Ceremony? Are you still seeing her?"

"That's a stupid question Sandra. I just asked you if you would marry me. I want to spend the rest of my life with you, not with Eleanor."

Sandra looked at him with a range of emotion on her face: shock, confusion, doubt.

"Oh, I'm sorry Sandra. I shouldn't have said it was a stupid question. No questions are stupid if they're serious."

She had turned away from him, studying her hands in her lap. Alex had dropped his arm from her shoulders. Silence sat between them. He sensed she had more questions but wasn't going to ask them. He had answers but was afraid how she would feel about them.

After a while she said, "May I see the ring?"

Alex opened the ring box. Sandra looked at it for a long time but did not remove it from the box.

"It's beautiful Alex. Is that an emerald? Did you pick that out because I like green?"

"Yes Sandra."

She studied his face for a long moment.

"I love you Alex Jorgenson,

"but I can't give you an answer right now.

"I have to think about this a while longer.

"Would you give me a month please?"

Alex said nothing, sitting with his confused thoughts.

"Could you come back and see me the July weekend. I will try to have an answer for you then."

"Will you take the ring, now Sandra?" he pleaded.

"No Alex, not now. If I answer yes, it will be because I want to marry you, not because of a ring."

They grew quiet. After a while Sandra lay back on the blanket, soaking up the sun. Alex lay down beside her. His mind was racing, and he had no doubt Sandra's was too. But the emotional conversation had been exhausting and soon he fell asleep. He woke a while later to see Sandra sleeping calmly by his side. He turned carefully on his elbow to look at her lovely face, being careful so as not to disturb her.

But he worried that she was getting too much sun. He got up to get her clothes and when he returned to the blanket, touched her shoulder to waken her. She looked at him and smiled, contentedly.

She put on her blouse and shorts and they moved the blanket to the shady spot under a maple tree.

They both realized they needed to leave the question alone, but Sandra asked, "so when can you come back to see me?"

"You suggested I come back the July long weekend."

"Okay. I'll be there."

They spent the rest of the afternoon on the blanket, leaning against the trunk of the tree, watching the comings and goings of the boats to the locks. Four o'clock eventually arrived and so did the taxi to take them home.

"You know Alex, I'll never forget this place, even if I never come here again."

"Me neither, Sandra."

They spent a quiet evening with Clara. She didn't seem to notice anything out of the ordinary, which was a relief.

But next day when Peter picked Alex up at the train station in Cobourg, he remarked, "Everything okay, Alex?"

"I don't know Dad, I guess so."

"Do you want to talk about it?"

"Not right now, Dad."

"Is it about Sandra?"

"Yes, Dad."

Peter muttered under his breath, "Hmmm." He waited.

"Sandra knows about Eleanor."

"Everything?"

"No, not everything. I couldn't tell her everything."

"I see. Well, maybe that's best."

"What am I going to do, Dad?"

"Give her time Son. That's all you can do."

"When are you going to see her next?"

"First of July."

"Good. Don't wait too long."

Alex' Choice

her Graduation Prom in March. That's when the photo was taken."

"So where do things stand with her now? Did you go to her Graduation Ceremony? Are you still seeing her?"

"That's a stupid question Sandra. I just asked you if you would marry me. I want to spend the rest of my life with you, not with Eleanor."

Sandra looked at him with a range of emotion on her face: shock, confusion, doubt.

"Oh, I'm sorry Sandra. I shouldn't have said it was a stupid question. No questions are stupid if they're serious."

She had turned away from him, studying her hands in her lap. Alex had dropped his arm from her shoulders. Silence sat between them. He sensed she had more questions but wasn't going to ask them. He had answers but was afraid how she would feel about them.

After a while she said, "May I see the ring?"

Alex opened the ring box. Sandra looked at it for a long time but did not remove it from the box.

"It's beautiful Alex. Is that an emerald? Did you pick that out because I like green?"

"Yes Sandra."

She studied his face for a long moment.

"I love you Alex Jorgenson,

"but I can't give you an answer right now.

"I have to think about this a while longer.

"Would you give me a month please?"

Alex said nothing, sitting with his confused thoughts.

"Could you come back and see me the July weekend. I will try to have an answer for you then."

"Will you take the ring, now Sandra?" he pleaded.

"No Alex, not now. If I answer yes, it will be because I want to marry you, not because of a ring."

They grew quiet. After a while Sandra lay back on the blanket, soaking up the sun. Alex lay down beside her. His mind was racing, and he had no doubt Sandra's was too. But the emotional conversation had been exhausting and soon he fell asleep. He woke a while later to see Sandra sleeping calmly by his side. He turned carefully on his elbow to look at her lovely face, being careful so as not to disturb her.

But he worried that she was getting too much sun. He got up to get her clothes and when he returned to the blanket, touched her shoulder to waken her. She looked at him and smiled, contentedly.

She put on her blouse and shorts and they moved the blanket to the shady spot under a maple tree.

They both realized they needed to leave the question alone, but Sandra asked, "so when can you come back to see me?"

"You suggested I come back the July long weekend."

"Okay. I'll be there."

They spent the rest of the afternoon on the blanket, leaning against the trunk of the tree, watching the comings and goings of the boats to the locks. Four o'clock eventually arrived and so did the taxi to take them home.

"You know Alex, I'll never forget this place, even if I never come here again."

"Me neither, Sandra."

They spent a quiet evening with Clara. She didn't seem to notice anything out of the ordinary, which was a relief.

But next day when Peter picked Alex up at the train station in Cobourg, he remarked, "Everything okay, Alex?"

"I don't know Dad, I guess so."

"Do you want to talk about it?"

"Not right now, Dad."

"Is it about Sandra?"

"Yes, Dad."

Peter muttered under his breath, "Hmmm." He waited.

"Sandra knows about Eleanor."

"Everything?"

"No, not everything. I couldn't tell her everything."

"I see. Well, maybe that's best."

"What am I going to do, Dad?"

"Give her time Son. That's all you can do."

"When are you going to see her next?"

"First of July."

"Good. Don't wait too long."

53. Yes or No?

ALEX HAD TO TELL SOMEBODY. And somehow, he couldn't tell his father. Maybe it was because Alex knew, this time – almost on his own – he had to decide this for himself.

He knew that things would sort themselves out if Sandra said yes, but what if she said, no?

He called Hugh.

"Hugh, it's Alex."

"Hey, what's up Alex? You've never called me in Cobourg since Grade Eight."

"I've got a big problem and I need some advice."

"So you called me; cool."

"What's the problem?"

"More like, who's the problem?"

"Oh, oh. Sounds like woman problems."

"Yeah, sure. It's about Sandra."

"Oh, really? What about Sandra?"

"I asked her to marry me."

"Whoa. Hold on a minute. You asked her to marry you? Way to go.

"She's a wonderful girl. Pretty. Talented, easy to be with. If she hadn't been your girl, I might have taken a run at her myself.

"So, what's the problem?"

"She didn't give me an answer."

"Oh. Hmmm. Why not?"

"She says she needs to think about it."

"Hmmm, that's a bit surprising. You two seem like such a natural pair.

"But she didn't say no, right?"

"No. She's asked me to give her a month."

"Had you two talked about marriage before, you know, hypothetically."

"Not really."

"Well, there you go. You probably took her by surprise."

"She said she always thought of us as like brother and sister."

"Hmmm, that's not good. You're not supposed to sleep with your sister."

353

"Stop it, Hugh.

"But then she told me she had found out about Eleanor."

"Oh. Now I see the problem.

"Eleanor is very sexy; women have instincts about these things."

"So, what am I going to do?"

"Did you tell her Eleanor is in the past?"

"Yes."

"And is she?"

"Yes, it's over."

"And did she believe you?"

"I don't know."

Hugh went silent for a few minutes, thinking.

"Alex, I'm no expert on women, and love – you're the philosopher here – but this is what I think.

"You and Sandra are destined to be together. I don't think she's going to say no.

"Women want a strong man in their lives. They have a need to feel safe and protected. You've always been that for her.

"But you have to stay confident and strong. Don't put any doubt in her mind."

"Alright Hugh, thank you. I feel better now."

"But Alex, this advice is going to cost you."

"How so?"

"I have to be your Best Man at the wedding."

Alex could hear Hugh laughing all the way from Cobourg.

Feeling more self-assured, Alex counted the days till June 30th. It was a Saturday. He finished his shift and raced home to clean up. The VW van was already packed.

As Alex was about to back out the driveway his dad met him at the driver's side door.

"Good luck, Son."

Victoria watched the van disappear down the street then asked, "What the devil is going on, Peter?"

"I don't know for sure, Victoria. The man's in love."

"Did he just figure that out now?" she said, smiling.

Alex took the shortest route he could cross country to Kingston on the busy holiday weekend, arriving at Clara and

Sandra's door less than two hours later. Sandra warmly greeted him at the door, planting an affectionate kiss on his mouth as Clara looked on approvingly.

"We've been looking forward to seeing you all week, Alex," Clara said. "I've kept supper for you – cold ham and potato salad. And fresh strawberries for dessert – Sandra and I picked them this morning; two six-quart baskets."

They finished dinner, yakking about their activities since Graduation Day, Alex at the lumber yard, Sandra's special cases at KGH, Clara's job as records clerk at the St. Mary's-of-the-Lake Hospital.

"What are your plans for tomorrow, Alex?" Clara asked.

"I thought Sandra and I might take a tour around Amherst Island for the afternoon, maybe take a swim at Long Point Bay beach."

Sandra instantly noticed her mother's face fall. "You could come with us, Mom. Why don't you give one of your friends in Stella a call, have an afternoon tea."

"Oh my goodness, what a nice idea. Thank you. I haven't been back to Amherst Island since we moved here last year."

Alex wasn't quite sure how this would fit with *his* plans, but he could see Sandra's instincts were best.

"Do you think, maybe, we could visit Blair at St. Paul's Cemetery?" Clara continued.

"You know, Mrs. Farquharson, I was thinking the same thing," said Alex.

"Hey, what about Max?" Sandra queried.

"He can come too, I guess," Alex replied.

The next morning Clara dug up a clump of daisies from her back garden and put them in a plastic pot, put the pot and her spade in the back of the van. They made the short drive to Millhaven but had to wait two hours for the ferry, backed up with Dominion Day traffic.

They off-ramped the ferry at the Stella terminus and headed down the Stella Forty Foot Road for the short trip to St. Paul's. They soon found Blair's grave, noted the tall and prominent tombstone with a well-tended garden plot in front, evidently Duncan's handiwork. They stood together studying the gravestone, each in their private thoughts, Clara with a few tears, Sandra with more, Alex moved as well.

"Maybe we should get this daisy planted and watered," Alex said.

He dug a hole big enough for the daisy in the space left between the two roses Duncan had planted.

Their chore completed and saying goodbye to Blair, Alex drove Clara to her friend's house in Stella.

"We'll be back by 4:30, I think Mrs. Farquharson."

As Clara went into the house Alex turned to Sandra, "I don't really want to go to the beach, Sandra."

"I know Alex, that's no place to talk."

"There's a nice quiet place on the South Shore Road where Hugh and I used to throw stones into Lake Ontario."

They parked the van by the side of the road that edged a sheltered cove of the lake; they settled by a big willow tree on a couple of large boulders just down the embankment from the road. Max was grateful for the freedom, chasing seagulls along the shore.

Alex picked up a few flat stones and pitched them sidearm across the water, skipping each several times. Sandra had a go too but she couldn't get hers to skip.

"Sit down with me now, Alex."

"I've had a long think over the last four weeks, Alex, and I have pretty much made my decision."

Alex could hardly contain himself but kept his mouth shut, studying his shoes, his mind on the ring box in his pocket.

"Alex, I wasn't prepared for you when you popped the question last month.

"And I was upset that there might be another girl in your life."

Alex glanced up at that. Upset? Eleanor?

Sandra continued, "But that made me realize how important you are to me.

"And I also realize I have not been fair to you the last couple of years since my dad died. I couldn't help myself."

"I know Sandra. My dad explained to me what you might be experiencing in grieving your dad."

Alex' Choice

"But Alex, I am very sorry for how I treated you. I love you so much, but I didn't let you know. I assumed you just knew it."

"I,..."

"Don't talk, Alex, please. Let me finish."

"Alex, I promise you I will no longer take you for granted."

"I want to marry you. I always thought we would be married. I don't want ever to lose you."

"But you must promise me that you are finished with that other girl, and from now on it will be only me."

"Yes, Sandra, only you."

Sandra looked at him, eyes wet, welling tears. She waited.

Alex said, "Sandra, I love you with all my heart. Will you marry me?"

"Yes, Alex Jorgenson, I will marry you!"

"You have just made me the happiest boy in the world!"

He reached in his pocket and pulled out the ring box.

Sandra watched him expectantly as he opened the lid and passed the box to her.

The tears were flowing now. "It's so beautiful."

She took the ring out of the box and slipped it on her finger.

"Oh, it fits perfectly. How did you know?"

"Because, when you showed me your graduation ring last year, I tried it on; your ring fit perfectly on my baby finger, so I knew what the size had to be."

"You're so clever. I love you."

Alex smiled hugely, overcome with emotion, happiness and relief. He stood up and took the last of the flat stones he had been handling nervously throughout their conversation, leaned sideways and pitched it across the still water: seven skips.

"Yes!"

About the Author

Alex' Choice is Doug Jordan's tenth book, and third novel, the sequel to *The Treasure of Stella Bay*. (2021)
Doug used to describe himself as a consultant by day in strategic, executive and career development, and author by night. But now the roles have been somewhat reversed.

In *Stella*, 12-year-old Alex finds the treasure, and the girl, but inquiring readers wanted to know – what happens next? Here's what happened next. Follow Alex through high school, then Queen's, as he struggles with change and disappointment, until finally, he must make a choice.

Doug has two epistolary novels, which have long lingered on his computer hard drive, that may get back on the front burner some day; they may need a bit of polish (likely more than a bit).

He published *Travels With Himself* in 2020, an account of his journey through change and transition following the death of his wife of almost 50 years. *My Story, Mostly*, published in 2022, is an autobiography intended for his three adult children and six grandchildren, as well as his *apos* in Pilipiñas, and for anyone who wishes to tell their own story.

You can discover his books and blogs at www.afspublishing.ca.

Doug has a Bachelor's Degree in Arts and an MBA from Queen's University, Kingston, but his education has never ended.

2024, Kanata, Canada

– Alex' Choice –

Praise for *The Treasure of Stella Bay*

Lorraine McKay, Gatineau

Stella Bay is a magical place to visit, and this book extends the magic through a nostalgic trip to the '60s. Doug Jordan tells the story vividly, saving the surprise till the end.

Maurice Dubras, Jersey, Channel Islands

What a delightful story – I had forgotten what it was like to be an eleven- and twelve-year-old boy! Having myself grown up by the sea in a small island community, as the reader, I could relate to some of the thoughts and emotions so cleverly woven into Alex Jorgenson's creative reflections and activities. The device of asking his father questions, some about quite profound matters, demonstrated a particular type of relationship, quite different than those with the other key characters. I loved the inclusion of events celebrated as they were in 1960s rural Canada, such as Victoria Day, seasonal rituals, including the communal skating on frozen lakes. All-in-all, a fluid and entertaining read, even exciting, which provides an insight into the 60s with the relative freedom that young lads then had to entertain themselves in the outdoors. I would encourage today's youngsters – and parents – to read, and 'compare and contrast' with what seems to me a much more restrictive environment 60 years on.

CARL NICHOLSON, of Ottawa and Jamaica

A good read. Well-told adventures of a boy growing up in small town Ontario in the 1960s: Boy Scouts, public school and Sunday school, dealing with bullies and parents and first love, the gang at the hideout and searching for treasure. A cornucopia of memories. Enjoy.

Leah Dunham, Kitchener, Ontario

Read this book! Your heart and soul will thank you. A treasure to be treasured. Mr. Jordan... more please!